CW01261740

'Heart-warming, funny and so relatable. This book made me want to cling to my life-long friendships – and listen to Fleetwood Mac.'
Laura Dockrill, author of *I Love You, I Love You, I Love You*

'A smart, perceptive take on Millennial womanhood, *That Time Everything Was on Fire* tackles the classic "stuff of life" in all its modern messiness. Spending time with the characters – in their hope, uncertainty and banter – was like being amongst friends.'
Gabrielle Griffiths, author of *Greater Sins*

'Relatable for every stage of your thirties – both joyfully and painfully. Every character is so richly drawn I feel like I know them – I've been to the pub with these girls, been through their break-ups, arguments and reconciliations. A must-read full of heart, especially if you're this age and worrying that you're the only one who hasn't got it all figured out yet.'
Stephanie Steel, author of *The Train from Platform 2*

'Sharp and observant, warm and touching. Downes moves skilfully and empathetically across her characters' turbulent and relatable lives. A soulful, sensitive read.'
Bonnie Burke-Patel, author of *Dead as Gold*

'This book is for any woman who is, has been, or will be, in her thirties, or anyone who knows one. *That Time Everything Was on Fire* is an assured and clever debut about lives pulled in different directions, about hope and expectation, and the friendships that both weather life changes and sustain us through them. With brilliant characterisation and compelling plot lines, Kerry Downes grabbed hold of my heart. I laughed. I cried. I loved it.'
Kate Kemp, author of *The Grapevine*

Kerry Downes grew up in East Yorkshire and has spent the last decade in South London, working as an NHS specialist audiologist. Her journey through fertility treatment over the last few years inspired parts of this novel. She's an alumna of Curtis Brown Creative's selective three-month novel-writing course and was shortlisted for the 2021 TLC Pen Factor Prize. She lives in Brighton with her husband and two children.

that time everything was on fire

KERRY DOWNES

H|Q

ONE PLACE. MANY STORIES

HQ
An imprint of HarperCollins*Publishers* Ltd
1 London Bridge Street
London SE1 9GF

www.harpercollins.co.uk

HarperCollins*Publishers*
Macken House, 39/40 Mayor Street Upper,
Dublin 1, D01 C9W8, Ireland

This edition 2025

1

First published in Great Britain by
HQ, an imprint of HarperCollins*Publishers* Ltd 2025

Copyright © Kerry Downes 2025

Kerry Downes asserts the moral right to be identified as the author of this work.
A catalogue record for this book is available from the British Library.

ISBN (HB): 9780008665746
ISBN (TPB): 9780008665715

This novel is entirely a work of fiction. The names, characters and incidents portrayed in it are the work of the author's imagination. Any resemblance to actual persons, living or dead, events or localities is entirely coincidental.

All rights reserved. No part of this publication may be reproduced, stored in a retrieval system, or transmitted, in any form or by any means, electronic, mechanical, photocopying, recording or otherwise, without the prior permission of the publishers.

Without limiting the author's and publisher's exclusive rights, any unauthorised use of this publication to train generative artificial intelligence (AI) technologies is expressly prohibited. HarperCollins also exercise their rights under Article 4(3) of the Digital Single Market Directive 2019/790 and expressly reserve this publication from the text and data mining exception.

Printed and bound in the UK using 100% Renewable
Electricity by CPI Group (UK) Ltd

For more information visit: www.harpercollins.co.uk/green

For Ezra,
who took his time

summer

Sam

'Enough Prosecco – it's time for whisky!' Daisy cupped her hand around her mouth to project her voice to their two friends heading to the bar.

Imo, the taller of the two retreating figures, turned around and flicked her thumb upwards to acknowledge the order.

Sam turned to Daisy on the bench beside her and, squashing her cheeks with both hands, said, 'It's *never* time for whisky.'

'They'll get you gin, mate; no one's forcing whisky on the bride.'

She looked at Daisy, considering this for a moment. 'Imagine a universe where I was cool enough to order a whisky on the rocks.' She shook her head in disbelief. 'Sexy as fuck.'

Daisy laughed. 'You're legitimately the coolest person I know, and no one says *on the rocks*.'

'James Bond does.'

There was a pause as they stared at each other.

'No, you're right, no one says that,' Sam concluded. She drained the remnants of her Prosecco, eyeing the empty glass with suspicion.

The two of them leant back against the wooden bench and gazed across the garden at the rest of the party, whirling under the festoon lights. Darkness was setting in, making the tired garden at the back of their beloved local pub look more magical than it deserved. They watched Sam's uncle twirling her cousin a little too enthusiastically on the dance floor as the sound system pumped out a recent hit. Sam bobbed her head along to the beat while Daisy looked on, the song clearly unknown to her.

'Still waiting for my Fleetwood Mac request,' Daisy said, strumming her fingers on the arm of the bench with faux irritation.

It was a deliberate gesture to their countless nights out together where, to Sam's amusement, the latest music was always lost on Daisy. Sam felt a wave of adoration for her friend and their shared history, a regular sentiment alongside grand-scale drinking – stronger, of course, today of all days. Repositioning herself, she shifted sideways on the bench and lifted her legs over Daisy's lap, lightly at first, as if seeking permission. Daisy adjusted the silk of Sam's gown over her knees, ensuring it didn't drape onto the floor. Pastel blue in colour – Sam had always known she'd never wear white; it didn't suit her pale complexion or fit with her alternative style, generally bright colours and vintage pieces, with a particular affinity for early Nineties sportswear. Plus, she'd paid about a quarter of the price of a traditional gown, purely because hers wasn't the colour of an elephant tusk.

'Mate . . .' Sam gasped, gripping her friend's tanned forearm, '. . . your speech! It was truly *brilliant*.'

Daisy's speech had won the loudest applause of the night, rousing heckling cheers from all the women in the room by rejecting the outdated traditional titles: being introduced as the best woman and toasting the bridesmates. She'd also outlined a self-deprecating comparison of the best man and woman's friendship credentials. Marvin's best man was his oldest friend, James, an impossibly good-looking and overachieving army sergeant who unknowingly made everyone around him feel inferior, and Daisy's speech had climaxed with a satirical roast of her competitor, eventually declaring a toast to 'the distinctly *average* man'.

'Do you really think?' Daisy asked, a smile creeping onto her lips. 'I'm so glad it went down well. Yours though—'

'I don't know . . .' Sam interrupted, sensing a compliment and feeling undeserving of it.

'No, honestly, it was magnificent.'

Sam smiled at the choice of adjective; Daisy often came out with words that didn't quite fit their generation, a result of her academic parents not diluting their vocabulary when she was young. It had been more apparent when they'd first met, aged eighteen – clearly Sam's generic use of language had permeated her friend over the years.

'Well, I think I might have overdone the Dutch courage part. Could you tell? Was I slurring?'

'No, definitely not.'

Sam didn't believe her but appreciated the committed delivery of the lie. 'Oh, and James is into you, by the way.'

Daisy frowned.

'I'm telling you,' Sam continued, 'the way to a cocky man's heart is apparently to publicly shame him: he's been staring at you for the last two hours.'

'What?' Daisy glanced around, unable to place him. 'There's no way that's true.' She slumped back against the bench. 'He'll go for girls from the home counties with double-barrelled names and floral tea dresses that show a bit of boob – your classic feminine with a whiff of sex and the possibility of horse riding the next morning.' She looked down at herself. 'I'm way too lanky and loud for him.'

'You're not loud *or* lanky; you just said that for the alliteration.'

'Fine, opinionated and gangly, then.'

Daisy was five foot ten with broad swimmer's shoulders and endless angular limbs, and she enjoyed a hearty debate. There was something almost masculine about the unapologetic way that she spoke and held herself, at odds with her long blonde hair and heart-shaped face, as though she'd escaped the pressure to play up to a feminine ideal of how to conduct oneself. Men tended to be intimidated or confused by her, and people generally assumed she possessed an unwavering confidence, but Sam knew that Daisy could be as unsure as the next person, particularly when it came to dating.

'You're more solid than gangly,' Sam said.

'Oh, and solidity is what James looks for in a lover, is it? Anyway, the best man and woman getting together would be beyond cliché.'

'It would be amazing!' cried Sam, who'd secretly always hoped this might happen. 'He's got a bit of that army arrogance going on, but he *is* a nice guy. Plus' – she smirked as though recovering a secret – 'you'd look weirdly good together, kind of like those couples who look like brother and sister.'

'Gross!' Daisy laughed, unable to deny their matching sandy blonde hair. She reached over to fix a wayward piece of Sam's hair, repositioning a kirby grip, then tilted her head backwards to survey the braided crown she'd intricately plaited and pinned into place that morning. 'You know, I'm pretty proud: it's still perfectly intact ten hours in.'

'Is it?' Sam patted her hair to feel the evidence, as though something unknown was stuck to the back of her head.

The action tickled Daisy, and she started laughing, or perhaps it was Sam's now undeniably slurred words which did the trick.

'What?' Sam joined her in laughter.

Reaching down for the tobacco tin in her handbag, Daisy said, 'I can't believe you're fucking married,' seemingly in awe of how grown-up they were. 'Has it been the best day ever?'

Sam beamed back at her, raising her shoulders up towards her ears for a second. 'I know. *Yeah, like actually the best.* I didn't think it would be this good.' Sam's eyes found her new husband on the dance floor across the garden, his right arm extended to the sky as his hand bounced to the beat. 'Big fan of marriage, so far.'

'You're not changing your mind about taking his name, are you?'

'God no! Samantha Thompson? Bore off.'

'Thompson's fine, but it must feel nice keeping your dad's name?'

Sam folded her arms, and her voice came out small when she said, 'Exactly.' She glanced back to the dancers and made an effort to return to an upbeat tone when she said, 'Marriage feels . . . *nice*; zero regrets six hours in.'

'Nice? Calm down, you might convince me at this rate.' Daisy had always declared that she didn't want to get married but had become more vehement about the idea following a painful break-up a few years ago – as though an aversion to the institution acted as a protective film of some sort.

Buoyed by alcohol, Sam said, 'I think you'll change your mind eventually. You'll have a cool whimsical wedding on the Yorkshire Moors where you'll casually arrive on a white stallion, swigging whisky in a dress made out of feathers.'

Daisy looked down, concentrating on the cigarette she was rolling. There was a pause before she replied, 'That's what married people say.'

'What, the stallion part?'

Her smile at this retort was weak.

'Joking,' Sam added. 'You're right; I'm sorry. I fully support your not partaking in matrimony.'

Daisy looked back at her and gave a brief lopsided smile of acceptance. She licked the paper of her cigarette, lit it, and took a cautious first drag. 'That does sound like a fucking cool wedding though.'

They spotted Imo and Jas approaching in their coordinated rust-coloured dresses, drinks in hands. Jas, a good eight inches smaller than Imo, bounced up the steps and reached the bench first. Her long black hair billowed behind her shoulders, loosely tonged.

'Sorry we took ages; we got chatting to Marvin's sister.'

Imo reached them and passed the drinks over. 'Whisky on the rocks for you, D.'

Hearing this, Sam raised her eyebrows at Daisy: you *see*.

'And Sam, we panic-bought and got you a Pornstar Martini.' She passed the extravagant orange cocktail over.

'Great choice.' Sam accepted the glass gladly. 'Very blushing bride.'

'I'm still so impressed that you wore trainers,' said Jas, sitting down next to Daisy and delicately positioning herself under Sam's shoes, the soles contrastingly blackened from just one day of Brixton's streets.

Imo squeezed in next to her at the other end, the only position to escape leg-supporting duty.

'It's nice to have us four together,' Jas said. 'I was imagining it'd be so busy, there wouldn't be time for just us.'

'But this is the *best bit*,' Sam said, looking across at them all sentimentally. 'The *fucking* best bit.' The three of them stared back at her with amusement, and Sam suspected her faint Scouse accent was showing itself more proudly than usual after many hours of drinking. She raised her glass, the orange liquid shimmering in the evening light. 'To the bridesmates!'

'The bridesmates!' the other three said in unison, clinking glasses with fittingly joyous faces.

However, before any of them had a chance to take a sip, Sam added, 'But promise me everything's not going to *change*,' drawing out the last word for heavy emphasis.

The three of them looked back at her, glasses held mid-air.

'I'm worried that soon we'll all be living in different places, having babies – some of us, anyway – and we won't have any time to see each other.' Sam had always hated change.

'Wait, wait, wait . . .' Daisy raised her hand in the air to amplify her point. 'Jas and I are still going to be living down the road from you in Clapham; Imo has lived in Putney for three years now. And you're the only one who's mad enough to be attempting procreation. We're only thirty, for Christ's sake!'

'Twenty-nine actually,' Imo corrected, raising her glass to no one in particular, a silent toast to her youth.

Daisy narrowed her eyes in Imo's direction. 'How are you so successful for an August-born by the way?'

'Plagiarism, my dear.'

Ignoring their side conversation, Sam continued, 'You're

right, and I've always looked forward to my thirties – I think it's going to be our best decade.'

Daisy snorted in disbelief. 'D'you know how Jemima describes her thirties?' Daisy had always called her parents by their first names, something her mum apparently insisted on.

'The best years of her life?' said Sam, hopeful.

'Nope.' Daisy shook her head. '*That time everything was on fire.*'

'Fire in a good way?' Jas asked, though they all knew from Daisy's tone that this wasn't the case.

'Well, she was probably raising you three tossers while trying to keep her career,' said Imo.

'I think things are different now,' Sam said, not liking the downward turn the conversation was taking. 'Anyway, it could take *a year* for me to get pregnant – Jas might even beat me to it.' She raised her eyebrows suggestively at Jas, who had been with her fiancé for almost a decade.

'Not just yet, babes; I want to make it to consultant first. Anyway, you could be pregnant by next month.'

'Oh, come on, I'm not going to be one of those gross honeymooners.' Sam moved her glass as she gesticulated, slopping some of the drink onto her dress. 'Shit,' she said, glancing down but not bothering to mop up the liquid.

Daisy half-heartedly rubbed at the stain but made little difference.

'Why not?' asked Imo. 'That happened to my friend at work: pregnant on the first attempt. She was horrified.'

Sam smiled at the predictability of this comment – the maternal desire had not yet set in for Daisy's cousin, Imo, and likely never would. She was an astoundingly successful financial analyst with a disinterest in children so pronounced it bordered on comic revulsion.

'Oh my god, Marvin would love that,' Sam said, smiling at the thought of it happening that quickly.

'Of course he would; he doesn't have to do all the shit parts.'

Sam ignored Imo and continued wistfully, 'I really hope I don't have to do all that cycle tracking and sex planning charts that some women do.'

'What the fuck! People have charts for when to have sex?' asked Daisy.

As a gynaecology registrar, Jas was naturally their go-to on conception matters. 'Mhmm, people can get really desperate.' They considered this in silence for a moment before Jas added, 'Who knows what'll happen – by this time next year we could be Us Four plus one!' *Us4* was their very unimaginative WhatsApp group name. 'And you two really would have the *fittest* children.'

It wasn't the first time someone has said this to Sam; Marvin's Jamaican–Irish skin combining with her milky hue and ash-blonde hair was apparently an obvious recipe for attractive offspring. She was still unsure whether to be annoyed or flattered by the comments but smiled simply at Jas, her eyes glistening in a drunken haze.

Hearing the first beats of Oasis's 'Wonderwall', Sam swung her legs off her friends and got up, grabbing the end of the cigarette from Daisy and taking a long drag, certain it was the last one she'd have for years. Raising her empty glass up towards the crowd across the garden, she joined them in shouting the lyrics of the first verse. The dancers spotted her and directed their singing and hand waving over to her in a loving serenade.

Sam reached up high, swaying her cigarette from side to side, her Nike high tops peeping out from beneath her dress, and bellowed the words to her husband across the garden, her three best friends on the bench behind. This was exactly how she'd dreamt her wedding day would be.

'Wow, it's like she's literally become Liam Gallagher,' Imo said.

'She's going to be absolutely smashed by midnight,' said Jas. 'Shall we get her some water?'

'Oh, come on, it's her wedding day! This is how it's meant to be,' Daisy concluded. 'What an absolute legend.'

Marvin eventually made his way across the dance floor to his new wife, his checked suit and bow tie still looking remarkably dapper.

'There you are, Lamp,' he said, swapping Sam's empty cocktail glass for a bottle of beer. Scooping her up in one swift move, he positioned her across him as though it was the end of the night and they were crossing the threshold of their first home.

'Jesus Christ, you're heavy.'

'Aw, you too, darling.'

'Why do you call her Lamp?' Jas asked. 'I don't think I've ever asked.'

'Oh, it's from *Anchorman*,' Daisy answered for him. 'Didn't you watch it on your second date or something? "*I love lamp*".'

'Riiight, oh that's cute.'

Marvin kissed Sam lightly but with intent, then proceeded to carry her to the crowd of dancers like she was the headline act. Sam arched her back and twisted around in his arms to face her friends, now swaying with their arms in the air and singing along to 'Wonderwall'. She kissed the palm of her hand

and hurled it towards them, with maximum effort from her upside-down position. Imo reacted first, reaching out wide to catch the kiss before throwing it to Jas, who thrust it deeply inside her clutch bag. Lastly, Daisy dived across them to guard the bag with her full body weight, roaring into the night, 'WE GOT IT!' as the other two collapsed under her in laughter.

The tradition had begun in their second year at university at a house party. As usual, the four of them had found themselves grouped together in a corner of the living room, preferring each other's company to the rest that was on offer. Imo's boyfriend at the time, a particular breed of patronizing prick, had blown a parting kiss at the four of them as he bid them goodnight. It was not ushered with irony or humour, but suggestion, his head moving in a circle to ensure his breathy lust reached all of them. Once he'd left, they sat stunned for a moment, torn between the need for mockery and concern over hurting Imo.

It was Imo who broke the trance, the insipid wet kiss having had the exact opposite of the desired effect. She snatched at the air, presumably enclosing the dirty kiss that had now reached them, before throwing it onto the floor and stamping on it. They erupted into laughter, and Sam then picked up Imo's foot, supposedly peeling off the shit-like kiss and throwing it at the rest of them. A battle to contain the demon ensued and ended with it firmly pinned under the sofa cushion, with both Daisy and Jas sitting on it to trap it for eternity. Imo broke it off with the boy the next day.

Over the years, there were less vile kisses that came their way, and the routine transitioned into containing acts of love. Kisses hurled at each other in either elaborate over-arms across an entire park or a subtle flick of the wrist caught and stashed in another's pocket with a wink at the end of the night. I love you too, the wink said.

As Sam turned herself back towards Marvin, still in his arms and laughing at the girls' efforts, he looked down at her, and they smiled unabashedly at each other. The image was caught on camera by someone from the party and, for many years to come, the framed photo would hang on the wall in Sam and Marvin's home. And on one particularly trying day, Sam would look over to it and, in a quiet voice to Daisy, conclude that that moment was the happiest of her life. That they had captured her very most best bit – as though no more joy was to come.

Daisy

The following morning, Daisy woke to a machine groaning as it crunched or pulverized something in the kitchen. A heavy checked curtain captured her attention on the wall next to the bed, and her eyes followed the mulberry lines cutting through the navy background fabric. She ran her tongue over the roof of her mouth and dry lips, summoning the reliable wetness, then spotted a half full pint glass of water on the bedside table and remembered him getting it for her before they went to sleep. She sat up and drank deeply, aware of the liquid entering her tender stomach.

Seizing the opportunity of his absence, she whipped the duvet off, grabbed her underwear from the side of the bed and tiptoed through to the impressive en suite – all biscuit-coloured stone tiles and a shower built for two. She splashed her face with water and picked at some mascara crust in the corners of her eyes, then borrowed his toothbrush, stealthily opting against the noisy electric function; in her experience, a surprising amount of people made a fuss over toothbrush sharing.

Opening the door quietly, she climbed back into the huge bed. Her strapless nude bra – necessary for the style of bridesmaid dress – appeared particularly drab and beige in the harsh morning light; it was probably the same one she'd worn at her university leaving ball almost a decade ago. She pulled the duvet up to conceal it, wishing she had the confidence to have remained naked. Was she ever that person, she considered, fingering the elastic seam of the bra beneath the duvet where it met her flesh.

James returned holding two black cups, the type without handles that you would cradle between both hands at upmarket brunch spots. He was wearing a grey T-shirt and some comfy-looking black shorts. He suited grey, she noted, almost with annoyance – he probably suited everything he wore.

He knelt on the bed to reach over to her with a cup.

Daisy repositioned the pillows to sit up, tucking the covers firmly under her armpits. 'Thanks.' Her voice was croaky and obtrusive in the otherwise silence. 'Could I get a . . .' She stroked her shoulder back and forth like they were playing charades. '. . . T-shirt or something?'

'Oh, sure,' he said with a boyish grin at the acknowledgement of her level of undress.

A line of dry-cleaned shirts, still in their plastic sheaths, hung together in the wardrobe. He selected a pale blue one, loudly whipping the plastic cover off.

'Oh, honestly, any old T-shirt is fine.'

But he was already walking towards her, crisp shirt held out, and she couldn't keep the amusement from her face. Used to dating men who chucked her faded T-shirts picked up for free at foam parties or hockey tours a decade ago, she didn't feel adult enough to pull off a man's shirt in the expected sexy, post-coital manner. Feigning confidence, she met his eye as she took the shirt, fastened only the middle two buttons, then flipped her long hair over the back of the collar. It felt like she was play-acting *the morning after* in a film written by her sixteen-year-old self.

'Suits you,' he said, playing along nicely.

He walked around to the end of the bed, then took a full dive back into his spot, his muscular build allowing him to land effortlessly in a side-plank position.

'Jesus!' she said, trying to prevent her coffee spilling. 'You're like an excitable Labrador.'

He picked up his coffee and positioned himself to sit up next to her. 'You're not the first to say that. I've had a Golden Retriever too.'

'You've *had* a Golden Retriever?'

'Yes, I've *fucked* a Golden Retriever; that's exactly what I meant,' he said flatly, quashing her lazy attempt at humour.

'It was the way you said it!' Daisy turned away from him to sip from her cup, regretting the comment.

'Bestiality jokes at 9 a.m. – what have I got myself into?' He nudged her shoulder with his.

She shielded her face with a hand and said, 'Leave me alone, I've just woken up. My usual superior level of wit hasn't kicked in yet.'

He smiled, then openly ran his tongue over his front teeth as he considered her. Even his smile had a sprinkling of arrogance: charismatic dimples and an American level of perfection to his dentistry. His eyes lingered on her, and she turned away from his scrutiny, taking in the room. The walls were a warm showroom grey, with no tack stains or marks at all – either recently painted or, more likely, rarely inhabited. A black dressing gown hung from the bare wooden door, and a handful of books, their titles teasingly out of view, were stacked on a mahogany chest of drawers alongside a saucer of coins and an open packet of chewing gum. The furniture was mismatched: old and well-made pieces, possibly inherited. She examined a framed print on the wall facing the bed, a weathered rowing boat sitting on the shoreline of some distant, jade-coloured sea.

'Did you take that?'

He followed her eyes. 'No, it's from Ikea.'

'Oh,' she scoffed, feeling both foolish and disappointed.

'I'm kidding, though it does look a bit generic GP-surgery art, doesn't it? It's Lake Malawi.'

'Oh,' Daisy repeated, sarcastically adjusting her accent to fittingly upper class when she added, 'Was that on your Gap Year?' Growing up at opposite ends of the country to her cousin, Imo, and with parents with opposing politics and salaries, Daisy had spent her adolescence rinsing Imo for her collection of friends called Henrietta and the way she pronounced 'grass'. She was aware this sort of prejudice was no longer acceptable but couldn't seem to refrain from mocking the overtly privileged.

She glanced at James, feeling rude, but he seemed only amused and thankfully resisted coming back with a story about how he actually worked in Woolworths for three years to save up for the trip. Instead, with an unexpected seriousness, he only said, 'No,' giving her a faint smile of forgiveness.

Daisy looked back at the photograph, panicking now that he must have visited Malawi with the army and that she'd mocked some sacred place to him where something terrible happened. When he didn't further elaborate, she was forced to fill the silence with, 'It's good coffee,' then wanted to die inside.

'It's Rob's – he's one of those coffee wankers with all the gear,' he said, sounding more relaxed.

She chuckled in agreement, though really she was also one of those wankers. 'Rob's your . . . brother who you live with?' Hazy conversation from the taxi was coming back to her.

He nodded slowly like she was someone who struggled with basic facts.

'And he's . . . ?'

'Away for the weekend.'

She looked away, unable to keep the smile from her face; they'd definitely started having sex in the kitchen last night. It had been coming up to six months since she'd last slept with anyone, and the emotion of the day – together with Sam's encouragement – had coerced her into accepting James's unambiguous offer of a shared taxi home. It had taken them all of three minutes to start kissing on the backseat.

She cringed at the memory and ran a hand through her hair. 'I can't imagine living with my brothers anymore.' Searching a strand for split ends, she added, almost to herself, 'Graham would love us to, though.'

'How many brothers are we talking?' he asked this with a hint of bravado, assessing potential threats.

'Only two.'

'Graham and . . . ?'

'Oh, no, Graham's my dad.' She swatted the comment away, not wanting to explain the irregular workings of her family.

'Why do you—'

'It's just a thing we do, always "Graham" and "Jemima" – never "Mum" and "Dad", even when we were little.' She adjusted the duvet over her thighs. 'I forget how weird people find it.'

James stuck his bottom lip out, considering the names, then disappointed her when he said, 'That is quite weird.'

She'd had this conversation countless times and struggled not to sound defensive. 'It's *uncommon*, sure, but isn't it better than "Mummy and Daddy"?'

'Fair enough.' He ran his eyes over her, pondering something.

She jutted her chin out and stared back in defiance of his intimidating observation. There were dark circles around his eyes, which seemed to give him an air of poetic depth that had been absent yesterday, making him less text-book perfect yet more handsome. His nose was slim at the bridge, almost feminine, his eyebrows darker than his golden hair and angled like he was a man with strong opinions. Fittingly, he had the broad square jaw of a soldier and, sitting below a wide philtrum, a contrastingly delicate cupid's bow.

She pulled her eyes away from his lips and said, with barely disguised dread, 'What?'

'Nothing,' he said after a beat.

'Don't say *nothing*; you look like you're trying to work something out about me.'

He turned away at last, crossing his ankles and focusing on

his toes. 'I just can't believe it: Daisy-fucking-Carlisle in my bed!' The words were almost shouted in rejoice. 'I've wanted this to happen for ages.'

She attempted to appear unbothered as she said, 'No, you haven't,' when in fact she felt the blood rising to her cheeks.

'I've fancied you for ages, ever since Marvin's birthday at that weird cave bar.' He said this as casually as telling her he'd played rugby for ages, which she suspected he had; he seemed the type.

She frowned. 'That was *years* ago!'

He tipped his head to the side, indicating that his point had been proven.

Daisy had always been aware of James at Marvin and Sam's gatherings – it was difficult not to be – but he'd always seemed indifferent towards her, so much so that she was unsure whether to believe this apparent confession; he was undoubtedly the type of man who knew what to say to women to make them feel special. She put her cup down and turned to face him properly, pulling her knees up above the duvet. His eyes flicked down to her skin, recently bronzed from days at Brockwell Lido and contrasting starkly with the pale blue of the shirt, and she felt momentarily powerful.

'It was a weird bar,' she said, pointedly ignoring his revelation. 'In Vauxhall or somewhere.'

Finishing his coffee, he held a finger out until he'd swallowed and could speak again. 'Elephant and Castle. And the cave walls were made of papier-maché.'

'That was it!' She considered him more closely; the idea that this could be anything more than a one-night stand hadn't occurred to her until now. 'I do remember us talking that night, actually.'

'You had a boyfriend.'

She laughed. 'Did I, now?'

'And then I went on tour—'

'But then you came back and barely spoke to me at any of Marvin's other parties—'

'I've only made about two since then! Plus, you're intimidating.'

'*I'm* intimidating?' She leant forward in protest.

'Of course you are. Until you speak.' He gave her his most charming of smiles.

'Wow – backhander!'

'No, you sound really down to earth, like you categorically couldn't be a bitch.'

Daisy looked up at the ceiling, hugging her knees as she considered this. 'But what you actually mean is, you couldn't possibly be intimidated by a girl from Yorkshire – so, essentially, you're admitting that you feel superior to northerners.'

'Fuck me.' He puffed air out extravagantly, wafting a tuft of hair by his forehead. 'Someone's a *little* sensitive . . .' He pushed her knees over playfully, pulling her down the bed as she yelped. '. . . about her cute accent.' Then knelt over her, holding her wrists down. 'What am I going to do with you?'

She glowered at him from below, feeling her heart racing in response to the weight of his body, then raised her lips to his, tasting the coffee and a hint of alcohol – a not unpleasant reminder of last night's proceedings.

His smile disappeared, and he pulled away, straightening his arms to hover above her. His cornflower blue eyes contracted. 'I really like you, Daisy.'

Their faces felt far too close for such an earnest statement, and she bit her lip, suddenly aware of his arms either side of her and the bed beneath preventing escape. 'I like you too!' She added a cheerful ring to her words, diminishing their power, as though they were merely complimenting each other's outfits.

James blinked back at her, then moved his eyes away to something in the corner of the room, perhaps offended by her indifference. Propelled by his unexpected revelation, she raised her hand and stroked the side of his face, the skin soft around his temple, turning to sharp along his cheek and jaw as the beginnings of stubble emerged. He turned back around, and it was as though they were looking at each other for the first time, no flirtations or ambiguous smirks, their expressions open and their faces exposed.

Daisy had been in one long-term relationship that ended when she was twenty-seven. They'd been together for four years, though she'd felt him pulling away for the last one, and the pain of him finally removing himself from her life was seared so violently into her being that she could still locate it in an instant, caressing it as you would the raised skin of a scar. It was foolish to have been so hurt by one man, so predictable and so far from the person she aspired to be. She'd since built up barricades substantial enough to withhold further pain, well versed in the art of keeping love affairs short, her vulnerabilities tucked neatly away beneath a carefree veil. But as James gazed into her eyes, she sensed something slipping away within her, the first stone from the wall around her heart.

It was James who turned away first, leaning back onto his calves with his head down, resting on her stomach. 'Shit,' he said, drawing out the word, then laughing.

She laughed too, acknowledging that something had been

unlocked between them. He remained leaning on her stomach, and she stroked a tuft of his hair, wondering what to say next. There was a pleasant crispness to it, the tracings of wax from yesterday.

'I should get going,' she said softly, her voice cracking with tiredness. She cleared her throat, and this seemed to clear the air too.

He lifted his head from her stomach and pulled her on top of him, their feet tangled together. 'No.' He drew the word out to such an extent that she couldn't tell if he was being cruel and she'd misjudged their moment before.

'Yes,' she said more firmly.

He took hold of her waist gently, his strong palms warm through the cotton of the shirt, and his eyes were almost pleading as he said, 'Come on, best woman, *stay* – just a few more hours?'

Around 8 o'clock that evening, Daisy clambered into the passenger side of Jas's black Renault Clio, the blue shirt worn sheepishly over her bridesmaid's dress. Jas was staring at her with a smile that showed most of her teeth, her eyes open wide enough to display the entirety of her irises like a surprised cartoon character.

Daisy and James had managed to slip off together unseen at the end of the wedding but, as Daisy's housemate, Jas had needed to know that she wouldn't be heading home. She'd been texting Daisy throughout the day, from aubergine emojis to GIFs of the axe scene in *The Shining* followed by question marks.

'You look like you're about to explode,' Daisy said, joining her in smiling.

'Babe, you've been there *all* day – of course I'm about to explode! Tell me EVERYTHING AND QUICK!' She showed no intention of starting the car.

'Okay, but let's go; I don't want him to see us sitting outside like a stakeout.'

'Fine. I can drive and listen.' Jas turned to face the windscreen and started the car. 'So how many times did you shag and are you in love?'

Jas loved to talk about sex and dating. Having met her fiancé, Ash, at the age of nineteen, she'd only ever slept with two people and openly moaned about how utterly unfair this was.

Daisy laughed at her reliable sarcasm. 'I can't believe we're still using the word "shag" at the age of thirty.'

'It's a strong word – don't overthink it.'

Jas leant forward to check the traffic at a T-junction as she edged out, and Daisy's foot automatically pressed down in an attempt to brake. Having always lived in cities, Jas's driving was assertive bordering on insane. Luckily James's flat was only ten minutes from their place in Clapham.

'So?'

'God,' Daisy said sulkily, as though it was a parent asking her awkward questions. 'Yes, we're absolutely in love and planning to wed next month. And three times . . . well, three and a half.'

Jas frowned at her, then glared back at the road, annoyed that something else was demanding part of her attention. 'The half being?'

'We kind of started but then gave up and ordered takeaway.'

'Oh my goddd, you ordered takeaway together!'

Daisy laughed. 'Twenty-first-century romance.'

'Three and a half is basically four times. I haven't had sex four times in a twenty-four hour period for a decade.'

'I actually wouldn't recommend it.'

'Oh piss off if you want me to feel sorry for you and your sore vagina.' Jas indicated and pulled onto the high street, gladly joining a traffic jam and putting the handbrake on. 'So, what's he actually like – I thought you weren't keen? But 8 p.m. the next day, babe, that's something.'

'I know, we just ended up talking all day. About everything, really.' Daisy traced her finger through the condensation on the window, creating a line, and then staring absently at the wetness on her fingertip. James had talked a lot about his family: his relationship with his two siblings, how they'd grown up in a small village in Surrey then moved to Brixton when he was a teenager. Having assumed she and him were polar opposites, Daisy was quietly surprised at how their upbringings had been similar in some ways. 'I wasn't *keen* keen. I thought he was your classic fuckboy and a bit, well, *basic.*' She whispered the word. 'But he surprised me today. He's actually super intelligent.'

'He went to Sandhurst, didn't he?' Jas asked, her tone suggesting Daisy was the unintelligent one.

'Yeah, I don't know why I thought that.'

'Probably because he's so fit?'

Daisy hoped this wasn't the case, aware of her tendency to jump to conclusions about people, particularly when it came to intelligence. She dismissed the thought, unable to compute any worthwhile self-reflection on so little sleep. 'He is quite intense though.'

'In what way?'

'Like, he *kept* telling me how much he liked me, which usually puts me off.'

'But, chick, remember the psychology behind that reaction?'

A few months ago, Jas had stumbled on an article in the Sunday papers and, attempting to diagnose Daisy's romantic temperament, had read it aloud to her. It detailed the psychological processes involved in dating: how being turned off by overkeen partners was often due to the possibility of intimacy setting off fears of being hurt. Since Daisy's break-up, there'd been numerous dates and some flings, but a pattern had clearly emerged where her interest in men seemed to correlate directly with their interest: the more they liked her, the less she was interested. It was the ones who didn't text back, the ones who seemed too busy or too beautiful to fall in love with her that occupied her mind. Her idea of compatibility had somehow become tangled up with anxiety, the adrenalin of simple desire outweighed by the heart-stopping concoction of lust with the risk of rejection.

'I remember. I was going to say: his keenness actually hasn't put me off this time. I think because of his whole self-important demeanour, and that he's so handsome—'

'Oh my god, *so* fit.'

'—that you assume he's going to be this arsehole who's not interested the next day, so when he *is* . . . it's actually really flattering.'

'But is it just flattery? As that's totally different from really liking someone.'

Daisy scratched her head; she found it difficult admitting to liking men, not just to her friends but to herself. She'd been brought up with the belief that relationships should come easily, that they should be a building block in making you the best version of yourself, but they shouldn't be a necessity. Her parents – who were together but unmarried – thought society's obsession with marriage and romance was faintly amusing (and were entirely baffled by friends spending endless hours obsessing over past lovers or arguing with their partners) and, as a consequence, Daisy couldn't help but view her own aching desire to attach herself to another – and her upset when it didn't work out – as a weakness.

She looked out at the pavement in the fading evening light, a dense tiredness pressing on her whole body as she said, 'No, I think I actually do like him.'

'Oh my god, Sam is going to go nuts! She's been hoping this'd happen for *years*.'

They treated themselves to the lift, the stairs seeming quite simply impossible.

Daisy slumped against the mirrored wall and exhaled heavily. 'Thanks for coming to get me.'

Jas winked in reply. 'No worries. I was desperate for the gossip.'

The lift pinged, and the doors opened to the navy carpeted hallway and stark white walls. Their flat was on the second floor of a new build just off Clapham High Street – perfectly formed and highly convenient – but with a distinct feeling of a high-end and characterless student hall of residence.

Entering the flat, Daisy tugged her espadrilles off, frustrated at the excessive ties around her ankles; she'd been living in Birkenstocks since April. 'I think I'm going to have a bath and head to bed early. Urgh, I can't even think about work tomorrow.'

Jas dropped the keys into a small basket on a side table by the door and headed to the kitchen area. 'You say that every Sunday.'

'Doesn't everyone? Not you because you deliver babies – you're literally bringing new life into the world while I'm writing about pizza toppings. And shit, no meal prep done.' Over the last couple of years, Daisy had spent a few hours cooking on Sundays: aubergine pargmigianas and slow cooked curries – new recipes each week – which could be stored in batches, saving her money on weekday lunches and time on busy evenings. She'd always loved cooking, and the process felt measured and mature, making her feel in control of the week ahead.

'Oh, babe, don't stress – there'll be something in the freezer,' Jas replied. 'I'll make you a chamomile tea to soothe the Monday-dread.' It was her antidote for anything remotely stressful.

Daisy started the bath running – a painfully slow process with a stylish but inefficient tap and an unnecessarily large tub. She plodded into her bedroom next door and slumped onto the bed, staring into space while she waited. After a year of living there, she'd acquired a vague awareness of the water depth by the increasing pitch of the gushing tap.

The bedroom wall was cold against her shoulders through the thin shirt, and she longed for the luxury of a headboard. A bright coloured lappa, bought in Uganda years ago, adorned the largest wall to the side of her bed, and Polaroid photos pegged to a thin piece of twine snaked around the opposite wall. There was one framed picture in the room: a screen print of black-and-white photography sitting against bold red and orange shapes. Bought by the girls for her birthday last year, it depicted four women in vintage swimwear sunbathing and laughing together on the surface of the moon, while earth loomed in the distance.

She missed having a chair in her room, one that would rarely be seen but could act as an acceptable way of piling up clothes rather than her current shameful heap on the floor. The room was only large enough to squeeze in a small double bed, a wardrobe, and a chest of drawers, with little floor space left over. Jas's room was significantly bigger, with an en suite and, accordingly, she paid much more of the rent.

Up until April last year, they'd been living as a three with one of Jas's school friends. Their budget had stretched much further with an extra person, and they'd lived in a large Victorian flat in Camberwell. The kitchen and bathroom were old-fashioned, and it was freezing in winter, but the ceilings were high, their rooms spacious and the garden ideal for house parties in summer.

The new flat wasn't Daisy's style at all: a couple of years old with heavy modern fire doors and a shiny white kitchen. But it was clean and habitable and in a decent location. They'd looked at a lot of places and both knew that the alternatives were either to increase their budget or to move further out. Paying more was not an option for Daisy, but moving a couple of miles out – in one of the most connected cities in the world – wouldn't have bothered her at all. She grew up in North Yorkshire and had spent her childhood roaming fields and swimming in the biting North Sea. London was a place she visited to see her mum's family: Imo and her parents. But Jas grew up in Croydon (which to her at the time seemed like a million miles away from central London and all its exciting prospects) and since settling in London after university in Newcastle, she'd vowed to stay in zone two.

Jas knocked lightly on the half open bedroom door with a steaming cup of tea. 'Want me to put it in the bathroom for you?'

Daisy noted that it was her favourite mug, a thin-rimmed ceramic with a hand-painted scene of her hometown of Whitby. She smiled and held out her hand in lieu of answering, and Jas stepped forward to gently pass it to her.

'You're my favourite.'

Jas perched on the end of the bed, folding her tracksuit bottomed legs beneath her. 'Speaking of, when are you going to tell Sam?' It was common and comfortable knowledge within their friendship group that Sam and Daisy were a duo in the same way that Jas and Imo were.

'Not now – she'll still be buzzing from the wedding, and I don't want to make it all about me and James. Can you check the bath for me?'

'Sure.' Jas skipped out and put her head around the bathroom door. 'A few minutes to go.'

'Thanks,' Daisy said, manoeuvring herself into an upright position. 'Are you in tomorrow night?'

'No, I'm staying at Ash's. He wants to go through the wedding spreadsheet.' She raised her eyebrows and stared at Daisy with a look of resigned horror.

'At least he's willing to be spreadsheet-guy and not leaving it all to you.'

'Yeah, plus he's got way more time on his hands than I have.' Jas continued to be astonished at Ash's working hours as a freelance graphic designer, the flexibility putting her shifts on the labour ward into an even harsher light.

'What's the guest list looking like these days?'

Jas set her mouth into a straight line, holding off a grimace. 'I think we've got it down to 270?'

Daisy shook her head in dismay.

'I know, I know. If he left it down to me, we'd all go for a wicked time in Pizza Express, then out to Infernos.'

'Jas, no . . . Pizza Express is so 2003.' Daisy pulled herself up from the bed with maximum effort and located her checked pyjamas under her pillow. 'But you really should consider Infernos for the after party. We could all pretend it was ironic or some deliberately woke move – a *fuck you* to the wedding industry.'

'Yeah, I can just see my aunts navigating those vodka red bull saturated carpets.'

'You and I both know that those floors contain many worse things than sugary drinks.'

Jas laughed and stepped out of the room to let Daisy pass. 'Are you going to text him tonight?'

'James?'

Jas made a goofy face to the obvious question.

'I don't know,' Daisy said, suspecting it would be shamefully keen. 'What do you think?' She bent down over the bath to turn the taps off, and the absence of running water felt startlingly quiet.

'You hate those dating rules; message him if you want to.'

Daisy offered a half smile, feeling uncertain; the more dates she went on, the less confident she became in her twenty-two-year-old self's flagrant disregard of said 'rules'.

'I'll leave you to it,' Jas said, reaching for the bathroom door to close. 'Catch you Tuesday? But update me if he messages you!'

Daisy laughed. 'I will. Good luck with the wedmin.'

'I hate that term,' Jas called from behind the closed door.

'Sorry. I hate myself for using it.' Daisy's voice echoed in the enclosed tiled space. She tugged the shirt over her head and unzipped the terracotta-coloured dress, the steam from the bath already making her feel more human. Her phone lit up from the sink unit, and she watched the messages come through one at a time.

James: Hey
So
I was wondering
There's this great bar
It's like a cave made of papier-maché
But also a bar . . .

Sam

The sunshine glared through the shuttle bus windows at Gatwick airport, and Sam shielded her eyes with the hand holding her passport. Marvin, standing above her with their cabin-sized suitcases between his feet, shuffled to the right a few inches to block the sun from her face. Sam dropped her hand and briefly smiled up at him in gratitude.

'It's weird that it's not raining; it *always* rains on the return leg,' she said, looking out at the glistening tarmac as the bus filled with people.

'Makes it easier though – coming home to sunshine,' said Marvin.

Sam pouted; she didn't agree, in truth. The weather in the UK had been great for the whole week they'd been away (her mum had sent her daily updates). Sam couldn't help but feel annoyed about this – not that she wanted her friends to be sitting miserably in torrential rain, but she wasn't expecting to be on her honeymoon in Croatia feeling like she was missing out.

There was something about a British summer that brought out a camaraderie like nothing else; a sort of collective celebration of unexpected good fortune. In Sam's experience, this was strongest in May and June when people were still full of hope, dusting off their barbeques and sliders from last year and revelling in the brilliance of their first pint in a beer garden or picnic in the park. July and August were usually tainted, firstly by disappointment in the scarcity of sunny days and eventually by panic that autumn was coming and neither the desired tan had been achieved nor had enough magical memories been made to see you through winter.

At least Croatia had been undeniably wonderful – infinitely hotter and more beautiful than London. They'd stayed five nights in Split in a chic boutique hotel, a significant step up from their usual accommodation style of eclectically furnished Airbnbs that always looked better in the pictures than in reality. The roof held a glorious infinity pool shaped like a half moon, where a DJ played chillout dance music from the early afternoon. They'd spent most days by the pool sipping cocktails before heading out into the town for dinner. On two nights they'd made it out to clubs – ordering shots and dancing until the early hours, then seeing out their hangovers with coconut water on the beach in the morning.

Sam was aware that going clubbing wasn't common

honeymoon behaviour, but she loved that about their relationship; it was so easy to slip into boring, TV-watching matrimony. She imagined telling her work colleagues about their nights out and them being impressed. Sam and Marvin had met when she was twenty-four and he twenty-six, when big club nights were a regular weekend fixture. Marvin was the first boy that she could truthfully say she'd enjoyed going on nights out with. Prior to him, she'd spent nearly a decade going to bars and clubs with female friends and having the absolute best of times. It was a revelation to her that someone you fancied could be just as fun.

Marvin took her hand as they headed through passport control, and she glanced down, his gold wedding band still unfamiliar to her touch. He smiled at her, knowing what she was thinking.

'Don't be mad at me if I lose my rings,' she said to him, her voice pleading and child-like. She was terrible for losing things; it was, in her opinion, one of her worst traits. Marvin was endlessly patient with her daily searches for the mundane items that make up life: phone, keys, purse, hairbrush, water bottle, etc. And for this she loved him even more.

'You won't lose them,' he said, then, as though remembering whom he'd married, added, 'Just don't take them off.'

She looked down at the new ring, coarse and twisted gold like a thin piece of twine, tucked neatly underneath her antique opal engagement ring. She flexed her fingers, admiring the pairing of the rings against the apricot-coloured gels she'd had done for the wedding. 'I'll try,' she said, looking up at Marvin and meaning it.

They arrived home in the early afternoon when the sun was

high in the sky and the whirr of traffic from the nearby main road at peak amplitude. They'd moved in six weeks before the wedding – not something they'd planned on doing, but it had taken five months for the sale to go through. Situated a few miles from where they had been renting in Streatham, the flat sat at the end of a tucked away cul-de-sac in Herne Hill, near to where Marvin grew up. Sam loved the area; it was quieter and felt more grown-up, somewhere she could imagine them living for years to come and happily raising children.

The flat itself wasn't the most aesthetically pleasing property: a slightly rundown two-bed on the ground floor of a 1970s ex-council block. But sacrificing the grandiose features of period properties in the area had afforded them a second bedroom and a small back garden. They'd pulled back the old carpets and had new floors laid, sourcing a high quality lino that gave the illusion of polished concrete and worked well with their mid-century furniture and bright rugs. The kitchen and bathroom needed replacing at some point, but it'd be a while before they could afford that.

'Is your mum in?' Marvin asked, fishing for the keys in his shorts pocket.

Sam's mum, Linda, had stayed at theirs for the week they were away, keen to help make a start on painting the flat. Sam's dad had been a decorator and, before she had a career of her own, Linda often helped him on big jobs when Sam was little.

Marvin pulled out his keys, which clattered against an old plastic Crystal Palace FC key ring. Sam marvelled at his forward-thinking, realizing that her own house keys were likely at the bottom of her suitcase, somewhere very safe and entirely inconvenient.

'I don't know. Knock?'

He tried the handle of the clunky white UPVC door, which gave easily under his grasp. Sam witnessed a fleeting look of annoyance on his face, and she silently cursed her mum for letting the side down – they'd told her numerous times to keep the doors locked even when she was in. The error was absolute fuel to the fire for Marvin's teasing about Sam's provincial upbringing in the Wirral.

'Hello? Linda?' Marvin called.

She appeared from the living area at the back of the flat, wearing cropped white jeans and a bottle-green sleeveless shirt, a chunky necklace with mustard-coloured gemstones sitting against her tanned clavicle. Linda had been twenty-six when she'd had Sam, younger than most of her friends' mothers and, although they would never admit it to each other, Sam was aware that they both liked this detail. When Sam was a teenager, her mum had been slightly more fashionable and less embarrassing at parents' evenings, and as adults, they found they had similar interests and lots to talk about. Their relationship was also propelled, of course, by the acute awareness that their family was now made up of only the two of them.

After the customary fussing over their luggage and enquiring about the specific details of the journey home – rather than anything interesting about the actual holiday – her mum showed them their newly painted bedroom. The pastel sage green they'd chosen flooded over the walls and ceiling, creating a calming cocoon. The room was perfectly laid out with no signs of the decorating process, the furniture back in place and a set of new blush pink curtains hanging from a black rail.

Linda clapped her hands together in delight at their enthused reactions. 'I did have a bit of help shuffling all the furniture back into place this morning.' Her mum walked backwards to lead them into the open-plan living space, the kitchen having been knocked through by the previous owners.

'Oh hey, lovers.' Jas was stretched out on the sofa in an orange summer maxi dress, one arm supporting her head like she was posing in an advert. Behind her was a large hand-painted mural, an array of abstract shapes and colour set off by the dark-blue surround of the rest of the room. Sam recognized it immediately to be by one of Jas's friends, an artist whose work she'd always admired on Instagram, and her hands went to cover her open mouth.

Jas jumped up to hug them then stepped back and squeezed Sam's mum's waist, both of them revelling in pulling off the surprise. Her mum put her arm around Jas, and the four of them stared at the mural.

'I thought it was safest to go behind the sofa, so you don't have to look at it all day long,' said Jas. 'A migraine for a wedding present isn't what I was shooting for.'

They all laughed and agreed that the placement was perfect.

Stepping closer to examine it in more detail, Marvin declared, 'Right, that's it, we're never moving.'

'You could take a photo of it, blow it up in a big frame, then take it with you when you eventually move?' her mum offered. Sam noticed her accent, the comforting Scouse more apparent against her friends' South London drawls.

'Great idea, Mum.'

Marvin made a pot of tea, despite the heat, and they sat around their kitchen table, a recent purchase made of old scaffolding boards. Sam spotted her mum running her manicured fingers over the rough edges, most likely itching to give them a good sanding. They recounted the highlights of the honeymoon, taking turns to speak in that way that couples tend to default to. Marvin showed them some photos on his phone and then, inevitably, they steered the conversation back to the wedding. Sam wanted to relive the day, hungry for further details: who spoke to who, which food they liked best, and what songs the band had played, since neither she nor Marvin could recollect many.

Once they'd finished their tea, Jas headed home, kissing Linda dearly on the cheek and inexplicably slapping Sam's behind on the way out. 'Sorry, I don't know what came over me. Juicy though.'

Sam had booked afternoon tea at the Ritz for her mum months ago as an anticipated thank you for all the help with the wedding and now the decorating too. She was heading back to the Wirral the following morning, so that afternoon was the only time they could fit it in. Sam changed into an overly appropriate vintage tea dress and kissed Marvin goodbye, and they walked the fifteen-minute stretch to Brixton underground station.

Her mum's pace slowed as she took in the sights and cacophony of the high street: two lanes of roaring traffic, cyclists, buskers, shouting market traders and a noticeable mix of age, class, ethnicity, and sanity among the pedestrians. Sam had always loved Brixton, but it was worlds away from the Wirral, and she was unsure what her mum made of it. Knowing these would impress her, Sam pointed out the more upmarket bars and restaurants as they passed. She was aware that the arrival of people like herself had driven rents up and forced many locals out of the area, but her internal conflict about the gentrification was given over today, quashed by the need for her mum's approval of where she'd chosen to live.

Growing up, Sam's family had always pronounced 'London' with a smattering of distaste, as though it was a place to avoid where possible, and one of her uncles still proudly refused to ever visit the city. Her decision to move down after university was greeted with a mix of disappointment and utter bewilderment, leaving her still desperate to prove the city's worth, a decade on. While her mum had been surprised at her daughter's decision, she'd never once tried to change her mind.

They got off at Victoria, and Sam led the way past Buckingham Palace and the Mall, and through Green Park. Her mum marvelled at the landmarks and insisted on taking selfies to send to her various WhatsApp groups. Arriving at the Ritz promptly for the 4 p.m. slot, they were briskly shown to a small round table by a waiter wearing the expected finest livery.

Her mum had always had afternoon tea at the Ritz on her bucket list, but it had never appealed to Sam – she assumed it would be full of tourists and extortionately priced scones. However, as they sat down on the luxuriously upholstered straight back chairs and took in their surroundings, Sam couldn't help but gaze around the room: a mix of gold and white surfaces with vast marble pillars, opulent chandeliers and huge palm-like plants spilling out of ornate pots. The space was surprisingly quiet, the clatter of silver cutlery echoing above lowered voices in the high-ceilinged room, and the atmosphere undeniably stuffy.

Once seated, they looked at each other across the white

tablecloth and couldn't help but giggle. Her mum suggested getting a glass of Prosecco each.

'That's a nice idea,' Sam said, wondering how much a glass would set her back. 'D'you know what, since we're at the Ritz, let's go all out and get *Champagne*.'

'Oh, no need. It'll be extortionate here, and you can barely taste the difference.'

Recently, through no intended malice, Sam's mum had made her feel silly and flashy about things she owned or wanted. 'True,' Sam lied.

The food and drinks arrived: perfectly cut sandwiches and miniature cakes so exquisite they looked like they've been swiped from a doll's house.

'Jas tells me Daisy's seeing the stocky blond fella from the wedding?'

Sam put her sandwich down and brought her hands together in a prayer-come-clap. 'Yesss! I'm so excited for them.' Daisy had sent regular updates when they were away, and Sam and Marvin had spent a great deal of time discussing their potential future as a unit of four. 'Well, they're not exactly *seeing* each other – it's only been a week – but he's been over at hers for three nights on the trot.'

'In my day, that counted as *seeing someone*. Oh, I am glad for her; he's gorgeous! And a nice bloke, I take it, if Marvin chose him as his best man?'

'Yeah, they've been friends since they were at primary school – he's perfect for her.'

'And I guess that'd make you a jolly foursome?'

Sam's mouth was full of cucumber sandwich so she raised her eyebrows conspiringly in response.

They worked their way up the tiered cake stand, moving on to drinking the requisite tea, and Sam asked Linda about her week in London, really only wanting to hear how her evening at Marvin's parents' house had been. Having only met Linda a handful of times, they'd kindly invited her over for dinner. Irritatingly, Linda gave a positive but vague summary of the evening before running through her entire week. She recounted everything from using contactless on the bus (*did you know you could do that?*), to her cappuccino in Covent Garden with her friend Sandra and the Margaret Thatcher song in the *Billy Elliot* musical they'd seen at the West End.

Perhaps due to tiredness, Sam struggled to find her mum's 'London adventures' endearing. She shuffled in her seat, smiling at the stories while attempting to suppress an uncomfortable feeling creeping over her. Sam had seen countless musicals and plays in the last decade since moving down to London, and here was her mum talking about *Billy Elliot* like it was one of the best evenings of her life.

Over the last few years, Sam had noticed that her mum had an innocence about her – a sort of child-like delight at things that many took for granted. Sam's parents had worked hard to give her everything they felt their childhoods lacked; Sam was the first person in her extended family to travel further than Europe and to get a degree. Her mum earnt a reasonable salary as a legal secretary and had paid her mortgage off years ago; in terms of wealth, owing to the circumstances of their respective generations, Sam was by no means better off than her mum. However, the privilege afforded to Sam by her parents' hard work had created a disparity between the way she and her mum viewed certain things. And in these moments of her mum's wide-eyed wonder at the world, Sam felt the familiar pang of pity strumming its ugly fingers on her chest.

They resurfaced onto the busy high street, blinking at the brightness. It was nearing 6 p.m. and there was a new coolness to the air. Her mum pulled out a patterned scarf from her bag and wrapped it around her shoulders, and Sam berated herself for not bringing a jacket.

'Your hair looks nice.' Sam reached out to touch a strand hanging loose over her forehead. 'New clip?'

Her mum's hair was straight and blonde and always worn short, swept over in a side parting and usually secured with a single hairclip. It had always reminded Sam of Cameron Diaz in the early Noughties.

'Oh yeah, thanks,' Linda said, bringing her hand to her hair. 'Sandra and I went to Oxford Street on Tuesday, and I bought a couple of bits.'

Sam had a sudden urge to shower her mum in decency, compensation for her earlier condescending thoughts perhaps. 'Shall we go for one last drink somewhere?'

'Oh, I'm fine to go home now, love. You've spent a fortune on me.' She linked Sam's arm and turned them towards Green Park to head back. 'And you must be shattered, waking up in another country only this morning?'

Sam gripped her mum's arm and gave in to her tiredness. 'I am pretty knackered, to be fair.' *To be fair*, she repeated in her head; she had a tendency to slip into her former dialect around her mum. 'I'll miss you when you go tomorrow though – I feel like I've barely seen you, what with the honeymoon and all.'

'Oh, don't be silly – today's been lovely. Anyway, I'll be

down every weekend as soon as you and Marvin start popping out babies.'

Sam had vaguely mentioned that she and Marvin were planning to start a family soon, but she hadn't gone as far as sharing that she came off the pill a month before the wedding; she wanted there to be some element of surprise when it did happen. 'Every *weekend*? Are you joking? You'll be moving in, whether you like it or not.'

Her mum laughed and patted Sam's arm.

'Do you think you'll come down again this summer?' Sam asked.

'Maybe, if you want me to?'

'I always want you to.'

Daisy

A month later, Daisy was standing over the kitchen sink eating some defrosted bread and marmite when her phone vibrated on the worktop to her left. She grabbed it, her heart rate rapidly climbing then stabilizing when she saw it was a message from Dan, a guy from Tinder she'd spontaneously agreed to go on a date with the following week. She dropped the phone back down with a clatter and returned to chewing her toast without tasting it, her eyes fixed and unblinking on the tiled kitchen splashback.

Wiping the crumbs from her hands, she picked the phone up again and scrolled down to her chat with James. She liked to check when he was last online – a simple and sad, distant glimpse into his life, and one of the only remaining ones available to her. Reading over his last message for the hundredth time, the sting was still there.

> **James:** Hey sorry for my radio silence over the last few days. I've been going over stuff in my head. These last few weeks have been really great but, to be completely honest, I can't see us working out in the long term. I think its best if we call it before anyone catches feelings. I hope things aren't weird between us for Sam and Marvs sake. Your a great girl. Take care, James x

The 'great girl' comment still stirred up a swirl of anger, further impounded by the poor spelling. She hadn't replied. What was the point?

James had pursued Daisy following their first night together. Initially, she'd been unnerved by his persistence, his assuredness in his desire for her, so blatant and unguarded – she wouldn't dream of behaving in such a way towards someone she liked, someone who could reject her. But here was a beautiful man who her best friend vouched for, telling her that he wanted her. It would have been entirely self-sabotaging to not even entertain the idea that there could be something worthwhile between them. So she willed herself to shed the protective layers that had built up over the last few years, shrouding her from further heartbreak. And eventually, she let James in.

The weeks passed in a blur of kissing in parks at dusk and outside pubs at midnight; of late-night dinners in cheap restaurants with forgettable food chosen purely for sustenance; of conversations spilling over into the early hours, fuelled by wine and the promise of more sex at dawn. The working days had dragged as she'd repeatedly checked her phone, itching for the hours to roll by so that she could jump on her bike and be with him again. Time had seemed to take on a peculiar elastic quality, the faithful chronology of the era before him long forgotten. It had been less than a month that they'd spent together, but it had felt like a whole summer – a tiny lifetime. It was the way he spoke, clipped but gravelly, the fullness of his lips and the way that he bit down on them when trying to recognize a song, the hollows below his hip bones and the feel of his upper arms, the way he grabbed hold of her hair with both desperation and tenderness when he fucked her.

After finally giving in and opening her heart to him, she was left trying to piece it back together, wondering how she'd got it so wrong, how she could have misinterpreted something so badly. She'd been over their last night together in her mind countless times. He'd seemed distant, which in turn had made her closed off, her words more guarded, sharp even. But there'd been no significant arguments or declarations; nothing else had occurred. Their messages to each other – their entire relationship's correspondence – sat in her hand like dynamite, accessible by the touch of a button. She read over their conversations in the dead of the night, mouthing his words and clutching onto them as evidence of her sanity. It hadn't all come from her; in fact, he'd led the way.

She opened Dan's message back up – an unfunny remark about asking for *'cow's milk per chance'* at coffee shops – the underlying message being that people who request dairy alternatives are pretentious gits. He probably liked fracking and foie gras too, she thought, grinding her teeth.

'Fuck it,' she muttered to herself, then fired out a message before she was able to change her mind.

Daisy: Ha! Anyway it's Friday – Friday is a good day. What are your plans tonight?

She saw him come online and held her breath as though movement might make her visible. Two blue ticks appeared under her message followed by a pause, then he went offline.

'Motherfucker.' She locked her phone then pushed her feelings down through her stomach to a place deep enough to not ruin her day.

At 8.15 a.m., Daisy set off on her bike for the office in Brixton. She'd been working for a small online lifestyle publication for three years now, mostly covering the food pages, critiquing restaurants, interviewing food bloggers that no one had heard of and chefs who photographed well. The pay was terrible but the job wasn't; she just wasn't sure it was right for her. By the end of each week, she'd be left with a nagging feeling that she was merely playing the role of what an acceptable life should look like.

Securing her bike on a side street near the office, she took her phone out of her rucksack and opened a message from Sam.

Sam: Guess what I'm eating

Daisy smiled and walked slowly as she typed.

Daisy: If it's a Portuguese tart pre 9am then we can be best friends

Sam: It's not. It's worse

Daisy: Hit me

Sam: A chupa chup I found on the classroom floor

Daisy: What flavour?

Sam: 🍎

Daisy: Wait, was it in its wrapper?

Sam: YES WHO DO YOU THINK I AM

Daisy: It's 8.42, you're an animal.

Sam: Thanks for your support.
What you doing tonight btw? We're still broke after Croatia so thinking tinnies in Brockwell Park. The Crescents are keen.

The Crescent boys were three of Marvin's friends from school who'd lived together for years on a street called Eden Crescent. Although only one of them remained there, the address still constituted their collective noun.

Daisy checked if Dan had replied, though she knew deep

down that he wasn't going to; her message to him was far too keen. She typed a reply to Sam as she walked towards her office.

Daisy: Great plan. I
IN*

Taking her helmet off, then returning to her screen, she saw that Sam was already typing a response.

Sam: Should warn you though – small chance James might come . . .

'Fuck's sake,' she spat, surprising a man in a suit walking past. It had only been ten days since she'd seen him. Perhaps this was better though, getting their first meeting out of the way rather than it building for months.

Daisy: F/?%!!!$)!(S'.V;':%')
Kidding
In a way
It's fine
I'M FINE
Will be awkward but better to bite the bullet
Will require many tinnies though
Excessive, mountains of tins please

Sam: K good. Think you're right. Re bullet sitch. Tinnies. Got it. Of the craft or lager/value-for-money variety?

Daisy: Craft safer. He seems like a man who would judge a woman drinking large cheap beverages

Sam: He wouldn't do that. You're a great girl remember.

Daisy: 🤮

Sam: WHATACUNT
Ok let's meet usual place. 6.30?

That evening, Daisy was pleased that the ground in the park was hard enough to cycle across the grass. The idea of swooping in on her bike was much more appealing than the painfully slow approach by foot – what to do with one's hands and eyes? But she was disappointed to see only Sam and Marvin on the grass at the bottom of the hill where they usually gathered.

'Oh hey!' Sam called.

Daisy dismounted and leant down to high five them both with one swooping wave, before removing her helmet and rucksack. She took a four pack of beers and a packet of crisps from her bag; usually she brought homemade snacks, cheese straws or crudites and tzatziki, but she'd come straight from work, so Kettle Chips were all she had to offer. She sat down cross-legged on the grass. Sam was wearing a colourful Adidas jacket, worn loosely over a black T-shirt, making Daisy's plain playsuit look drab in comparison.

'This is terrific.' She tugged the sleeve of the jacket. 'Your guys' commitment to retro sportswear is so impressive,' she added, taking in Marvin's New Balance trainers, which she was sure she'd had a similar version to aged nine. 'I'd look like an Eighties PE teacher in that jacket.'

'That's actually just what I was going f—' Sam's sentence was cut off abruptly with a hiccup.

With a sense of wonder rather than judgement, Marvin nodded towards his wife and said, 'She's drunk already.'

Sam placed her hand on her chest and stared into the distance, waiting to see if the hiccups caught on. 'I actually am. I've only had two but they're about seven per cent.'

'Jesus, bloody teachers,' Daisy said in a pointedly Yorkshire accent.

Marvin smiled. 'I wish you were more northern.'

Daisy opened a beer with a gorgeous cracking sound. 'Me too. I think we're all slowly blending into each other. We'll all talk like Imo eventually.'

Marvin laughed at this. 'You two would never sink that low.'

'Damn right,' said Sam. 'She sounds like she's never left Wimbledon.'

'Ain't nothin' wrong with that,' said Marvin, who, apart from a brief stint in Brighton, had lived in South London his entire life. He stretched his legs out in front, leaning backwards and resting his head on Sam's lap.

'Oh, D, James isn't coming anymore,' Sam said quickly. 'He's always a bit flaky.'

'Tell me about it,' Daisy said with humour. Not wanting to say more in front of Marvin, Daisy attempted to deliver multiple thoughts to Sam through her widened eyes.

From above Marvin, Sam looked back at her with alarm as she obviously failed to understand.

'Is everything cool with you guys now?' Marvin asked.

Sam held her beer up to her eye line and examined the graphic cartoon scribblings on the side of the can, childish in her distraction.

'Yeah.' Daisy's voice came out in a higher pitch than usual as she attempted to appear casual. She couldn't trust that Marvin wouldn't go back to James and share her upset over the situation – an indignity she was keen to avoid.

'Sam filled me in on the basics,' Marvin continued. 'I know that you guys were pretty full on for a few weeks. I hope he wasn't too much of a prick about it in the end.'

'No, not a prick. Just . . .' She looked up to the clear sky, eyebrows raised as she searched for the right word. 'Confusing. He was the keen one, then he suddenly wasn't. And a lovely text to finish it.' Her words brimmed with bitterness. She shrugged and looked away, hating how self-pitying she sounded.

'I still can't believe it,' said Sam, who'd been particularly vocal about her disappointment in James. Turning to Marvin as though he was to blame, she added, 'He practically lived at hers for a month, told her he'd never met anyone as amazing as her before . . .' She used her fingers to provide quotation marks and, as though reciting a romcom, took on an American accent to impersonate him. 'Said "he could see himself really falling for her", and then finishes it with one shitty message.'

'Sam.' Daisy's tone was authoritative; this was not a conversation she wanted to have with Marvin.

But Sam continued, her tone exasperated, 'I'm sorry but I still don't get it; it's just not like him at all!'

There was a silence for a few seconds before Marvin responded. 'You know he's not American, right?' He smiled, but Sam didn't, so he continued, 'Daisy, I'm sorry, I don't wanna get involved.' He held both hands up, palms splayed as though putting a stop to Daisy's non-existent words. 'I just know that, at the end of the day, he is a good guy and he wouldn't have wanted to upset you.'

Sam rolled her eyes at this, and Daisy looked away. Her friends' collective outrage at the behaviour of men towards her was passionate and unrelenting, yet she rarely came away from these conversations feeling better. To have people she loved berate men for not loving her only seemed to highlight the loss of their affection more acutely.

'It's fine, Marv. He clearly just changed his mind about me. I've done it to plenty of guys before. At least he didn't *ghost* me.' She'd recently added the word to her small repertoire of zeitgeist vocabulary and couldn't help but pronounce it with flair.

'Well, that'd be pretty hard to do since he'll definitely see you again through us,' said Marvin.

Daisy stared back at him.

'Not that he would *want* to ghost you . . .'

'More a cut-throat message kind of bloke,' she said, her casual façade waning as traces of disapproval made their way onto her lips. 'Anyway, let's stop talking about it. And don't you guys say anything to him!'

Marvin flicked Sam's calf and craned his neck backwards to check she was listening.

'I won't! He knows my stance on the whole situation anyway.'

The light was changing now as the evening drew in and the park took on a rose-tinted glow. A middle-aged Asian couple kicked a football to each other in the distance. The woman kept picking up the dupatta of her cream salwar kameez and flinging it back over her shoulder after she ran for the ball. Daisy's eyes searched the people around them for a child or a teenager, an explanation for the activity, but they were alone – the game obviously their choice – and this made her smile again as she listened to the faint tap of the football between them.

To the left of the unlikely footballers, Daisy spotted two of the Crescent boys approaching in the distance. 'Oh, here's Matty and Ellis.' She waved with both hands, and Sam and Marvin turned around, tracing her line of vision and waving too when they spotted them.

After exchanging greetings, Daisy shuffled towards Sam. The two of them wordlessly arranged themselves to sit back-to-back, leaning on each other to continue their conversation. The boys started playing frisbee, and Daisy and Sam half watched while discussing their days. They pulled their jackets tighter around their shoulders, the air cooler now as the sun retreated. The park was still busy with many people like them trying to squeeze the last moments out of the day. A young couple, with a baby in a black sling across the man's chest, walked by, and the woman, wearing a denim boiler suit and sunglasses despite the fading light, turned and smiled at Sam and Daisy.

'They look like a famous couple,' said Daisy quietly, once they'd passed.

'I think they're just cool young parents,' said Sam, still watching them. 'That's what I want to be like: still coming to the park for a few drinks with Marv and the baby.'

'You're only saying that because they're dressed stylishly – this could be the first time they've left the house in weeks.'

Sam laughed. 'True.'

Daisy turned her head but couldn't read Sam's expression

from the angle. She'd always talked about having her first baby aged thirty, as though life was that easy to plan out. Daisy wondered if she too should be having these maternal desires. When they were at university, motherhood had seemed so far into the future that it was almost an abstract notion, one that Daisy had openly voiced her uncertainty over; it made for an interesting conversation. What she hadn't shared, however, was a long-standing assuredness, deep down, that as her age increased, so would her desire for children. The evidence was all around her: the vast majority of women chose to have children. But now she was thirty and her best friend was actively trying to get pregnant, yet her own anticipated desire for the same future was still to arrive.

They watched the game of frisbee play out in front; Daisy wanted to join in but not enough to leave the comfort of Sam's tipsy chatter and the warmth of her shoulders. She checked her phone: no messages. Perhaps it was the beer, or possibly just that she was with her best friend but, for the first time in days, she felt that she could breathe again.

winter

Sam

Sam walked her regular route from her and Marvin's flat to Brixton tube station. It was unseasonably warm, and she had to remove her beanie and undo her coat after a few minutes. She longed for the cold winters of her childhood, where the air was crisp and sharp in her lungs and snow a frequent visitor. The tepid wet weather felt surreal in December, the Christmas decorations adorning the shop windows early intruders.

Heading through quiet residential streets where houses hadn't yet been broken up into flats – a sign of incomprehensible wealth – she peered through the windows as she passed, hungry for a glimpse of the lives of people inhabiting three million pound homes. Most of them had plantation shutters in the large bay windows, their residents clearly aware of the prying eyes that passed.

She reached the tube and removed her heavy wool coat to join the statues on the escalator. Positioning herself on the right, she slowly descended into the day, observing, with interest, the enthusiastic souls on the left who strode towards it. As usual, she used her travel time to catch up on messages, laughing particularly at one from Imo who'd just returned from her firm's mandatory debauched Christmas party in Barcelona.

Imo: Here's a game. Which one of these events did NOT occur:
a) guy from floor below took his penis out in the bar and walked around showing it to everyone
b) I snogged Alex from the M&A team
c) I was forced to lie on the bar and have champagne poured into my mouth while everyone chanted 'Chug'
d) One of the partners did coke off Cat's stomach before they ducked
e) I was sick in a bag on the plane on the way home
*fucked (bastard PG iPhone)

Sam: It's d). That cannot be true. You've been watching Wolf of Wall Street. Cat is hot and like 26 no? Partner is surely 50 and in my mind resembles Jack Nicholson on that boat with those women.
OH GOD WAS IT LIKE JACK NICHOLSON ON THAT BOAT WITH THOSE WOMEN?
WHO IS ALEX? THIS IS EXCITING
DO PEOPLE STILL SAY CHUG?
IS PENIS-IN-HAND GUY ALEX?

In a very different conversation, her mum sent a photo of a wreath she'd made at a floristry course.

Sam: Looks amazing. Can you make me one please? Sure it'll be fine to post . . .

As the tube paused at Vauxhall and the Wi-Fi returned, the replies came through.

Imo: It was b). Alex doesn't exist. I would never pull someone I work with – do you not know me at allllll woman?????? Cat is 28 and he's like ? early 40s. Married with kids and pretending to be a normal person. She felt really shit the next day, think it was a moral lapse.

Mum: Fat chance. Class was £40 and only one glass of bubbles!!!!!!!!

Sam: They're double that in London. That's a bargain! You should've smuggled your own booze in.

Sam: Fucking hell! Hope she gets that promotion. KIDDING. Hope she's ok.
Yes true, you don't ever pull work people. Well done.

Imo: Penis in hand was some guy called Mark who started 6 months ago. IMAGINE

Mum: Your Aunty Jess made us drink a bottle beforehand so we were a bit meerry when we got there.

Sam: You're typing like you're a bit merry right now

Mum: It's 8am!!! I hope you're joking!

Sam: Yes, obviously joking Mum

Her thumb hovered over the text box, wondering if her tone was too sharp. She switched back to Imo.

Sam: Jesus, has Mark been arrested for indecent exposure? Or at least resigned?

Imo: Nope, just carrying on like it never happened

The train arrived, and she squeezed out of the carriage with a large crowd, holding her phone up to her face and waiting for the signal to come back.

Sam: Gossip: one of Imo's colleagues got his todger out at the bar at their Christmas party

Mum: What the hell!!!!! Did she get a picture?

Sam giggled to herself as she reached the top of the escalators at Pimlico, tapping out with her phone and weaving her way to the quieter side streets that led to her school. She had started at Parkmoor almost three years ago, teaching the five-year-olds of the city's one per cent how to add, spell, and colour. Initially she'd been apprehensive about moving to the private education sector, but eventually she'd put her vague concerns to the back of her mind and gladly accepted the 8k pay rise. She'd chosen teaching partly for the stability – her dad had worked for himself and decorating jobs were 'often like buses': too many, then none at all. As a family, they hadn't exactly struggled, but money had been tight at times and, as a result, Sam would always be acutely aware of the balance in her bank account. She'd known that if she wanted to stay in London and get her foot on the property ladder, she couldn't overlook the opportunity for such a pay rise.

At the time, Daisy had been outraged at Sam's decision, insisting that she was selling out and sacrificing her morals for a bit more cash. It didn't offend Sam. She knew that Daisy had been brought up differently – not exactly wealthy, but her parents had a pretty big house in Yorkshire and academic careers. Daisy could afford to hold such high morals because she had more security to fall back on. Imo also helped diffuse the situation, since she'd attended private school herself and actively encouraged the move, accusing Daisy of being a naive and ill-informed Champagne socialist.

The longer holidays were a huge bonus to the private sector and, only ten days into December, it was already the penultimate day of school. The morning passed with relative ease, and only a handful of the children were unable to contain their mounting excitement at the impending tombola and sugar treats available at the Christmas fair that afternoon. Sam enjoyed the school fairs: there was always a warm atmosphere and, although she did have to speak to lots of the parents and vaguely keep an eye out for unruly children, staff were generally able to relax and drink mulled wine (though never enough to appear tipsy). She tended to station herself in a corner with colleagues who were equally excited at the opportunity to drink while being paid.

The grand hall was Nutcracker themed this year. Decorations made by the children – some more impressive than others – adorned the wooden panelled walls, and a large round table stood in the centre, housing an exciting array of raffle prizes. Craft stalls selling various handmade trinkets and decorations ran along the length of the hall, many of them run by mothers of children at the school.

After polite conversation with many of the parents, Sam sat down next to two teacher friends, Komal and Stacey.

'Shotgun the Fortnum Mason hamper this year,' said Stacey, looking over to the raffle table.

'I'll take the Champagne,' Sam said.

'I thought you weren't drinking at the moment?' asked Komal.

'What do you think this is?' Sam lowered her paper cup to reveal her mulled wine.

'Ohhh. It's just that you had a Diet Coke before, which is so not like you,' said Stacey with a frown. 'So we thought, you know, maybe . . .'

They both stared at her like idiots.

'Jesus, no!' Sam felt distinctly uncomfortable with this unexpected accost. 'When did you two become the drinks police? I had a coke because it was 2 p.m. and I didn't want to be pissed by 4 p.m.'

'All right! Sorry, we got all excited for you,' Komal said in a sickly-sweet voice, squeezing her elbow.

'Oh god no, we only just got married.'

'In May – hardly *just*,' corrected Stacey.

Sam drank her mulled wine – suddenly tart and difficult to swallow – and turned to the rest of the room, hoping for a distraction. Before either of them had a chance to ask anything else, she changed the topic to their Christmas party. 'So, are you two getting changed tomorrow or going straight there in work stuff?'

★

That evening, sitting on the sofa after dinner, Sam shared the conversation with Marvin as he finished washing up.

'They honestly looked at me like I was ruining their day by drinking, bursting the bubble of their weird fantasy of me being pregnant.' She picked up her mint tea to take a sip.

Marvin pulled the plug at the kitchen sink, wiped his hands on a tea towel, then joined her on the sofa. 'People are always like that for a bit after a wedding; it's drilled into them from all the cheesy films in the world: you get married, then you immediately get pregnant.'

'But they really don't know me that well – what if I'd just had a miscarriage . . . or a termination?'

'Did you tell them that we were trying?'

''Course I didn't tell them!' she said, a notch louder than needed.

'All right!' he said, raising his hands in surrender and laughing a little at her exasperation. 'Good, I was only checking. You've told the girls.'

She sensed something accusatory in his voice. 'What? Daisy, Imo, and Jas? That's completely different – of course I've told them! But work people? God no. They'd all be looking at me expectantly, monitoring my alcohol and . . . shellfish intake.'

'How much shellfish do you eat at . . . you know what, I don't want to—'

'We just have prawns occasionally,' she interrupted before he could insult her school again. 'It's not like we're having bloody lobster banquets for lunch each day.'

'Can you not eat prawns if you're pregnant?'

'No . . . I don't know! Anyway, we've got off topic. There's no way I'm telling anyone from work. Imagine if the Head of Early Years or some other amazing position came up and everyone knew I was trying to get pregnant – they'd be like: what's the point, we'll just have to replace her in a year.'

'You don't get replaced; it'd be maternity cover. Plus, that's one hundred per cent illegal.'

'Yes, but it blatantly still happens all the time. And even if people actively try not to discriminate, there could be an unconscious bias there where they'd tell themselves that I didn't perform that well at interview or whatever. So no, I will not be telling work people.'

They were silent for a minute, and Marvin played with her fingers in a distracted way, tugging each upwards until it flicked back down.

'So, just to be clear,' Marvin said, 'I don't think that you *should* be telling work people. You're talking like you're trying to convince me.'

'No, I know. You just asked me like you thought I might be planning to.'

'It's your job, your friends – it's your decision at the end of the day.' He shrugged. 'But yes, I think it'd be a bit weird if everyone knew we were trying.'

'God, I hate that term.'

'Trying?'

'Yeah. But there isn't really an alternative.' She shuffled down, deeper into the sofa and into the crook of his shoulder. 'Have you not told any of your friends?'

'What?'

She shifted her head to look up at him, determining if he was genuine. 'Have you not told any of your friends that we are . . . having purposeful unprotected sex, in the hope of creating a child?'

'No. But when I do, I'll be sure to use those words exactly.'

Sam bit her thumbnail as she looked at him. 'None at all? I thought you'd have told Matty or James.'

'I probably will tell them; it just hasn't come up yet. I think guys tell each other once the deed's done.'

'"The deed" sounds dodgy.'

'Okay. Once the seed is planted.'

'Quite literally.'

'Speaking of.' He raised his eyebrows suggestively at her.

'What, you want to sow your seeds right now?'

He continued to bounce his eyebrows up and down, his face serious.

'Are you not really full after tea?'

'Never too full for . . . gardening.'

'Okay. We've gone too far.'

Marvin tutted. 'You had to ruin it before I could get in something about a hose.'

She smiled. 'I might change my mind in an hour, but I'm really knackered. Plus, I'm getting my period so there isn't much point in terms of . . . sowing.'

'You didn't tell me you were getting your period?'

'I'm telling you now,' she said, irritated. 'It hasn't arrived but my boobs are sore; I was really hot last night. I can just tell.'

Since they'd started trying to get pregnant, Sam had become acutely aware of her premenstrual symptoms. A few days before her period arrived, she'd experience night sweats and a general low-level irritation at the world. She usually tried to delay telling Marvin, since delivering the news and watching him absorb it wasn't the most uplifting of tasks.

'Argh.' Marvin sat forward on the sofa, rubbing at the stubble on his jaw, disappointment seeping from him like a tangible mist. 'That's a shame,' he said at last, smiling weakly at her. 'I was thinking it'd be really nice if we knew over Christmas. Like this exciting secret between the two of us, and we could plan the year ahead.'

'That would have been nice,' she said softly. 'You'd have had to subtly drink all the Christmas Eve cocktails for me.'

His features softened. 'And that would have been a disaster.'

Their smiles faded, and he rubbed her thigh, patting it to draw a line under the conversation.

'Remind me what you're doing this weekend, again?' he asked.

'Saturday I'll be hungover.'

'Oh right, it's your Christmas thing tomorrow, isn't it?'

'Yep,' she said without enthusiasm. 'I'm sure it'll be fine when we get there. Daisy's work party is tomorrow as well, so she might come over and hang out on Saturday for a duvet day.'

'Mmm. Good idea – you can ride it out together. Is she still pulling that guy from her building?'

'Jono? Yes.'

There was a silence between them for a moment, and she wondered if he too was still disappointed that Daisy and James hadn't worked out.

'He works for some architect's firm, a few floors below, so it's not like they're colleagues,' she added.

'Ah, okay.' Marvin considered. 'And does he sound nice?'

'Too soon to tell.' Sam smiled blandly, not wanting to betray her friend.

Two days later and, as predicted, Sam was exceptionally hungover.

'Oh, Lamp,' Marvin said with sympathy when he saw her sitting up in bed staring into the space in front of her through remnants of black eye make-up, ineffectually removed at 3 a.m. He placed a glass down on the bedside table with some paracetamol.

She looked slowly at the glass and then to him, fully dressed in sports kit, and her heart swelled with the kind of love only achievable through tequila-derived hangover anxiety.

'I don't want you to go,' she said simply, taking hold of his shirt gently like it was a rare piece of material she'd never come across.

He stroked her cheek with his thumb and said, 'Daisy'll be over soon.'

'But she won't stroke my hair.'

'She might if you ask nicely.' He kissed the top of her matted blonde hair. 'You literally stink of booze. Like, impressively so. Was it a good night?'

She nodded slowly, her face a picture of glumness.

Marvin couldn't help but laugh.

Looking up at him, she saw herself through his eyes and laughed too. 'Don't,' she groaned and fell back into the covers. 'I need caring for. I need you to be my carer for the day. Please, Marvin. In sickness and in health.'

'I brought you Berocca!' He took hold of her ankle sticking

out from the duvet and gave it an affectionate squeeze as he retreated to the hallway. 'Love you, babe.'

'Love you.' Her voice was muffled from her face-down position on the bed.

At 1 p.m., Sam opened the door to Daisy and took in her hair tied in a messy top knot, dungarees over an old stripy T-shirt beneath her checked coat. 'Okay, good. You look how I feel.'

Daisy looked down at her outfit as she stepped through the door. 'You said you felt like utter shit?'

They walked through to the living area, and Sam plonked herself dramatically back down on the sofa. Daisy pulled out a kitchen chair opposite her and started unpacking her rucksack full of snacks that Sam had begged her to bring: cheese scones, Pringles, and Lucozade. Daisy had made cheese scones in their second year of university, and they'd swiftly become their hangover cure, with the girls frequently begging her to restock the freezer with a life-saving supply.

'I take it back. You always manage to maintain an air of glamour in a hangover, like a kind of off-duty celebrity. But an eccentric one who only dresses in natural fibres.'

'I hate to disappoint, but this is definitely a Primark polyester situation,' Daisy said, fingering the neck of her T-shirt.

'Even so, you've still got that natural aura going on.' Sam thrust the palm of her hand at her in a circular motion as though cleaning a window.

Daisy laughed a little, opening a can of Pringles and taking a stack before throwing them over. Sam had always marvelled at Daisy's low-key beauty regime, particularly her hair – a dark caramel blonde that many women would highlight but that she had always kept natural. Sam had been dyeing her hair since she was fourteen and wasn't actually sure what her natural colour was anymore. Daisy also managed to look lovely in the morning, fresh-faced with her clear skin, strong eyebrows and green eyes, whereas Sam felt completely washed out without make-up.

Before they'd met at university, Daisy had reminded Sam of the current chart topper: Joss Stone. Daisy and Imo had built up a kind of status on campus: two tall cousins with mismatched accents who barely left each other's sides, smoked constantly, and didn't exactly exude warmth. Imo had blonde highlights back then, making their resemblance easier to spot. A few weeks in, Sam got chatting to Daisy in the cafeteria and laughed more in fifteen minutes than she had in total since unpacking in her new bedroom. The cool exterior didn't match up with the eccentric charm of the golden girl before her, dry witted and excitedly sporting a new fleece from a local garden centre.

On their first night out together, Sam had affectionately told Daisy about the Joss Stone similarity, but Daisy's face was blank. The gaping holes in her knowledge of popular culture was mind-boggling to Sam who, along with all her friends, had Radio 1 on at all hours and inhaled the celebrity news in *Heat* magazine each week. Sam had grown up in the Wirral and spent her adolescence traipsing into Liverpool for shopping trips and nights out. She was both mystified and intimidated by Daisy – this wild girl who seemed to have descended from the Moors, smoked roll-ups instead of Marlboro Lights, and listened to music Sam's parents liked. But their shared sense of humour and shock of being surrounded by southerners who'd descended on Newcastle – seemingly straight from the corridors of boarding schools – had soon secured their friendship. Under each other's influence, Sam eventually accepted that her parents had had a point about Bob Dylan and Joni Mitchell, and Daisy binged three seasons of *Grey's Anatomy* in reading week. Over the years, they'd morphed more solidly into a middle ground but retained enough individualism to still hold a torch for each other's quirks.

'Stop fawning over my aura with your anxious eyes,' Daisy said as she placed two scones in the microwave.

'Sorry. I can't help it.' Sam always experienced a low-level anxiety alongside her hangover after work parties. 'Oh my god, you actually brought cheese scones! Are they the Marmite ones?'

Daisy gave a wink of confirmation.

'Fucking *yes*, I'm actually salivating. Now tell me about your night. Did you go home with Jono?'

The microwave beeped, and Daisy opened the door, clattering plates and knives as she buttered the scones. 'I want to hear about your party first!'

'It was boring. Fine. Same as always. I drank too much – thought I had a point to prove because people had made pregnancy comments – went too far. Standard.' Sam reached for her water glass and took several gulps, forcing the liquid down. 'No, it wasn't that bad. I only have a few regrets.' She eyed Daisy, reluctant to continue.

Daisy walked over and handed Sam a plate, the perfectly round fluffy scone sitting in the centre, the mouthwatering smell of baked cheddar filling the room. 'Such as?'

Sam took the plate and sighed, puffing her cheeks out. 'I thought it'd be a good idea to play "Never Have I Ever".'

'Oooh,' Daisy grimaced. '*Never* with colleagues.'

Sam rested her head on the arm of the sofa and, staring at the ceiling, said, 'Also fell over in the street . . .' She lifted her tracksuit bottoms to show a marbled green bruise on her left knee.

'Right.' Daisy gestured to the knee. 'Anyone see?'

'Not sure . . . maybe not?' Sam bit into the scone, the dense dough filling her mouth and immediately suppressing the persistent nausea of the morning. The subtle kick of marmite added a gratifying richness, and Sam chewed with pleasure, licking the salty butter from her lips.

'Great. All fine then. A boring night. And . . . you're definitely not pregnant?'

Sam finished chewing, pointing to her mouth and shaking her head in disbelief before giving Daisy the sign for perfect with her right hand. She swallowed, then said, 'Got my period yesterday.'

'Ah, sorry, kid. Do you think that's why you had so much to drink?' Daisy sat down at the other end of the sofa next to Sam's tie-dye bed socks, taking a hefty bite out of her own scone.

Sam shifted her feet up to make more room. She'd been considering this question herself all morning. 'I don't know, maybe. I mean, it was the Christmas party. I don't binge drink that much anymore, do I? Not like ten years ago.'

'No, definitely not,' Daisy said through the mouthful of scone. 'But last month, when you got your period, you also got really drunk with Imo, so . . . I hate to sound like a therapist but I'm *sensing a pattern.*'

Sam picked at a stain on the sleeve of her sweatshirt; an unidentifiable blob of crimson – possibly some jam from last weekend – had formed a tacky mound on the cuff. She was making up her mind about whether to feel attacked by Daisy's statement, despite suspecting as much herself.

'Maybe,' she said at last, looking up at Daisy. 'I know it's only been eight months, but it's still disappointing every time. And really shit having to tell Marvin, like kicking a puppy.'

Daisy offered a sympathetic tightening of her lips.

Sam put her plate down on the sofa and brought her knees up to her chest, wrapping her arms around them. 'It's funny, last week I was worrying about if I was pregnant, then how the hell I'd get out of drinking at the Christmas party. It'd be so obvious, I'd just have to feign illness and not go.'

Daisy reached over to her rucksack and removed two bottles of Lucozade, passing one to Sam, then said, 'Would it be so bad if people knew, though?'

'Well, it's the waiting until twelve weeks thing,' Sam said through a mouthful of crisps. 'I know you don't *have to* wait, but I personally wouldn't want everyone at work to know if I did miscarry.' She swallowed and rested her head on the back of the sofa. 'Urgh, that word—'

'—Miscarriage? It's so "pointing the finger", isn't it?' Daisy sat up taller, the topic pricking her interest. She loved to get into conversations about societal attitudes – particularly concerning women or climate change – and while Sam usually agreed with her views, she struggled to summon the same level of passion.

Too tired to enter a conversation on the narrative around pregnancy loss, Sam quickly skipped to a different topic. 'Anyway, Jono?'

Daisy took a deep breath and stretched her feet out on the sofa, her legs in line with Sam's like they were playing a game of sleeping fish. 'Well, I stayed at his again last Saturday and we've been messaging quite a lot this week. Then last night we ended up kissing in the bar in front of a few people.'

'Oh my god! So everyone knows now?'

'Yeah, but remember, it's not like we actually work together – we basically share coffee and an occasional social activity with his company. Plus—,' She fiddled with a button on the back of the sofa as she said, 'it's been a few weeks now . . . I think it could potentially go somewhere.'

'Shit!' Sam said, genuinely surprised. Daisy hadn't been remotely serious about anyone for the last few years, apart from James. 'Amazing, a little Christmas romance!'

Daisy's eyes flashed to Sam's, and there was an edge to her voice when she replied, 'Right, you never know, it might even last until New Year's.'

Sam frowned, privately appalled at her lack of tact. 'D, I didn't mean it like that. I meant, like, it can be a bit shit to be single at Christmas sometimes – I definitely felt that, anyway – so what better time for a new relationship to start?'

Daisy swigged from her Lucozade while eyeing Sam keenly. 'Okay, because a "little Christmas romance" sounds quite like a "holiday romance", i.e. short-lived. Which, let's face it, with my record, it probably will be.' She leant over to the coffee table to place her bottle down, then sat back up and, with a renewed seriousness, said, 'But I can't cope with even *you* assuming that.'

''Course not,' Sam said, scrunching up her forehead and shaking her head, though in truth, she suspected Jono was a mere distraction, a plaster over the wound that James had inflicted.

Daisy had a tendency to get with unsuitable men who clearly

weren't interested in anything long term. Sam viewed it as a kind of subconscious self-preservation strategy; there was no danger of the liaisons lasting more than a handful of meet-ups – enough for her to come away at the worst singed, never scorched. At the other end of the spectrum were a few unlucky bastards who were bowled over by her but utterly failed to capture her full attention. James had seemed a hopeful anomaly who didn't quite fit either category, but then he changed his mind about the prospect of anything long term. Sam still caught him looking over at Daisy on the few occasions they'd all been together; she was certain he still had feelings for her.

'Anyway, you can meet him later,' Daisy said, reaching across for her Lucozade again. 'He's staying at mine for the first time, so he'll pick me up from here.'

'Oh great,' Sam said, willing her features into an expression of enthusiasm.

Daisy

The following Friday, Daisy headed into town to meet the girls. They'd had the date in the diary for months as their last get together before all heading off to different corners of the country for Christmas. Daisy made her way through the pinstripe pack of men crowding outside the pub near Imo's. She ordered two tonic waters at the bar, then joined the crowds spilling out onto the pavement outside. Choosing a spot against the wall, she placed the drinks on the windowsill, then subtly topped them up with a hipflask of gin she'd brought from home. It was something she hadn't had to resort to in years, but following lots of evenings out and Christmas present buying, she was heavily into her overdraft. Recently it felt like her friends were becoming richer, their tastes more refined and their homes more polished, whereas she was feeling the financial strain more than ever. She hated that everything was more expensive in London as a single person, that people were forced to pair up to afford the cost of living.

Hugging her coat around her, she took the tobacco tin out the front pocket of her rucksack and started to roll a cigarette.

'Daisy!' Imo appeared, squeezing past a large group in front. 'Look at you! You're like a parrot among pigeons.' She hugged her then stepped back to further take in her red and black checked coat and scuffed trainers.

'All right? Did you mean to pick the most unlikely place I would ever be found? I feel like a canary in the trenches.'

'Oh good one – shall we continue with bird similes throughout the evening?'

Daisy smiled and lit her cigarette.

Imo said, 'No, I haven't actually been here before, but it was recommended by someone – good drinks and music. Is this for me?' she said, gesturing to the other glass on the windowsill.

'Oh, yes, I assumed a G&T would be fine.' Daisy passed it over, straining to identify the generic indie song from inside – Imo usually listened to mindless dance music that the rest of them hated.

''Course, thanks.' Imo took the glass, then, spotting Daisy's confusion, said, 'Oh, I meant good music for *you guys*; I'm selfless like that.' She took a sip from her drink. 'Jesus! That's strong. Is it a double?'

'Er, yep.'

She took another sip and whooped suddenly, turning several heads which she failed to notice. 'Double gin – what were you thinking? Kidding, I'm almost acclimatized.' She checked her watch as she sipped tentatively. 'So Jas won't be here until about 7.30 p.m. Sam's the same, right?'

Daisy and Imo had agreed to meet as soon as they'd finished work, despite the others not being able to make it until later. Though they'd never voice any such sentiment to each other, Daisy was quite sure that Imo agreed their time together as a pair was both precious and too fleeting these days. The lifelong bond and shared family backdrop enabled a different level of communication to her friends; there was no one in the world who could talk such shit to Daisy and, in doing so, leave her feeling restored.

'I think closer to 8 p.m. – some staff meeting bollocks.'

Imo narrowed her eyes. 'Why anyone would choose to be a teacher, I do not know.' She rummaged in her large black Mulberry handbag for her cigarettes, her chestnut hair falling forward from its neat blunt bob.

Daisy opened her palm to display her lighter.

'Ah, saviour.' Imo leant in, cupping her hand around to make a shield as the cigarette was lit, then angled her mouth to blow the smoke swiftly to her right. 'No one smokes anymore, do they? It pisses me off.'

'I'm down to one a day. Unless I'm drinking; then it goes to shit.'

'One a day? Christ, don't join the others and leave me out here puffing away alone like an old *Ab Fab* extra.'

'An extra? You're like one hundred per cent Patsy. No, I can't see that happening for a while, unfortunately. But I'm sick of spending a tenner a week and worrying about my impending death. Doesn't it concern you that we've been doing this for over fifteen years now?' They'd smoked their first cigarettes together on a family holiday in the south of France.

Imo looked at her and exhaled, then flicked ash onto the pavement. 'No.'

'No?' Imo's stubbornness was, at times, exasperating.

'No, not really.'

'You have no concerns about what smoking does to your health?' Daisy took another sip of her gin, cringing before wiping her lips with the back of her hand in an attempt to remove some of the taste. Was it triples she'd created?

Imo smiled at her reaction. 'I'm not one of those deniers; obviously I know that smoking has major health implications, is terrible for the NHS, blah blah blah . . . But we're also living longer than ever before.'

'Too long, if anything.'

'Exactly. We have the best diets we've ever had; I work out, like, once a month. We've got no idea what's going to happen in life, so we should at least *try* to enjoy it. Gen Z with all their smoothies and meditation and political awareness. I mean, *Jesus*.' Making quotation marks with her fingers and feigning a well-spoken old lady's voice, she added, 'Youth is wasted on them.' She gulped down some more of her drink, grimacing, before adding, 'You're quite Gen Z actually, aren't you?'

'I'll take that as an insult, following your previous sentence.'

'No but you drink and smoke and *dabble*, so it's okay. Otherwise we couldn't possibly be related, least not friends.'

Daisy chose to ignore this and said simply, 'Gin face?'

'Sure.'

They both gulped from their glasses and then stared at each other, poker faced, silently reeling from the assault.

After swallowing several times, Imo said, 'I think that helped. It's like you're telling your body everything is fine.'

'I actually think Gen Z have got things pretty right. And even if they haven't, they've been dealt a completely shit hand: massive student debts, no chance of buying a property; their lives revolve around social media, and they're even more fucked than us when it comes to climate change!'

Imo sighed. 'You're probably right. Still think they could do with a few lines though.'

Daisy leant her head back on the windowpane, a smile nudging at the corners of her mouth. 'You're such a city cunt.'

'Said the northern hippie.'

'Hippies would be embarrassed to associate with me.'

'As would city cunts with me. Just kidding. They all *love* me.' And at that very moment she spotted an acquaintance approaching from behind Daisy. 'Charles! How lovely to see you.'

'Imogen.' He leant in, and they kissed on both cheeks.

'This is my cousin, Daisy.'

Daisy raised her hand stiffly into a wave, which could also be interpreted as a stop sign. She much preferred the northern routine of a nod, wave, or possible handshake upon introduction, rather than the double kiss shenanigans that this set had adopted from the French. 'Hi,' she said, smiling without revealing any teeth.

He mimicked her wave, with possible sarcasm or awkwardness, she couldn't tell. His eyes tracked her up and down to take in her non-corporate clothes and make-up free face. 'Hi there, how's it going?' he said with little interest. 'So, Imogen, it's been *time*.' He elongated the vowel sound as a sort of onomatopoeic time scale. 'Wasn't Geneva the last time I saw you? Remember the drinking game with Freddie? That was so epic.'

'Er, *do* I? "Hats off Badger!"' she shouted out, cupping her hand around her mouth to project the words.

Charles laughed, a staccato gasping hoot which Daisy couldn't help but curl her top lip at.

'That was such a fun week,' said Imo, her manner all of a sudden coquettish. 'Are you lot going to Stockholm in Feb?'

'We certainly are, old girl,' he said suggestively.

'Fantastic,' she said, smirking at him. She raised her drink to his and said, 'I'll see you there. It was *so* nice to bump into you.'

He tipped his glass to hers and, realizing he was being bid goodbye, added with some disappointment, 'Yes, you too.'

'Have a good night now. Don't go too wild – I know what you're like.'

'Ha! No, 'course not.' He winked, and Imo opened her mouth widely in mock surprise, pointing to him in a 'You got me!' fashion.

'Bye, Charles,' she said, smiling now.

'Bye,' Daisy added politely.

He raised his hand to them both and turned, sipping on his pint casually, then bumping into the man next to him. They pretended not to notice.

'What the fuck was that?' Daisy whispered fervently.

'I know, amazing, right?' Imo sounded genuinely proud.

'"Hats off badger?" Who even are you? Are they all like that?'

She shrugged. 'Not all. Plus, he's sweet. They're not all bad people, Daisy.'

'No, I'm sure they're not. It's just . . . is anyone northern? Or not Caucasian?'

'Oh yeah, no: diversity is terrible. There's a lot of Europeans, some Asians. But there aren't any female partners, no one with disabilities . . . northerners? I don't think you guys really qualify as a minority group, darling . . .'

'Obviously I'm not comparing us, but are there any?'

'There must be . . . Yes, there are a couple. I think one of the partners might be from Birmingham actually?'

'That's not the north.'

'Oh, come on.'

'It's just depressing how nothing has changed,' Daisy said with dismay. 'What's that fact about CEOs? There's more called David in the UK then there are women. Is that it?'

'I think so.' Imo leant heavily against the wall beside Daisy, scanning the tide of suits in front of her. 'But it is changing; it really is. There are some really progressive firms coming through. There's a lot of women in finance now, so there will have to be a management shift eventually.' She turned to Daisy and said, 'I know you think I'm a shallow bitch, selling my soul to the corporate machine, but it's not all like that. I'm actually good at what I do, and I want to change it from within.' She looked back out at the men in front. 'I just have to play their game for a bit to get there.'

The conversation paused as Daisy looked out, considering the people around them. She turned back to Imo and said with a smile, 'Well, if that was anything to go by, you're very good at playing their game.'

Imo laughed loudly. 'Oh, I know. I was born for this shit.'

Daisy folded her arms and turned to face her cousin. 'What

was I born for, please? You obviously chose the right profession *for you*, whereas I'm still dossing around in a job I don't really like, googling surf instructor vacancies in my lunch hour.'

'You can't surf?'

'Exactly. I'm royally fucked.'

Imo smiled and considered Daisy as she sipped through her straw. 'Okay, so let's think of what you like: books, beaches, food . . .'

'And dogs.'

'And dogs,' Imo repeated. 'So I'm thinking like a mobile library with a cute dog that serves homemade ice cream and travels the coast of Britain. Hey!' she almost shouted, jubilant to have solved Daisy's decade-long career dilemma.

So desperate for a solution, Daisy actually gave the idea a moment's serious consideration before laughing at herself. 'Could be some hygiene rating issues with the dog and ice cream combo, but I'm sure nothing that we can't overcome.'

'That's the spirit.' Perhaps spotting a weariness in Daisy, Imo added in a quieter voice, 'It'll come to you. I don't know what exactly, but I don't think you belong in an office. Unless it's in a treehouse and you're working for Greenpeace. Drink?' she asked, gulping down the last of hers.

They headed inside once their reserved table became free: a cosy corner spot with a curved leather banquette. The pub's soundtrack switched to Christmas songs, and the air was alive with mulled wine spices and buttery pastry from their signature Wellington dishes. The lighting inside was a mixture of candles and old-fashioned lamps, not dissimilar to the Victorian street lights that lined the pavement outside, and the combined effect threw a honeycomb gold over the walls.

Jas arrived at her promised 7.30 p.m., a whirl of five-foot-two energy, elated at having finished her shift in time for the meal. They ordered a further round of G&Ts and settled into their corner, raising their voices to be heard over the hundred others around them.

'So, what's the latest with the wedding?' Daisy asked, turning to Jas. 'Can we book our flights yet?' Jas and Ash had finally set the date for May the following year and chosen a venue in Seville.

'Yep, it's legit happening, book away.' She gave an elaborate flick of her wrist, batting the subject of weddings away. 'In more exciting news . . .' She paused for dramatic effect as she took off her black polo-neck, getting it momentarily stuck on her head and reappearing with a messed-up fringe and laughter. 'Guess what I'm doing tomorrow?'

Imo held a palm out to Daisy's face, ensuring she didn't cut in with the first guess, then frowned at Jas as though pulling the information from her brain with psychic powers. In slow and over-pronounced words, she said, 'You're getting . . . a fringe cut.'

'For fuck's sake,' Daisy muttered with amusement.

'My fringe is fine, bitch.' Jas laughed, patting her hair.

'You're delivering triplets?'

'No,' Jas said, looking at Daisy with interest, 'but that would be cool – only done twins so far. No, I'm being *interviewed* on Radio London!'

'What!' they both shrieked. 'How come?'

'The media department at the hospital hooked me up; they

were looking for a gynae doctor to do a weekly slot for teens about sexual health, contraception, you know, the lot.'

'Oh, you'll be awesome at that,' Imo said.

Jas had always been passionate about this subject. In their very first year at university, she'd helped second year medical students on a sexual health stall in freshers' week, handing out free condoms and leaflets about STIs. It was actually how Sam had met her: wandering up, intrigued by rumoured freebies, then ending up chatting with her for nearly an hour. (Jas loved to explain to people that it was sex that had first brought them together). Since graduating, she'd volunteered for numerous school talks on everything from consent to puberty and was involved in a charity working with FGM victims.

'Thanks – I hope so,' she replied. 'If it goes well, then I'm thinking of setting up Instagram and TikTok accounts – so they can DM me with questions and stuff they daren't ask anyone else.'

'Jas, you are *perfect* for this,' Daisy said. 'You should talk about body positivity too – your specialty.'

Jas sat up higher and proudly ran her hands down the sides of her torso as she wiggled, 'Yes, babe! Although' – she slumped back down – 'maybe that's a bit off topic.'

Imo shrugged. 'Whatever, mate, it'll be your thing – you can choose the topics. What are you going to call the account?'

'Well.' Jas tipped her head to one side and said, 'It's not particularly inventive but I was thinking "Ask Dr Jas"?'

'Perfect.'

Imo took her phone out and said, 'And is that abbreviating doctor? @AskDrJas? Because I've got a *friend* with this rash . . .'

★

Their glasses soon emptied again, and Daisy headed back to the bar.

'Wow,' a woman next to her said quietly to her friend, having tapped her card to the machine. 'This is literally the cheapest place in the City.'

'I can't believe you haven't been here before; I *lived* in here when I was a trainee,' the friend replied.

Imo's reasons for choosing the bar suddenly became clear. Since landing a job with one of the City's biggest financial firms aged twenty-three, on a salary significantly higher than Daisy's current one, Imo boasted the biggest disposable income that Daisy knew of. She had obviously chosen the bar with Daisy in mind, not wanting to patronize her by insisting on buying all of their drinks. Daisy simultaneously felt a rush of fondness and guilt at having not yet paid for any alcohol. Imo usually tended to exhibit a complete lack of awareness of regular people's means.

'Oh, Daisy, you didn't have to get a bottle,' Imo said as Daisy returned to the table with a bottle of Sauvignon Blanc in a smeared metal cooler.

'What, because the four of us won't manage it?' she replied, pretending not to notice Imo's concern about her spending.

'Sam won't be drinking much; she said her Christmas party was her last hurrah,' Imo said. 'I don't see why – people get pregnant when they're drunk all the time. In fact, potentially most people are conceived under the influence.'

'Maybe don't say that to her, though,' Jas warned. 'I think she's sick of being given advice.'

Imo laughed. 'That's not *advice*; it's just a thoroughly un-researched fact.'

Once Sam arrived, another bottle was bought, and Imo's voice increased a few notches in volume. Sam was delighted to have broken up from school and amused them by reeling off all the over-the-top Christmas presents from the parents of her class. She'd already decided to regift a designer purse to her mum.

'You've already got Linda loads of stuff, though?'

'I know but . . .' There was no need for her to remind them that it was just the two of them at Christmas. 'It's more her style.'

'Marvin's going up with you this year, isn't he?' Jas asked.

'Yes,' Sam said with an effort to sound upbeat. She always missed her dad most around Christmas time, and even Marvin's cheerful presence couldn't erase that.

The subject changed to Jono, as Jas was desperate to hear more about him.

'Give us his bio – like, what's he into, etc.?'

Daisy surprised herself at how attractive he sounded as she listed his attributes: he was half Greek, from Bournemouth, and could surf; his favourite TV show was *The Sopranos*; he was the ultimate early riser, a terrible cook but appreciated everything she fed him; and he always replied to her messages.

'Hell, I'd be swiping left,' Jas said, pouting and miming an eager swiping action. 'D, he sounds like such a catch?'

Imo placed her hand on Jas's and said with a sarcastic earnestness, 'Babe, you mean right, swipe *right* for fitties.'

'Oh, really?' Jas looked devastated. 'I was trying to fit in with the dating lingo.'

'I know, but quite frankly, you've embarrassed yourself.'

Jas laughed then gave a comedic bottom lip of sadness. 'I'm so annoyed I didn't get to meet him at ours last weekend.'

'You've met him, haven't you?' Imo asked Sam.

'I have. Last Saturday when he picked Daisy up.'

There was a silence where they waited for her to elaborate.

'And . . . ?' Jas asked, smiling brightly up at Sam. 'What's he like? Does he match the profile IRL?'

'Oh, I mean, he literally came in for thirty seconds.'

Daisy reared her head back, frowning. 'It was more than that! Like a good five minutes?'

Sam met her eye, then looked at Imo opposite as she said, 'Okay, *five minutes* – not long is what I'm saying.' She gave a subtle widening of her eyes to Imo, as though Daisy was being unreasonably pedantic.

Daisy's temper flickered. She swallowed and sat back, arms folded. 'It's long enough to form some sort of opinion on a person – you two had a full-on conversation.'

Jas looked between Sam and Daisy, licking her lips and clearly regretting raising the subject.

Sam's eyebrows were fixed in a raised position. 'We talked about hangovers and his journey from Parsons Green – nothing worth repeating.' She turned to Jas and added in a lighter tone, 'He was sweet – nice polite manner . . . brown hair . . . nice coat—'

'Brown hair, nice coat?' Daisy repeated, incredulous. She knew that Sam was still disappointed that she and James hadn't worked out – her initial anger at him seemed to have transitioned to disappointment in Daisy for not forgiving him, for not trying harder to make it work – but this reaction to Jono was unexpected.

'I don't know!' Sam laughed and raised her hands in a comic surrender, avoiding Daisy's furious eyes. 'He was *nice* – I've nothing against the guy!'

'It *does* sound like there's a "but" coming though,' Imo said delicately.

'There's no "but",' Sam said, then after a pause added, 'I guess' – she raised her hands in the air again, floundering for the words – 'he just seems quite *safe*, after James. Which is a good thing!'

'Ooh,' Imo said, her eyes cast downwards to a beer mat that she fiddled with as a distraction from the awkwardness.

'Safe is okay,' added Jas quickly. 'You mean a nice guy, right? We're in our thirties; who doesn't want safe?'

Imo raised her long arm in the air like she was in a classroom.

'Imogen!' Jas said, throwing a beer mat at her. 'Not helpful!'

Sam ignored Imo and addressed Jas when she said, 'Exactly, that's what I meant: nice.' But her eyes were skittish, dancing around to avoid Daisy's.

Daisy remembered Marvin entering their lives in their mid-twenties. Sam had introduced him in a pub in Hackney after they'd been dating for only a few weeks. He'd broken the arm of his glasses in a club the night before and had scruffily sello-taped them back together; they sat wonkily on his face above his wide smile, making him immediately endearing to them all. They'd played Monopoly, and Marvin had bankrupted himself in record speed. Daisy had left the pub and practically skipped home; from the outset, Marvin was exactly the type of person you pray your friend will find.

Daisy didn't need Sam to gush about Jono, but she hadn't expected her to be entirely dismissive. She traced the rim of her wine glass with her forefinger as a mild sense of humiliation settled over her. 'No offence, mate, but after the whole James debacle, I'm not quite as trusting of your opinion on potential suitors.' She delivered the line with a false cheeriness, the last word taking on a bizarre regal accent, but it failed to detract from the passive aggression of the sentence.

'Well, you liked him at the time.' Sam dipped her head to one side, addressing her wine glass when she added quietly, 'And we all know you still do.'

Jas and Imo's silence felt complicit, a group attack.

Daisy laughed through her nose, then picked up her glass, gathering herself before replying. She was ashamed of how much time she'd spent thinking about James; it had been only a month they'd spent together – not even long enough to class as a relationship – and it was both true and pathetic that she still liked him. She knew there was no use denying the accusation, so she simply sat back, folded her arms, and took a deep breath.

'*Well*,' she repeated Sam's word with barely disguised distaste, meeting her eye as she said, 'I like Jono more.'

The words came out with such conviction that even Daisy herself started to believe them.

summer ii

Sam

Staring at the ceiling, Sam waited for the irritating beep of the thermometer to signal that it'd done its job. She pushed the cold metal deeper into the veiny crevice under her tongue, feeling the coolness melt away as it united with her own body temperature. After a few moments, she heard the beeps and removed it, reading the screen: 36.4 degrees Celsius. She grabbed her phone to input the data into the app. It flashed up with a message: 'You have entered your fertile window for this month.'

She imagined it being said in an irritating female robot voice, then spent a few moments considering why robots often had an assigned gender. A question for Daisy, for sure. She looked over to Marvin, still asleep next to her, having trained himself to sleep through the beeps over the last few months. Unable to resist his warm, slumber-like state, she cuddled up to him, wrapping her arms around him from behind. He woke momentarily to grasp her hands around him more tightly.

Fifteen minutes later, Marvin's alarm went off and woke them both.

'Shit, I fell back asleep,' said Sam, sitting up slowly. 'I remembered to do my temperature though. The app said I'm fertile, so we need to have sex tonight.'

'Lamp, you're turning me on right now with your sexy timetable.'

Unable to muster a retort so early in the morning, she fell back on the bed and said, 'Oh god, what have I become?'

He walked around to her side of the bed, pulled her up and kissed her. 'It's fine. I'll put it in the diary.'

Once they were both dressed, Sam looked over at Marvin and said, 'Isn't that shirt a bit hipster for school?'

Marvin looked down at his vintage patterned shirt that they'd picked up in Brixton village a few months ago. 'I've got a date,' he said earnestly, pushing his thick-framed glasses up his nose as he grabbed his phone and wallet. 'Happy Anniversary, Lamp.'

'Shit!' she gasped, stepping away from him as though stung. 'We were literally talking about it before we went to sleep last night!'

He smiled and kissed her on the forehead, clearly not perturbed, then swiftly headed out of the bedroom as she stood still, overwhelmed by her forgetfulness.

'Sorry!' she shouted after him. 'See you at eight.'

'We said seven, babe. I'll be the one with the rose in my mouth,' he shouted before closing the door.

She doused her hair in dry shampoo for the third day in a row, smiling to herself until she caught sight of the garish pink thermometer on the bedside table, staring at her in the mirror. She'd been tracking her cycles closely over the last few months, inputting data into the app about all sorts of bodily symptoms that had previously gone unnoticed. But she still wasn't pregnant.

★

Arriving at work, Sam headed to the staff room to make a tea. She survived a few minutes of small talk with some of her lesser-known colleagues before escaping to her classroom to 'set up for the day'. In reality, she planned to browse Vinted. She took out her phone and, as she could have predicted, saw two anniversary messages, one from her mum and another from Jas. Despite having the most demanding profession as well as the most friends and family members out of the four of them, Jas was unfailingly reliable when it came to remembering birthdays or important dates. Since this wasn't a strength of her own, Sam viewed it as a remarkable talent. A year after Sam's dad's death, when everyone else, it seemed, had moved on – their cards and sympathies exhausted on the previous year's efforts – Jas sent flowers. It was something that Sam had never forgotten. She pressed dial on Jas's number.

'Sammy!'

'Hey, I wasn't expecting you to answer. How's it going, newlywed?'

Jas and Ash had married in Seville a few weeks before, with a grand ceremony in the courtyard of a swanky hotel, which only Imo could afford to stay in.

'Well, it's been nearly three weeks; do I even still qualify for that title?'

'Oh, no way, you're an old hand at it now,' Sam said, grinning down the phone. 'It's actually quite annoying how your relationship before is kind of wiped out and people just calculate how long you've been married, isn't it?'

'Er, yes, like, hello! I've put in a good eleven years before getting here – let's not forget! Speaking of: happy anniversary, gurl.'

'Aw, thanks for the message – I'm glad *someone* remembered.'

'Shit, did you forget?'

'Why would you assume *I* forgot?'

'Chick, come on. We know Marvin isn't gonna be forgetting *any* anniversaries.'

'True,' she said and plodded over to the window to watch the morning traffic. 'But I hate always being the shit one in the relationship.'

'Would you rather it be the other way around?'

'No,' she said sulkily. 'But maybe he could just mess up once, to highlight my brilliance.'

'I'm sure that'll happen at some point, sadly. Anyway, are you gonna talk to him about the fertility stuff?'

'Yeah, but not tonight,' Sam said, pressing her index finger onto the glass and examining the faint print left behind. She'd been putting off the conversation, and she wasn't sure why. 'It's not exactly the most celebratory topic. But soon. It's been a year and, you know, I'm going to be thirty-*two* in September.'

'Oh, babes, thirty-two is *young*; you've got loads of time.'

'I know, but I always had it in my head that I'd start at thirty – and I still want three, remember, and not that close together.' Sam recalled a mum of twins in her reception class, who also had a six-year-old and always looked like she needed a good lie down. 'I still want some sort of semblance of a life.'

There was a pause, and Jas's voice softened. 'Three, hey? You used to say four when we were at uni.'

'I know – a bit optimistic on teachers' salaries. Three's more realistic. And look at Daisy's family; I always thought she was so lucky having two brothers.'

'True. I think I'd be happy with two. I quite liked it being just me and my sister,' Jas said.

'Anything's better than one, mate. Being an only child sucked.'

Jas laughed. 'Imo didn't seem to mind.'

'But she had Daisy! I know they didn't live near each other, but they went on every holiday together. I just have weird cousin Karen—'

'Oh, is that Karen with the eyebrows?'

'—with the eyebrows,' Sam said at the same time. 'Yes and she's ten years older than me.'

'I get it. I can totally see you and Marv with a mad household full of kids. So maybe arrange a check with the GP, so you know what you're working with. They'll do blood tests for you to check your hormone levels, and Marv can do his business in a cup for analysis.'

'*His business*?' Sam laughed.

'That's what I say to patients! Is that weird? I always thought it was better than ejaculate . . .'

'I mean, it's very British.'

'Which is *fine*. Anyway, chick, I need to go – first patient's here. But look, happy anniversary, I really hope you guys have an awesome night. And get drunk! Forget about the baby stuff for tonight.'

'I'll try.'

'Sam, a year is nothing.'

'I know,' she said lightly, willing herself to agree.

★

The school day crawled to a finish, the classroom hot and the children dreaming of alternative lives that included ice lollies on the beach. Sam freshened up in the staff toilets, redoing her hair and make-up, and adding what she felt was a tempestuous flick of liquid eyeliner. She emerged as a new and improved version of herself and bumped straight into Blake, a new teaching assistant. As with any new member of staff who was male and under fifty, there'd been considerable interest in him since he joined at Easter. Although for once, Sam agreed that her colleagues had a point: Blake was six-foot with wavy brown hair and chiseled cheekbones.

'Blake!' she said, startled and stepping back from him. 'Sorry—'

'Shit! Sorry, I was in my own world there.'

'No, my fault, I'm just rushing off to meet my husband – first anniversary,' she said as way of explanation for her make-up. The ridiculousness of the term 'husband' had not been extinguished a year in, but she was unsure if she'd ever mentioned Marvin's name to Blake before.

'Oh, no way? Me too.'

She smiled, unsure of the joke.

He raised his eyebrows at her apparent consideration of not just his sexuality but of them being coincidentally married on the same day, before saying flatly, 'Joking.'

'Right!' Sam laughed and tucked a stray piece of hair behind her ear to occupy her hands.

'Congratulations. I hear the first year is the hardest, though I'm sure that's complete bullshit.'

Sam felt a kind of camaraderie among teachers who swore, having met far too many who failed to break out of their censored classroom vocabulary. 'Oh yeah, I'm sure I've got that to come: mid-to-late forties, I reckon?'

'You've bought the red sports car and he's pissed about it.'

'Not to mention my affair with my nineteen-year-old secretary, Winona, a feisty redhead.'

He laughed genuinely, and she noticed his teeth weren't perfect, making him less intimidating. It occurred to her that perhaps he could be a new work friend. Navigating friendships with men had always been a challenge. Having grown up in a fierce gang of girls who viewed boys with interest from afar, she wasn't sure how to handle them when she got to university. After several awkward blunders as supposed friends made passes at her on nights out, she spent years worrying that she was inviting these advances. By her early twenties, she'd resigned herself to the fact that she was better suited to befriending women. The opal on her ring finger had made the situation a little easier for the past couple of years. There could be no mistaking her joking for flirting – nothing serious at least – and it provided an unspoken but concrete barrier. Conversations were finally on a mutually acknowledged platonic basis. There would always be the odd man who would not be deterred by a wedding ring and others who somehow rendered useless the platonic powers of the ring. After only a brief conversation with one such man at a friend's barbeque last year, her mind kept inadvertently returning to him for weeks afterwards. He was not a man she would have dared enter a friendship with.

'Anyway, what are you up to this weekend?' She heard the small-talk nature of the question but was generally interested since she knew nothing of his personal life.

'Oh, just in the workshop mostly, seeing a couple of mates,

the usual.' Noticing her confusion, Blake added, 'I'm into woodwork, furniture-making – that's why I'm only here three days a week.'

'God, I didn't even know you were part-time, sorry. That's so cool.'

'Oh, I don't even know everyone's name yet, never mind their working hours. But thanks, it is . . . cool.' He emphasized her last word with friendly mockery.

'Anyway, I really should . . .' Sam indicated the exit with her forefinger.

'No worries, have a great night.'

Stepping out of the sunshine and into the dimly lit bar, Sam scanned the room for Marvin. As her eyes adjusted to the lighting, she took in the concrete-clad walls and industrial aesthetic and remembered why they didn't usually choose this place in summer. She spotted his colourful shirt at the bar and stayed standing by the door for a minute, watching him speaking to the bartender. She liked these moments of observing him before he saw her. When you spent so many hours of each day, each week, each year with your partner right in front of you, it was so easy to forget to look at them, to truly look and to remember why you chose them.

Marvin was one of those people who emanated warmth in every circumstance. Even when he was tired or in a bad mood and it was raining outside, he still managed to give off a sort of decency, an effervescence that drew people to him. His scientist-like thick-rimmed glasses and high forehead seemingly balanced out his dimpled cheeks, which took on a childish apple-roundness when he smiled, and he still stood with the classic shoulder stoop that came from being the tallest in a class when puberty hit unfavourably early. Sam watched the bartender observing him as he scanned the drinks menu and felt a familiar pulse of gratitude that she got to share her small piece of earth with this man.

She squeezed in beside him and took hold of his upper arm lightly. He turned towards her suddenly, clearly fearing an over-friendly stranger.

'Samantha! You're on time!'

'I'm often on time.'

He smiled knowingly and kissed her on the cheek in greeting. 'Of course you are, babe – sorry, you just caught me off guard, so I didn't have time to do *this*.'

Turning away from her and adjusting something out of sight, he spun around, dramatically slow, arms folded and head tilted with a paper rose in his teeth. Sam laughed at his faux-sleazy expression and took the rose carefully from his jaw, examining the intricate peachy-orange-coloured folds of the petals and delicate green stem.

'Happy Anniversary, Lamp.'

'Oh my god,' she said, still inspecting it, 'did you make this?'

'Did I? DID I? Yes. That's about the seventh attempt though.'

'And it's the colour of my bouquet! This is too good.' She held it to her chest like a little girl with a new doll. 'Hey . . .' lowering her voice now, 'do you want to stay here? I'd forgotten how dark it is; we could go and find somewhere outside in the sun if you prefer?'

'Nah, it's fine – who doesn't love a prison aesthetic? Plus, we'll get seats here.'

'What the hell? The drinks are orange too!' she said as he

passed a vivid orange Aperol Spritz. 'Are we having an orange-themed evening?'

'Yep, we're headed to Sainsbury's next.'

She laughed and they clinked glasses.

'Your present hasn't arrived yet, I'm afraid,' she said, 'but I'm hoping it will tomorrow.' They'd agreed to a ten pounds limit and to stick to the paper theme, so she'd somewhat unimaginatively printed and framed a photo from their wedding. He'd always been better at presents.

Marvin shrugged, unbothered.

'So how was work?' she asked, leaning against the bar and sipping from her glass.

He frowned. 'Let's not do work. Let's summarize our first year of marital bliss and our wedding night highlights.'

'Wedding night highlights?'

'Wedding highlights? I didn't say night, you filthy harlot.'

'You did!' she cried.

They moved over to a table that had become free, and Sam changed the subject.

'So I talked to that new TA guy today and I think he'd be a good match for Imo. He's, like, at least six foot.'

'Is that the only reason?'

'No.'

He waited for further information, inclining his head to one side, and when it didn't come, said, 'Imo's never going to get with a teaching assistant.'

'Yes she would! She's not a complete snob. Plus, he's part-time – he's into woodwork as his main job.'

'So part-time TA, part-time tradey? Do you know your friend at all? She thinks I'm a waster as a secondary school teacher.'

'No, she doesn't! That would mean she thinks my job is shit too, and I *know* she doesn't.'

'But it's okay for you because you're a woman – she's got that old traditionalist sexist thing going on subconsciously. Thinks all men should be bankers or farmers.'

'She does not!' she said with laughter, though considered Imo's parents probably did think in this way. 'Plus I don't think being into woodwork makes him a tradey.'

'Woodwork is carpentry, no? That's definitely a trade. Why do you say it with such distaste? Is that school getting to you?'

'I did not!' Her voice rose unnaturally high on the last word; comments on her acquired snobbery riled her more than anything.

'I'm kidding, Lamp,' he said, laughing.

'My *dad* was a tradey! It was the way he said "woodwork" – I imagined more like carving spoons in a forest than sanding floorboards.'

'And you can see Imo with a spoon-carver, can you?'

She sipped her drink while eyeing him steadily, aware that she had lost the debate.

'Imo's fine as she is. I don't know why you're always trying to set her up. Isn't she always having Bumble hook-ups?'

It was true that over the last few years, Imo had been on more dates than Sam could even hazard a guess at. She often had funny stories to tell and rarely seemed upset when things didn't work out for more than a few weeks – unlike Daisy, who seemed to be finding dating less enjoyable with every year that went by.

'Yeah but . . . never good ones. They never get to the point that we're allowed to meet them; she sacks them off before that.'

They sipped their drinks and paused between conversations, watching the large group on the table next to them celebrating a birthday. Turning back to Marvin, Sam said, 'Anyway, before we head to the restaurant and get too drunk, I wanted to talk to you about the baby stuff.'

'Okay,' he replied, drawing out the latter syllable to accentuate his uncertainty.

'Nothing bad, but, as it's been a year now, I think that we should book an appointment with the GP and get the basic checks done.'

'Okay.' He licked his bottom lip.

'Okay? Is that all?'

'Yeah, that's fine, if you want to. I just think that we haven't really been trying until the last six months, not properly, so it's not fully a year. But I'm happy to go.'

She'd suspected this might be his reaction. 'But we have been, Marv. I wasn't tracking my temperature or doing the ovulation tests at the beginning, but I do know my cycle and roughly when I'm ovulating, and I made sure that we had sex around those times, so I'd say that's fully a year – over really, as I came off the pill before the wedding, didn't I?'

'Oh. Right.' He looked down at his drink and started poking the ice with his straw. 'You never used to mention about your ovulation times before – I thought I was just, you know, stabbing in the dark.'

She smiled at his choice of phrase. 'I'd read all this stuff about trying to keep the romance alive and not telling your partner about every single thing, but I was vaguely monitoring it from the beginning. And I think *trying* means having regular sex and not using protection. Using thermometers and meticulous cycle-tracking is just, well, trying harder.' She sighed heavily, hoping that the words were sinking in.

'Okay . . . yeah.' He rubbed the stubble on his jaw, absorbing the information. 'That makes me more worried than I was.' He took a sip of his drink, knocking it back with sudden vigour. 'When you say it like that – over a year of regular sex and no pregnancy – it sounds quite bad. We must have had sex . . . what, like, a hundred times in the last year? What the hell were we worrying about at school?'

'Well, I was worrying about GCSEs, not about my skank girlfriend being pregnant.'

Marvin had dated a girl for three years in the latter part of school, and it had become a strange tradition to feign jealousy of this woman she'd never met.

'Oh, because everyone waits until they've left school in the Wirral?'

'Yes, that's factually correct.'

They smiled at each other and sipped the remnants of their drinks, and Sam watched him running over the information in his mind.

'I'm sorry that you've been having to think about it more than I have,' said Marvin, serious now.

She shrugged. 'I think that responsibility just comes with the vagina. Part of the package. Along with all the other changes if it does happen – my body, my job; it's a lot actually.'

He reached for her hand across the table. 'I thought you'd be excited to have maternity leave?'

'I am, I think. But you don't know what it'll be like: at home with a baby all the time, I might find it really hard. Who knows.'

'We could always split it. Six months each? Hell, I would *love* paternity leave.'

She laughed at the excitement in his voice. 'You would love it. You'd be so much better at it than me: having a routine, getting out the house, having all the yummy mummies fawn over you. Fifty-fifty sounds good.' They grasped each other's hands over the table, as though saying a prayer before dinner. 'Thanks for being a good one.'

'A *good one*? Stop it, Lamp.'

She laughed and drained the last of her drink from the glass, making a loud sucking noise with the straw. 'Anyway, maybe we shouldn't be planning those kinds of things at this point.' She removed her hand gently from his grasp and put it under her chin, resting her elbow on the table. 'It might never happen, Marv.'

He blinked sadly, then subconsciously copied her pose, his head suddenly too heavy to support itself. 'It will, Lamp. I'm sure it will.'

He looked at her, with attempted reassurance, but she saw a flicker in his eyes, something that wasn't there before tonight: a doubt.

And she couldn't help but ignite the flicker, bringing it into their lives with words, 'But what if it doesn't?'

Daisy

Daisy woke to the sound of gunfire coming from the living room. She sat up suddenly, taking a few moments to adjust to her surroundings. Jono's bedroom was still very much his own space, despite her moving in three months ago. Her things were unpacked into her designated drawers and suitcase stored away under the stairs, as though taking up too much room might alert him to her presence. She climbed out of bed and made her way to the living room, noticing the sound of her bare feet padding on the sleek laminate flooring, unwelcome guests in a stark spaceship. Pushing the door open, she saw Jono standing with his back to her in boxers, a Tough Mudder T-shirt, and an elaborate headset, gunning down people on the television screen.

'Rock374, lower ground level clear, I'm heading towards foxtrot station zero. Do you copy?' he said into the microphone attached to the headset.

Someone obviously replied as he barked with laughter and said, 'Sick, see you there.'

It occurred to Daisy that she had very recently had sex with this man.

'Jono?' He didn't answer so she raised her voice. 'Jono!'

He turned towards her and, in her opinion, did not seem appropriately alarmed to be caught in such circumstances. He pulled the headset away from one ear, waiting expectantly.

'It's half seven; what in god's name are you doing?'

'Oh shit, sorry, gorgeous, did it wake you? The sound quality isn't as good through the headphones,' he said, turning his eyes back to the screen, and showing no intention of turning the volume down. 'Sorry, I've nearly finished this level . . .' He chanced another glance at her, away from the screen. 'I'll come and bring you a coffee in a second.'

It was Jono who'd suggested she move in. Initially she'd resisted; they'd only been together four months. But the contract on the Clapham flat was coming to an end, Jas was finally moving in with Ash before the wedding, and the rest of their friends were fairly settled in house-shares or with partners. She'd considered asking to stay at Sam and Marvin's for a bit, but she didn't want to encroach on their first home together; plus, she knew there would be a time limit on her being there as they'd need the room for a nursery. She'd browsed SpareRoom and other similar websites, but the ads were uninspiring; she'd reached the age where she didn't want to live with strangers again. Jono lived in a large modern flat in Parsons Green with his friend Andre from school and, since she already stayed there half the week anyway, moving in seemed the obvious next step. Andre's easy-going presence also made it a less daunting decision – they could pretend it was a flat-share rather than a significant move in their relationship.

Jono entered the room, carefully carrying a cup of coffee. She noticed immediately that it was too milky, but smiled anyway, arranging the pillows to sit up against the wooden headboard.

'Thanks. I can't believe you're up at seven on a Saturday. And what's with the . . .' She gestured to the headset, which he was still unashamedly wearing.

'Oh, it's a mic.' He removed it for her to examine more closely. 'And I've set it up so that I hear the guys through this and the rest of the sound from the Soundbar – better quality that way.'

She sipped her coffee and pretended not to notice his attempt to pass it over, knowing she'd have nothing to say, similar to when people showed her their engagement rings: most likely blood diamonds stuck on silver bands that all looked the same.

'Me and these guys from Ohio and New Zealand usually get together to play, and Andre often joins. The times can be a bit awkward because of the Kiwis.'

'Crikey, I didn't know you were such a *gamer*.' She couldn't help but let the distaste slide off her tongue.

'You don't have to get all bitchy about it,' he replied, her derisive tone apparently unambiguous. He stood up, backing away from her. 'It's just something I enjoy doing. How is it any different from you reading all the time?'

She ran her tongue over the front of her teeth as she mulled over this remark, aware of her occasional habit of condescension. Computer games had always been banned from Daisy's home, her parents preferring she and her brothers created games outside instead. As with so many other things, their views had obviously permeated her mind at some point over the years.

'Okay, point accepted. No more judgement here.' She knew the words weren't true as soon as she finished the sentence, eyed the headset again, and experienced another jolt of aversion. 'It would be quite nice to wake up next to you occasionally though, rather than an empty bed and the sound of the smoothie maker or your machine gun from the next room.'

His face softened, and he placed the headset back on with enthusiasm. 'We've got plenty of other days for that.'

Daisy didn't have the energy to explain that she wasn't referring to sex. 'So you're still coming later on today, aren't you?' Imo was doing a three-month secondment in Copenhagen and had arranged a picnic and rounders game as a leaving party.

'Yes, 'course, I'll be there after squash.' He kissed her on the forehead and retreated into the living room.

She picked up her book from the bedside table, examining the battered Penguin Classic cover, and considered his point about their respective hobbies; she really could be a snob at times.

★

A few hours later, Daisy skipped up the stairs to the top deck while the bus remained stationary. The front four seats were mysteriously free. She edged forward with trepidation, looking right then left. Seeing no vomit or chicken shop remnants, she felt a delicious sense of victory as she settled down in the best seat, directly above the driver. The tube would have taken half the time, but she still held a romantic notion of London buses; she loved riding at the top and taking in the sites and people. She shuffled up, making space on the seat next to her for a large man in a pink shirt and straw hat. The bus was soon packed with people, everyone excitedly making their way to various places for the sunny weekend.

Imo had organized a picnic and rounders game on Tooting Bec Common, and the plan was for them to meet at Jas and Ash's new place in Balham before joining everyone else in the park. Daisy didn't particularly like Imo's wider circle of friends and was feeling a little flat about the afternoon. She took out her phone to text Sam.

> **Daisy:** If there are dickheads there, can we boycott rounders and just sit and drink with Jas and Ash?

Sam started typing immediately, and it comforted Daisy to think of her also sitting on a bus, knowing she too would have tried to get the front seat on the top deck.

> **Sam:** Mate
> There will be dickheads
> HELL YES to antisocial drinking with JASH

> Catchy, no?
> Also, you KNOW I can't play rounders
> Imo will shout at me and things might get NASTY

Daisy smiled to herself. Sam really was one of the least sporty people she knew and Imo the most competitive. Another message popped up on her screen.

> **Jono:** Have a smashing day babe, I'll try and join later.

Daisy's grandmother, Ida, used the word 'smashing' a lot, and it didn't feel quite right coming from Jono. She knew that he wouldn't come later, and she tried to assess if she cared. Slotting boyfriends into friendship groups was difficult, and she often enjoyed herself less when they were there. Marvin and Ash had been a part of their group for so long that they were no longer additions to the group – welcome extensions perhaps. Whereas with Jono, she often found herself glancing over, worrying about what he was saying and how he was getting on with everyone. Sam seemed to have warmed up to him since her negative impression when they first met, but Daisy sensed that she still wasn't bowled over.

Jas and Ash's flat was on the first floor of a beautiful period terrace, on a road running directly from Balham station to Tooting Bec Common. Waiting at the door, Daisy lifted her long hair off her shoulders, wrapping it into a makeshift bun and holding it there a moment in place of a bobble. The breeze lapped pleasantly at the film of sweat on the back of her neck. Looking around at the houses on the street, she noticed the building opposite had achingly beautiful wisteria draped over the doorway. It was the kind of house that she dreamt of, full of character and high ceilings but not too proud and assuming. It contrasted hugely with Jono's industrial block of flats: trendy and hard-edged. She could imagine Sam and Marvin at his place with their mid-century furniture and on-trend art, but her own eclectic belongings seemed out of place.

Jas opened the door and threw her arms around Daisy, startling her from her daydream.

'Daisy! I missed you so much.'

'Aw, you too, kid,' she said hugging her back warmly. 'I brought beer and children's pop.' She held up a blue carrier of drinks she'd picked up only minutes ago. 'Plus some picnic bits I made for later.' She indicated her rucksack with a tilt of her head.

'Amazing, come in. Sam and Imo are here already. You look *fit*, by the way.'

Daisy looked down at her now slightly creased jumpsuit and attempted to smooth it down, 'Oh, thanks.'

Jas was the queen of compliments, and they were never fake; she genuinely believed her friends were *beautiful* women, and she called them out whenever they talked negatively about their appearances. She was fiercely body confident and wanted everyone around her to be equally so. Growing up self-conscious about her height and weight, Jas then went to medical school, realized just how exceptional a healthy body was, and endeavoured to waste no more time worrying about subjective imperfections.

They headed up the narrow staircase to the flat.

'So, friend, Zone 3, ey?' Daisy teased. 'Practically the countryside.'

Jas turned to her, eyes wide in a *Don't* expression.

They reached the second floor and entered the flat: a recently refurbished two bed adorned with copper accessories and colourful geometric-patterned cushions. The navy kitchen units were rendered more homely by a mass of wedding and moving-in cards lining the highest cupboards. The kitchen island was heaped with plastic-packaged picnic items and bottles of beer and Prosecco, and Imo, Marvin, and Sam were standing around it, chatting.

'D's here!' Marvin announced with a smile, and the girls echoed him with greetings.

'Hey guys.' She approached, hugging Marvin and Imo, then high-fived Sam with pointed awkwardness.

'You two never hug,' Imo noticed.

'I saw her yesterday!' said Sam. 'It's weird hugging people you see all the time.'

'We save it for special occasions. Not that this isn't one . . .' She slapped Imo on the back, a little too hard.

'Jesus!'

Ash joined them from another room, and Daisy gave him a hug. They chatted briefly about their honeymoon in the Greek islands, and Jas started pouring glasses of Prosecco.

'I'll have a beer if that's all right, Jas?' said Marvin.

'Of course, everyone help themselves to whatever.'

Marvin wordlessly offered a bottle of Beck's to Daisy, knowing she too would prefer this. Over the years, their familiarity with each other often edged into sibling territory.

'You're not *not* drinking today, are you?' Imo asked Sam with an undertone of threat.

'I'm drinking,' Sam replied, indicating to Jas to top up her glass then casting her eyes downwards.

Daisy pointedly glared at Imo.

'What? It's meant to be a party! I don't want everyone to be sober. She'd be the same if it was her thing, or would have been a year ago anyway.'

Her words seemed to twist the knife deeper. 'That's probably true,' Sam replied.

'I'm only saying it because you're so fun when you're drunk.'

'She's fun when she's sober too,' Marvin piped up with humour in his voice, then put his arm around Sam and pulled her into his shoulder.

'Not quite *as* fun,' Sam said, looking down at the table and sipping from her glass in defeat.

'Exactly,' Imo said, pleased with herself.

'Tell them what the GP said,' Marvin said, squeezing Sam towards him in encouragement, as though coaxing a story out of a shy child.

'Oh god.' Sam rolled her eyes. 'So I went yesterday to get some checks done, since we've been trying for over a year now,' she added in explanation to Ash, who might not have known this. 'And he's this little old-school doctor, must be pushing seventy. He barely looked away from his computer screen when he asked me how often "we were having intercourse", etc., and then eventually he looked me up and down and went, "You're slim, young, your husband doesn't smoke, all will be fine. Just relax, take yourself on holiday" . . .'

Imo grimaced. '"Take yourself on holiday?" Fuck off, mate. Why don't you take *yourself* on holiday!'

They all laughed at how little sense this made.

Jas brought her hand to her face as she shook her head. 'It's not only suggesting fault on your part for supposedly being uptight, but also suggesting that no young, fit, and healthy people have fertility issues!'

'Did he give any *useful* advice?' Daisy asked. She could see that Sam was doing her best to put an entertaining spin on the appointment when it probably wasn't that funny at the time. Recently, expensive-looking vitamins had appeared on Sam and Marvin's kitchen table, and Sam had started having weekly acupuncture appointments for some assumed fertility increase.

'He vaguely asked about my diet and lifestyle but barely listened to my answers. I think he'd already decided I "just needed to relax".'

Imo said, 'God, isn't it unfair that people get pregnant on one night stands after eating burgers for a week and doing ketamine all night? Well, hats off to you, darling; I'm not sure I could cut down on everything like you have. I'm happy being Aunty Imo to your guys' offspring.' She gestured to them all.

'Don't include me in that – I'm still very much undecided,' Daisy said, happy to direct the attention away from Sam, whose smile was no longer holding. 'Actually edging towards the child-free option lately.'

Imo considered her for a moment, their eyes locked, then said, 'You'll cave. She'll have them' – she indicated Sam with a tilt of her head – 'then you'll copy.'

Daisy heard this a lot, the expectation that she would change her mind. It didn't used to bother her as, deep down, she'd agreed. But over the last year, as she'd considered that the expected yearning in her womb might never actually present itself, the comment had started to irritate her. There was an unmistakable presumption in those words that she would be making the wrong decision. She was disappointed to hear it even from her cousin, someone who had always pointedly said that she, herself, would not have children. She folded her arms and sat back in her seat, raising her eyebrows briefly.

Sam eyed them both and added, 'Or, we'll have IVF triplets and then just give you all one each at weekends.'

Imo smiled and said, 'Thanks, babe, but we don't want them.' Then, as a peace offering, she raised her glass to Daisy in acknowledgement of her potential child-free conspirator.

After finishing the drinks, they all walked down to the Common, where several of Imo's friends joined them at different points throughout the afternoon. They set up in a lesser-known section of the park, their various picnic blankets and rugs spread side by side like towels on the beach. The sun peeped through the clouds intermittently, flooding them with warmth then cruelly retracting it; they applied sun cream, then reached for extra layers five minutes later. A pleasant smell of barbecued meat hung in the air, and the distant beat of dance music from another group's speakers carried across the field.

Daisy took pleasure in passing around her homemade sausage rolls and mini-quiches; welcome anomalies from the pre-bought spread, they were snapped up in minutes. Splurging the remainder of her meagre wages on high-end ingredients was her ultimate treat, and she could spend all morning wandering around the food stalls of Borough Market. At least the compliments on the pastries made her feel it was money well spent.

The first rounders game kicked off with Jas an enthusiastic bowler, Ash and Marvin fielders (spending some time trying to do cartwheels together), and five of Imo's other friends covering the posts and backstop. Sam begrudgingly stepped up to play, joining Daisy and Imo's team, and was swiftly stumped out on her first bat. When Daisy was caught out by Marvin five minutes later, she joined Sam and another girl on a picnic rug to watch Imo's inevitable demise as the only person left batting.

'Hey, it's Steph, right?' Daisy confirmed. 'I'm Daisy, Imo's cousin. I think we met at Imo's flat warming a few years ago?' She noticed that Steph was sporting a significant pregnancy bump under her dress.

'Hi, oh, maybe.'

Sam shuffled up to the side of the rug to give Daisy more room. Steph repositioned herself too, straightening her legs out and leaning backwards, exposing her bump more obviously. Seeing Daisy glancing at her stomach, Steph looked down and sighed, puffing her cheeks out sulkily. 'I can't believe I've got three more months of this hell left.'

Daisy felt the sting of the words for Sam and chanced a quick glance in her direction. Seeing her empathetic grimace at Steph's reported misery, she felt a surge of protective love for her friend, desperate to reach this said state of hell.

'Have you and Marvin thought about having one soon?' Steph asked, raising her eyebrows and smiling like she'd just told a dirty secret. Daisy was unsure how to save Sam from having to answer and sat back, looking on.

'Yeah,' Sam said with an edge of indignation.

Steph carried on smiling her stupid fucking smile, urging Sam to continue, her answer not acceptably detailed.

'We've been trying for some time actually—'

'Oh, how exciting!' Steph interrupted. 'Don't worry, it took us a few months but, like, 90 per cent of couples get pregnant within the first year, so you'll be fine! Are you tracking your cycles?'

'My what?'

Daisy silently saluted her friend's sarcasm.

'Your cycles, you know, your—'

'I'm kidding; yes, I'm tracking them. And it's actually 80 per cent in the first year, 90 per cent in the first two.'

Daisy looked between the two of them, a smile nudging at the corner of her mouth. You ask, you get.

'Oh,' Steph said, frowning. Her hand went subconsciously to her stomach. 'Yeah, that's right, sorry.' She sipped from her pink paper cup and pretended to watch the game of rounders for a moment. 'Well, I'm sure it'll happen soon for you guys.' She smiled a tight-lipped smile. 'I'm just going to say hi to Cordelia.' She gestured to a bird-like woman who'd arrived, then heaved herself up, smiling awkwardly at them as she turned away.

'Is there seriously someone here called Cordelia?' Daisy joked.

Sam offered a half smile back. 'Was I a real bitch just then?'

Daisy turned to her. 'Absolutely not! She asked you a completely intrusive question and then gave you unasked for, patronizing advice. I'd say you held it together pretty well. I wanted to smack her in her smug-ass face.'

Sam raised a smile at this.

'Or push her over. Do you want me to push her over? Not like, injure the baby style, just a thuggish nudge.'

A laugh escaped Sam's closed mouth, an exultant raspberry.

'Don't people know that you don't ask those sorts of things?' Daisy continued. 'I assumed it was an unwritten rule.'

Sam turned to her and said slowly, 'People ask me *all the time*. Just this week I've now had . . . three comments.'

'Are you joking?'

Sam scratched at some dirt on the side of her trainer. 'Nope.' Her tone was overly casual, having the opposing effect.

Daisy watched her for a few seconds, noting a new hardness in the setting of her jaw. 'How are you feeling about it all at the moment?'

Sam shrugged her shoulders in an exaggerated manner, then looked away at the rounders game like she was bored of the conversation. 'Increasingly shit but trying not to think about it all the time – trying to "relax" I guess.'

'Taking yourself on holiday soon then?'

'I wish.' Sam looked back at Daisy, and the brusqueness of her voice melted away when she said, 'Fifteen months of disappointment isn't the easiest.'

'No,' Daisy said with feeling, 'I imagine not.' She picked at the grass, its squeaky texture familiar in her fingertips.

Staring ahead at the players, Sam added, 'I've got to the point where, when people ask awkward questions like Steph just did, I actively try to make them feel more uncomfortable than I do. I used to be all, "Oh I dunno, maybe one day!".' She chortled. 'But in the last few months, I seem to have progressed to giving a really bleak answer. That soon shuts them up.'

'Then maybe that's a good thing,' Daisy suggested. 'Maybe you're making them realize their insensitivity; you might even stop them badgering other women in future.'

Sam shrugged. 'I feel like it's turning me mean.' She too now pulled at the grass, ripping it out mercilessly and piling it next to the picnic rug. 'Like, I've even got to the point where

I actually envy people who've had miscarriages. When Jas was talking about her sister in April, all I could think was: *at least she can get pregnant. Plus, it was first trimester and she can just try again.*' She looked up at Daisy, her eyes wary with shame. 'Fucked up, right?'

Daisy tipped her head to one side and said, 'A *bit* fucked up—'

Sam covered her face with her hands.

'—but also understandable: it's not that you don't sympathize, you just want to know that you *can* get pregnant.'

'Hmm, still think I'm becoming a horrible, bitter person.'

Daisy looked at her, considering what to say next. Keen to steer the conversation back to firmer territory and keep the day joyful, she settled for, 'Don't be ridiculous,' before reaching her arm out to pull her over into an over-the-top hug.

Sam yelped as she was tipped sideways, toppling over with her right leg splayed in the air. Finally, she started laughing. 'Always so bloody rough!' she said from beneath Daisy's shoulder.

Daisy added a knuckle rub on Sam's head in response. 'You're the least mean person I know, Samantha Rose Finchley,' she said as they sat back up.

Sam pulled her green dress down and looked back at Daisy for a second, her eyes shining a desperate blue. She dabbed her right tear duct, wiping away the moment. 'That's gotta be Jas, though: least mean person alive.'

Seeing that the rounders team had finally caught Imo out, they both clapped and cheered, despite being on her team. They stood, preparing to field.

'Fine,' Daisy said, 'second least mean person I know.'

'What about Marvin?'

'THIRD,' she shouted, attracting glances from people around.

This made Sam laugh properly.

'Oh my god!' Sam stretched her neck forward and raised her palm to her forehead to shield the sun. She focused on a man with a dog approaching from fifty metres away. 'I think that's Blake from school.'

'Who?'

'It *is*! Blake!' She cupped her hands around her mouth to call, then waved with both arms and started walking towards him.

Daisy followed, unable to resist the opportunity to harass a cute-looking dog. 'From work? He looks . . . handsome,' she said with some confusion, trying to remember if Sam had mentioned him before. While Daisy had grown up with two brothers and always had male friends, she'd never really known Sam to.

Blake spotted Sam and waved back, continuing to do so until he was close enough to start talking.

'Hi,' he said from a few metres away. 'I always find excessive waving minimizes the awkwardness of these approaches.' His voice was light and familiar sounding.

Sam laughed. 'Yeah, that doesn't make it awkward at all. Hey! What are you doing here? And who is *this*?' She bent to stroke the dog, a small black spaniel of some sort.

'Oh, this is Wolf. Hey, I'm Blake, by the way.' He leant over to shake Daisy's hand. His eye contact was piercing, and she felt exposed, ungrounded somehow by his presence. His dark green shirt, worn loosely over a white T-shirt, billowed out in the wind and she was grateful for the distraction, breaking eye contact momentarily.

'Hi. Daisy,' she replied, noticing the roughness of his palms, the sensation lingering when they broke away from each other. 'You two work together?'

'I've mentioned Blake before, haven't I?' Sam said from below as she stroked the dog. A rhetorical question implying that she most definitely had mentioned him. 'Aw, he's shaking – is he cold?'

'Ah, *she* actually. And no, she's a rescue so can be a bit panicky around new people.' He bent down to rub her under the chin. 'Can't you, old girl?' Daisy was relieved to hear him address his pet in his normal, unaltered voice. 'She'll soon settle if you keep stroking her.'

'How long have you had her?' Daisy asked, bending down to join them but refraining from stroking the trembling creature. 'And is Wolf an ironic name? She seems more *terrified* than terrifying?' She looked across at Blake, whose face was now very close. Noticing laughter and brow lines deeper than her own, she suspected he was in his mid-to-late thirties. A small gold sleeper sat in his left earlobe beneath his unruly brown hair, swept back away from his forehead. He must have been the most rock 'n' roll thing to happen to that school in years.

'Two years and er, yeah, I guess. Ironic and literary.' He looked at Daisy, his brown eyes apologetic somehow. 'Hi, my name's Blake, and I'm a huge wanker.'

Sam laughed openly at this, seemingly back to her usual self, their prior conversation forgotten.

'No, but before you judge . . .' He stood back up and Sam followed, leaving Daisy with Wolf.

'When I got her from *Battersea Dogs Home* – see, not all wanker – she was branded with the unfortunate name Virginia.'

'Ahh, *Woolf*!' Daisy and Sam replied in unison.

'Who calls their dog Virginia?' Daisy asked.

'Well, Daisy, I'm glad you ask,' he said, his tone sarcastic and teacher-like. The unnecessary use of her name caused a minor dance in Daisy's stomach. He continued, 'The answer to that is in fact literary wankers who abandon their dogs.'

'You could have gone for Mrs Dalloway,' Sam suggested.

'Really? I'd have to become an eccentric Dame before I could confidently shout that across the park.'

'I hated that book,' said Daisy, attempting to support his name choice but instead coming across as more bookish and serious than she'd intended.

'Did you study it at school?' Blake asked, wrapping the dog lead around his right palm.

'Uni.' She wrinkled her nose in dislike.

'I think that ruins a book for a lot of people. Have you read *A Room of One's Own*? It's so impressive and weirdly relevant.'

Daisy realized her mouth was open and that she had not replied. She looked back at Woolf and couldn't fathom how the day had suddenly included a dog-rescuing, millennial Heathcliff giving her Virginia fucking Woolf recommendations.

'I completely forgot you lived around here,' Sam said, changing the subject from books that didn't interest her.

'I'm on the other side of the park, towards Streatham. I met a friend for a coffee and am heading back to get some work done now. Is this your crew here?' He gestured to their spread of blankets twenty yards behind them, everyone now pausing from rounders for drinks and food.

'Yeah, it's our friend Imogen's thing, so mostly her mates. You should come and meet Marvin!' Sam said.

They walked back to their spot, and Sam introduced Blake to everyone, then left him chatting with Marvin. Daisy stayed with the boys, noting as she did that Marvin seemed genuinely excited to meet Blake. She found herself considering Jono and knew with certainty that he would be suspicious of a new male friend. She realized with sadness that she would also be suspicious of him with a new female friend. Sometimes she envied Marvin and Sam for getting together so young and avoiding the inevitable cynicism that took hold after a decade of London dating.

'Blake, would you like a drink?' Daisy asked, realizing that she was essentially inviting him to stay for longer than a quick introduction.

'Ah, thanks, but I've got to work this afternoon, so I probably shouldn't be on the beers.'

'Carpentry, right?' Marvin said, pleased with himself. 'We've got non-alcoholic stuff: coke, zero per cent beer . . .'

'Oh okay, then yeah, whatever, man. Surprise me.'

'I think I even saw some cans of Irn-Bru. Did you bring them, D?' Marvin asked, bemused. 'You're the nearest to Scottish we've got here,' he added, walking off before she could answer.

Daisy and Blake were left standing alone together, side by side at the edge of the group which had now swelled to over thirty people. She could feel his presence to her side like a phantom limb, pulsating with life.

'You don't *sound* Scottish,' he said, looking at her with his head to one side.

'I'm about as Scottish as Marvin is.' She stepped closer to him and, at a level befitting grave secret-telling, added in a confessional tone, 'I did bring the Irn-Bru though. Imo's friends tend to be of a certain bank-working/yacht-sailing breed—'

'Oh, the type to bring Moët to a picnic?' he asked, spotting two empty bottles strewn on the grass in front of them.

'Exactly!' Daisy smiled, knowing her cousin would likely have brought these herself. 'So it kind of amused me to bring random fizzy pop from the corner shop.'

'I see,' Blake said, interested. 'A quiet rebellion.' He leant his head towards her, continuing to look out at the people in front of them, and rubbed his chin in collaboration.

She experienced an obscene and carnal urge to smell him.

'But why Irn-Bru? Because I could think of much more lethal items.' He pronounced the last two words with pauses between them.

'What are we talking,' she said with as much seriousness as she could, 'Lilt? *Tizer*?'

He turned to her, his face disconcertingly close now, and said with a teasing intensity, 'Don't.'

She laughed at this and stepped backwards. 'Tizer was so good.'

'*So* good. But dirty as hell.' His voice returned to a normal volume. He leant down to stroke Woolf, who was looking up at him.

Daisy folded her arms and continued in a light tone, 'I don't know why I went for Irn-Bru – me and my brothers used to have it as kids on holiday, and the Scots obviously love it.' She looked at Blake, realizing she couldn't place his accent. 'Where are you from, Blake?' His name seemed unnatural on her lips and, from the way he looked at her before he answered, she suspected he knew as much.

'Originally? Leicester.' He looked down at Woolf, now sitting patiently by his feet. 'Don't tell me I sound southern, please.'

There was a weariness to his words. Her accent had also diluted itself over the years, and it saddened her when people seemed surprised that she was from Yorkshire, uprooted both physically and linguistically.

'I wasn't going to,' she replied.

Blake put his hands in his pockets and looked back at the crowd of people. There was a brief silence before he said, 'God, I hope Marvin chooses the Irn-Bru.'

'He's choosing right now I think,' she said, spotting Marvin rummaging through their cool bag.

She felt Blake's eyes on her and turned towards him.

With a seriousness she wasn't expecting, he asked, 'So what's your story, Daisy?'

Her mind emptied itself of anything interesting to say, and she felt a heat rise in her cheeks under the intensity of his gaze. Fiddling with her necklace, she pulled a hopeless shrugging face, when thankfully Marvin returned. He passed Blake a non-alcoholic beer, and she and Blake made brief eye contact, united in their disappointment.

'Sorry, I got waylaid. Is Jono coming, by the way?' Marvin asked, shattering the Irn-Bru spell.

'Oh fuck,' Daisy said, realizing she hadn't checked her phone in hours. She bent over to find it in her rucksack and saw four missed calls from him. She stayed crouched down, leaving them to chat, and fired off several apologetic messages and a pin of their location.

'He'll be here in half an hour,' she said to Marvin. Her reluctance to look at Blake certified her eye-wandering guilt.

They played the second half of the rounders game, and Blake joined Imo's team, out wide as a fielder with Daisy. She was pleased when he didn't compliment her strong overarm as most men tended to, their voices predictably droll. She could feel his presence to her right during the game: a lighthouse signalling danger which she refused to look at. Blake left shortly afterwards, bidding Sam and Marvin goodbye and giving Daisy a static wave over the bodies between them. She returned the gesture, smiling in what she hoped was a friendly rather than flirtatious manner.

Daisy was happy with Jono; he'd told her he loved her over breakfast in bed a few months ago, and it had been easy to say back. They spent their evenings cooking together and watching Scandinavian crime dramas and still had sex most nights. He made her coffee every morning without fail, and when he laughed, his nose crinkled in a way that made him less attractive but more lovable. Last weekend, they'd drunk two bottles of wine, painted each other's faces with erotic motifs, then laughed so hard they had to lie on the floor, gasping for breath.

But there were moments. Moments that chipped away at the love, which she was then unable to rebuild. There was that time they argued about his comment in the pub that 'anyone who works hard enough can get ahead', in relation to inequality in London; she'd been astounded by his inability to recognize his white male privilege and the basic principles of meritocracy. And the time that he went for her throat during sex, uninvited and unconsented – a nod to his pornographic tastes: a violent king of the bedroom.

Recently she'd become aware that she was sinking lower in Jono's estimations too. He'd looked at her with such disdain last week when she'd written 'fuck le climate' in the dust on his friend's grotesque SUV. It followed a fierce dinner party debate about climate protesters storming the prime minister's home. They were on the same side, but her graffiti was clearly a step too far. She, his petty, childish lover. She wondered if this was what marriage was like: not the anticipated slow ebb but a violent hacking away of love by unretractable actions.

winter ii

Sam

Sam set out early on a Saturday morning to buy some Christmas presents in Brixton. It was the first day of December and perfectly cold and crisp with bright-blue skies. She wandered around the independent shops in the village, pleased with the selection of unique gifts she'd picked up, then caught a bus to Clapham Junction to meet Jas for lunch. The bus pulled up, and Sam clambered off, hauling her canvas shopping bags on both shoulders. She checked her phone for the time, then quickened her pace when she saw that she was five minutes late.

Jas had chosen a cosy pub, and Sam spotted her as soon as she entered. The place was all oak beams and leather armchairs with elaborate foliage draped in boughs and tasteful decorations adorning the fireplace. Their table was close to a roaring fire, and Sam headed over to it, dumping her shopping bags underneath. She hugged Jas and warmed her hands by the fire before removing her coat.

'This is perfect,' Sam said, taking in the room. She settled herself in the seat opposite Jas, pulling her tights up at the knees and straightening her blue vinyl skirt. 'So how are you? It's been forever.'

'I know! I'm good – how're you?'

'Fine, fine. Sorry I've been rubbish on WhatsApp lately, just end of term shit, you know.'

'Not at all, you're never rubbish,' Jas replied, picking up the menu to look over as they talked.

'Oh, I've got to tell you about the test!' Sam said, still high on relief at having got the appointment over with. 'I had it yesterday – the one to check my fallopian tubes aren't blocked.'

Sam and Marvin had been referred to a fertility unit at their local hospital and sent for further tests.

Jas raised her eyebrows, her smile unsure.

'Sorry, is this weird? Me telling you? Is it too like you're at work with me jumping right into gynae procedures?'

Jas put the menu down and clasped her hands together on the table. 'No, Sammy, 'course not. I just didn't realize you were having it yesterday. Was it okay? Did it really hurt?'

'No – I was dreading it, but it was absolutely fine! No blockages, and they showed me the screen and the little passageway that the dye had drawn.' She wiggled her finger up an imaginary picture of her reproductive system, as the radiographer had done when showing her the results. 'All very clever. I feel like I'm learning a lot about my anatomy on this *journey*.'

Her tone was light-hearted, but Jas responded with an unexpected heaviness. 'That's so great, Sammy.'

She studied Jas a moment, then felt she should change the subject. 'Shall we order at the bar or do they come over?'

'Chick, there's something I need to tell you.'

'Oh, okay.' Sam leant forward and softened her voice. 'What's up?'

Jas whipped her long hair behind her right shoulder and licked her lips before speaking. 'Ash and I are pregnant.'

'Oh.' Sam automatically drew herself backwards in her seat then gathered herself and said, 'Jas, that's amazing. Congratulations!' Her voice picked up in volume. 'Come here!' She got up out of her seat and bent to hug Jas, seizing the opportunity to arrange her face out of view.

'Thanks,' Jas said from within the hug.

Sam stood back and smiled, her eyes wide and unblinking. 'How many weeks?'

'Only seven. I know it's early, but I had a scan on Thursday to confirm the heartbeat, and I felt weird not telling you guys.'

"Course.'

'And I wanted to tell you first.' She scratched a patch of skin on her cheek, then brought her hand down to her lap, grasping it tightly in the other. 'Sam, I've felt so awful about it.'

'Jas, no . . .' Sam reached for Jas's arm across the table, noticing that there were tears in her eyes, and the plummeting feeling in her stomach was at once overtaken by the need to reassure her friend. 'Hey, mate, come on. Honestly, I'm fine.'

'Really?' Jas said, unconvinced.

Sam frowned, aware of the first prickles of irritation at Jas's pitying eyes. She held her smile intact and said lightly, 'This isn't about me; it's about you guys, and I'm so happy for you. Marvin will be too.'

Jas swallowed. 'But it's not fair; you guys were meant to be first.'

Sam rubbed Jas's arm. 'There's no such thing as "meant to be".' Her tone was sharper than she'd intended, and she took a deep breath and added, 'Anyway, we'll get there, one way or another.'

Jas smiled, her eyes still glassy.

Sam continued in a bouncy tone, 'And I hate to make you not feel special, but you're not the first person to have told me you're pregnant since we started trying. Probably about the ninth actually. Teachers are bloody fertile mammals, let me tell you.'

Jas laughed at this and delicately dabbed at the corners of her eyes with her napkin. 'Yeah, but, they're not one of *us four*.'

'No, they're not,' Sam said quietly, sitting back as she allowed herself to digest the information. The thought of their group now including a baby was conflicting, both magical and painful. She absolutely wanted Jas and Ash to be able to have a family – of course she did – but the revelation only brought her and Marvin's circumstances painfully into focus. She circled around the word envy as an explanation for the uncomfortable feeling in her gut, but it was too ugly a term for her to willingly accept. She swallowed the growing lump in her throat, looked up at Jas, and asked, 'When are you telling the others?'

'Tomorrow.'

Sam's smile dissolved at the thought of Imo and Daisy's excitement; she'd imagined their reactions to her own such news countless times. 'Right, I'll order some drinks,' she said, forcing her voice to return to cheerful, her face set in a strange gleeful mask. 'We need a toast. I'm going to have a mulled something or other.' She was aware that she was talking too quickly but couldn't seem to stop. 'You're obviously not having wine, or maybe you are? No judgement here. What shall I get you?'

They said goodbye at the crossroads by the station, hugging for a moment longer than usual. Sam thought about the tiny being inside her friend, cells multiplying every second. The high street was now busy with afternoon Christmas shoppers. Sam made her way into a department store, determined to carry on with her day. The foyer was brightly lit and lined with cosmetic stalls and hard-selling beauticians. She found herself wandering into MAC, where an overzealous make-up artist soon had her sitting in a seat and trying out different products. Christmas songs blared from the speakers, and the mulled wine and rich lunch churned in her stomach. She suddenly wanted to be anywhere but there.

Leaving the store, she headed back out onto the street in search of the nearest bus stop and was distracted by a busker playing 'Silent Night' on an accordion. Immediately transported back to childhood carol concerts, she found herself standing motionless in the middle of the street with the sudden need to call her mum. She took out her phone and selected her number.

'Sammy, I'm just with someone. Can I call you back?' She sounded worried and mildly irritated. 'You're all right and everything?'

Sam swallowed and replied chirpily, 'Of course! Just out Christmas shopping and wanted to hear your voice.' She bit her lower lip as a lump in her throat threatened the false cheeriness of her voice.

'Well, can I call you back later, if it's not urgent?'
'Sure.'
'Okay, okay, bye Sammy, love you.'
Sam swallowed. 'Love you too.'
She hung up and walked to the bus stop, wishing that she could catch one to her mum's house and sit with her that

evening with tea on their laps in front of the television and forget about everything else.

'Samantha, love, are you okay?'

Sam looked up from the ground and realized that she'd walked straight past their front door. She blinked several times to bring her eyes back into focus. Their next-door neighbour, Mrs Wilson, was standing by her recycling bin in her slippers, looking at her with concern. She looked to be in her mid-seventies, with short, thick hair dyed a dark blonde and thin rimless glasses.

'Oh.' The sound escaped Sam's mouth without her consent.

'You look all out of sorts, pet. Come inside. I'll fix you a cup of tea.'

There was no questioning tone to her statement, and Sam did as she was told, stepping into Mrs Wilson's immaculate front yard, a complete contrast to her and Marvin's depressing square of crumpled flagstones, brambles, and weeds.

'Go on, head straight through – kitchen's at the back; you can't get lost.'

'Thank you,' Sam said, walking up the small ramp to the front door. Still hesitant to lead the way, she pressed herself against the wall so that Mrs Wilson could pass by.

'Go on through, pet. We'll put the kettle on.'

'Okay,' Sam said, walking slowly to the back of the flat with trepidation. She wasn't in the mood for small talk and was already regretting accepting the offer of tea. Marvin was out playing football, and she'd really rather be on her own for the rest of the afternoon.

The layout of the flat was very similar to theirs, except that the Wilsons' kitchen still existed as its own entity, with a small opening into the living room for trays of food to be passed through. It felt strange to Sam, like a model of their home but one that someone hadn't quite paid enough attention to. The kitchen cabinets were the sort of pine that was popular in the Nineties, and square pink and white floral tiles lined the countertops. It was too small to fit a table and chairs, and Sam felt unsure where to stand. The sound of the television from the living room was audible through the closed partition. She'd only seen Mr Wilson a few times before; he seemed significantly older than his wife and recently had been using a wheelchair. The small gardens to the back of their block of flats had waist-height fences between the rows with small gates, allowing residents to walk through to the next one in a bid to encourage community. Sam often saw Mr Wilson sitting outside in the mornings with a cup of tea and gave him a friendly wave.

Mrs Wilson joined her from the corridor with a cheery smile. 'Pop your bags over there and pass me your coat. Have you been Christmas shopping? That's probably why you look so pale. Have you had lunch?'

The questions flew at Sam before she had time to answer. She complied, removing her coat and passing it to Mrs Wilson to hang on a hook in the hallway. 'Yes, I have, thanks – I met a friend.'

Sam took in her navy trousers and pale-blue polo-neck, a gold cross on a delicate chain sitting on top of the fabric.

'Sorry, I was in a bit of a daydream back there, thinking about something. Can't believe I walked right past ours.' She rubbed the roots of her hair, pumping volume into her bleached locks as if this might give her more credibility. 'Bit embarrassed, really.'

'Oh, don't be silly! I always see you and your lovely husband coming and going. You two work very hard, don't you?'

'I don't know about that,' Sam said, considering the three weeks she'd soon have off. 'But pretty long hours during term time, I guess.'

'Are you a teacher as well as Marvin?' She took three stripy mugs out of the cupboard and filled a new-looking white kettle.

'I am. I'm primary though.' She was not surprised to hear of Mrs Wilson's familiarity with Marvin; he could chat with anyone.

'Oh, little ones, how fantastic.'

Sam felt the conversation moving towards their plans to have a family and braced herself for it; the older generation could be the worst for these sorts of questions. She leant against the doorframe and stared at the blue light on the kettle as electricity fired the elements into action.

'And is it a different school to Marvin? He teaches the older ones, doesn't he?'

'Yeah, he's secondary – very different. I work up in town.'

'That's good. Nice to have a bit of separation. Derek and I always worked together and it, er' – she laughed – 'well, let's say it had its pros and cons.'

'What did you both do?'

'Gardening. Just a small business with the two of us.'

'That makes sense now; your garden's always perfect. You have a lovely home as well, Mrs Wilson.' She cringed at the formality of her voice, aware of her habit of lapsing into this tone with older people. 'What I can see of it, anyway.' She looked back towards the hallway they'd passed through, a warm peach colour. There was no furniture in the corridor, and Sam realized this must be to allow Mr Wilson's wheelchair to pass through.

'Oh, call me June. And thank you – we've always loved it here.' She poured the water into a teapot and fixed a jug of milk and the mugs onto a small round tray. 'Been here over forty years now.'

Sam's mouth opened, incredulous; apart from her childhood home, she'd never lived anywhere for more than three years.

'I know, long time.' June took down a battered tartan tin from one of the upper cupboards and laid out an assortment of biscuits on a small plate. Sam noticed the precision with which she arranged them, each one different from the other and all equally spaced. June then thought better of it and selected a second custard cream, placing it neatly next to its twin.

'Would you like me to carry something?' Sam asked, noticing the plate of biscuits wasn't going to fit onto the tray.

'Oh yes, pet, if you could take these into the living room,' – she passed the biscuits and tilted her head towards the nearest door – 'that'd be very helpful.'

Sam took the plate and knocked lightly before pushing the door open. Mr Wilson was sitting on a small upright sofa with a blue throw draped over his lap. He picked up the remote control and turned the television off, then turned to smile at her. The room had cream wallpaper with accents of burgundy, the lower half striped with coral and separated by a floral border. It took Sam right back to her home as a child. A large flatscreen television, at odds with the rest of the room, sat on a mahogany stand in the corner, and framed photographs and ornaments lined every available surface.

'Hi,' Sam said, forcing a polite smile despite still feeling out of sorts. 'I'm Sam from next door. I don't think we've properly met.' She placed the biscuits on the Formica coffee table and leant over to shake his hand.

He shuffled forward on the sofa, taking her hand in both of his and bowing his head deeply. His reply came out as a whisper but still sounded confident in its delivery. 'Sam from next door. At last we meet.' His eyes almost disappeared into slits when he smiled. 'I'm Derek.'

Sam tried not to register any surprise about his voice, or lack of one. 'Nice to meet you, Derek. You'll have to get June to stop calling me Samantha.'

He chuckled at this, again without a lot of sound.

June joined them with the tray of tea and set it down next to the biscuits. 'Sorry, pet, I didn't realize you hadn't met Derek.' She lowered her voice as though he wouldn't hear from right next to her. 'He's had the throat cancer, you see, a few years back.' She pointed to his neck as way of explanation.

'I'm sorry to hear that.'

Derek took a custard cream from the plate, then passed it towards Sam. She realized why two custard creams were laid out and couldn't help but smile at this gesture; perhaps Marvin would lay two Jammie Dodgers out for her in forty years.

'Oh, I'm okay, thanks,' Sam replied. She was trying to cut down on sugar and was already feeling guilty about the chocolate-covered cereal bar she'd eaten that morning.

He frowned at her, insistent, so she relented and took a shortbread finger, promising herself tomorrow would be a healthier day. Derek then held his bitten down biscuit up to her in a confectionery toast.

'He was lucky really,' June continued while pouring the tea. 'Sugar?'

'No, thanks. Just milk.'

'He only lost his voice box in the end, so he can still eat and drink and make himself understood. And he's two years' clear now.'

Derek raised his eyebrows at Sam in a way that seemed like he was obliging June's storytelling rather than expressing genuine awe at news he was well aware of.

June continued, 'It's just his hips that are a bother these days. His last one failed, and they're not sure about replacing it again; he's high-risk anaesthetic, you see.'

Derek rolled his eyes in June's direction but in a playful rather than cruel way – a secret message to Sam. June's reeling off of his ailments was obviously a regular topic of conversation for visitors. Sam noticed a cheeky glint in his eyes and suspected he was younger than she'd first assumed. His face was thin, with a strong nose and fine white hair around his temples. His brown eyes stood out against the paleness of the rest of his features, and his bristled, snow-coloured eyebrows were positioned to somehow give him a look of perpetual surprise.

The conversation changed to their block of flats. June took obvious pleasure in describing what the area used to be like and how it had changed over the decades. Derek pitched in with the occasional anecdote and, once Sam had stopped fretting that she wasn't going to be able to understand him, she realized he was actually easy to follow. They told her about their gardening business, which they'd run together up until their late sixties. Derek's passion was roses, and he took the time to write down a couple of hardy ones that Sam might be able to grow. She took the piece of paper gladly, tucking it into the pocket of her skirt.

'We'll help you sort yours out, come summer,' Derek said with a wink.

There were lots of family pictures on the walls, several of a blond boy and girl that Sam assumed were their children. 'Do your children live close by?' she asked, smiling up at a photo of them as teenagers in the Nineties.

'Ah, that's Joanna and Stephen – our niece and nephew.'

'Oh, sorry.' Sam realized her mistake. She'd done the exact thing that she hated people doing to her.

Derek smiled back at her, but his eyes flicked down towards the carpet.

'No, no, don't be sorry – easy mistake to make.' June sipped from her mug, then said, 'We did have a little girl, a long time ago – Sarah – but she died just before she was born, sadly.'

'God, June, I'm so sorry.' Sam looked between the two of them, surprised at this honesty. 'That must have been . . . incredibly hard for you both. I'm sorry; that was insensitive of me. I shouldn't have assumed.'

June shook her head firmly and smoothed a piece of hair at the front of her head. 'It was a long time ago now. It's nice to say her name, actually.'

'It means "princess", doesn't it?'

'Yes, that's right.'

'I had a friend at school; I always remember that for some reason.' She shook her head again and looked down at her tea. 'Marvin and I aren't sure that we can have children. That's why I was a bit upset earlier.' She was surprised herself when she heard this sentence.

'Oh, love.' June focused on her with a new tenderness. 'It's a hard time, that. We certainly know.' She looked towards Derek.

Sam bit her lip, not trusting herself to speak.

'But you're both very young, so don't give up hope now,' June said with a kind smile.

This sort of comment usually irritated Sam, but she really must have seemed young to them. 'I don't feel that young these days,' she said with a false laugh.

Derek cocked his head to one side and said, 'Honey, anyone without grey hair is young to us.'

Sam smiled, and they all sipped their tea in unison. The silence wasn't uncomfortable; it felt as though they'd crossed the threshold from small talk to confidantes. No one had shared their experience of fertility problems or pregnancy loss with Sam, and she certainly wasn't expecting her elderly neighbours to be the first. She felt fractionally lighter, an ease within herself that had been absent for some time, almost within reach.

'Who's the detective around here then?' she asked, looking towards a bookshelf in the corner lined with paperback thrillers.

'That's Derek,' June said. 'He can't get enough of crime novels.'

'I picked the wrong career,' Derek said.

'Do you mean writing or solving crimes?' Sam asked.

'Oh, police – I'm no good with words. Quite literally these days!' This made him laugh, which then caused him to start coughing.

When he'd recovered, Sam said, 'I'm more into the easy reads: comedies and love stories mostly, but my friend Daisy has always got a crime novel or a thriller on the go.'

'You'll have to invite her around to borrow one of Derek's. They're just sitting there collecting dust.'

'Aw, she'll love that. Thank you.' Sam's phone vibrated from her handbag by her feet, and Derek tilted his head in puzzlement to see what the rumbling sound might be. 'Sorry, that's my phone.' She bent down and rummaged inside to locate it. 'It's just my mum.'

'Do answer it, Samantha; don't worry about us,' June said.

But Sam declined the call, feeling it would be rude and uncomfortable having the conversation in their living room. She bid Derek and June goodbye, thanking them for the tea, then called her mum back as she was unlocking her front door.

'Hey Mum. Sorry, I was just speaking to the neighbours.'

'Is that the elderly couple next door?'

'Yeah, they're not that old though. Maybe mid-seventies? I mean, they're not *young*. Anyway, how are you?' She walked through to the kitchen area, dumping her bags on the table.

'Not bad. We had a bit of drama last night though.'

Sam heard a tinkling of laughter in the background and someone saying, 'You can say that again!'

Her mum joined in with a chuckle and said, 'I've Julie from next door with me. Someone broke in, you see.'

'Oh, Mum! I'm sorry, how horrible. What did they take?'

'A few bits and pieces – nothing to worry about. I think they ran off when they heard me upstairs.'

Sam stopped unloading her bag. 'You were *in* the house?'

'Yes,' she said, as though Sam was being slow to catch on.

'Mum! That's terrifying. What time was it?'

'About 3 a.m. I think it was the kitchen window smashing that woke me up.' She said this in an admirably matter-of-fact way.

'That's how they got in,' Julie pipped in.

Sam gripped the phone with both hands. 'What did you do? Call the police from the bedroom?'

'Well, no. I just shouted at them.'

'You *shouted* at them? Mum!'

'I wasn't stupid. I made my voice really deep like a man's. I knew they'd just be kids—'

'You couldn't know that! They could have been violent murderers for all you knew!'

'You're not making me feel any better, Sammy.'

Sam put her hand to her forehead. 'Sorry, god, I just can't believe it. Why didn't you call me sooner – you must be so freaked out thinking about them in the house?'

'Oh, I didn't want to worry you. And Julie's been here all day.'

'I've been looking after her!' Julie added.

'Right, well, I'm getting on a train tonight.'

'Don't be so dramatic – there's no need! The police have been over—'

'Lovely they were,' said Julie.

'Oh, they were, so kind, both of them. And we've cleaned everything up.'

'Uh . . .' Sam faltered, feeling redundant. 'What about the window?'

'That's all sorted. They're coming tomorrow to replace it, and I'm staying at Anne's tonight.'

'Okay.' Sam slumped down on a kitchen chair. 'I'd still really like to come up; I'm sure work'd let me take—'

'Sam, there's no need,' her mum said more forcefully. 'You're coming up in a few weeks anyway; I don't want you wasting your money on last-minute train tickets. I'm fine, honestly.'

They ended the phone call, and Sam sat at the table in silence for a few minutes, running the awful scene over in her mind, acutely aware of the distance between her and her mum.

Muffled voices from next door pulled her back to the present and, at last, she stood up and finished unpacking her shopping, comforted by the thought of June and Derek so close, pottering around behind the thin wall of their homes.

The following Friday, Sam and the girls had tickets to see All Saints at Brixton Academy. Sam was getting ready at home, listening to their greatest hits and trying to summon the feeling of excitement for a night out that she used to have each weekend in her early twenties. She selected a Nineties button-down vintage dress, choker necklace, and Doc Martens, and styled her hair into space buns before saying a silent prayer that none of her ex-pupils or colleagues would be there.

'You look amazing,' Marvin said when she entered the living area, ready to go. 'Like a vampire-slaying Baby Spice. Come here, right now.'

'That's exactly the look I was going for.'

He took hold of her waist and pulled her onto his lap on the sofa, and she wrapped her arms around his neck, kissing him gently.

'So, I think you should really go for it tonight,' he said, looking up at her. 'Forget about all the baby stuff, the Jas thing—'

She frowned as though Marvin was speaking out of turn, unprepared to admit even to himself that her friend's pregnancy news was still sitting heavily upon her heart.

'Just *enjoy* it,' he added.

'I'll try.'

'Seriously, have a few drinks – you deserve a night off from it all.'

He squeezed her side and pulled her in towards him, and she submitted, resting her forehead on his. 'Fine, I will.' She lifted her head up, a glimmer of excitement in her features. 'We might even go big and go to the Fridge.'

He pulled back and widened his eyes with disbelief. 'Come now, babe, don't be giving me Fridge chat – you can't do that to me when I'm staying in.'

She kissed him, then stood up. 'It probably won't happen,' she said as a genuine smile spread over her lips.

She met them at a pub around the corner from the Academy. They crowded around a small table and shouted over the unnecessarily loud music, mostly about how young everyone around them looked. Sam couldn't help but be acutely aware of the alcohol they were getting through; she knew she'd be ovulating in the next few days and wondered if the damage she was doing to her body tonight would degrade her egg quality and scupper another month of trying.

There was no mention of Jas's pregnancy which, initially, was a relief to Sam – she knew they'd all be monitoring her for signs of upset when it was brought up. But as the hours rolled by and it still wasn't acknowledged, the blatant omission of the subject actually made Sam feel more uncomfortable as she imagined the three of them making some grandiose martyred vow to not bring the matter up. She sat back in the chair, biting her nails, and watched her friends as though watching a film. Imo elaborately regaled them with a story about some mad night out and, by the end, Daisy and Jas were doubled over in laughter, wiping tears from their eyes. Sam laughed along half-heartedly, feeling distinctly removed from the conversation.

They arrived at the gig as the supporting act was still on stage, leaving time for Sam to accompany Daisy to the toilets while Jas and Imo queued for drinks. The toilet queue was huge, snaking right along the corridor. They took their places side by side against the wall, and Sam felt better now that it was just the two of them, actually less alone than when they were in the pub as a four.

She looked at Daisy fondly, noticing her standard get-up of skinny jeans and a plain T-shirt, her silver necklace with a wishbone charm sitting on top; dressing up was never really her thing. 'Which song are you excited for?'

'"Never Ever",' Daisy replied after a pause.

'Is that the only one you know?'

'Fuck off. I actually know *a handful*, just not every single word like you three eejits.'

They turned to each other and smiled.

'So, I need to tell you something, and you need to *remain calm*,' Daisy said, turning her whole body around to face Sam, leaning one shoulder heavily against the wall.

'Please don't tell me you're pregnant too.'

Daisy threw her head back and let out a single 'Ha!'

It felt like a barrier of some sort had been broken at last, and Sam felt her shoulders relaxing.

'Jesus, no.' Daisy eyed Sam as though trying to convey a message, then folded her arms and leant back on the wall. 'Now it sounds much less dramatic: I had coffee with James last week.'

Sam copied Daisy's posture, folding her arms, her face

puzzled; Daisy had seemed happy with Jono lately. 'Are we talking coffee *sex* or coffee *coffee*?'

'Coffee *coffee*, of course.'

They edged up the line, finally making it into the entrance of the toilets. Daisy stood against the door, propping it open, and Sam just outside.

'We've never really stopped messaging, not for more than a couple of weeks anyway.' Daisy moved aside for a woman to exit the toilets, then turned back to Sam. 'Sometimes I'll think "Right, that's enough now", but then he'll come back at me with something he knows I'll find funny or a really witty water picture.'

Sam formed a question with her eyebrows.

'Oh, it was a stupid thing he did, a joke of some sort. He knew I loved the sea, so he used to send me photos of beaches, then it started to be anything with water, eventually grimy puddles/ glasses of water, you see where I'm going . . .' She tugged at the end of her hair, scattering a couple of strands that came loose and watching as they silently floated out of sight. 'It's like I can't completely move on and fully commit to Jono because James is there all the time, a few clicks away.' She gestured to the phone in her hand, an irritated shake of the device. 'So I thought meeting up might finally put things to bed' – she glared at Sam before she could mock her choice of words – 'and help me really make up my mind about Jono. But I think I'm even more confused.' She rubbed at her forehead with the palm of one hand.

Sam's head was hazy with alcohol, and she was mindful of saying the wrong thing; Daisy had been really offended when she'd called Jono a 'safe' choice when she first met him. She folded her arms and asked carefully, 'Are things not good with Jono?'

Daisy shuffled further along the wall, letting Sam replace her position as the door keeper. 'They're not bad.' She bit her knuckle and didn't elaborate further.

Sam had suspected James still liked Daisy, but she hadn't realized quite how often he'd been messaging her – it was surely proof of his feelings for her. Excitement mounting at the thought of them back together, Sam made a concerted effort to speak levelly when she said, 'I think you need to put James aside for the moment and try to work out what you really feel for Jono.'

They scooted up the queue, finally nearing the front.

'Well, I thought I loved him, *love* him – present tense,' Daisy corrected herself without humour, then sighed and bent down, resting her hands on her thighs to prop herself up. 'I'm thirty-two; I'm *sick* of dating; we live together and . . . what we have is . . . it's *good*, you know, we have fun together. He's a good person.'

'You keep saying "good".'

Daisy blinked once, then looked back at Sam with a new weariness, submissive as she said, 'Good not great – that's the problem, isn't it?'

Sam offered a sympathetic half smile, relieved she hadn't had to be the one to say it.

Daisy continued, 'But am I really going to destroy everything just because I'm arrogant enough to think that I could find something better, something great?'

Sam folded her arms and stared back at her. 'Daisy, breaking up with someone who's not right for you doesn't make you arrogant, it makes you . . . not a coward.'

Daisy suppressed a smile. 'Were you about to say brave and couldn't bring yourself to?'

'We're not American, mate. I've no rousing speeches in me.'

Daisy tilted her head to one side and pursed her lips. 'That was still pretty rousing. So you agree that he's not right for me?'

'That's not what I said.'

'Okay, too *safe* then.'

A year had passed since she'd met Jono, and they were at least able to joke about it now. 'We've been through this!' Sam laughed a little. 'I just meant he seemed like one of those guys who was going to fall madly in love with you and never dream of leaving you.'

'But what you really meant was *beneath* me.'

Sam looked away. They'd never ventured this far into extracting meaning from her comment. 'That's a horrible expression,' she said quietly, turning to place her back against the wall next to Daisy. 'It wasn't that exactly.' She stared at the dirty black tiles on the floor. 'It was more that he wasn't the sort of person you'd really fall for – like I didn't think there was any danger of that happening because you're so different: you don't have the same values or passions!'

Daisy pulled a face like she was about to contest this statement, but there was a reluctance in her expression, as though she felt she should object rather than wanted to, and Sam took the opportunity to continue.

'Like the comment you told me about reading: that he said computer games were the same thing. But, Daisy, you read more than anyone I know! So I think it'd be a shame if you ended up with someone who didn't have an *ounce* of passion for . . .' She looked upwards, unable to summon an appropriate author.

'Shakespeare?'

'Not even Shakespeare . . . but Stephen King! Or Enid Blyton!'

Daisy put one hand on her hip and said, 'We don't *know* that Jono doesn't love the Famous Five.'

Sam tipped her head to one side in false consideration, and their smiles gradually faded.

'And James?'

Sam stared back at Daisy and said slowly, 'He behaved atrociously – that message was ridiculous! But he has apologized, and maybe there was more to it than him just dodging commitment. Maybe he was going through some shit we don't know about? Boys don't always share that kind of thing.' A cubicle became free, and Sam stepped forward, raising her voice as she closed the door to add, 'You know how I feel about James, D – he's Marv's best mate. I've always liked him.'

They met back up with the girls just as the band were coming on stage. Jas passed Sam a pint of beer in a plastic cup and, now drunk enough to push the feelings of guilt from her mind, she took it gladly. They found a spot in the middle that was large enough for the four of them to squeeze into. Jas put her earplugs in as usual and gave Imo the finger when she opened her mouth to inevitably tease her for being *Doctor Sensible*. The band pumped out their catchy hits with accompanying dance routines, and Sam relaxed into the gig, feeling more like herself as she swayed to the music, the alcohol in her body distilling its pleasant and familiar warmth. The room was full of women their age, and a sort of collective fervour emitted by a mass group being transported back to Year Three. Sam noticed Daisy wasn't singing along with as much confidence and smiled at the predictability of this.

Towards the end of the set, 'Never Ever' came on, and they

all turned to each other, wide-eyed with excitement. Jas put her arms around Daisy and Imo and brought them towards Sam to create a group slow-dance. They shouted the lyrics in each other's faces, clutching shoulders and beaming. As the chorus broke, they parted ways and turned back to face the band, throwing their arms up in the air.

Sam watched as Jas and Daisy hung on to each other and danced in front of her, and Imo stood stationary with both arms thrust in the air like a fanatic in church. Swaying along to the beat, Sam felt strangely aware of her arms, hanging limply by her sides; she couldn't seem to lose herself in the moment, like her friends had, like she used to. She'd always been someone for whom happiness came easily, but suddenly she felt like an outsider looking in, watching her friends from an invisible sideline. She raised her arms in the air, swinging them from side to side, but this act felt like an even bigger betrayal of her mood, and her face started to ache from the effort of a forced smile. A wave of sadness began to build up within her, rising so high it threatened to engulf her.

As the concert ended and they filtered out to the street, Sam made her excuses to go home. She'd been holding in tears for the last twenty minutes and didn't want to ruin the night.

'Hun, are you sure?' Jas asked, taking hold of her wrist, her brow furrowed. 'I won't stay too late, but we could just go back to the pub for one more? Have a lime 'n' soda with me?'

'No, honestly, I've got a bit of a headache. I'll be a drain on the night.'

'Darling, you could never be a drain,' Imo said, putting her arm around her.

As the Uber approached and Sam jogged over to it, Jas shouted after her. She turned around to see the three of them in a row, hurling an overarm kiss at her at the exact same moment. She watched them fly through the air, then made elaborate catching motions as though they'd pelted three oranges, grasping the third against her chest with her wrists. They laughed, waving her off, and she sunk into the backseat of the taxi.

'Good night, miss?' the driver asked.

She looked out the window and listened to the electric purr of the engine.

'Yeah, great, thanks,' she replied as a solitary tear rolled down her cheek.

The car pulled up outside their flat. She noticed that the lights were still on inside. Catching sight of herself in the dimly lit mirror in the hallway, she paused. Her Nineties outfit suddenly seemed acutely tragic. The space buns were wonky and her make-up faded, an unattractive shine coming off her forehead, her eyeliner smudged and only an outline of brownish lipstick remaining. She wiped her lips with the back of her hand and vowed to research what Botox actually was in the morning.

'Lamp? You're back early?' Marvin called from the living room.

'I am,' she replied, pulling off her Dr Martens and jacket.

He paused the television and started singing an All Saints hit in an overly camp voice.

She squeezed in next to him on the sofa, and he kissed her on the forehead, pulling her against his chest.

'You don't seem that bedraggled?' he said.

'You sound disappointed.'

'I am. I was expecting a 5 a.m. entry.'

She exhaled loudly. 'Too old for that.'

He fiddled with a piece of her hair. 'Was it fun, though? The girls all okay?'

'Yeah.' The word came out as though she was convincing herself. She sat back up to face him. 'It honestly was a nice night.'

He waited for her to continue.

'I think, probably because I haven't drunk a lot in a while, I had this moment when we were watching the band and . . .' She faltered, staring ahead, unsure what exactly did happen. Then her voice broke, and her eyes filled with tears. 'I just felt really fucking sad.'

'Oh, babe,' Marvin said, reaching out to touch her lower back. 'What happened?'

She wiped her eyes with her forefingers and quietly laughed, as though the outburst was mere silliness. 'I dunno. I guess it did feel a bit weird with the Jas thing, but at the gig, everything was fine. I kept thinking I should be loving this, the others are.' She leant forward, resting her elbows on her lap and fiddling with a thin gold bracelet on her wrist. 'It was like I'd forgotten how to be really happy.'

'Lamp,' Marvin said with surprise in his voice. 'I'm sorry. Come here.' He drew her in for a hug, grasping her tightly, his cheek warm against hers.

They pulled back from one another, and Sam added, 'And I already feel guilty about all the booze we got through.' She gave a short sharp laugh, and then her smile dropped, her eyes cast downwards, focusing on a box of matches on the coffee table. When she spoke again, her voice was low and heavy.

'I feel guilty all the time, Marv' – she glanced up at him, nervous with her confession – 'about everything: what I eat, what I drink, how often I exercise.' She reached up and rubbed her forehead, almost shielding herself from his gaze. 'The fact that I felt utterly devastated when one of my best friends told me she was pregnant.' Her voice crumbled, and she clumsily wiped her nose with the back of her hand. 'The fact I can't give you a kid—'

'Hey, hey, hey, Sam, what is all this? There's no you giving me anything – don't be ridiculous. I hate the thought of you feeling like that.' He took her hand, grasping it firmly. 'And I get it about Jas and Ash; I felt the same.'

She looked across at him then and saw her sadness reflected in the lines of his face.

'It's not that we're not happy for them,' he added.

They sat in silence for a moment, their hands entwined, Sam feeling slightly better that she wasn't the only one to have found their pregnancy difficult.

She drew in a long, steady breath. 'I keep having to remind myself that we were happy before we started trying – there was no baby then, either. But then I still find myself . . .'

'I didn't realize you felt like this,' Marvin said, sitting forward on the sofa. 'You always seem . . .' He shook his head. '. . . like you're taking it all in your stride, like, intimidatingly so. I've felt like I've needed to get my shit together because you've been coping so well.'

She shrugged, unsure exactly how to explain her coping mechanisms, then adjusted her grip to interlock their fingers together. 'Well, I've been trying to *think positively*, not catastrophize, but then . . .' She watched her fingers flexing open and closed against his as she continued quietly, 'Recently I've been thinking of Mum – and Dad – and our relationships, and how I might never have that.'

Marvin joined her in staring down at their hands. 'It's not the baby thing, is it? It's thinking about the future, about not ever having a family.'

Realizing Marvin's fears echoed hers, Sam felt less alone yet distinctly more upset. It was as if they'd finally stopped tiptoeing around the possibility of a childless future and instead opened a window to glimpse at an alternative version of their lives.

She closed her eyes, swallowed, and said, 'I keep saying I'm okay, that if it doesn't happen, then it'll be sad but we'll be all right, but now . . .' She let go of his hand and pressed her fingertips against her eyelids. 'It's like I'm saying the words, but I don't actually believe them anymore.'

'Sam,' he said with tenderness. 'We *will* be okay. And it hasn't even been that long! It could still happen—'

'I know it could.' She broke off as emotion threatened her voice again, then looked up at him. 'I'm not saying I'm giving up, Marv. I'm just saying that I feel sad about it. All the time.'

Two weeks later, Sam waited in the flat for Jono to drop Daisy's things off. She'd broken up with him a few days ago, and Sam and Marvin had offered their spare room to her for a few weeks until she had a plan. Sam was relieved that the relationship was finally over; Daisy had been in complete turmoil about breaking up with him the week before Christmas, but surely it was better than pretending. At least they could both now move on separately and start the New Year afresh.

Sam put *Miracle on 34th Street* on and painted her toenails a festive silver, willing herself into a social mood to join Marvin and his friends for drinks in Soho in a few hours. She hadn't seen Jono for months and was feeling strangely nervous about his knock on the door. She was sure he knew that she was never hugely keen on him and suspected he'd partly blame her for Daisy's decision. Daisy had brushed off these worries and told her to just accept the boxes and bid him farewell, which only encouraged Sam's theory that he might be holding onto some resentment.

The knock came just as Mr Kringle was arrested – surely not a good sign. She padded over to the door carefully, her metallic toenails still drying. Jono was standing further from the doorway than was necessary, holding a large cardboard box with two black bin bags at his feet. The bags felt like a last-ditch derogatory kick. Sam simultaneously noticed the paleness of his complexion and the emblem on his coat: an expensive and popular brand with well-known links to animal cruelty, an item which Daisy would certainly frown upon.

'Hey,' he said, making no movement.

'Hi.' She smiled, attempting to keep things civil. 'D'you wanna pass me the box so you can bring the bags in?'

He looked down at the bags, then stepped forward. 'It's pretty heavy; I can carry it in.'

She stepped back from the doorway to let him in. He placed the box on the floor in the hallway, then backed out to collect the bags.

'How have you been?' Sam asked, filling the silence.

He put the bags down with a surprising gentleness and said, 'You know how it is. Or maybe you don't.' Standing tall again, he added with a tilt of his head, 'It's a shit feeling, but I'll get over it.'

Sam offered a sympathetic smile. She'd expected more bravado from him, possibly complacency.

'I just never expected it from her,' he said, running his hand through his hair. 'She was always on her high horse about stuff, giving *me* shit about morals . . .'

Sam shrugged and said gently, 'People change their minds sometimes; it doesn't make her a bad person.'

'Change their minds?' He stared at her, then laughed. A short sharp burst of disbelief. 'She didn't tell you, did she? Daisy and Sam, who tell each other everything, except when it makes one of them look bad.' He walked towards the door, then turned back to her before stepping through it. 'She was cheating on me.'

Sam opened her mouth to deny this, to at least attempt to appear unbothered by the revelation, but nothing came and she was left staring back at him, embarrassed that she didn't know, that she hadn't guessed.

'Friend of yours, I believe? Nice guy, ey? Real honourable.' He turned around and closed the door gently, an inherent politeness prohibiting the tempting slam.

Daisy

Daisy spotted him before he did her, his black road bike and assured posture immediately recognizable after those months of looking out for him last summer, at cafés, bars, in parks and doorways, waiting, seemingly always waiting. He reached the traffic lights opposite and dismounted as the bike still moved, unclasping his helmet with his right hand and striding towards a cluster of locked bikes. They'd agreed to meet at Spitalfields market for a drink and wander before Daisy went home to Whitby for Christmas. They weren't accustomed to seeing each other in the daytime, sober; it had been her suggestion, and James had willingly accepted, even requesting her help choosing gifts for his siblings.

The last couple of weeks hadn't been as intense as that first summer together. Her relationship with Jono obviously complicated things – she'd discovered she didn't actually have the stomach for an affair and had felt sick with guilt since their meet-ups left the platonic stage a fortnight ago, but it wasn't just that. She was much more on guard now, less willing to jump in. The dynamic between them was different this time around, as though the seasons had directly affected things and winter had brought out a darkness that hadn't existed between them before. Embarrassed by how upset she'd been when he'd ended things, Daisy attempted to offset this by acting cold and unbothered, when in fact she was still drawn to him in a way that she hadn't been to many people in her life. James seemed less idealistic this time around, giving none of his prior showerings of flattery and false promises. Mostly, Daisy considered this positive – she was more able to contemplate her own feelings towards him without being swept up by his excitement – but she still found herself desiring his affection, grasping his rarer compliments and storing them away for moments of doubt.

He had at least seemed genuinely mortified about his final message to her, blaming an aversion to conflict, which Daisy pointed out was ironic given his choice of career. She still thought ending it in such a way was a cowardice, but the fire the message had once ignited had been put out with time.

He spotted her from across the road. They both waved, then spent an awkward thirty seconds looking elsewhere as he waited for the lights to change.

'Hey,' they both said once they were finally within a few feet, elongating the word as though saying cheese into a camera.

They kissed on the cheek as friends would, then she looked back at him, expecting something more, some look of significance that would mark the complexity of their relationship. But he gave nothing.

'So, how, er, how are you? How are things?' he asked as they started walking in the direction of the market. He was wearing grey gloves and clapped his hands together as he walked, rubbing them as you would to keep warm, despite it being a mild day.

She couldn't help but smile at his awkwardness, her eyes dancing with mockery, but he either chose not to laugh at himself or didn't notice her teasing expression.

'Yeah, good, thanks.' They walked on a few steps, and she decided to play along. 'How was your week?' She pointedly drew out the dull question, dipping the words in ironic uncertainty, like they were acquaintances or, more accurately, lapsed friends.

But he didn't react to her charade and only gave an equally dull answer about his working week.

She stopped in the street and folded her arms. 'Why are you being weird?'

He carried on a couple of steps, then turned to her, mouth

open a few seconds for dramatic effect. 'Err, what have I done now?'

Daisy dropped her arms and relaxed her shoulders, ready to dispel any forthcoming comments about her being a *crazy woman*. She gave her most patronizing of smiles. 'You're being awkward, like we've never hung out before.'

'Oh, I'm sorry. Am I not being *boyfriendy* enough?' he said without aggression, only lightly teasing. 'Should I have lovingly embraced you in the street?'

'It's not a question of being *boyfriend*-like—'

'I guess not, since you've already got *one of those*.' The last three words were almost whispered, slipping into something spiteful, a reaction to her calling out his awkwardness, making him feel small.

It wasn't the first time he'd behaved like this, seemingly enjoying her betrayal of Jono and how it tormented her. He'd been oddly interested in their relationship, and Daisy wasn't sure if the fascination was competitive (which could be construed as flattering), or if he merely enjoyed the danger and deceit that came with her being attached to someone else. She expected the latter and, on some self-sabotaging level, had even started to hope for it.

'Actually, I don't.' Her voice rung out, and a woman in a leopard-print coat turned around to look at her as she passed. Daisy had been saving this nugget of information for the right moment, a precious jewel she was keeping close to her chest.

He stopped walking, a smile spreading over his lips as he regarded her with wonder.

This was how it had been with them over the last few weeks: a strange game of goading each other under the guise of flirtation until one of them snapped. He seemed to like her best when she was sarcastic and cruel, grinning at her like she was the sexiest and wittiest thing alive. It made her push further, and those rare moments when she made it past his seemingly impenetrable wall of vulnerability made her feel invincible.

He took several steps towards her, grinning with admiration, his whole façade softer; she'd appeased or sated him for the time being. 'Well, well, well, Daisy Carlisle, you don't mess about.'

She tipped her head from side to side and said, 'Well, technically . . .' then felt a current of shame hit her; she was by no means cool nor cruel enough to joke about her infidelity.

'How was it?' His voice was gentle then, caring even. 'When did you do it?'

'Tuesday.'

Jono's reaction had been a quiet jealous rage. He wouldn't believe that it had only started the week before, snatching Daisy's phone and demanding to see her and James's messages. When she'd refused, he'd slumped down on the sofa and politely asked her to leave.

Saving Jono one last indignity, she chose not to share the details of their break-up with James, saying only, 'I feel better now it's done.'

They continued walking, and she sensed something shift in James, a tilt of his head or something else she'd learnt signified worry.

'I didn't see that one coming,' he said, his voice unnatural. He was a poor actor.

She carried on looking ahead and said flatly, 'What was it about my behaviour that made you think me and him were in it for the long run?'

He looked across at her, an unsure smile at her dry tone. 'No, I just meant, like, I didn't think you were going to end it this quickly. I thought you were . . .' He shrugged and put his hands in his pockets. 'I mean, I thought me and you were just—'

'We are,' she interrupted sharply, unable to hear any more of his stumbling, '*just,* or just *not* depending on how you look at it.' She felt a grim satisfaction in his obvious discomfort at the thought of them becoming anything significant, as though it was the long searched-for proof that her attachment to Jono was what attracted James to her again. 'It's been on the cards for a while,' she added casually. 'Me and him breaking up makes no difference to' – she wafted her hand in a circle – 'whatever this is.'

He took her hand then, and the tenderness of the action shocked her, such a blatant display of affection in public. 'Okay, it's just that we haven't talked about that kind of stuff – I wasn't expecting you to finish with him.' A piece of blond hair fell forward onto his face, and he swept it back, frowning like a film star with the weight of the world on his shoulders. 'I know I haven't exactly helped the situation, but I hope I wasn't the reason.'

His gloved hand felt oddly huge in comparison to her bare one, and she had a fleeting desire to remove hers from his grasp. Instead, she gripped his hand harder as she said, 'Babe, don't flatter yourself.' She heard her voice and knew that she'd reverted to Imo's tone and phrases, a habit she had when feeling exposed. 'You might have been the catalyst, but you certainly weren't the . . .' She grimaced and looked squarely at him. 'Can't think of any scientific metaphors.'

He raised one thick eyebrow and said, 'Prize?'

This did at least make her smile, so fitting with his arrogance.

'Does that work? I guess if one's sole reason for science is the pursuit of rewards rather than curiosity.' He looked lost, so she added, 'You weren't the *main reason* I ended it. So, sure: certainly not the prize.'

He tilted his head and spoke out the side of his mouth, 'There's a lot of pressure on a prize. Catalyst sounds sexier to me.'

She made a breathy, 'hm' sounding laugh as a flat feeling settled over her.

They reached the market, a warm glow of lights from the stalls contrasting with the stark steel roof pitched above them. Daisy walked over to the first stall that sold an array of T-shirts screen-printed with geometric shapes resembling London landmarks. She took the corner of one in her hands, fingering the fabric with her free hand like she was assessing its quality, the softness and familiar texture a strange comfort.

James steered her away, looking out at the traders for something to his taste. 'So I need to get something for my mum as well. My dad's easy: Ralph Lauren jumper every year . . .'

She half listened, holding the conversation in her mind just enough so as to be able to recall the last sentence when it was her turn to speak. While she wasn't expecting them to become anything significant or close to a couple overnight, she was hoping there was at least some prospect of this in the future, that they might soften to each other in time and, like Sam said, end up being great together. She'd anticipated her new availability might cause some panic in James, but she'd also expected some level of excitement at their new freedom. Otherwise, what the hell were they doing?

Aware of a bitter taste in her mouth as he guided her around the stalls, she dropped his hand and gripped his arm instead, still not ready to let go.

Daisy's time in Yorkshire over Christmas provided the restorative powers she'd hoped. She arrived crumpled and hungover, her body itching with shame and her mind reeling with rage: James hadn't replied to her messages since they'd met three days ago. She missed Jono but didn't allow herself to message him apart from a simple line on Christmas Day.

Most of her time was spent at her grandmother's house: a narrow terrace painted the colour of sunshine, tucked away in the coastal village of Robin Hood's Bay, a few miles from Whitby. It had dangerously low ceilings and drafts all year round; Daisy had spent the week in a heavy cardigan worn over a woolly jumper, trying not to think about how cold her nose was. The ground floor was dark, but there were incredible sea views from the second floor. The village had always been popular with artists – Graham said it was something to do with the light, and she knew what he meant. The sunsets in Robin Hood's Bay cast an ochre glaze over the village that she hadn't come across anywhere else in the world.

Ida was eighty-two now, and it was difficult to witness her losing some of her independence: the arthritis in her knees was so pronounced that she struggled to climb the stairs and could no longer tend to her vegetable garden with her usual tenacity. But she was still able to cook. Ever since Daisy was a child, she and Ida would while away hours in the kitchen together.

She didn't ask much about Daisy's life in London as they cooked this time around. Her disappointment in Daisy's current job was palpable; she'd always been ambitious for Daisy and couldn't understand why she'd chosen a life staring at a computer screen. It was something they used to discuss openly, but the longer Daisy stayed on at her company, the farther apart the conversations became. There was little left to say on the matter.

Sam had been somewhat cool towards Daisy over the Christmas period, still upset that she hadn't been told about James. She'd feigned anger at Daisy's selfishness towards Jono, but given that she'd practically told her to get with James when they were at the gig a few weeks before, Daisy suspected she was more hurt about being left in the dark. The truth was that she hadn't wanted the added pressure of Sam's hope.

By the time Daisy returned to London, Sam seemed to have forgiven her; they hugged warmly in the kitchen – a rare greeting between them that started off tenderly and ended with Daisy aggressively rocking them both from side to side with so much energy that they nearly fell over and parted in laughter. They spent an afternoon with Marvin and their delightful neighbours. Derek tottered in with a walking frame, dressed in a tweed blazer and black leather shoes, which had obviously been polished for the occasion, with June behind in a burgundy polo-neck, black skirt, and tiny black boots. They ended up staying for four hours, transitioning from tea to June's sloe gin and playing charades. Daisy lent Derek a hardback thriller she'd been given for Christmas, and he insisted she come over and choose one of his books in return.

After talking to June and Derek about her and Ida's cooking, Daisy decided to bake one of her signature ginger loaves for them as a New Year's gift. She rose early on New Year's Eve and enjoyed having an hour to herself in the kitchen before the party preparation began; Sam and Marvin had arranged a gathering to see in the New Year at theirs.

As the cake slowly turned brown in the oven, Daisy made herself a coffee in the cafetière and flicked through yesterday's paper, feeling more like her old self. Sam emerged around 9 a.m., still in her George Michael Christmas pyjamas, her hair dishevelled. Spotting her, Daisy grabbed a foil party horn from the side and tooted it with gusto.

'Happy last day of the year!'

Sam reared back from the noise, frowning at Daisy through a strand of hair. The radio was on, and Daisy turned it up as Stevie Wonder came on.

'What are you doing? It's so early?'

Daisy tooted again and then started dancing with her coffee mug.

'It's the party tonight and the end of a shitty, shitty year! Wait . . .' She picked up her phone and selected DMX's 'Party Up', connecting it with the Bluetooth speaker and boosting the volume.

Sam watched her, still frowning as the music assaulted her, then climbed onto the sofa and repeated, 'Happy last day of a shitty year!', dancing along with Daisy.

Hearing the noise, Marvin came through in his grey dressing gown. Daisy blew her horn at him, then carried on dancing, her mug still in one hand. Marvin looked from her to Sam grinding on the sofa, then stepped up onto the other end and joined them in dancing.

'Is that ginger I smell?' he said through a twerk.

★

They spent the afternoon decorating the flat, making black-and-gold pompoms out of tissue paper and sending Marvin out to get more ice and mixers. The girls got ready together, with Sam doing their make-up as they listened to Destiny's Child.

Finishing with a smattering of mascara on Daisy's fair lashes, Sam stood back to admire her work, her face still drawn in concentration. 'Nailed it.'

Daisy widened her eyes and lowered her front teeth over her bottom lip, grinning insanely.

Sam let a burst of laughter out and said, 'You look like a horse, a troubled mare called . . . Winifred.'

Daisy dropped the face and said, 'Poor Winifred. Maybe I should approach James like that tonight, make him see what he's missing.'

Sam shook her head as she rummaged in her make-up bag. 'Has he still not messaged you?'

'Once or twice. But nothing since the "Ha!" on Boxing day,' Daisy said with humour, despite a growing unease about seeing him tonight.

'Jesus.' Sam pulled a lipstick out and leant into the mirror to apply it, her words coming out comically as she spoke without moving her lips. 'You need to talk to him tonight, find out what's going on.'

'Well' – Daisy interrupted herself by sipping from her bottle of beer – 'pretty sure he's done the classic: no longer interested now I'm available.'

Daisy had spent a lot of time thinking about James when she'd been home for Christmas. Those few weeks spent together last year had been so fleeting, so transient – there hadn't been adequate time for him to let her down, until it was over. But this time around was different. James's frequent pushing and pulling, his intense desire followed by a complete withdrawal of himself, meant she was constantly running on adrenaline with him: anxiety during the silences followed by endorphin hits when he finally texted back or finally looked at her in that way he had. She found that she was sharp and even cruel to him sometimes, as though this was the only way to instil balance between them; their time together seemed to entail flirting, teasing, arguing, then fucking.

It was being around her parents over Christmas that had given Daisy some perspective and allowed her to really consider what she had, or didn't have, with James. She'd been telling herself that their relationship was passionate – after seeing him, she briefly felt beautiful and alive. But she didn't often feel happy. And she wasn't sure she liked who she became around him: this biting and bitter person, desperate for his enamour.

Daisy's parents' relationship wasn't passionate in the sense of the word that she knew, but, even after all these years, it was strong and it was easy, and it was what Daisy wanted for herself. She wanted to be with someone who made her heart sing – someone *great*, who loved her equally, who made her feel that she was enough. And she wasn't sure that James could ever do that.

Daisy put her bottle down and folded her arms. 'Anyway, me and him would never properly work; we're not right for each other.'

Sam turned away from the mirror. 'Don't say that!'

'I'm sorry to ruin your little wet dream about us being the perfect couple.'

'It was such a nice dream! Anyway, it's not over yet – you look banging tonight, no Winifred in sight.'

Daisy scratched her forehead, her patience waning. Sam was so insistent on them being the perfect match for each other, she never actually asked if this was truly the case. 'Your lipstick's smudged.'

Sam turned back to the mirror and saw the bright red smear above her lips. 'Oh shit.'

The first guests arrived around eight o'clock, spilling in wearing heavy coats over glitzy tops and velvet dresses. Imo walked in with a bottle of tequila in one hand and a bag of limes in the other.

'Daddy's home,' she announced, her gold sequin dress shimmering against her dark bob.

Jas rarely made their New Year's nights. She had some sort of pact with her school friends that they always spent it with each other, which usually meant months of moaning about the idea of being in Croydon again.

The living area gradually filled up, with most people crowding in the kitchen area. Daisy sat on one of the units, surrounded by bottles and carrier bags. She chatted with the Crescent boys for a while, then had a cigarette outside with Imo as they traded Christmas highs and lows. James arrived while she was in the garden. She spotted him through the window, then couldn't seem to shake his presence as she waited for him to approach, excuses regarding his silence inevitable. Sam's friend, Blake, arrived around 9.30 and was welcomed by a group from their school. He was different from how Daisy remembered, still tall and attractive but paler and with shorter hair. He looked up suddenly, as though he could feel her eyes on him, and she jolted her gaze back to Ellis, speaking in front of her.

The room was now rammed with people, their voices raised as they competed to be heard. A speaker pumped out a Spotify playlist, meticulously devised by Marvin over the last week. The windows looking out over the garden were completely steamed up, beads of condensation tracing lines down the velvet glass, an uncomfortable chill intermittently cast on the people standing by the door as people edged in and out.

After ten minutes, Blake headed over to the kitchen area with a four pack of beers in his hand. Daisy watched out the corner of her eye as he stooped to hug Sam, who then introduced him to some people from her old school. Daisy swigged her beer, then turned back to the boys as Ellis erupted into laughter at something she'd missed. The noise stood out above the music, making people turn towards their group. She looked back towards Blake and saw that he was looking directly at her. She raised her eyebrows and smiled like she hadn't noticed him before now, slid down from the countertop, and stepped the few feet towards him.

'Blake, isn't it? I think we met a while back, in the park.'

'I remember,' he said with warmth. 'How are you, Daisy?'

The sound of her name on his lips combined with the intensity of his gaze created a flash of something within her: an excitation of neurons somewhere within her brain firing out signals, automated and important. It took her a second to recognize the following sweeping sensation as relief – relief that it was not only James who could have this effect on her.

'Yeah, good,' she said, meaning it for the first time that night. 'Have you got a drink?'

'Sam's just grabbing me one.'

'Was I?' Sam called from her spot by the fridge. 'Shit, yes, what did you want again?'

'Just a beer'd be great. These aren't quite cold enough – have you got room?' Sam opened the small fridge, and Blake saw that it was jam-packed with bottles. 'That's cool. I'll just leave these here and slyly drink other people's.'

'That's the spirit,' said Sam, handing him a bottle. The doorbell rang, just audible above Foals' '2am', which was blaring out the speaker in the corner. 'Oh, excuse me,' Sam said, leaving the two of them.

Daisy smiled at her friend's formality but wasn't sure how to voice this to Blake in a way that would be funny. Blake sipped from his beer and turned his head to take in the room. Daisy too drank from her can. The room was noisy with chatter and music, making the silence between them more poignant.

'It's a nice place,' he said, turning back to her. 'Sam said you're staying here at the moment?'

'Yeah,' Daisy said, surprised that Sam had told him this; she made out they barely saw each other at school. She wondered if he knew the whole story. 'Just for a couple of months I think – it wasn't the best end to the year, so I'm squatting here for a bit.'

'Sorry.' Blake grimaced and rubbed at his forehead. 'I didn't mean to pry. She didn't mention why you were here – I thought . . . I assumed you wanted to – never mind.' He waved his hand in front of his chest as though trying to erase the last minute.

'No, it's fine. There's no major sob story: I broke up with my boyfriend, that's it.' Her confidence in the delivery of this message was unmistakable: she wanted him to know this information. The beer was making her more brazen than usual.

'Ah, I'm sorry to hear that.'

His dark eyes bored into her, and she looked away, afraid she'd smile too widely when they were discussing her break-up. An unforgivable flirtation. There was another silence between them as Daisy rummaged through her brain, wondering what she normally found to talk about with people.

'D'you want to do a shot?' she asked. 'With me. Do you want to do a shot of tequila with me?' The words tumbled out of her.

He raised his eyebrows, his beer frozen in the air on its way to his mouth. 'Tequila? With you?' He smiled as he repeated her words.

She shrugged. 'You can't do tequila alone . . .'

'We are, absolutely, not alone right now,' he said, looking around at the crowd.

She was certain these words were said in innocence, but the suggestion was impossible to ignore. There was a flicker of dismay in his features at the betrayal of his mouth. Daisy smiled and looked down at her beer, acutely aware of the air entering and exiting her lungs. A girl in a green silk shirt squeezed past Daisy, pushing her closer to Blake, and she saw James's eyes on her from across the room for the first time that night. She looked up at Blake, now unnaturally close. He was wearing a navy sweatshirt with a small triangle motif, the collar of his shirt just visible, tucked underneath. She drew her vision up from the stubble on his neck to meet his eyes.

His tone was serious when he said, 'I think you should get that tequila.'

★

He poured the liquid into two miniature glasses as she chopped them each a wedge of lime. Daisy picked up the salt, and they both shifted their gaze away from each other as they licked the back of their hands. She tipped the salt onto the shiny wetness on his skin, then covered her own in white crystals.

'A toast?' he said, picking up his glass.

She strummed her fingers back and forth on her chin. 'Pressure to come up with something that isn't about new beginnings . . .'

He smiled at her a moment too long, then said, 'Then let's just be French and say *santé*.' He clashed his glass into hers and raised his eyebrows, making pointed eye contact in the fashion of the toast.

'*Santé*,' she replied.

They licked the salt off their hands, holding each other's gaze this time, and threw the liquid back. Daisy turned away from him as the taste bombarded her, the sensation like fire. She grabbed the lime and bit down on it gladly, then swallowed and blinked away the onslaught.

He pulled his lips inwards and blinked several times himself, picked up his beer, took a gulp and said, 'That was terrible.'

She puffed her cheeks out and exhaled. 'It really was.'

They held each other's gaze a moment until they were interrupted by one of the teachers from his school, who greeted Daisy, then took Blake by the arm to lead him to their group across the room.

★

The party continued, reaching full capacity by ten o'clock. The room was jammed with people, as was the corridor and patio outside the back door. Sam and Daisy's eyes met across the room, and Sam raised her arm up high, her wine glass reaching up in the air, above all the heads between them. Daisy did the same with her beer, and they both grinned inanely at each other. James appeared at Daisy's side at this very moment. She brought the bottle back down and returned her face to normal. For half an hour at least, she'd genuinely forgotten he was there. They hugged and kissed on both cheeks and ended up chatting about their Christmas breaks rather than anything of worth. As she listened to him talking, she took in the line of his jaw and the golden tone of his skin, even in December.

'I'm sorry I've been a bit quiet lately.' He leant closer to her to avoid having to raise his voice above the music. 'I just thought you'd need a bit of time, after all the stuff with Jono.'

She pursed her lips, refusing to accept this explanation and forcing an uncomfortable silence to make him continue.

He offered a brief smile as though caught out. 'I still really like you, Daisy. I don't know where we're at . . .' He opened his palms to her.

Daisy ran a hand through her hair, her heart rate rising at these words. She hated her body's reaction to James, its betrayal of her mind. She folded her arms and looked away. 'Then how come it's taken you two hours to come and talk to me?'

'Nerves,' he said, a wry smile spreading upwards.

'Nerves?' she repeated, amused. 'Sure. You do come across that way.'

They grinned at each other before his eyes flicked down to her lips.

When the guest list topped fifty people a week before the party, Sam and Marvin had booked an area in a pub for 11 p.m. for the sake of their neighbours. At 10.30, Marvin started ushering people out, encouraging a mass exit to the pub. Sam insisted on booking an Uber, not wanting to walk in her blue velvet platforms, and many people jumped on this.

'It's New Year's – they'll be double the price! Plus it's like, twenty minutes away,' said Daisy from the doorstep. She couldn't understand why people chose to wear high heels.

Marvin had already set off walking with James and another of their friends, and everyone left seemed set on getting taxis.

'Imo?' Daisy said, her voice already resigned to the answer.

From beside the front door, Imo frowned and blew cigarette smoke to the side, the question too ludicrous to deserve a reply.

Daisy stepped back inside to find someone else and was met by Blake in the narrow corridor. She'd lost sight of him inside and had feared he'd left.

'Oh hey!' she said, smiling. The drink had significantly loosened her up. 'Are you walking to the pub?' she asked, taking in his padded black coat and knitted beanie the colour of sand.

'Yeah, Sam said it's only twenty minutes away?'

'Exactly! D'you wanna walk with me?'

'To the pub? With you?' he said with a wide grin, echoing their former stumbling conversation.

'Yes.' She laughed now. 'Do you want to walk to the pub with me?'

'Well, you can't walk alone . . .' He followed her through the front door and down the few steps.

★

They walked side by side in silence for the first minute, his trainers and her boots both quiet on the pavement. Music and laughter from distant parties drifted towards them. Daisy could feel the alcohol in her system; it was that lovely level where the world seemed easy but focused.

'So, what's your story, Blake?'

He looked at her, and she could see that he remembered. 'I seem to recall you not really giving an answer when I asked you that,' he said.

She shrugged, her smile refusing to dissolve. 'You can go first.'

'Okay, well, what would you like to know?'

'Erm . . . why are you hanging out with work people on New Year's?'

He laughed loudly at this, which surprised her.

'Are you slyly asking if I have any friends?'

They reached the end of the street, and she gestured to cross over, bumping into him slightly as they changed direction.

'Oh sorry, I don't actually know where we're going.'

Daisy took hold of his upper arm and gently steered him to the left. Her grasp lingered as she considered keeping hold, but instead she put her hand back into the pocket of her denim jacket. It was unseasonably warm, and she was glad she'd risked not bringing her big coat.

'Yeah, so the friend thing,' he said. 'It's a good point; tonight was a bit of a wild card.'

Daisy allowed herself to consider if he came with the hope of seeing her, and the thought provided a rush of excitement.

'Ben's here,' he said. 'Have you met him? He's one of my best mates.'

'Err . . . I don't think so. Does he exist in real life?'

'He *does*.' He laughed again at this, and Daisy felt triumphant to have brought out further amusement. 'I've known him for years. He got me to apply for the job at Parkmoor – he's been a teacher there for ages.'

'Ahh okay, so he's technically not a work friend.'

'Correct.' He glanced at her. 'And my other mates . . . they're a bit scattered, I guess.'

Daisy considered how the same could be said of her own friends and family.

He continued, 'I also have the added complication of a lot of my London mates being friends with my ex.'

'Ah.' She grimaced, turning towards him. 'Not on good terms?'

'Not bad terms, no. Just not sure I'd want to spend New Year's Eve with her.'

As they continued walking, Daisy ran over questions in her head about his ex but deemed them all inappropriate. 'Do you mind if I smoke?' she said, spotting a bench up ahead.

Even this seemed to amuse him. 'Why would I mind?'

She sat down on the bench and pulled her tobacco tin out of her jacket pocket. He joined her, sitting a foot away.

'You ever smoke?'

'For fifteen years.'

'Wow. Sorry, is this making you want one?'

'No. I stopped ages ago – six years now.'

'Wait, how old are you?' she asked, smiling.

'Fifty-one.'

She clamped her lips together in a smile. 'Right.'

'I fucked it, didn't I? Went too high.' He turned towards her, resting his right ankle on his left knee, and said, 'What could

I have got away with? That you'd doubt, but you couldn't be absolutely sure I was joking?'

'Hmm.' She pouted her lips in concentration as she examined his face, taking in its symmetry. His stubble looked to be a week or so old, framing his jaw flatteringly. She wondered if it was always this length and how rough it would feel against her lips. 'This is a dangerous game,' she said, sealing her cigarette with her tongue and looking away. 'I'd go forty-five. I'd be surprised, and interested in your skincare routine, but I couldn't confidently discount it as a lie.'

'Forty-five,' he repeated, accepting the number thoughtfully.

She lit her cigarette and inhaled, watching as some fiery sparks left the tip, luminous against the surrounding darkness. 'So how old are you, actually?'

'Thirty-seven.'

'Nice.'

'Thank you,' he said, finding her funny again. 'Are you going to ask me how I'm feeling about the big four-zero?'

'Oh, is that a thing? Should I have checked in with you about it?' she teased. 'I really don't get the whole "fear of ageing" thing. I've always looked forward to getting older. It's like each year I'm a step closer to figuring things out, what I'm meant to be doing with my life, etc.' She breathed smoke out, then, in a quieter voice, added, 'But then I don't quite ever make it there.' She shuffled on the bench, aware that she was doing a poor job of playing the easy-going and confident woman who men wanted to be with.

Blake stared ahead, examining a block of terrace houses facing them. 'I think you're just describing the human condition. We're all constantly searching for some kind of purpose, and no one actually knows what the fuck they're meant to be doing.'

'D'you think?' She turned to look at him then, noting how he matched her serious tone, seamlessly transitioning from their former playful manner; she'd anticipated some level of mockery in his response.

He looked back at her, the question rhetorical, then they both turned back to the other side of the road, their attention caught by a group of teenagers passing, one of them walking backwards to keep up with the conversation with the others behind.

'I don't know,' Daisy said. 'I guess it's stupid to be expecting life to get easier when the whole world's obsessed with youth. Graham – my dad – always said your twenties are the decade that provide the stories you'll tell for the rest of your life.'

'He's probably right, but it doesn't mean they're necessarily the best to live through at the time.'

'Maybe.' She bit her bottom lip, wanting to agree. 'My parents are kind of ageing anarchists; they're all about *carpe diem*.' She said this with amused disapproval, though really, she felt a swelling of pride.

'Ah.' He pointed like something had clicked. 'That's where your quiet rebellion stems from then.'

'Maybe.' She was touched that he remembered their Irn-Bru conversation in the park, looking away to conceal her smile. 'They've always encouraged us to kind of reject traditions and do what we really want, do what's right for us, you know – not just get married and have 2.4 kids because everyone else does.' She cast a nervous glance his way and took a drag on her cigarette. 'Not that there's anything wrong with that.'

He shrugged and said noncommittally, 'Works for a lot of people. So are your parents super laid-back?'

'Mmm . . . I wouldn't say that exactly – I've still felt pressure to live up to their expectations: to lead a really exciting life, have lots of adventures while also getting A grades.' She stared down at the end of her cigarette, a thought arriving in her conscience. 'I think I make *bad* decisions sometimes – like I'm fighting between what I think I should do and what I really want to do – and because of that, I've ended up with a completely chaotic existence.' She gave a brief, pathetic laugh. 'Maybe I would have been happier staying in Whitby and following the marriage and babies template.' She loved her hometown, but the idea of returning there after university seemed so unadventurous that it was never given any serious consideration.

Blake didn't say anything for a moment, and Daisy glanced at him, then away again, conscious now of her venture into self-analysis. Feeling him studying the side of her face, she turned back and held his gaze this time, allowing him to really look: past the misgiving calm of her green eyes to the tangle of connections and mayhem within. There was a stillness to his gaze, at odds with the disorder within her, and she found herself wondering about auras as an explanation to how pleasant he was to be around.

His tone was casual when he said, 'For what it's worth, I don't see chaos in you.'

She smiled briefly and looked down at the arm of the bench. 'Well, that's something at least.' She pulled her jacket tighter around her body as though it might restore a barrier of some sort. 'You ready to carry on?' She gestured with her head in the direction they were walking.

'Yeah,' he said, standing up and tucking his hands into his pockets.

She pulled her long hair over her right shoulder, throwing her heavy blanket scarf around the back of her neck. 'So how long have you lived in Streatham for?' she asked, directing the conversation back to lighter subjects.

'Coming up to six months now. I tend to move around a bit: I've lived all over East London, Devon, stints back home in Leicester here and there, a year in Lisbon . . .'

'Amazing. Where did you go to uni?'

'I didn't,' he said.

'Oh, shit, sorry.'

'You don't have to apologize; I don't see it as a negative.'

'No, 'course not,' she said quickly. 'I meant, I'm sorry for my assumption. Such an embarrassingly middle class faux pas.'

He smiled but didn't disagree.

'So . . . you have a friend called Ben, you're a teaching assistant and a furniture maker who lives in Streatham. You have a cute dog, an ex-girlfriend, and you read Virginia Woolf.'

He laughed. 'I'm not an avid Woolf fan; I've just read a few of hers.'

'What else do you read?'

He put his hands in his pockets and looked down to the ground as he answered. 'Bit of everything. Shit answer, sorry. I basically didn't read anything until I was about twenty-six. And then I read a lot.' They veered left onto a busier road, and he turned towards her, walking backwards as he said, 'Okay, my turn now. You're Sam's friend from uni, originally from Whitby? Recently single . . . currently homeless . . . not well read . . .'

She burst out laughing. 'Fuck me, that was a bit close to the bone. And if you say the word "banter" then I'm going home.'

He turned back around to face the way they were walking, and Daisy could see that he was smiling widely, a dimple visible on the cheek facing her. His dark hair peeped through from beneath his beanie, and the small gold hoop remained in his left earlobe.

Not wanting the walk to end, Daisy tried to slow her pace without it being noticeable. 'I don't know what to add to that. But, yeah, I grew up in Whitby, North Yorkshire. It's a nightmare to get to but . . . it's part of me, as cheesy as that sounds. I don't quite feel like myself if I'm away from the sea for a long time. I'm not sure exactly why I came to London. Actually, I am: Sam.'

'Yeah, she said you guys are super close?'

Daisy nodded as she examined the pavement. 'Her plan was London, so . . .' They walked a few more steps in silence before she said, 'I don't regret coming; there's so many things I love about it. But lately it feels like everyone's got their act together and I really don't; like, I really don't think I'm in the right career, but then I don't know what to do instead.' She saw he was frowning, so continued, 'Oh, I work for an online publication: Click-It? I do all the food stuff – interviews with chefs, recipes, the odd tasting.' Ashamed of her privilege, she added quickly, 'It's okay – obviously there's a multitude of worse jobs.'

She prepared herself for his excitement over the free tastings, as usually happened, but instead he replied, 'I used to be in a job like that. Not *like* that, but one that didn't really fit me: it was office-based, no flexibility, no creativity. I quit five years ago after doing some woodwork evening classes and, well, I don't earn as much, hence doing the TA stuff alongside it, but I'd never go back.'

Daisy digested this information as they walked, unsure if she was relieved or offended that he wasn't at all impressed by her job. 'Wow, that's really . . . brave,' she said, then felt silly and continued swiftly, hoping to distract from the comment, 'I dream about quitting all the time. I honestly think I'd be happy being a dog walker, outside all the time. Or doing something with my hands like a ceramicist.'

He looked over at her and made an affirming 'Hmm' sound. 'Let's have a look at those hands then?'

She stopped walking and frowned at him.

'Seriously, let's see.'

'You never said you were a hand talent scout?' She pulled her hands out of her jacket pockets and held them up, palms towards him.

He took each one in his, examining them as a doctor would, and she glanced between his face and the backs of her hands, regretting not asking Sam to paint her nails for the evening. Daisy had never paid any attention to her nails and thought of her hands as entirely unremarkable; she hoped Blake wasn't going to try and compliment their softness or something equally false.

'Cold,' he said, almost to himself.

It was true. His hands were remarkably warm in comparison, his skin faintly textured and rough against her own.

'Hmm, I see. Tiny.'

She laughed at the concentration on his face. 'Is that your diagnosis?'

'Yep, far too tiny for computer work. I don't know how you've managed all these years.'

He dropped her hands, and their eyes met as they stood opposite each other on the street. They were so close that she stepped back instinctively, her heartbeat rising, then yearned for his closeness again.

'I think we're nearly there,' she said, not wanting to look away from him.

'Yeah,' he said quietly. His eyes flickered over her face, then softened as he smiled.

They turned back in the direction they were heading, and the pub came into view at the crossroads. The night suddenly seemed less appealing, imagining the noise and people inside. She remembered that James was there, and the prospect of navigating his confusing advances almost took her breath away.

'So, we've got an hour 'til midnight,' Blake said, checking the time on his phone. 'What shall we drink? And don't say tequila.'

The 'we' in his sentence brought her attention back to the moment, and she turned and grinned at him.

They entered the pub, squeezing past a crowd congregating in the entrance. The place was packed with people of all ages, the air sticky and warm. A Christmas song was playing in the background, almost drowned out by the roar of conversations. Apart from the inviting golden glow of the bar, the lighting was low, and Daisy found it difficult to spot anyone.

Blake unzipped his coat and leant over to speak into her ear. 'Do you know which area they reserved?'

She felt the warmth of his breath on her neck and suppressed the urge to turn to him. 'I'm guessing it's in the other room.' She pointed to the opposite corner of the bar, where an archway opened up into another high-ceilinged room. There was a sea of people in between them and the archway.

'Shall we get a drink first then?' he said.

She bounced with enthusiasm as they wove their way into the mass queuing at the bar. They ordered whisky sours and then set off through the crowd to the other room, Daisy's hand gently resting on Blake's elbow as he led the way. After they were promptly separated by a woman pushing between them, Blake tenderly took hold of Daisy's hand as they continued through the crowd, and Daisy felt her heart soaring at the touch of his fingertips.

They reached the second room, where the noise transitioned from the low-pitched whirl of chatter to a pronounced music beat. Spotting their group in the corner, they headed over, parting hands in the less-crowded room. Daisy was unsure who let go first.

'D!' Sam spotted her and shouted over, squeezing past people to reach her. 'Where've you been?' she said, draping her arm around her heavily.

Blake was absorbed by the group around them, leaving Daisy's side.

'I walked with Blake,' she said, removing her denim jacket and scarf and adding them to the heap piled on one of the leather seats. She stood with her hands on her hips, taking in the room.

'Oh, okay,' Sam stuttered, struggling to process this information. She swayed slightly on the spot without Daisy to lean on.

Daisy took hold of her arm, bringing her closer and, with widened eyes, said, 'Will you come outside? I need to tell you something.'

Sam pulled a face and swiped at the air with one hand. 'It's so cold. Just tell me here.'

'Okay.' Daisy leant in, flicking her eyes to Blake, who was now standing a few metres away. She clapped her hands together as though in prayer, then pointed them towards Sam as she spoke. 'So . . . I *really* like Blake.'

'Blake?' Sam repeated, as though Daisy was speaking another language. 'But you still like James?'

'I do, but we're not—'

'And what about *Jono* – you just broke up *because* of James! You're literally chasing drama!'

'No, I'm not! And we didn't break-up just because of James; you know that.'

Sam shook her head a few too many times. 'This is your problem, Daisy,' she slurred. 'You don't know what you want.'

Daisy pulled backwards and folded her arms, frowning at her friend. 'I've just told you what I want. And I wasn't aware I had a *problem*.' Her eyes flicked over to Blake, and he seemed to feel her glare, glancing up at her with a serious expression that she felt in her gut.

Sam shook her head again. 'I think it'll be way simpler if you just pull James tonight.'

Daisy looked back at her, exasperated. 'Why do you keep—'

'James!' Sam shouted, spotting him close by.

'Sam! For fuck's sake, I don't want to speak to him right now.'

But Sam put her arm around Daisy, not recognizing her anger. James approached and put his arm around Daisy's other shoulder, encasing her in a claustrophobic squeeze.

'Hey,' he said to both of them, then to Daisy, 'I haven't seen you all night.'

Sam untwisted herself from Daisy and tottered off, and Daisy made a mental note to murder her tomorrow.

'That's a lie: we were just talking in the kitchen.' She turned her shoulder away slightly, an indication for him to release her, but he either chose to ignore it or was too drunk to notice. She could smell the alcohol on his breath.

'You love this song,' he said, indicating the Joy Division song blasting from a nearby speaker, which everyone loved.

'Doesn't everyone?' She'd noticed that men did this: hung on to snippets of information and brought them out as evidence of some prior intimacy, a reminder to whomever was listening that they *knew* you.

James ignored this and switched to a serious tone. 'I want to be with you at midnight.'

She sipped from her straw, feeling comparatively sober. She couldn't help but be flattered by this statement, though she disliked herself for feeling so. 'Why?' she asked, staring ahead and refusing to soften for him.

'You know why, D.' His face was only inches from hers.

She closed her eyes for a moment, then opened them and looked at him. 'James, you've barely spoken to me since finding out about Jono — since I've been available.'

'I told you before: I thought you'd need some space?' He ran his other hand through his hair and kept hold of a chunk like he was battling some inner turmoil.

She looked away, irritated by his inability to admit to any wrongdoing, but he moved his head over, forcing her to meet his eyes.

'I want you to come home with me tonight,' he said, bringing his hand across to stroke the side of her cheek.

Daisy had spent so long hoping for this moment, and now that it was here, she felt only a sweeping sense of disappointment in herself and the inevitability of it all. She met his eyes before removing his hand from her face, then remembered Blake: he was standing across the room, staring at her. She rearranged her face into a casual smile and stepped back from James, forcibly removing his arm from her shoulders.

The next hour passed in a blur. Daisy got sandwiched in a booth with Imo and her old housemate, who unknowingly acted as cordons between James and herself. She needed a moment to think, and it was near impossible when he was in such close proximity, telling her he wanted her. Her mind felt blunt, lethargic with an evening's drinks, and Imo's voice washed over her like she was underwater.

Blake stood in the same position, laughing easily with a skinny guy she assumed was Ben. She felt caught out, knowing the moment with James must have appeared intimate to an onlooker; perhaps Blake thought they were together, or worse, perhaps he'd guessed the extent of her deceit. She thought back to their conversation on the walk there, how alive she'd felt when he took hold of her hands and how freely she'd been able to speak; it'd felt close to contentment.

She never felt this way with James. Her desperation for his affection and resultant disappointment in herself was wearing her down. It was holding her back. James was never going to be the partner that she wanted – someone she felt passionately for but that she could also rely on, someone whose presence and love felt easy, solid. Regardless of what Sam said, they weren't right for each other and never would be.

Daisy stood up and clambered out the booth, determined to make the right decision. James was dancing with Sam and Marvin close by. He spotted Daisy and manoeuvred himself her way, continuing to dance on the spot.

'Hey, can we talk a second?' She folded her arms and smiled primly, waiting. 'James?'

He contined dancing his ludicrous moves so she spoke up. 'I think we need to just call it, between us . . . agree that our time is up.'

Finally, he faded out his dancing, slowing his arms down over a few seconds like he'd been put into slow motion. She saw that she had his attention and wondered if this was the first time a girl had declined going home with him.

'I think we want different things,' she continued, 'and I don't think we're very nice to each other – in fact, I don't particularly like myself when I'm around you.'

He put his hands in his pockets and ran his eyes over her features. She noted, with annoyance, how beautiful he was. 'Okay,' he said.

'Really?'

'Yeah.' He tilted his head to one side and said, 'I still think you should come home with me tonight though.'

This still managed to make her laugh, but when her laughter died, she took hold of his wrist and squeezed it gently, then turned and walked away.

With a tiny seedling of victory sprouting shoots within her, Daisy headed to the bar, a lightness in her step. Another whisky sour in hand, she headed back to the other room, determined to find Blake. The space that he occupied was empty, so she bounded up to his friend, Ben, and was told that he'd gone outside to call someone. Daisy chatted happily to Ben for a while, her body fizzing with anticipation, but as twenty minutes passed and the midnight countdown began, it became clear that Blake had gone, that he had left without even saying goodbye.

Imo grabbed hold of Daisy's shoulder as midnight struck and hugged her with a fierceness that was bordering on violent. As the first chords of 'Auld Lang Syne' played out, Daisy swayed along with everyone and Blake's absence settled over her, creating a painful gulf in her chest. She was too late; she'd missed yet another opportunity for something good, something great, even. Marvin raised Sam up onto his shoulders and marched her around their circle as she revelled in the cheers and laughter. Daisy watched her lapping up the attention, oblivious to the events of Daisy's evening, and their last conversation repeated in her mind, gaining in spite. James stood nearby, clapping along, and Daisy had the overwhelming feeling that her life was heading in the wrong direction.

Jas opened the door to see Daisy's bike haphazardly slumped against the metal railings of the front steps, the lock slung lazily around the bike's bar. An unrelenting mid-January darkness had already settled across the city, even though the working day was yet to finish. Daisy was standing in her fluorescent yellow cycling jacket with rain dripping off her face, the hood a forgotten pool behind her.

Jas looked between the bike and Daisy and back again.

'My period's late,' Daisy stated, blinking at her friend in the doorway.

Jas opened her mouth to speak, then closed it again. The rain hammered down around them, drowning out the familiar groan of the distant traffic. 'How late?' she said eventually.

Daisy ran a hand through her drenched hair and said, 'I don't know.' It came out sour and disagreeable. 'A week, maybe more.'

'Are you normally regular?'

Daisy stared back, her eyes wild. She'd come to Jas for reassurance and now realized this was foolish; her friend's usual upbeat tone was gone, a new hardness in its place.

'Daisy, are you normally regular?'

'Yes; never this late.' The words came out sulkily, a forced confession.

Jas tipped her head to one side and offered a consolatory smile. 'Chick,' she said, almost under her breath, and the warmness returned. 'Come in – it's pouring.' She reached out and took Daisy by the arm, guiding her into the hallway. 'Ash won't be home for a few hours; let's go up and talk.'

Daisy sat on the tiled floor of the windowless bathroom, opposite Jas, who leant against the closed door. They stared at each other in silence as they waited the required two minutes.

'This brings back memories,' Jas said.

'*Very* different circumstances.'

Jas didn't disagree.

They fell into silence again until Jas looked down at her phone and said, 'It's time. Do you want me to look?'

'No,' Daisy said, determined. She pulled herself up to

standing and lifted the flimsy piece of blue and white plastic from the sink. The two blue lines stared back at her, cold and hard and certain. Her first thought was for her friend who had longed for this, longed for these simple, silly blue lines.

Ten days later, Daisy stood at the corner of Crystal Palace park, her mittened hands wrapped around a thermos flask of tea. She'd gone off coffee, the smell suddenly unbearable. She spotted Sam emerging from across the road, her bright lilac puffer jacket contrasting with the surrounding grey of winter. They waved simultaneously, then broke eye contact until Sam arrived.

'Hey,' Daisy said.

'Hey, how're you feeling?'

Daisy turned towards the entrance of the park, and Sam followed. 'Yeah, better. Thanks,' Daisy lied, swallowing the unrelenting nausea back. 'Tell me about the class.'

Sam had started going to an oil painting class on Saturday mornings. She'd always been good at art and had decided a class was the push she needed to make time for it. There was an unspoken understanding that it was also a necessary aid for her swirling mind, an antidote to the current stress of her life.

Sam chatted away next to Daisy, describing the people in the class, the teacher's surprisingly unimpressive and therefore unintimidating own attempts, and the way the three hours raced by with her mind the stillest it'd been in months.

'That's great. Well done you for finding it and getting yourself down there.' Daisy's stomach churned as she considered how her own news was, without doubt, going to undo any positive impact art therapy could have achieved.

They headed to the south of the park, planning to find the Victorian dinosaur statues that Daisy remembered visiting as a child, though she couldn't be less interested today. She gripped her flask tightly and considered whether it would be best to find a bench and sit down or to be on the move so that she wasn't looking directly at Sam as the words left her mouth.

'So, tell me what's happening with you and boys,' Sam said. 'I feel like I've barely seen you this week.'

Daisy had suggested moving to Imo's after that night at Jas's. She'd told Marvin and Sam that she'd outstayed her welcome, when in fact she simply couldn't bear to be around them with such a secret growing within her. But they'd insisted she stay.

'Nothing happening with Jono or James these days?'

It didn't escape Daisy's attention that Sam had omitted Blake. She'd asked Sam for his number on New Year's Day, and Sam had looked at her with such surprise; she clearly didn't remember their conversation from the night before, but Daisy still ran over the words in her head: *this is your problem; you don't know what you want.* The thought of her friend trying to pinpoint 'her problem' stung, possibly because there was some truth to her words. Why was she still failing at relationships, squatting in her friends' flats and staring out the window at work, wishing she was somewhere else? And now this, an unplanned pregnancy with a man she hadn't spoken to in weeks.

It turned out that Sam didn't have Blake's number, but she had reluctantly agreed to ask him for it, apparently finally convinced that things were over with James and Jono. But the following morning, Daisy thought better of it and begged Sam not to ask; he'd left the pub without even saying goodbye.

'Nope,' Daisy said glumly, 'nothing new with boys.'

'Well, James'll be in touch again soon – there's no doubt about it.'

Daisy exhaled sharply, the following ripple of laughter turning the reaction meaner than she'd planned. She tipped her head backwards, looking up to the sky briefly before asking in a level voice, 'Why do you still have such faith in him? He's *genuinely* not very nice to me.'

Sam stopped walking and folded her arms, running her eyes over Daisy's face as though she'd only just noticed her. 'Not nice, how? What's he said?'

Daisy sighed loudly, regretting opening up the conversation. Not only did she have no idea where to start in explaining the myriad micro-aggressions she and James had heaped upon each other over the last year, she'd also intended to avoid all topics of contention this morning – wading into an argument before following it up with her pregnancy news surely wasn't the best route to keeping their friendship afloat.

'No, Dais, tell me?' Sam's voice was patient, her expression concerned, protective even. But there was also a trace of exasperation in the weight of her vowels – a persistent reluctance to hear more complaints about a man who she'd decided, long ago, was worthy of Daisy.

Daisy swallowed, feeling that she'd overreacted. 'Nothing in particular, just the same old lack of contact, etc.'

'Okay, well, yeah: he needs to pull his finger out when it comes to messaging. I'm not, like, blind to his faults or anything. Oh, I nearly forgot . . .' Sam fished around in her black canvas tote bag, pulling out a pale-blue envelope. 'From June and Derek.'

Daisy stared down at the blue square. 'What for?'

'I told them how ill you'd been this week with the stomach bug, and June was worried. You know what she's like.'

'Oh.' Daisy clenched her jaw and took the card like it was a telegram delivering bad news. 'They shouldn't have.'

'They've gone down to Kent this weekend and obviously wanted to send you some get well love before they went.'

Daisy clumsily folded the card inside her coat pocket, the guilt of her lie practically dripping from her hand. 'They're so sweet.'

They headed down some stone steps, Sam reaching the bottom first and turning back to Daisy as she waited for her. The sky behind framed her with dramatic rolling clouds like a Turner painting. Daisy looked down at her feet as she descended the last steps, unable to meet Sam's gaze; how was it that her best friend couldn't see?

They walked on to the south of the park, reaching the ponds and staring sombrely at the disappointing dinosaurs, excited children whizzing past them on scooters. After circling the still water, they headed back the way they came, Daisy's heart rate climbing as she considered there wasn't much of the walk left.

Making a concerted effort to control her breathing, she said, 'Jas mentioned you didn't go to the IVF info day in her department last week?'

Sam brought her forefinger to her mouth and chewed on the corner of the nail. A smattering of black paint from the art class sat in the nail bed, the skin beneath angry and raw. 'When did she say that?'

'I don't know – whenever I last saw her.'

Sam raised her eyebrows and focused on a towering Indian

Chestnut tree ahead, and Daisy suspected a line of some sort had been crossed.

'I just don't want it to become my whole life.' There was a desperation to Sam's voice, the joy of the painting class forgotten already. 'I can do all the temperature checks and weeing on sticks and living the life of the bloody Amish, but not those big groups.'

A gust of wind hit them as they wandered back onto the expanse of the park, and Sam zipped her jacket up to her chin.

Daisy switched the thermos between her hands before asking, with tenderness, 'Why not?'

'Because!' Sam stopped walking and turned back to face the way they'd come, searching for something behind. 'It doesn't make me feel better talking about it!' She closed her eyes and pinched the bridge of her nose, squeezing the moment away. When she spoke again, her voice was small. 'Going to those counselling groups and information days feels like a really big step and . . . I don't think I'm ready to accept that that's my life; I don't want to be one of those women sharing pictures of my AMH results and hunting for a scrap of hope that this'll happen for us one day.' She folded her arms and kicked at a stone wedged in the earth. 'I think it's a self-preservation thing: like I need some distance from it all or I'll implode.'

Daisy wasn't sure what AMH was and didn't feel like this was the right moment to ask. She gripped the thermos tightly and opened her mouth to speak, unsure of what to say next.

But Sam spoke first. 'Everyone keeps saying "how exciting" about starting IVF, and I don't feel excited *at all*. One of Marvin's friends even congratulated me.'

Daisy's chest constricted. She swallowed and forced herself to speak. 'I think people are just hopeful that it'll give you a baby.'

'Well, they obviously don't know how rarely it works!' She folded her arms and looked at her shoes as she said, 'Thirty-two per cent chance if you're under thirty-five – almost a seventy per cent failure rate.' She shook her head as though dismissing the stats. 'Anyway, let's talk about something else, please. How's Jas?' She started walking again, at a faster pace.

'Jas?' Daisy stumbled on, unsure. 'Yeah, she's good, I think.'

'Actually, sorry.' Sam tucked her hair behind her ear. 'I'm not sure I can hear about her today.' She thrust her hands in her pockets and looked right at Daisy. 'I couldn't say that to anyone but you.'

Daisy nodded, her words grave and dutiful as she said, 'I get it.'

They walked on past the park coffee shop with its curved tiles mimicking dinosaur scales, both of them watching their own feet on the dusty path as they trudged uphill. Sam kept the conversation ticking on, sharing her anxiety about a baby shower she had to attend at work that week, and Daisy followed along, offering sympathetic sounds here and there.

A numbness spread through Daisy's limbs as she came to accept the reality of the situation: whether she shared the truth or held onto such a secret, her and Sam's friendship would be forever altered. When they reached the top of the hill and gazed down at the park, Daisy swallowed the urge to scream.

Imo picked Daisy up from the clinic. Both Jas and Imo had offered to go in with Daisy, but she'd refused. There was only one person in the world she wanted with her, and that person thought she was at a yoga class. She climbed in the passenger side of the dark-blue BMW and slammed the door harder than necessary, the paper pharmacy bag of pills demanding their attention with its loud crinkling in the silence of the car. She leant back in the seat and looked out the window at the bright-blue winter sky.

'All good?' Imo asked.

'Yeah.'

'So you've taken the first set of pills?'

'Yep.'

Imo shifted in her seat and took the keys out of the ignition, turning herself towards Daisy. 'When will it start?'

'The next few hours.' Daisy continued to look out at the sky, clutching the paper bag on her lap. She'd been told to expect heavy bleeding and cramps – the overused words which gave no real indication of where the experience would fall on the scale of mild to horrendous. Accounts online detailed anything from a standard period to trips to A&E with agonizing pain and clots the size of a plum.

'I've got some painkillers; it'll be fine.' She turned back to face Imo, who was looking at her with an unsettling level of concern.

'And, er—' Imo folded her arms and looked uncomfortable. 'Emotionally – you all good?'

'*Emotionally – you all good?*' Daisy stared back at her. 'Is that seriously how you're assessing my mental welfare?'

'You know what I mean. I'm just checking you're not going to get home and work out when the thing's birthday would have been before hanging yourself from the shower rail.'

'You don't have a shower rail,' Daisy said absently, no longer shocked by her cousin's dark humour.

Imo smiled at her, impressed with the comeback.

Daisy looked back out at the parked car in front and added, 'I'm fine. We're lucky to live in this country and have the option. I'm not going to be made to feel ashamed about it.'

''Course not,' Imo scoffed.

'If anything, I should be proud, proud to have done the sensible thing – the responsible thing.'

Imo raised her eyebrows in a way that suggested she didn't entirely agree with this turn of phrase.

'Just because I'm in my thirties and I'm middle class, doesn't mean I'd be able to raise a child well.'

'I'm not saying you would.'

'I'm not going to let it be this massive life-altering thing that happened to me.' Daisy noticed a scratch above the number plate of the car in front, a harsh straight line that looked to be purposefully carved into the paintwork. The thought of metal scraping on metal made her shudder, and the prickles of anxiety she'd felt in the waiting room earlier returned to her stomach in spikes.

Imo's tone was disconcertingly kind as she said, 'Daisy, you didn't want a child, particularly not one with James, and particularly not now.'

Daisy stared down at the bag in her hands. 'I'm not regretting it or anything; the only bit I feel weird about is . . . kind of, *morally*. Like . . .' She closed her eyes as she said this: 'what if we do have souls that early and . . .'

'Er, I'm sorry?' Imo leant backwards to get a good view of the entrance to the clinic. 'Did some pro-lifers get to you in the waiting area? *Souls?*' She frowned at Daisy like she was a child who'd just sworn. 'Are you high? What painkillers are you on? You're six weeks; we're talking about a clump of cells; I've had bigger blood clots.'

'Gross.'

'Look, you've taken the morning after pill before, haven't you?'

Daisy looked at Imo, knowing that she didn't have to respond as she knew the answer.

'This isn't that different. It's like the morning morning morning after pill.'

'Wouldn't it be the morning after after after pill?'

'Whatever.' Imo picked up the car keys and reached for her seatbelt. 'Just don't be torturing yourself because you feel terrible that this happened to you and not to Sam.'

'But why *did* it?' Daisy's voice broke unexpectedly, and Imo let go of the seatbelt, leaving it to clang loudly against the door. 'What is actually wrong with the universe? Why *couldn't* it have just happened for her and not me?'

Imo joined her in staring at the car in front. 'I don't know,' she said with defeat. 'There'll be women all over with unwanted pregnancies and just as many praying each day to be pregnant. It's a massive fucking menace of womanhood.'

Daisy stared ahead like she was frozen to the spot; silence filled the car like a scream.

'I really want apple crumble,' Daisy mumbled with the least energy possible to form words. 'Like, more than I've ever wanted apple crumble before.' It reminded her of Ida's baking, of the comfort of childhood.

'Okay,' Imo said, like this was a completely normal request during a termination. 'With custard?'

'With custard.'

They sat in silence for a moment, then Imo said, 'Are you sure you don't want to tell her?'

Daisy broke from her trance and turned to Imo, her voice stern, 'How? *How* do I tell her this? I don't mean it figuratively – literally, what words do I use?'

Imo looked back at her with a resigned expression that made Daisy feel worse.

'She'd never forgive me.' She shook her head. 'She'd try to, but it would always be there.'

summer iii

Sam

This was a mistake, Sam decided, eyeing the circle of women around her with wary interest. She cast her gaze down to the pamphlet in her lap with its calming blues and picture of a couple holding hands. A woman sitting to her right was talking about her despair at not falling pregnant after a year of trying. Sam imagined balling the pamphlet up and throwing it at the woman. A year was nothing. Instead, she stared at the floor and jiggled her leg in her seat, willing the seconds away.

'Samantha, did you have anything you wanted to share with the group?' The nurse turned towards her, along with several faces from the small circle of chairs.

'Oh, Sam is fine.'

'Okay. Sorry, love, I was going off your sticker.' She indicated the white paper label on Sam's T-shirt, on which Sam had scrawled her name at the beginning of the session.

Sam brought her hand to the label self-consciously. 'Yeah, sorry, I'm not sure why I wrote that.' There was some comforting laughter from the women around her. 'Nerves, I think.'

'Don't be nervous, Sam. We're all here to listen and support each other. So tell us a little bit about your journey or just why you've come today.'

Sam did not want to get into her 'journey', not here with

all these strangers. Why had she come? 'Erm, well, I started IVF last week – I'm still on the downgrading process . . .' she added apologetically, knowing that this part was by no means the hardest.

People in the group nodded, accustomed to these new terms that felt foreign on Sam's lips.

Aware of a threatening lump in her throat, she dug her thumbnail into the palm of her hand, then continued in a small voice, 'But even before I started, I was feeling pretty low and kind of a burden on the people around me.'

The nurse looked at her, brow furrowed with concern, and Sam could not bear to look at the kindness ebbing from her. Several of the women offered tight-lipped smiles.

'Actually' – Sam cleared her throat, her voice regaining its volume – 'do you mind if I read something?' She bent down to rifle through her bag, pleased to have a distraction from the suffocating examination. Noticing her neon socks and vintage Reeboks, contrasting starkly with the drab black loafers of the woman to her left, she made a mental note to stop dressing like a teenager when attending the clinic.

'I'm not very good at this kind of thing.' She located her notebook and sat back up, addressing the room with a little more confidence. 'But I read something the other day about infertility that described it better than I ever could.'

'Of course, that's a lovely idea, Sam.'

The nurses here always overused names. She opened her notebook to the relevant page.

'Oh, you copied it down?' the nurse asked with surprise, as though she'd suspected illiteracy.

'Yeah, it was online, and I just thought . . . it felt quite nice to write the words out and go back to them sometimes.' She sighed. 'You know, to remember that other people are feeling similar.' She paused and cleared her throat, looking down at the familiar words.

'Infertility is like a shadow of grief, shimmering in the background of every aspect of your life. It rarely knocks you down completely, but it is there. Gnawing the edges of experiences that were formerly joyful and all-encompassing, a blanket of numbness, gradually smothering. And who can understand such an experience other than those forced to enter its dark vicinity.'

She folded the notebook up and stared down at the floor.

'So true,' said a woman opposite her, her yellow polka-dot dress at odds with the mood in the room. Others around the circle made sounds of agreement.

The nurse looked around at the women, taking in their reactions. 'Thank you, Sam. Those are very powerful words, which obviously resonate with a lot of people in the group here. Is there a particular part that jumped out at you? Ooh, I sound like an English teacher now, don't I?'

There was an overly generous amount of laughter.

Sam paused to consider. 'Just, all of it really.' Then, feeling this wasn't an acceptable answer, she added, 'Lately, the part about other people not being able to understand unless they've been through it.'

'Right,' the nurse said. 'And many people say that, actually. It's one of the main reasons we hold these groups. Are you able to talk about your feelings with your partner?'

Sam thought back to her and Marvin's conversation the previous night, and her mouth clamped shut. She shrugged her shoulders and, after a moment, said, 'Yeah, most of the time.'

The girl next to her asked in a strong Italian accent, 'What about your friends? Do you have some that you talk to, that understand?'

'My friends?' she asked, momentarily stunned by another person questioning her.

Sam looked down and fiddled with the strap of her watch, remembering the three of them presenting it for her birthday, years ago. 'My friends are great,' she said, fastening and unfastening the watch strap. 'But, I guess we're all in different places at the moment, so it's difficult for them to really get it.' She tightened the strap so that it pinched the soft flesh of her wrist, then looked at the floor and added, 'Impossible, actually.'

Daisy

Sitting on the sand next to her friends, Daisy stared out at the ocean. Airlie beach was as beautiful as promised: white sands lined with palm trees like a scene pulled directly from a magazine. Quieter at this time of year too. She listened to the gentle lap of the waves on the shore and thought about the sea back in Whitby. The smell was different here, as though the air had been cleansed of brine and seaweed, only fragments left, and she found she missed the salty stench of the North Sea. If she closed her eyes, they sounded the same, though this made her feel dizzy, so she opened them again.

Following the termination, Daisy had handed in her notice at work and booked a three-month trip around Australia. It had wiped out her meagre savings, eradicating any hope of buying a flat in the next decade, but she needed a change; she needed to get away – from the temptation of James and from her friends whose lives were all moving in the opposite direction to hers.

Living at Sam and Marvin's had been difficult, and she'd taken to spending more time at Imo's and Jas's places, avoiding evenings in alone with Sam. Four months on and she wholeheartedly regretted not telling her about the pregnancy at the time. It was too big a secret to hold on to, and now it was too late. Not only would Sam hate her for what had happened, she'd hate her for keeping the truth from her.

The distance from Sam had allowed Daisy to fully process her feelings about the termination. She knew she had the capacity to view it as an almost medically mundane event, a necessary procedure that didn't have to be wrapped up in heavy emotion and become part of her identity. But then she thought about how unfair it was that she'd fallen pregnant with such ease, how she hadn't really even considered keeping it, and how she hadn't had the courage to even tell Sam about it. She was constantly wading through this sea of guilt as Sam was a constant in her mind, and it was difficult not to resent this. Sam didn't even seem to notice the change in Daisy, her quietness, her absence. She was so caught up in her own struggle, she was entirely blind to Daisy's.

Daisy hadn't told James. Imo was adamant that she should have, and perhaps she was right. But he hadn't been in contact since New Year's, and Daisy had no desire to get in touch; she couldn't trust herself around him, and she couldn't be sure that he wouldn't tell Marvin. She still thought about Blake. Apparently, he'd left the school – moving back home to Leicester so suddenly that Sam hadn't had chance to say goodbye. Daisy had searched all social media platforms, but he was nowhere to be found.

★

Their group was in the Whitsundays for two weeks before heading up to Cairns. Daisy had found it surprisingly easy to settle into the trip and make friends. The majority of people on the tour were in their twenties, making Daisy one of the oldest, but it had taken only a few nights out to bond with them all, their feelings chemically enhanced by the romance of MDMA. Daisy had been particularly drawn to a German girl called Victoria. She was confident and unapologetic, similar to Imo in many ways. The five-year age gap was noticeable to Daisy only in a positive way. Victoria worked freelance in the film industry and lived in a house-share in Berlin. She talked about going out most nights to gigs, bars, and film screenings, making Daisy realize how boring they'd all become back home. It was refreshing to be around people who still partied until the early hours each weekend, for whom friendships were still the centre of their worlds and, most importantly, who were so far from even considering having children.

The sun was appearing on the horizon, bathing the bay in a rose tint. A faint wind blew, and Daisy nudged Dean, sitting next to her. In a croaky voice, she sang the first few lines of a Fleetwood Mac song. Perhaps she was still high.

Dean swayed his head along obligingly but didn't offer up the next line. 'Is that the Beatles?'

She looked at him, disappointed but expressionless, then gazed back out at the sea. 'Fleetwood.'

After a moment, in the manner of someone who's been taking drugs for six hours, Dean said, 'At sunrise, everything is luminous but not clear.'

After suppressing her laughter, Daisy stared out at the waves and ran the words through her brain. They seemed very appropriate. Since her arrival two months ago, her life seemed to have taken on a fluorescence that it had lacked in London. She was having adventures again, making memories – but she knew this way of life couldn't last forever. When she thought of back home, she still couldn't see where she fit in or what she wanted to do career-wise, and when she thought of Sam, her heart ached with the weight of the secret.

'Dean, did you just pull that out the bag?' She ran her eyes over Dean's features, wondering fleetingly if she should sleep with him. She was definitely still high.

He grinned and revealed his phone in his hand. 'Sorry to disappoint; I googled sunrise quotes.'

Daisy remembered that he was twenty-five.

Victoria was lying next to Daisy, sleeping quietly on the sand. Her black button-down dress had ridden up, revealing more of the large tattoo on her thigh: a landscape of mountains and trees, tastefully done with a fine needle. Victoria's tattoos made Daisy's one star on her wrist seem even more lame than usual; she and Imo had got matching ones on a family holiday in Portugal when they were seventeen.

Dean leant onto his left hip, stretching his right leg out in from of him so that he could reach the pocket in his shorts. He took out the wrap and dabbed at the golden crystals, rubbing them into his gums. Seeing that Daisy was watching him, he offered it to her.

She frowned. 'It's nearly 6 a.m. – the night is over.' Her voice felt scratchy and her jaw tight.

'Never,' he said.

She shook her head and looked down at her bare feet,

wiggling her toes into the sand. When they were younger, Sam was always chasing the night. It was usually around eight drinks in that she'd clutch Daisy's arm, look fiercely into her eyes, and say, 'Let's make it a night we'll talk about for the rest of our lives.' Daisy suspected one of the reasons she'd been drawn to Sam was some innate need to live up to her parents' expectations of a youth full of stories. She couldn't remember the last time she and Sam had had a big night together. She needed to call her.

'Right, let's go swimming,' Dean said, leaning behind Daisy and slapping Victoria's arm to wake her up. 'Tori, swim time.' He stood up, waiting for her to come around.

Victoria blinked several times, then sat up. Daisy passed her the two-litre water bottle she'd been sipping from for the last two hours, her own thirst unquenchable. Victoria glugged from the bottle, then obediently stood up.

'Right, let's do this,' she said.

'Are you fucking joking?' Daisy said, 'I need to go to bed, not swimming.'

'Daisy, this is exactly what you need. It'll get rid of your hangover.'

The problem with partying with people much younger was that their hangovers only required a swim in the sea and some fast food, whereas Daisy took two days of nausea and crippling anxiety to feel human again. She watched them both strip off to their underwear and run into the waves, shouting as the water hit them. Victoria turned to face Daisy, waving as she flopped backwards like a giant starfish bobbing on the waves. A laugh escaped Daisy's mouth, and then she was standing, muttering obscenities, and running across the sand to join them.

Sam

'Okay, ready?' Marvin asked.

'Wait, let me take a photo.' Sam reached for her phone.

'A *photo*?'

'It's the trigger shot. It's a big deal,' she said. 'This could be my last injection. And even if it's not, it's still exciting. It's like the magic wand that releases the eggs.'

'Or like when they pull the lever down for the National Lottery to release the balls?'

'Yes! Perfect metaphor, because those balls make a few lucky people very happy.'

They smiled, and she snapped a photo of them pretending to inject. They checked the picture together. Marvin's face was comic-book-mean – a bad man with his weapon – and Sam's was exaggerated excitement.

'Oh, good! We both went for understated realism,' Marvin said. 'It's 9.03 p.m. now, so we're late.' The clinic had been very clear that the trigger shot needed to be taken at 9 p.m. sharp for the eggs to be ready for collection in theatre at 9 a.m., thirty-six hours later.

'Yep. Don't fuck it up.' Sam removed the ice pack from her stomach to allow Marvin access.

'Here, we go,' he said, as he pinched her flesh and steadily inserted the needle.

Two days later, Sam woke up in theatre to people in scrubs moving around her bed. A woman she didn't recognize said, 'Okay, you're coming around now. All went well.' She fiddled with the bed and lowered it.

'How many eggs did I get?' Sam croaked.

The woman stepped closer to the bed and said with kindness, 'The embryologist will tell you when you head back downstairs.'

Marvin was waiting for her where she left him on the ward. He looked anxious. 'All okay?'

'Yeah.' She smiled. 'How was your part?'

'Fine,' he said with a begrudging smile. 'Been practising for this moment since I was thirteen. I will say that they need to update their magazines though – we're talking Nineties ladette vibes.'

Sam chuckled and took hold of the inside of his wrist. 'Well, didn't you always love *The Big Breakfast*?'

They were called into the embryologist's office and sat down opposite her desk like two children sent to the headteacher's office for a scolding. The dated teak armchairs could almost pass as stylish mid-century designs were it not for the cheap blue plastic cushioning of the seats. Sam felt the chair sag with disappointment beneath her, sinking lower than she'd expected. Making brief eye contact with Marvin, who'd obviously noticed the same thing, she felt the threat of inappropriate laughter and purposefully looked away. The room was a pale green colour – perfect for making the complexions of the sick appear gravely so – right down to the doors, blinds, and speckled lino flooring. The smell was clinical but inoffensively so, a comforting suggestion of sterility.

They made polite introductions and were promptly told that eighteen eggs had been collected. Sam and Marvin immediately turned to each other, delight flooding each of their faces, and he grabbed her hand to squeeze.

'It is a high number, but we need to see how many fertilize. This should happen today and overnight, so I will call you tomorrow to see how many have. In rare cases, no eggs fertilize, in which case I'm afraid there's nothing we can do for this round.' The embryologist folded her arms, her expression stern.

'Wow. That would be pretty disappointing,' Marvin said, the delight swiftly leaving his face.

She ignored him and continued, 'After tomorrow, I'll call you each day to give you an update. If we do have some viable embryos, we'll be aiming to transfer one on day five. Are you clear on the medication timetable?'

'Yes. Mostly. But when do I need to start the progesterone pessaries – and *where* exactly am I putting them?' Sam asked, unable to meet the woman's eyes as she imagined inserting the tampon-shaped pillars of hormones, their consistency like a bar of soap.

'They've put one in during surgery, so you'll do another one tonight, then each morning and evening. It needs to be in the *back passage* until transfer, then after that you can insert vaginally if you prefer.'

Sam nodded, then kept nodding – a verbal response to such an instruction entirely beyond her.

Walking though the car park to find their Uber, Sam stopped a moment. Closing her eyes and lifting her face towards the sun, she let the relief wash over her. *Eighteen eggs*. When she opened her eyes and caught up with Marvin, she noticed confusion in his face.

'Did she mean that they put something up your arsehole in surgery?'

Daisy

Daisy's phone lit up on the table of the dimly lit bar. She saw it was a photo of Jas in scrubs, pointing to a pineapple pin badge on her chest and kissing her fingertips. Another message immediately came through, a selfie of Imo wearing her pineapple pin on her work blazer, her arm pulled back into an overarm to propel the kiss.

'Shit!' Daisy said, dropping her phone on the table and rifling through her bag for her unopened badge. Jas had spent a month organizing this; she'd always been good at sending cards and arranging gifts, but recently she seemed to be taking things to a whole extra level for Sam. It was clearly her way of dealing with the guilt of her own blossoming pregnancy and for being implicated in the deceit of the termination; she was still angry at Daisy for keeping it from Sam.

The pins were apparently to support women undergoing fertility treatment, a sign of sisterly solidarity, with the pineapple being some kind of appointed symbol. Weeks ago, Jas had paid for the postage of a badge to the hostel Daisy was heading to, for this very moment. She hurriedly unwrapped the cellophane and fastened the badge onto her T-shirt, then got Victoria to take some photos of her casting her right hand forward to finish a throwing action. Daisy quickly selected the best one with the badge clearly visible, then posted it to the group.

Sam: CAUGHT IT ♥
AH GUYS you got the pins! You're too cuuuuuute. Welling up over here with the hormonal overload.

Jas: ♥
How'd it go babe?

Sam: WE GOT 18 EGGS BITCHEZ!

Daisy started typing, glad to be receiving the information at the same time as Jas and Imo. The nine-hour time difference had taught her that most interesting things in life occurred in the afternoon and evening. By the time Daisy read the girls' updates the following morning, the conversation had usually moved on considerably.

Jas: 18!!!!!!!!!!!!!!! OMG!!!!! Amazing Sammy!

Daisy: TERRIFIC news! Well done kid.
Was it okay?

Imo: Daisy isn't that the age of your current fling?

Daisy: Dad joke.

Imo: Fair. @Sam I don't know what a good number is but the general vibe is celebratory so I'm guessing 18 is bloody good going. Congrats babe. 8 hours til wine time.

Jas: 18 is INCREDZ high. Remember we usually make one a month!

Sam: Thanks guys. Was ok. Just glad it's over and hope they fertilize ✌

Brad, their Aussie guide for the trip, returned to the table.

'Who you messaging, London?'

He'd adopted this rather unoriginal nickname for her. He was twenty-eight and seemed to believe that driving the minibus of them around the country was the greatest job on earth. Everyone on the trip seemed to love him, and Daisy felt old and dreary in her dislike of him.

'Just my friend Sam, from back home.'

'Oh, how did the egg freezing thing go?' Victoria asked.

'She's not freezing them, but yeah, good I think.'

'Shouldn't you be thinking about freezing yours?' Brad said.

Victoria smacked him with her nearest hand.

'Hey!' He laughed. 'I'm not being a dick. I thought that's what independent women were doing these days if they weren't hitched by thirty?'

'*Thirty?*' Victoria repeated.

'Well, mid-thirties then – London's age.'

Victoria rolled her eyes in Daisy's defence. Dean joined from the bar and sat next to Victoria, sipping from his pint glass as he lowered himself onto the seat.

'They do if they're loaded and really want children,' Daisy said, her tone casual.

'And you don't?' Brad asked.

'I don't know. Certainly not now and, yeah, possibly never.' She said this like the thought had just occurred to her.

'Hear, hear!' Victoria said, raising her glass. 'Kids are bloody boring. I don't get why the world is so obsessed with them.'

'You don't want kids?' Dean asked, catching up on the conversation.

Daisy shrugged. 'Maybe not.' She picked up her beer and

sipped from it, hoping the conversation moved on soon; she no longer enjoyed this topic of debate.

Dean said, 'That's really brave.'

Daisy and Victoria made eye contact before laughing.

'Dean! Why the fuck is that brave?' Victoria said. 'It's her decision, and it's not exactly radical anymore.'

'Well, it's not entirely her decision,' Brad said. 'If you were with a guy who wanted kids, you'd totally go there.'

Daisy frowned. 'So you think every woman wants children and I'm just saying I might not because I'm single and in my thirties, so don't currently have the option?'

Brad tilted his head to one side. 'Your words, not mine.'

Daisy glared back at him and considered throwing the revelation of her termination at him, but she knew it proved nothing – she didn't want a baby then, with James, or without him more likely, but it didn't make her certain that she wouldn't ever want one. 'Fuck you, Brad,' she spat, 'you don't know shit about women. And Dean, it's not *brave*, and the fact you think that just shows how immature you are.'

The boys made eye contact with each other, then both reached to pick up their beers at the same time.

Victoria surveyed them all and said, 'Okay, let's change the subject, guys. Tonight's going to be fun!' She stood up and smoothed out her black pleather skirt. It looked cheap, and Daisy wondered which shitty store she'd bought it from. 'I'm getting us shots. Daisy, come to the bar with me?'

'I'm going for a smoke,' Daisy said, rising from the table and heading outside.

Sam

Imo arrived at 7 p.m., bearing a bottle of red wine and a large white cardboard box. The clinic had advised that having a glass of wine was perfectly fine now that the eggs were out, and Sam had a few days to wait before transferring an embryo back in. Sam opened the box to reveal a huge birthday cake in the shape of the number eighteen with professional white icing and small golden eggs placed delicately on top.

'Oh my god!' Sam said through laughter. 'Imo! How . . .' She sat down at the kitchen table and laughed even harder. 'This is utterly ridiculous.'

'I think you mean perfect? I was in Waitrose getting the wine, and there it was, waving at me from the bakery section. I reckon someone had ordered and not collected it.'

'Did you say it was for a party?'

'No, I told the truth. And d'you know what the baker lady said?'

'She probably had no idea what you were on about.'

'No, she actually stopped in her tracks, said "My sister went through all that; her son's just turning three", disappeared with it for five minutes to put these eighteen golden eggs on it, then said, "Good luck to her; I'll have my fingers crossed". You know, like she really meant it.'

'Aww.' Sam stared down at the cake with a new level of awe, examining the golden eggs, individually placed with kindness, and for the hundredth time that week, felt like she might cry.

She ran through the day for Imo, not leaving any details out and making her laugh about the post-surgical sanitary towel the size of a nappy and Marvin's 'arsehole' comment. She'd noticed a creeping nausea throughout the day, presumably an aftereffect of the anaesthetic, and couldn't bring herself to have any cake or wine.

'No!' Imo said, hearing this. 'And you've only got five days of fun before the thing goes back in?'

'Yeah, I'm not sure about "fun". I was only going to have a glass tonight. I'm sure we can freeze some of it like people do with wedding cakes.'

'Oh right. Is it your first anniversary when you're meant to have it?'

'Nope,' Sam said with raised eyebrows, 'it's the christening of your first child. Imagine how awful it was for really traditional housewives who couldn't conceive back in the day. Every time they opened the freezer, there it'd be as a big fat reminder.'

Imo looked at Sam. 'Right, we are not freezing that cake. Marvin can eat it all, or you can bring it into work and tell them it was your cousin's eighteenth or something.'

Imo changed out of her fitted work dress into expensive-looking loungewear, the bottom of her trousers tucked into cashmere socks. She browsed Netflix, skimming over the choices at lighting speed as she asked, 'How's Daisy getting on?'

'Yeah, good, I think,' Sam replied, settling herself at the other end of the sofa.

Imo stared at her, awaiting more information.

'I haven't heard the latest – only what's been on our Us4 chat.'

'Really?' Imo frowned, surprised by this admission.

A sink hole seemed to have opened up between Sam and Daisy over the last six months, and Sam simply did not have the energy to rectify it at the moment: every ounce of herself was going on this quest for a child. She told herself every day that she would call her that night, but then the evening rolled around after another trying day, and she didn't have it in her to listen to Daisy's shining adventures on the other side of the world.

'Yeah.' Sam tried to keep her tone light; it was too painful to discuss, and she needed to remain upbeat today of all days: successful embryo transfers were actually linked with the mother laughing on the day. 'I think she's having an amazing time out there; I have nothing but boring stuff to report when I speak to her.'

Imo considered Sam, her hand still pointing the remote at the TV. 'I know what you mean, but I think she'd always want to hear from you.'

'Yeah, you're right. I'll call her tomorrow,' Sam lied, fiddling with a tassel on the corner of the cream throw on her lap. The thought of Daisy and herself drifting apart entirely was both obscene and, for the first time, faintly possible. She looked at Imo squarely and, with more honesty, added, 'It's hard because we've always been roughly on the same page, and suddenly she's partying 'til dawn and I'm living the life of some kind of sick, depressed . . . nun.'

Imo didn't follow.

'In and out of hospital, not drinking . . .'

'Right! I get it. Not sure how a nun'd feel about the anal skulduggery.'

Sam smiled. 'Why does everyone fixate on the arse situation? They've also rummaged inside me and extracted certain parts – surely that's worse?'

'Yes, but that's the whole point. That's what you've signed up for. The arsehole pessary just seems a bit . . . sneaky.'

'I had to sign a form allowing them to do it beforehand.'

'Oh, Jesus. There really is a form for everything these days.'

Sam leant forward to reach her water glass and gasped, clutching her stomach.

'Shit, babe, are you okay?'

Breathing heavily, Sam said tentatively, 'Yeah . . .' She placed her hands onto her abdomen, feeling the unfamiliar roundness. 'I think I might have some hyperstimulation; I feel really sick.' She noticed Imo's confused face and added, 'It's this side effect that can happen where your ovaries go a bit insane.'

'What's it called, the side effect?' Imo said, unlocking her phone.

'Ovarian hyperstimulation syndrome or OHSS. Don't google it; it'll scare us.'

Imo clearly ignored her and started reading aloud. 'Affects five per cent of women who have IVF; ovaries go into overdrive and swell, sometimes to the size of grapefruits.' She looked up and added more quietly, 'Can result in breathing difficulties and . . .'

'. . . even death in rare cases,' Sam finished for her. 'Yes, I'm well aware of that.' She stood up and walked slowly across the room, keeping her hands on her stomach. 'I don't like grapefruits.'

Imo looked back at her, bewildered.

'What I mean is, I don't eat them. I don't know how big they are – are they like a melon?'

'A melon? Are you fucking joking? Imagine suddenly having two melons in your abdomen – that would certainly result in death. They're like big oranges.'

'Okay, you're not making me feel better. And how big are they meant to be usually? Ovaries, not grapefruits.'

'Erm . . .' Imo typed on her phone again. 'About 2 to 3 cm, like a walnut. Why is everything to do with women's bodies compared to food?'

Sam smiled weakly, very much aware that the same was done for growing foetuses. 'I think a bit of swelling is common. Let's just watch a film and hope it passes.'

Imo eyed Sam warily as she winced when she leant back on the sofa. 'Are you sure? We could call Jas?'

'No, honestly, it's fine. Just find a film.'

Daisy

Daisy woke to a searing pain in her right arm. She groaned and sat up, realizing that she was on top of her bed covers and that Victoria's bed was empty. Her head was pounding and her mouth dry, but the pain in her arm was like a burning white light, eclipsing all other problems. She examined the arm and saw that her forearm was swollen, a green bruise dappling the skin like mould. She tried to turn it over to examine the underside but cried out with pain. Tears sprung to her eyes, and she let herself cry, but the shuddering sobs sent renewed jolts of pain through her arm. She slowed her breathing and eased her legs off the side of the bed, realizing she was still in her jeans and T-shirt from last night.

She stood up, placing her swollen arm gently on her chest as though in an invisible sling, and looked around for her phone. Her left hand shook as she pulled the covers back, revealing the newly smashed screen of her phone. She grabbed it, a whimper escaping her mouth followed by a more confident 'Fuck', when she saw that it only had seven per cent battery. She took the charging cable from her bedside table and tried to line it up with the phone, using her left hand only. When her fourth attempt slipped out, she dropped her head backwards to look up at the ceiling and let out something between a scream and a growl. Positioning the phone between her knees, she eventually managed to get the cable in. She tried calling Victoria, but there was no answer.

As she waited for the phone to charge, she dug out a packet of paracetamol from the mess on the bedside table and knocked back four with some stale water. She gripped the edge of the bedside table and swallowed several times as her stomach lurched and threatened to throw the pills back up. Relieved to find the shared bathroom empty, she pulled down her jeans to examine a large bruise and scab on her right knee, then squeezed toothpaste directly into her mouth and gargled water with it.

Staring at her reflection, she attempted to piece together the night in her mind. They'd stayed at the Anchor for hours, doing too many shots, then had gone on to somewhere else – a club presumably. There were snippets of a lit-up dance floor . . . and the stars. They must have been on the beach; she remembered looking at the black starry sky with Victoria and being upset about something. After that, it was a blank.

Sam

'Right, I'm calling Marv,' Imo said as Sam returned from the toilet, tears welling.

Marvin sprinted back from the pub and attempted to comfort Sam as she slowly paced up and down the kitchen. Imo made several panicked phone calls. Jas didn't pick up, and a nurse from the gynaecology department advised that the on-call doctor would phone them back. They helped Sam into bed, hoping to make her more comfortable. She let out a low-pitched groan as they lowered her onto the mattress and the pain intensified.

Imo came over to the bed, helpless hands raised level with her chest, with nowhere for them to go. They settled around her own face, squashing her cheeks towards her nose as her dark hair fell forward. 'Is it getting worse?' The words came out strangely through her squashed features.

Sam took in Imo's ridiculous gurning face and said, 'My organs feel like your face.'

Imo realized what she was doing and dropped her hands to her sides. 'Seriously though, I'm fucking worried about you.' She fired off more messages to Jas, berating the on-call doctor for not calling sooner.

'Give the woman a chance; you only called ten minutes ago,' said Marvin. 'She'll be doing ward rounds, not sat with her feet up eating a KitKat. Jas, on the other hand, is dead to me.' He pulled his phone out of his pocket and left the room.

Imo sighed and sat on the edge of the bed by Sam's feet. 'Sam, I'm so sorry this is happening to you. You've had such a shitshow already – you couldn't be less deserving of this right now.'

Sam looked over to her and said quietly, 'Don't be so nice to me; it's weird and making me cry.'

'Okay, noted.' They sat in silence for a moment, then Imo took hold of Sam's leg through the duvet. 'We should message your mum, let her know you're not well. And Daisy.'

Sam imagined Daisy right now, probably still sleeping off a big night out or waking up next to a stranger, and felt a hot anger for the ignorant ease of her friend's comparative life. 'I don't want to worry them when it could be nothing.'

Marvin returned with Jas on loudspeaker.

'Hey Sammy, Marv's filled me in. I'm so, so sorry to hear that you're going through this.' Her voice was desperate, possibly even teary. 'It definitely sounds like OHSS – do you want me to come over? I can be there in twenty—'

'Jas, no, you're about twelve months pregnant – you're no use to us!' said Imo.

'But should we be going back to the hospital?' Marvin asked.

'If it gets really painful, then yes, go. You'll be on a bed on the ward, and they'll give you codeine and, if it's really severe, drain some of the fluid from around the ovaries. But if it's bearable to wait it out at home, then you might be more comfortable there with the guys looking after you.'

They ended the call, and Sam insisted on staying put. The thought of getting out of the flat and the bumpy fifteen-minute ride to the hospital wasn't something she could bear thinking about. Imo decided to stay the night in the spare room in case they needed to get Sam to the hospital in the early hours, so Marvin helped her make up the single bed. When he returned, he wrapped his body around Sam and read quietly to her from a trashy magazine, something she always asked him to do when she was unwell. Sam closed her eyes, letting the words fall over her and willing the minutes away.

Daisy

'Broken in two places,' the doctor said as he pointed to the small dark fissures on Daisy's X-ray. 'This one here on the radius and then a hairline fracture of the ulna. No surgery needed, but you will have a cast on for six weeks.' His face seemed wary of her reaction to this and, absurdly, she found herself wanting to comfort him. 'Must have been some fall?' He raised one eyebrow at her, and she wondered if this was his way of inviting women to divulge details of domestic abuse.

She turned back to the X-ray screen, feeling strangely comforted by the images. 'Can I keep them?'

He laughed, presuming she was joking, then promptly turned away, leaving her with a young Filipino nurse with bleached blond hair. He took a large laminated colour chart out and asked her to choose which she'd like for the cast. Daisy ran her weary eyes over the array and felt completely unable to make this decision. She imagined this part must be fun for children, their parent helpfully pointing towards their favourite colour – or a friend or partner daring her to go for the neon range. The seconds ticked by as Daisy stared at the sheet and the distinct feeling of loneliness took hold of her.

'I can see you in the green?' the nurse offered, indicating a square the colour of grass.

Daisy looked up at him and blinked, releasing a tear which plopped steadily down her cheek. Her voice came out in a hoarse whisper, 'Yeah, whatever. Thanks.'

He smiled at her with pity and whisked the chart away, before leaving the room to find her emerald swathe. Having the cast made was so painful that she vomited into a cardboard kidney dish, and the vile yellow liquid sat on the side as the nurse finished up. The cast extended above her elbow – keeping her arm locked at a right angle for three weeks until a shorter removable one could be fitted. The claustrophobic thought of not being able to straighten her arm made her want to throw up again.

She was given numerous medical forms to fill out, a task which seemed impossible with her left hand. She tried calling Victoria and Dean, but neither of them picked up, and she didn't feel close enough to anyone else to ask for their help in such mortifying circumstances. Taking several more painkillers, she headed to the hospital canteen, ordered a coffee and some plain toast, and started the painstaking task of filling the forms out left-handed. Her writing was so bad that it would have been quite funny were she not alone to witness it.

She took out her phone to take a picture of a particularly curly word to send to Sam, imagining it would be a left-field way to break the news, but stopped when she saw several messages from Victoria, just legible under the cracked glass.

Victoria: 5 missed calls? You miss me that much?! How's your knee? That fall was pretty epic.

Daisy reread the message. She'd assumed there hadn't been any witnesses to her injury, least of all her closest friend there. She tried calling Victoria, but the call was declined.

> **Victoria:** Sorry – can we message instead – not great timing . . .
> Currently in Brad's bed and he's still asleep . . .

Daisy didn't have the patience to comment on this revelation.

> **Daisy:** I broke my arm in two places. At the hospital now.

She expected the news to trigger Victoria to get the fuck out of bed and call her, but after a few seconds, she saw that she was typing.

> **Victoria:** Holy shit!
> You get a cast?!
> You were pretty fucked!

Her overuse of exclamation marks irked Daisy even more, and she flexed her neck, trying to remain calm.

> **Daisy:** Weren't we all? I can't remember falling, what happened?

Typing took significantly longer than usual, and she felt a rising irritation at her slow left thumb and slower supposed friend.

> **Victoria:** It was down the concrete steps to the beach?

We were down there for ages – you were going mental about the stars!
Then when we left, you fell?
You didn't seem that bad! Can't believe you broke it.
Fuckkk!!
OMG need to tell you about Brad.

Daisy locked her phone as the memory flooded her brain. They'd been on the beach looking up at the sky, and she'd started throwing kisses towards the stars to reach the girls. It had seemed funny at the time – particularly when Brad had called her a *fucking maniac* – but now just seemed overwhelmingly sad.

Sam

Nearly two weeks later, Sam woke up to two missed calls from Daisy and one from Imo. She sat up in bed immediately, and her first thought was that Jas must have had the baby. Shamefully, her second thought was how any stressful news might affect the microscopic embryo implanting within her. It had been inserted six days ago, despite the doctor recommending they freeze their embryos and wait a few months until Sam was fully recovered. But she'd waited long enough.

She walked through to the living area so as not to wake Marvin in the bedroom, then selected Daisy's number tentatively; they hadn't spoken on the phone in over a month.

'Hey!' Daisy's voice sounded strained, deeper than usual.

'Hey,' Sam replied in a cheery tone. 'Imo tried calling me too. Is everything all right? How's your arm?'

'It's . . . it's Ida. She had a stroke yesterday and was brought into Scarborough hospital.'

Sam pressed the phone firmly against her ear as she waited for Daisy to continue.

After a long pause, Daisy said, 'She died, Sam. A few hours ago.'

Sam stopped in the middle of the room. 'Oh god, Daisy, I'm so sorry.' There was a pause, and Sam could hear distant music down the line. 'Where are you?'

'In my room – in the hostel. There's a bar below,' she added as explanation to the din.

There was a silence, and Sam took a deep breath, aware that she was not speaking enough but unsure what to say next. She sat down cross-legged on the rug in the living area, grimacing slightly from the pressure on her still-tender abdomen. 'Do you know when the funeral will be?'

'Next week probably. I'll need to check my arm's okay to fly.'

'D'you think you'll fly back after, to finish the trip?'

'No,' Daisy said in an overly casual tone.

Sam sensed that she was hiding something; possibly something had happened out there, or perhaps Daisy hadn't been having as good a time as her Instagram posts suggested. 'Really? That's a shame to miss the last month though?'

'Well, it'd cost me fifteen hundred for the flights; it's not like I'm nipping over from Europe. And there's no way I'd miss Ida's funeral.' Her tone was defensive, angry even, as though Sam was suggesting something preposterous.

''Course, no, you couldn't do that,' she said quickly, before they sunk into further silence. Sam pictured their friendship like a light that was going out, in need of a new bulb, once luminous, then gone completely. A shooting star in a vast sky. 'I can't wait to see you,' she said quickly, hating the stiffness in her voice. 'Obviously I wish it was, you know, in better circumstances.'

'Will you come? To the funeral?'

'To the funeral?' This wasn't what Sam had meant. She ran over the end of term in her mind. It was impossible to get time off from school: even for her own grandma's funeral, she had to take unpaid leave in a previous job because their connection wasn't classed as immediate relatives. She was also very aware that she could be knowingly pregnant, or not, by next week, and it stung that Daisy seemed to have forgotten this.

'Yeah,' Daisy said, with a hint of something close to a threat, 'it'd be nice to have you there.'

Sam swallowed and, sensing the importance of the request, said, 'I'll speak to Andy – the head at school,' she added, suspecting Daisy might no longer be familiar with these people in her life, 'see what I can do – once the date's been confirmed.'

'Great.' Daisy puffed air out, making a harsh crackle down the phone. 'I just can't really believe it.'

Her voice felt softer, more Daisy, as though Sam's attending the funeral had eliminated a barrier between them.

'It'll take time,' Sam said gently. 'I'm really sorry, Dais.'

'Thank you.' The words cracked, her voice trailing off to a whisper.

Nine days after the embryo transfer, Sam noticed a line of dried blood in her underwear. Her heart pounded, and she became aware of an acidic churn in her stomach at the thought of telling Marvin. She calculated her cycle; it was a few days early for her period to arrive. The previously mythical phenomenon of implantation bleeding roared into her cortex and, for the first time, she felt her heart soar with hope.

Three days later, following a blood test that morning, the phone call with the results came in at 12.40 p.m. Sam was sitting at the kitchen table; she had been waiting all morning for the sound. She stared at the lit-up screen for a few seconds before answering with a shaking voice. She could tell from the way the nurse said her name. That was all it took. There was a nervousness, as though she'd been dreading calling.

'Sam, I'm really sorry to tell you that you're not pregnant.'
Sam bit down on her lower lip.
'Are you still there, love?'
'Yeah, sorry. Erm . . .' She stood up and walked over to the kitchen window. The grass had grown long over the last month; they needed to cut it this weekend. 'It's okay. It was our first time, so . . .'
'I know, Sam, but it's still hard. I'm so very sorry it didn't work for you this time.'
'Yeah.' Sam's voice wavered, and she cleared her throat. 'Thank you for telling me.'

She ended the call quickly and put her phone down, leaning forward on the kitchen counter and watched a pigeon doddering about on the lawn, its head bobbing in time to a mysterious beat. A sparrow landed nearby on a fence post – its movements swift and agile in comparison – then flew away, and the pigeon was left, looking even more stupid than before.

Sam dialled Marvin's number and swallowed several times. Expecting the call, he answered straight away. 'Lamp?'

When she heard his voice, she understood that it didn't

matter what words she used as he too would know from her voice. 'Marv, it was negative.'

He didn't so much answer as make a wounded sound of acknowledgement. 'I really thought . . . after you had that bleeding, I started to . . .'

'I know,' she said, bringing her hand to rub her forehead. 'Me too.'

They finished the call, and Sam dropped her phone onto the counter harder than she intended. It smacked down, highlighting the quiet that followed. The hum of the fridge entered her consciousness and was then difficult to dislodge. The room suddenly seemed suffocating. She unlocked the back door with loud metallic clunks and stepped out onto the cool grass, which peeped out around her bare toes. The pigeon looked at her and flew off, leaving her standing alone. She lifted her head up to the sky, the white expanse dilating her pupils. The sun appeared from behind a cloud, dousing her in warmth for a moment, then she shielded her eyes, took a deep breath, and turned around to head back indoors.

A pile of clean laundry sat on top of the washing machine, and she decided to iron it before calling her mum to break the news. She turned the radio on and started to drag the iron down the hem of a dress, watching as the wrinkles started to disappear. A Smiths song came on, stirring up fragments of memories and feelings that she couldn't quite grasp. As the chorus broke, Sam felt a pressure rising in her chest. The corners of her mouth cast downwards, and her eyes filled with tears. She shifted the dress over the ironing board and reminded herself of the statistics: it was never going to work the first time. She ran the iron over a new layer of scrunched fabric, keeping her mouth rigid as tears slid down her cheeks. A gasp escaped her mouth, and eventually she put the iron down, sank to the floor, and cried like she hadn't in years.

Daisy

The plane descended towards Manchester airport, and the green patchwork squares of England came into view. Daisy rested her forehead on the glass and stared out at the miniature roads and buildings. Rain was clouding the air with a thin grey haze, and the buildings were littered with amber freckles as people turned their lights on, despite it being only late afternoon.

In the end, she'd been relieved to cut her time in Australia short. Leaving the hospital to recuperate in her shared hostel room had been a grim wake-up call to the reality of the trip. Victoria had appeared in the afternoon, initially gushing with sympathy, then swiftly offloading about her and Brad's hook-up. Together with the others on the tour, she'd brought beers up to their room, filling Daisy in on the adventures she'd missed. But no one had remembered to help with her bags, and no one had looked back when they'd left Daisy in her room, absently bidding her goodnight before rushing back to the bar. Overnight, she'd become painstakingly aware of the fickle nature of the friendships she'd made and how lacking in worth their conversations were. She'd loved the beaches, the sights, and the sea, but she'd seen enough. Her heart ached for the grey and the gusts of Whitby.

The plane touched down, and Daisy felt the familiar relief that they were on firm ground again. She was looking forward to seeing everyone but felt panicked when she considered not only Ida's empty home but also the prospect of job hunting, where she was going to live, and her rapidly declining bank balance. Five hours of interrupted sleep wasn't helping her brain sort through these issues.

Two train journeys later, Graham picked her up from the station at Scarborough in his old blue Land Rover Defender. Their dog, Maeve, a young black Labrador, sat patiently by his feet, standing to wag her tail when Daisy got close.

'Christ alive, they'll spot you from space!' he said, indicating the bright-green cast on her arm. He hugged her tightly, swaying her from side to side, and said, 'Hello, Trouble.'

She stepped back to take him in with a smile. He looked older, his hair now entirely grey and his jawline less pronounced.

'Where's the tattoo, the dreadlocks? Don't tell me you haven't *found yourself*?'

'Fuck off,' she said playfully.

'Oh charming – the first words she utters are *fuck off*. What have we raised?'

Daisy bent down to see Maeve. 'Hey girl! Did you miss me?' She stroked the dog's glossy head and took the lead from Graham.

'Is this all you've got?' he asked, taking Daisy's small rucksack she'd used as hand luggage and pretending he hadn't seen her other huge bag. She ignored him as she dragged it over to the back of the car.

They climbed into the front seats, and Graham started the engine, a spluttering roar that sounded like it could cut out at any minute. They'd had the Defender for most of her life, and she'd given up nagging him to replace it. She raised her voice above the engine to fill him in on the details of her journey, including each meal and snack. She yawned loudly when she finished, the fatigue pressing down on her like lead.

'Jemima's made you a sandwich for when we get in, then you can go straight up to bed.'

She smiled and turned to him. Her mother always made sandwiches when they got in from long journeys. 'Ham and pickle from the farm shop?'

'Yep.'

'Amazing.' She tipped her head back on the headrest. 'I'm really sorry about Ida.'

He glanced over to her, then quickly back to the darkening road. 'Me too, kid.' He reached across with his left hand and found a cassette among the jumble near the gearstick. 'You were always her favourite, you know.' He pressed play and, for the rest of the journey, Phil Collins competed with the clatter of the engine.

Jemima met them in the hallway with a knowing smile. She was wearing a turquoise kimono with thick grey woolly socks, an exotic bird retired to Whitby. Daisy didn't have any conversation left in her so gave her a hug, wolfed down the sandwich, then climbed the stairs to her childhood bedroom and slept for nine hours straight.

She was wide awake by 4 a.m. the next day, and after half an hour of unsuccessfully trying to fall back to sleep, she got up and showered. Her suitcase was still standing on the landing where she'd dumped it last night, but she found some jeans and a black sweatshirt in the chest of drawers in her room. She purposefully left her phone in the kitchen and headed out for a walk along the cliff tops. It was still dark as she set out, but by the time she reached Whitby town, the sky had turned a magnificent burnt orange. Everywhere was deserted apart from a few fishermen setting out on small, weathered boats. She headed up the steps to the Abbey and sat on a bench, taking in the familiar view while catching her breath. A thin smattering of clouds sat on top of the fiery expanse, creating an illusion of billowing smoke and flames rising from the deep purple sea; it was as if the town was playing up to its setting for Dracula. She took a deep breath in and felt a part of herself returning.

The next two days were spent in a confusion of laundry, jet lag, and time with her parents. She visited the local hospital and got her cast changed to a much more manageable one. This one was only up to her elbow and could be removed for showering. Jemima drove her to the appointment and asked very little about Australia. This irritated Daisy, despite the fact that she didn't actually want to talk about it; she couldn't shake a sense of mild humiliation, like she'd been pretending to be someone else when she was out there. She scrolled through her Instagram and deleted some of her posts, deeming them irrefutably narcissistic. When did she become someone who uploaded photos of herself out to dinner, tagging the restaurant as though the post was to do with her job rather than a blatant brag?

She clicked on James's profile. Her checking of his activity had decreased substantially since being in Australia, but she was still surprised to see two new posts on his profile. His photos were a mix of scenes from holidays and travel, and nights out with friends – a surprising number of which were in black tie. Either the British army held an unsustainable amount of formal dinners, or James really liked how he looked in a tux. She clicked on his latest picture of rugged mountains at sunrise and saw that he'd been in the Lake District, climbing Scafell Pike. It was posted back in May; it hadn't occurred to Daisy to check his profile in over a month. A mix of shameful pride and relief swelled in her chest at this realization. Clicking back to the search bar, she typed in 'Blake Gibson', scrolling down the list of familiar accounts, none which matched up with the man she'd met in the park.

After dinner that evening, Jemima took her customary hour-long bath, while Daisy drank whisky with Graham in the living room. It was the best room in the house. Blue floral wallpaper, a wall full of books, and a bay window with heavy wooden shutters that faced out over fields towards the sea. They talked mostly about Ida: snippets of stories that were new to either of them or reciting well-worn memories, the classics that were brought out regularly. On the second evening, the conversation moved on to Daisy's job search.

Graham leant back in his sagging velvet armchair, staring ahead at the sunset through the bay window. 'I think it was a wise move, getting out of your last one.'

'You do? I thought you'd be on at me to find another job?'

He frowned. 'You'll find another one soon enough. You've always worked, ever since you were fifteen.'

Daisy relaxed a little, pleased that her work ethic hadn't been overlooked. 'Do you think Jemima thinks the same: that I was right to leave?'

'I do actually. She knows you've been unhappy for a while; we've both noticed.'

Daisy chewed on her thumbnail as she regarded him. 'Unhappy at work?'

He tipped his head from side to side and said plainly, 'Not just at work.'

Daisy took a large gulp from her crystal-cut glass, feeling the burn at the back of her throat as she considered this insight. She was unsure why the notion of her parents discussing her unhappiness was so mortifying. Her eyes flicked between Graham and a large painting of a swirling river and old stone bridge that hung above the fireplace. 'I wouldn't say that I've been *unhappy.*' The word reverberated between them. 'Maybe . . . unsettled?' she offered in exchange.

Graham turned himself towards her to hear more, stretching his legs out in front of him and crossing them at the ankles. His battered brown slippers sat on top of one another like Jenga blocks. He was subtly very good at opening up a conversation and encouraging people to express themselves in ways that they weren't even aware they could. His gentle questions and earnest expression as he awaited more information seemed to instil confidence and trust in people.

She considered her words carefully, knowing he was expecting a detailed response. 'I think, for me, my twenties felt like life was wide open, almost overwhelmingly so. Then we all turned thirty and it's like I missed an announcement of some sort: suddenly everyone's got everything in order: house, career, partner, money, kids.' She counted them off on her fingers. 'Everyone except' – she jabbed goofily at her chest – 'yours truly,' offering a brief self-deprecating smile in the fashion of *ta da*! When Graham didn't say anything, she looked down and picked at a fingernail. Her current no-ties circumstances were entirely down to her own choices and, she knew, ultimately weren't the sole source of her discontentment. She thought of Sam, Imo, and Jas, and how different their lives were turning out. Her voice was quieter when she added, 'I just didn't expect it from them all this quickly.'

Graham didn't reply straight away, and she wondered if he too was disappointed in how her life was turning out. But his eyes were kind and his voice gentle when he said, 'So what do you think is making you feel . . . *unsettled*?' She appreciated him keeping up the charade of her happiness and offered a grateful smile. 'The fact your friends' lives are differing from yours, or the fact you haven't ticked anything off this list of apparent essential criteria?'

She tipped her head back in resignation and looked at the ceiling rose above. 'Both, I think.'

'Okay.' Graham clapped his hands together as though they were getting somewhere. 'So what's most important to you on that list? What needs addressing first?'

'Uh . . . somewhere to live is pretty important.' She tapped her forefinger with the other as though checking off the list.

'You staying up here with us for a bit then?'

Daisy didn't want to offend him by explaining that living with one's parents at the age of thirty-two didn't quite produce a big green tick on the list of life achievements. 'Yes please, until I sort a job' – she crossed off another finger – 'if that's okay?'

Graham pouted thoughtfully.

'And I mean a decent job, one I actually like. They're the two most important things,' she added, knowing this was the sensible answer.

'Are they?' Graham asked, his eyebrows furrowed.

She looked between him and the floor. 'For the moment, yeah. I'm still not sure I want kids, and you'd bloody *ground* me if I prioritized getting a boyfriend over finding a job.'

Daisy and her brothers had been brought up to believe that relationships should come easily – that they should be a building block in making you the best version of yourself, but they shouldn't be a necessity or expectation. Graham and Jemima had been together for over forty years, stubbornly and happily *unmarried*. Students of the Seventies with new ideas on the way of life, they were both set on living independently, on focusing solely on academia, until they'd met one another. Their union meant a change of track, but they managed to stay true to their philosophy by shunning co-dependence where possible.

Graham chuckled into the rim of his glass. 'And I'd be absolutely bloody right! Look at your cousin, anyway: she's always happily unattached.'

'True,' Daisy said in defeat.

They both leant back in their chairs at the same time, then she looked across at him fondly and said, 'I'm not a hundred per cent about the no-kids thing, by the way.' She considered discussing the termination but worried that Graham's genetic tie to the could-have-been child would mar his point of view on the subject.

'Quite frankly, I don't think anyone's ever a hundred per cent either way,' he replied.

'But who then regrets their decision? How do I know I won't regret not having kids in fifteen years?'

'You can't know. But that doubt on its own isn't a big enough reason to have them.' He lifted his glass to take a sip, then added, 'Just don't be too stubborn to admit to a change of heart if that is the case in future.' He raised his palm as he saw that she was opening her mouth to object. 'And that's not me saying that you'll end up wanting them, only that you *can* change your mind if you want to. It's not a weakness of character.'

'Noted,' she said, relieved that he hadn't told her she'd be making a huge mistake.

'And I wouldn't worry about Sam, Jas, and Imogen – friendships tend to ebb and flow a little – you'll come back together in time.'

Daisy nodded faintly but felt uncomfortable with his analogy. She turned away to the painting on the hearth and imagined the bridge coming apart in the middle, shattering into pieces, and plunging into the river below.

Sam

The following evening, Sam and Imo caught the train up to Yorkshire together. Imo looked more expensive than ever, positively shining after a ten-hour day in the office and, despite Sam's new midi-dress and trainers, she felt crumpled and lifeless in comparison. It had only been two days since the news of the transfer failing, and a quiet sadness had settled over her.

The funeral had landed on a Saturday, meaning Sam couldn't exactly use work as an excuse to not go. Of course, she'd been fond of Ida and had met her several times, but travelling up to Whitby and away from Marvin still felt like a big ask at this point. Her period had arrived that morning, feeling heavier than usual, though perhaps this was just in her mind: the loss of something more evident. Daisy didn't seem to register the gravity of her request for Sam to attend the funeral and, so far, there'd been no show of gratitude for her decision to do so.

Sitting next to Imo's lively chatter as the train charged through endless fields, heading further and further north in the fading summer light, Sam experienced an uncomfortable feeling in her stomach in anticipation of her reunion with Daisy. She couldn't bear for them to be distant and awkward with each other, but it felt as though so much had changed in the ten weeks since she'd seen her. She reminded herself that nothing really had: Sam was still spending her days with Marvin in their flat, drinking decaf tea and buying crap online as pregnancy pillow adverts bombarded the sidebar. It was like her life was stuck and only a baby could unstick it.

Exiting the station, they heard Daisy before they saw her.

'Heads up!' she shouted, climbing out the passenger side of her dad's old Land Rover and hurling an overarm kiss at them from across the car park.

Imo reached out wide to catch the kiss in her free left hand, rejoicing at her apparent skill. Sam gave a clap that was so lifeless it was barely audible, and Imo looked disappointed in her dejected attitude. Just as Sam was about to plaster on a smile and will her voice into something upbeat, Imo reached across to tuck the kiss into the breast pocket of Sam's leather jacket, tapping it with tenderness. Sam placed her hand on the pocket over her heart and gave two small nods of gratitude as she fought an overwhelming urge to cry. The moment was interrupted by Daisy inexplicably careening towards them in a galloping sidestep, observed proudly by her dad, who was leaning out the driver's window. She barged into them both at speed, wrapping her long arms around them in a tangle of a hug, all limbs and teeth, and Sam gripped her friend's shoulder fiercely, the blade beneath her fingers so familiar to the touch.

The embroidered aggressive message across Imo's pink satin sleep mask was the first thing Sam saw when she woke early the next morning. She turned over and stared at the ceiling, listening to Imo's purring breaths as she thought about Marvin. She missed him. Their grief had brought them closer together over the last few days, united in their shared disappointment. She heard someone on the landing and recognized Daisy's distinctive walk: wide strides and heavily landing size eights, even on carpet.

'Jesus!' Daisy whispered, stepping backwards in the kitchen. 'You frightened me! Why are you up so early?' She looked Sam up and down, taking in her sports kit. 'Are you going *running*? It's only just gone seven?'

'Sorry. I was lying in bed awake and heard you get up, so thought I might as well.'

'Okay.' Daisy's tone was suspicious; Sam had never been an early riser. 'I'm going to do the cliff walk if you want to come, instead of a run?'

Their eyes met and, for an awful second, it seemed as though Daisy was regretting the suggestion of the two of them being along together. Daisy looked away quickly and added, 'We can bring Maeve.'

'Yeah, great,' Sam said, unsure how they'd got to the point of needing an animal chaperone.

★

They set out under a sky heavy with clouds, the roar of the wind on their collars and the swish of grass against their boots as their steps fell in sync. Maeve ran ahead, delighted at the unexpected walk, and they watched her alternate between sniffing the ground and bounding along.

'So, what's with all the running?' Daisy asked.

Sam shrugged and folded her arms. 'I know, not very me.' They continued walking for a few more steps, and Daisy looked across at Sam, waiting for her to continue. 'I started a few months ago. I never go that far and didn't do it around the transfer, but yeah, it turns out that exercise actually makes you feel better.'

'And here I was thinking that was an old wives' tale.'

'You've always been good at sport; I just never got to a point where I enjoyed it. Traumatized by year eight netball. Kirsty Braithwaite, *such* a bitch.'

'Was she centre? The centres were always bitches.'

'Yes, she actually was!' Sam laughed, relieved at their returned ease of conversation. 'What were you? I bet you were gold attack or some glory position.'

Daisy stopped walking, a smile spreading across her lips. 'Did you just call it gold attack?'

Sam turned back to her. 'What's it meant to be?'

'*Goal* attack.'

'Ohhh, that makes so much more sense.' Sam looked out across the sea as a small boat passed by in the distance, tucking her hands in her coat pockets and smiling genuinely as they walked on.

They talked about Australia, Daisy filling Sam in on the last few weeks there. Sam struggled to keep up with all the names of the people on the trip but asked about the places they'd visited, trying to picture Daisy there with all these adventurous people.

'It was fun for what it was,' she concluded, 'good to get away at the time, but I'm glad to be home now.'

Sam wondered if she meant the UK or Whitby as her home.

'Anyway,' Daisy continued, 'how are you and Marv doing with it all after last week?'

Sam looked down at the ground, unsure how to summarize 'it all'. 'Surviving,' she said, disliking the term but unable to give a better answer. She waited for Daisy to follow-up with a more specific question.

'Last night I told Graham that I don't think I want children, and he took it well.'

Sam looked at her, both irritated by the immediate swing back to talking about herself and surprised by this frankness with her dad. Sam's parents had always hoped she'd have a family of her own and would definitely have been upset if she'd told them such news. She wondered if Daisy was exaggerating their conversation but obliged by saying, 'Wow. Do you feel like you're really sure then?'

Daisy called ahead to Maeve as they reached the end of the coastal path, and the dog obediently bounded back towards them. 'Not completely,' she said as she bent down to secure the dog's lead, 'but I might never be certain.'

They joined the pavement of the road leading into town. Daisy's boots made noticeable thuds on the tarmac compared to Sam's silent bounce from her rubber trainers. A café had just opened, the owner still setting the chairs and tables out front, so they headed in to buy coffees before finding a bench facing the harbour. A middle-aged man in a burgundy jumper worked away on his boat below; perched on the bow, he ran a tool back and forth over the wood, and they both watched, transfixed.

'How are you feeling about today?' Sam asked, glancing Daisy's way.

Daisy exhaled. 'Okay, I think. Ready for it to be over, in a selfish way.'

'It's not selfish.' Sam shook her head. 'It's a difficult day. And it's hard to move on before the funeral's happened.'

At Sam's dad's wake, a decade ago, Daisy had found her sitting alone on her bedroom floor, her black dress ballooning around her like a used parachute. As the guests circled downstairs with polite chatter over a half-hearted buffet, Sam had sobbed into her best friend's shoulder.

They both turned to look out at the horizon, the memory sitting between them like glue. Sam reached over with her half empty coffee cup in a silent toast, for Ida and for Daisy being there in that tragic moment in her childhood bedroom, ten years ago.

Daisy tapped her paper cup to Sam's but continued looking out at the boats, and Sam couldn't read her expression.

After a moment, she said, 'I'm sorry if it seems really spoilt to you, me saying I don't want kids.'

Sam blew air out sharply through her nose. 'Spoilt?' she repeated, incredulous and a little relieved: it had felt like Daisy was going to say something worse, something uncomfortable. 'Isn't it the best thing you can do for the world, with climate change – not breed?'

'I mean, like . . . I can have them, probably, and I'm choosing not to.'

'Oh god, don't be silly.' Sam frowned. 'I was listening to a podcast the other day where they interviewed women who are child-free by choice. It was really good; I'll send it to you.'

'Thanks,' Daisy said without enthusiasm, then reached out to stroke Maeve's silky ear.

Again, Sam had a distinct feeling that she'd said something wrong. Maybe everyone was sending her such podcasts.

Daisy added, 'The only thing about those kind of interviews is that they always seem so sure of their decision — what about those of us who aren't a hundred per cent? Plus, they always have ridiculously amazing lives.'

'Oh, like incredible careers, hot partners, and shit loads of money?'

'Yes, exactly. What about the ordinary people?'

'Are you fishing for me to tell you you're extraordinary?' Sam cracked a smile.

'What: jobless, single, and living with my parents?'

Sam raised her eyebrows. 'Well, it actually is quite out of the ordinary for a thirty-two-year-old.'

'Fuck off!' Daisy laughed, and there was a flash of something when their eyes met, a glimmer of their former banter. Then Daisy shuffled on the bench and folded her arms across her chest. 'What I mean is, there's a pressure to justify not having children — your life needs to be really, really good. I'm clearly not going to be CEO of whatever airline who does screen writing on the side, but I still don't want to waste it sitting on my arse and watching Netflix.'

'You mean you want to do all the stuff that people with kids dream of doing — dashing off to Paris at the drop of a hat and going to the theatre mid-week?'

'Exactly,' Daisy said. She opened her mouth a fraction, as though to say more, but nothing came.

The ceremony was held in the grounds of a crematorium in Scarborough. It wasn't the most picturesque setting, so they kept the service short, then made their way to Ida's favourite pub in Robin Hood's Bay. It was an old-fashioned place with burgundy carpets, vast wooden tables and hundreds of beer mats glued to the ceiling. Daisy joked that Ida only loved it because of the acoustic properties the beer mats created – there was little reverberation, meaning the hard of hearing became conversational wizards again. Behind the bar was a narrow doorway that opened out onto a pebbled patio, sitting adjacent to the rocky beach, which had been hired for the afternoon. A few rickety picnic benches filled the small space, and some treacherous stone steps led down to a jetty where small boats could be moored as their owners stopped by for a pint. The sun shone brightly as the waves lapped calmly on the rocks below. Sam wasn't particularly a beach person, but it really was lovely there.

About twenty people outside of Daisy's family turned up, apparently a good turnout given Ida's age, and the afternoon passed by with triangular sandwiches and pints of local beer. Sam caught up with Daisy's older brother, Arkley, who she'd always found warm and easy to talk to on her visits up to Whitby over the years. She accepted it as a kindness that he didn't mention his impending fatherhood, his wife now visibly pregnant.

By six o'clock, everyone had left apart from Daisy's family. They headed inside to gather around a large corner table. Imo gestured to Daisy to go outside for a cigarette.

'She's trying to quit, Imogen. Don't be the bad influence!' Jemima said.

'She got me onto them! I was an innocent sixteen-year-old with lovely clean lungs—'

'That's bullshit,' Daisy said.

'They were thirteen,' Sam confirmed, rising from the table to join them outside.

They left the table to various shocked cries: 'Thirteen!'

The three of them sat on the ground in a row under the metal railings, dangling their legs down towards the beach as they looked out to the sea. The tide was going out, revealing glistening dark rocks and snatches of golden sand.

'I can't be bothered to roll; can I have one of yours?' Daisy asked.

'Sure. Too pissed?'

Daisy shrugged her shoulders.

'Shouldn't you guys be vaping by now?' Sam asked.

Imo pulled a disgusted face while Daisy grimaced but said, 'Probably. I tell myself I'll be less likely to fully quit if I make the switch though.'

'Hmm, maybe,' Sam said, then added, 'Can I have one please?'

Imo and Daisy both turned to stare at her, cigarettes held aloft.

'Don't look at me like that – it's only one.' This would be her one cigarette of the year, she promised herself. 'I'm not doing the next transfer for another month.'

''Course, babes,' Imo said.

They both watched Sam as she lit up and inhaled, looking up and ceremoniously blowing the smoke to the sky. She collapsed into a coughing fit straight after, and they laughed with her, Imo slapping her on her back.

'Awful,' she said through watery eyes, the burn in her chest unpleasant but reminiscent of better times.

They smoked in silence for a moment, watching the waves and a group of teenagers skimming stones nearby.

'So, we need to find Daisy a guy, Imo,' Sam said playfully, the tobacco and alcohol making her romantic.

'*Find* me a guy?' Daisy repeated, smiling but her eyes unamused.

Sam ignored her and continued, 'Like James, but not James. Someone better.'

'Well, darling, isn't a job a little more pressing?' Imo replied, her eyes flicking to Daisy. 'But what about that guy at New Year you were into?' She frowned as she recovered the memory, then turned back to Sam. 'He was your teacher friend, wasn't he?'

'Blake,' Daisy said. 'He's left her school now, and he wasn't into me. Anyway' – she turned to Sam – 'don't be all, "We need to find Daisy a guy" like it's the Nineties and I'm some desperate case. And what about Imo?' She turned to her cousin and considered her. 'Although you don't seem to *mind* being on your own. You're good at it. And you're rich enough.'

'What does that matter?' Sam asked, mimicking Daisy's former expression of a disagreeing smile. Recently Daisy kept talking as though there was a huge disparity in their finances because she didn't yet own a flat. It irritated Sam, because she felt, on some level, Daisy had always displayed an unawareness of her privileged upbringing, often talking like she and Sam came from the same roots because they'd both been raised in the north. Sam was well aware of and entirely comfortable with the working/middle class difference in their families, but it irritated her that Daisy pretended not to be. She was sure that Daisy's parents would help her out with a deposit for a property in the end. And how could she possibly believe that someone who handed their notice in and spent their savings on travel was seriously worried about money?

'It absolutely matters!' Daisy replied. 'Not just for rent. Think of every hotel room you stay in with Marv — split between you. Even a food shop and bloody *train travel* is more expensive. And calling the railcard "Two Together" is just . . .' She mimed a dagger to her heart.

Sam laughed a little; she hadn't actually considered hotel room prices for single people before. Perhaps she was being too dismissive of Daisy's money worries.

Imo sat up straighter, bringing the attention back to herself. 'I don't mind being on my own, but that isn't to say I prefer it. Which leads me onto some news, actually. I've been waiting for the right moment.'

Sam stubbed her cigarette out and lifted both legs off the side, crossing them and turning away from the sea to face them; she enjoyed hearing about Imo's conquests, and this sounded significant.

'Oh my god. What is it?' Daisy said, her eyes wide with intrigue. 'You're not . . . oh my god. I won't guess—'

'Just listen!' Sam said.

'I've met someone,' Imo said. 'Through work. We've been seeing each other since January, and it's quite serious.'

'Since *January*? Amazing! What's he like?' Sam asked.

Imo smiled. 'She's incredible. She's from the Netherlands, lives in Copenhagen but is in London for work every month.

She's a bit older: forty-two. A company director – not my company.'

Daisy's mouth dropped open as she continued staring. 'A director! Holy shit!'

The three of them laughed, and Imo smacked Daisy's upper arm.

'Ow! No, but seriously, you two will be riiiich. But, oh my god! A woman!'

'You've never even pulled a girl before, have you?' Sam interrupted, clapping in delight. She hadn't seen Imo light up about someone in this way for years. 'How did it happen? Are you in love? Tell us everything!'

'And she's how old? Forty-two?' Daisy asked.

'Yeah, ten years' difference. She's got two kids.'

Sam felt her mouth drop open again.

'I know. Two boys: eleven and fourteen.'

'Stepmum Imo!' Sam said. 'Is it that serious?'

'I haven't met them yet, but I'm planning to next month. It's just different from any other relationship I've had.'

'Well, yeah, there's no penis involved,' Daisy said. 'How did you know what to do?'

'Oh, I fucking didn't. I think she thought I was being coy but I was like, "No, no, I literally have no idea what I'm meant to be doing".'

All three of them laughed.

'She's been with other women since her divorce, so that definitely helped.'

'And what's she like? Sex aside, is she similar to you? What's her name, for fuck's sake?'

'Her name's Mathilde. She's brunette, kind of Sam's length

hair.' She turned to Sam, assessing her shoulder-length cut. 'She's quite short, which makes me look even more giant than usual, kind of petite but curvaceous? She's super intelligent, puts me in my place. Dry sense of humour.'

'She basically sounds like your perfect match,' Sam said.

Daisy put her hands on either side of her face and smiled at her cousin. 'Imo. Fuck. I don't think I've ever seen you like this about someone.' She dropped her hands. 'I'm so happy for you. Have you told your parents?'

'Christ no! Haven't navigated that yet. You know what my dad's like.'

Sam looked between the two of them, trying to follow; she'd only met Imo's dad once but was aware that he could be quite domineering.

'Mmm.' Daisy grimaced. 'Not the most progressive fellow is old Uncle Peter. But I think he might surprise you, once he understands how happy you are.'

Sam could tell that Daisy didn't really believe this and knew that Imo would be thinking the same.

Imo dipped her head from side to side, weighing up the point before disagreeing. 'This is a man who dislikes my swearing because it's "unfeminine"; his ideal daughter is Kate Middleton, not a potty-mouthed banker who, it turns out, likes women.' She stubbed out her cigarette and tucked her hands under her knees, her face drawn into a rare show of vulnerability. 'Anyway, keep a lid on it for now. I don't imagine I'll be telling them anytime soon.'

''Course,' Sam said, unsure how to comfort her.

Daisy mimed zipping her mouth shut, then pointed her cigarette at Imo. 'Does Mathilde have any Kate Middleton likeness – in manner or looks? Could cause some inner conflict in your dad, offset the shock a little?'

Imo snorted. 'Can you really see me with a Kate?'

Sam and Daisy responded identically with positive grunts. 'Yeah, actually.'

Imo raised her eyebrows and muttered, 'Huh,' clearly complimented, and they all then laughed at the conversational turn.

Sam looked between the two of them. 'Shall we hug it out?'

They encircled Imo from either side, wrapping their arms around her and falling back onto the pebbles in a heap of laughter. A phone beeped, and another vibrated from their mass of limbs.

'Whose was that?' Imo said, sitting up and dusting off her designer dress.

'Not mine – I left it inside,' Sam said.

'Oh my god,' Imo said, staring down at her own phone. 'She's had the baby at last!' She turned her phone to show a photo of Jas cradling a tiny bundle with a full head of hair.

Sam looked down at the delicate pink face nestled into her friend's arms, the miniature hands held up like a doll, fists still clenched. Jas's face was drawn but elated, her eyes shining with happiness or possibly disbelief. Sam could not move for the intensity of the emotions that hit her: joy, sadness, envy, and love – love for her friend who was now a mother and always would be.

She pushed her tongue against the roof of her mouth to control any tell-tale quivering of her jaw before saying in her brightest voice, 'Amazing!'

'Oh wow!' Daisy reached for the phone to have a closer look, but Imo snatched it away and gripped it tighter, staring intently.

'A girl, it's a girl! A tiny Jas! A baby. I can't believe it!' Imo repeated, tears clearly welling in her eyes.

Sam and Daisy looked at each other, then Daisy erupted into laughter.

'Imo!'

'What has happened to you?'

'Pull yourself together!' said Daisy, yanking the phone out of her hands. 'Oh my god,' she said, looking at the picture properly.

Sam rested her hand on Daisy's shoulder to look as well. 'So much hair,' she said wistfully.

Daisy quietly covered Sam's hand with hers and said, 'I hope Jas is okay.' She lowered the phone, turned to Imo and said, 'Now, should we talk about what just happened there or . . .'

Daisy

Three weeks later, Daisy headed down to London to stay with Imo for a few days and catch up with people she hadn't yet seen since returning to the UK. She'd spent her time in Whitby searching and applying for jobs, holed up in her bedroom or local cafés where she'd try to make a latte last as long as possible – heavily into her overdraft, she really needed a salary soon. Each job application took days, and she felt depressed about the prospect of working in most of the roles – and, if her invite to interview rate was anything to go off, her reluctance was clearly infecting the applications.

She'd been over for dinner at a friend from school's house one evening; it had been nice. They'd got on better than Daisy had anticipated and had made plans again in a few weeks, but the majority of her time had been spent with her parents or alone. The girls had called once or twice but were all seemingly busy, and their Us4 chat was quieter than usual. Daisy's daily walks with Maeve were unfailingly accompanied by podcasts or audiobooks, as though she couldn't bear to be alone with her thoughts. She was absolutely ready for a weekend in London, seeing friends, just like old times.

Daisy: On the train ladz.
Tea was £3 – what in the world.

Imo: That's cheap. The north has got to you.

Sam: £3 FOR TEA IS A DISGRACE

Daisy: Imo I'll be there in three hours
I'm guessing you have zero food options

Imo: I actually have a readily prepared pasta salad waiting for you in the fridge.

Sam: Who made that then mate?

Daisy left a voice note crying 'Mathildddddde' in a goblin-like voice. Jas followed suit. As did Sam. Still to meet Imo's girlfriend, they'd taken to mocking the way that Imo said her name.

Imo: You bitches are NEVER meeting her

Sam: Good one bro

Daisy: Jas what time do you want us tomorrow?

The message remained unread, and Daisy assumed Jas had put down her phone to attend to baby Layla. She clicked her phone locked and stared out the window as the train approached the grand arches of King's Cross Station. A trail of people led her to the underground, where the air was stifling. As soon as she got a seat, she removed her denim jacket and pushed it into the top of her canvas backpack; London had always felt like an entirely different climate to Whitby. Her cast had been taken off the day before, and having the full function of her right arm again was exhilarating. She took out her battered copy of *Murder on the Orient Express* but failed to open it, opting to people-watch instead. Two teenage boys sitting opposite shared a set of headphones, the top of their heads touching in subtle intimacy as one of them tapped his Nike trainer to the beat. To her left, a woman of a similar age to Daisy stood holding on to a pole in a matching violet trouser suit, a small teddy bear-like dog in her other arm. The noise of the tube was comfortably familiar though not exactly pleasant.

Daisy looked around the carriage, unsure of her feelings about returning to the city she'd called home for over a decade. So far, she hadn't been hit by a wave of belonging that should accompany a return home. She'd always felt like a northerner occupying a space in London: not exactly an intruder, but by no means a Londoner. In Whitby, she'd become the girl 'up from London' to the locals, simultaneously omitting the ties to her town of birth and insinuating her presence there was temporary.

She arrived at Imo's at 2 p.m. to her stark white table laid with the promised pasta salad and fresh apple juice.

'Looks great – you actually made this yourself?'

Imo usually dined out or bought high-end preprepared food.

'Daisy, it's pasta; don't belittle me.'

Daisy took a forkful, eyeing Imo's glowing complexion. New relationships did that. 'Mmm, it's good. She's obviously taught you well. How often are you flying over there?'

'About every three weeks. And she comes here for one weekend a month usually. It works. Copenhagen's amazing.'

'Yeah, I'd love to go. It's pretty expensive though, is it not?'

Imo tipped her head to one side as she considered this while chewing, then said, 'Babe, are you using eye cream?'

Daisy dropped her fork with a clatter and stared at her cousin, open-mouthed.

'I'm just saying you look baggier than usual. I'm family: I can say this shit to you.'

'*Baggier?*' Daisy felt below her eyes with her forefingers.

'Well, you're thirty-two now – you need to invest in your skin. I've got some really good shit in the bathroom, so knock yourself out with it this week and you'll notice the difference.'

Daisy glared at her. 'Not that I care about the natural ageing process, but fine, maybe I will. Your eye area does look particularly dewy.'

'Thank you. So how are you surviving living with Gremima?'

Daisy finished chewing before answering. 'Surviving is the word. No, they're fine. I don't want to be ungrateful; we're actually getting on okay. It's . . .' She looked away and, too embarrassed to admit to loneliness, shrugged and offered, '*dull*, I guess.'

Imo copied her shrug. 'Well, what did you expect?'

'I don't know, I don't think I thought it through this far – I just had to get away, didn't I, from James and Sam—'

'You didn't *have* to. Look.' Imo put her glass down on the table and met Daisy's gaze. '*You* made the decision not to tell Sam, so now move on from it.'

'I have moved on from it.' Daisy frowned back. 'But sometimes I think maybe it'd be best to, you know, come clean.'

'Best for who?' Imo asked, folding her arms. 'You didn't tell her because you thought it would hurt her. Why would it be different now?'

Daisy put her right elbow on the table and rested her chin on her hand. 'But it's horrible because it's always there, this *thing* between us. Like, didn't you think she was a bit weird with me in Whitby? A bit cold?' She dropped her hand and leant back in the chair, turning to stare at a large Coco Chanel print on the wall. 'It's fine. Telling her isn't going solve everything.' She put her hand over her face and let out a frustrated groan, her good mood from the journey down now entirely dissolved. 'This whole year's been a disaster.'

'What! You quit a job you hated, you went around Australia with a group of kids, got roaringly drunk and smashed up your arm—'

'Don't. I still can't think about that,' Daisy said without humour.

Imo sat back in her chair and regarded her cousin. 'Daisy, when did you get so serious? You just need to laugh a little at these parts of life.'

'That's easy for you to say with your perfect relationship and home.' Daisy gestured to the pristine flat around them.

Imo watched her for a few seconds and said, 'The year's not over yet. If you want a different life, then put some effort into making it happen.'

'Put some effort in? All I do is search for jobs—'

'I'm not just talking about jobs. Anyway, my flight's at five so I need to head soon, and I don't want to argue with you. I'm just saying, things will pick up. Have faith.'

Daisy forked another mouthful of pasta into her mouth and chewed without pleasure as she glared at Imo. She swallowed loudly and said, 'Thanks for the pep talk, George Michael. I'll head out and buy that lottery ticket.'

Daisy's dinner plans with an old work colleague fell through at the last minute, so she spent the evening on her own, enjoying the contents of Imo's fridge, her obscenely large television, and admittedly luxurious eye cream.

The following day, she woke up early and wasted an hour scrolling Instagram while lying in bed. She got up at 8 a.m., showered and assessed her eye area, then headed down to the corner shop to buy the *Guardian*. Predictably, Imo had some great coffee and an impressive silver spaceship of a machine, so Daisy passed a few hours devouring the paper and drinking cup after cup. By midday, she was more than ready to leave the flat so set off early to Balham, walking the first half of the journey along the river in Putney.

Imo called as she was walking, presumably to check that she hadn't yet burnt the place down – or for positive feedback on the eye cream.

'Did you tell your parents about Mathilde?'

The directness of Imo's voice startled Daisy, and she looked up, as though squaring up to an opponent. 'Mathilde? Erm, yeah, but I asked them not to say anything—'

'I fucking told you not to!'

'Well—'

'Jemima's just *told* my mum on the phone!'

'What?' Daisy was aghast. Her parents were the best secret keepers and the least interested in gossip; she'd never expect her mother to be so careless.

'And now they're obviously feeling fucking betrayed, like all the family knew except them.'

'Shit, Imo—'

'Absolutely *not* how I wanted to come out.'

'God, I'm so sorry. I can't understand *why* Jemima would have done that.'

'It was by mistake,' Imo said, her tone changing from angry to exasperated. 'I'd said I was staying with a girlfriend as in, like, the neutral use of the word, and Jemima obviously thought my mum knew when she used the term.'

'Bloody hell, what an idiot.'

'I don't blame her, Daisy. I blame *you*. I specifically asked you guys not to tell anyone.'

'I didn't think they really counted—'

'What, my mother's *sister* didn't count?' She breathed heavily down the line, making a harsh rasping sound.

'You're right, Imo. I'm really sorry – that was massively dumb of me.'

'Well, it's done now – that's forever going to be my "coming out story".' She sighed again with frustration.

Daisy rubbed at her neck, pulling at her skin until it felt sore. 'What can I do to fix this?'

There was silence on the line before Imo said, 'Just fucking sort yourself out. Stop being careless with people.'

Imo hung up, and Daisy dropped her arm to her side, cut

by the suggestion of her wider lack of care. Imo was lashing out, rightly so. She turned towards the Thames and took hold of the cold metal handrail that lined the stone wall separating her from the water, then dropped her head backwards and let out an audacious groan to the placid clouds above.

She arrived at Jas's five minutes early and tentatively rung the bell, wondering if Sam and Jas knew what had happened. Jas opened the door slowly like the big reveal on a home renovation show. In her arms was a tiny person with a mop of black hair, sleeping soundly. She looked even smaller than in the pictures.

Jas grinned and said with frustration, 'She'll only sleep *on* us. Highly inconvenient for general living.'

Daisy stepped in closer to take in Layla's features. 'She's amazing, Jas,' she whispered, placing her finger on her cheek to feel the softness of it. 'I can definitely see Ash in her.'

'I know, that's what everyone says. Apparently it's a common thing when they're newborns – they look like the dad so that they recognize it as their own.' She raised her eyebrows in disbelief. 'Anyway, it's been forever!' Jas hugged her with her free right arm, and Daisy decided that Imo couldn't have told her yet. She hugged her back, relishing not yet being in the doghouse.

They headed upstairs to the flat, Daisy following from behind. Not wanting to add to the conversation of women 'getting their figures back' after birth – as though they'd been carelessly lost like a set of keys – Daisy refrained from commenting on Jas's. She was already staggeringly body confident anyway. Instead, she opted for, 'Your hair looks good, all thick and glossy.'

'Thanks, but it's falling out.'

'What?' Daisy frowned as she sat down at the kitchen island.

'Yeah, during pregnancy you don't shed hair like normal; that's why it gets really thick. Then, post-partum, it comes out in clumps.'

'Jesus,' Daisy said, gritting her teeth. 'Imo pointed out my eye bags yesterday.'

'Oh, she's kind like that.'

Daisy considered telling her what'd happened but decided she'd wait until Sam arrived so that she didn't have to run through the story twice.

Jas managed to transfer a sleeping Layla into a cushioned pod on the sofa, and they took the opportunity to start making lunch. At points, it felt like when they were flatmates, except that Jas's attention flickered over to Layla every few minutes.

'Sorry, I thought she'd woken up,' Jas said, holding her forefinger up to signal Daisy to stop talking.

Daisy stared at the finger in her face and tried not to take offence.

'It's going to be any minute now,' Jas continued; 'she'll probably start screaming as soon as Sam arrives.' She slumped onto a barstool and fondled a packet of salad leaves, rustling the plastic in her hands but making no movements to start making the lunch.

Daisy volunteered to put together the harissa chicken salad, and they talked about the birth and Layla's first few weeks. The conversation moved on to Jas's radio slot and @AskDrJas Instagram account – they were going so well she'd chosen to continue doing them through her maternity leave. Daisy listened keenly, interested about the wide range of queries sent in; she loved watching the weekly videos where Jas answered various questions from femidom use to accessing PrEP.

A high-pitched squeal interrupted them as Layla stirred. Jas swept her long hair over her head, holding it on the back of her neck as she closed her eyes for two seconds before rising from the stool.

'Don't worry; I'll sort this,' Daisy called over the crying. 'And it might actually be better for Sam if she's met with the reality of a crying baby rather than the perfection I got earlier.'

'You're probably right,' Jas shouted back as she rocked Layla on her chest.

Layla was still crying when Sam arrived ten minutes later. Jas did her best to settle her while apologizing repeatedly.

'Jas, stop. We get that this is what babies do,' Sam said.

Daisy glanced over to the kitchen, wondering when they'd eat as the chicken would dry out if she had to reheat it. 'D'you want me to have a go?' Daisy asked. 'I'm sure it'll make no difference but at least it'll give your arms a break.'

'Really? That'd be great, actually. I've fed her, changed her – she can't be tired . . .'

They carefully made the transaction, with Daisy doing her best to support Layla's head.

'Oh she's so tiny!' she said over the din of Layla's wails, her mouth a ruby oval. Daisy took her over to the window to see if the change in light might startle her into silence. 'Nope, you don't care about the scenery of Balham, do you?' she said in a higher-pitched voice than usual. 'D'you want a go?' she asked Sam, then regretted it as she saw a moment of hesitation.

'Sure,' Sam said, rising from the sofa.

Jas looked over from the kitchen and met Daisy's eyes.

'Hi baby,' Sam said, looking down at her. Layla continued to bawl, her toothless mouth extended. Sam rocked her back and forth, then blew gently onto her forehead. Her crying became less energized, so Sam blew harder, circling her breath over her tiny brow. It seemed to startle Layla; her eyes widened then focused on Sam's chest as her crying ceased.

'Oh my god, the child whisperer,' Daisy said.

Sam blinked several times, staring down at Layla. 'I feel like she's looking at my boob like Edward Cullen looked at Bella in that science class.'

'Gross, who's Edward Cullen?'

Sam's eyes flicked over to Daisy, and she said with distaste, 'Don't do that.'

'What?'

'*Pretend* that you don't know *Twilight*. I hate it when people show off about not following popular culture, like it makes them superior to not know a single *Love Island* contestant.'

Daisy let out a snort of laughter, then hesitated before replying, 'I actually don't know any Love Islanders, but I don't walk around feeling superior about it.'

Sam gave a brief raise of her eyebrows to show she disagreed. 'Well, you definitely know *Twilight*.'

Daisy's patience waivered. 'I know *of* it, but I don't know the characters' names, Jesus!' Sam had always found Daisy's poor knowledge of popstars and reality TV amusing; she was clearly annoyed at her for some other reason.

'Okay, guys, let's not argue about sexy vampires!' Jas called out in a pointedly lowered voice to remind them to keep the volume down now that Layla was finally content in Sam's arms. She walked over to them and placed her arm on Sam's back. 'I think she's looking at the pattern of your top,' she said, gesturing to Sam's black-and-white gingham blouse, as though this might clear the Edward Cullen riddled air.

Still holding Layla, Sam sat down gently on the sofa. 'Mate, we really should have had a baby shower for you – sorry for not getting our shit together in time.'

Daisy glanced at Jas, not knowing what to do. Jas's baby shower had purposefully been held when Sam was in the Wirral visiting her mum. Jas had been certain this was for the best, that it would be too painful for Sam to go, and while Daisy had disagreed, she couldn't exactly be lecturing her on keeping things from Sam.

'The girls from school arranged a little thing but you were away, remember?' Jas said, her tone casual. 'It was that weekend in May you were up north?'

'Oh.' Sam looked at Daisy and smiled briefly, embarrassed to have got it wrong. She returned to Layla in her lap, stroking her cheek. 'How come I didn't hear about it?'

Jas's eyes flicked between them both like a hare caught in a trap. 'I'm pretty sure I mentioned it but . . . it wasn't really a proper thing. I know you guys think they're lame anyway – Daisy didn't come either.'

'Daisy was in Australia,' Sam said, not looking up.

Jas leant on the back of the sofa and licked her lips, considering what to say next.

'Sounded shit – I wouldn't have gone anyway,' Daisy said, feeling that humour was the only way through.

But Sam carried on rocking Layla, her face downcast, and for a horrible moment, it looked as though she was about to cry.

Jas edged around the sofa and sat next to her. 'Sammy,' she said, her voice tender, the pretence gone. 'I'm really sorry if I did the wrong thing. I just knew you'd feel you had to come because you're a good friend, a really good friend. And I didn't want to put you through that when you were about to start IVF.'

Sam nodded several times, then reached over to pass Layla over. 'I know you meant it kindly, but it still hurts.' She looked up at Jas. 'Don't decide for me what I'm capable of.'

Jas swallowed. 'Okay.' Then she whispered, 'I'm sorry.'

Sam patted Jas's thigh to draw a line under the conversation and changed her tone to more upbeat. 'Now show me some pics. What did you wear?'

Daisy watched Sam, unable to tell what she was thinking. Perhaps she was angry that Daisy hadn't told her. She looked away, back to Jas, and asked, 'And did Imo partake or just roll her eyes and smoke cigarettes in your face?'

Jas nervously reached for her phone. 'Bit of both really.'

She pulled up some photos from the day, and Daisy and Jas watched as Sam flicked through them, a brave smile fixed below her joyless eyes as she saw the banners, presents, and numerous guests that attended.

'Your outfit,' Sam said with confusion or possibly awe.

Daisy had seen the photos already. Jas had worn a sheer black Seventies nightgown over a black bra and knickers, fully displaying her incredible stretched stomach and new figure.

'I know, a bit ridiculous.' Jas's eyes ran desperately over Sam's face.

'No, perfect.'

★

They ate lunch together, all three of them making an effort to keep the conversation flowing, to act like everything was fine. They discussed Imo and Mathilde and when they'd meet her. Daisy sat quietly, unwilling to relive the conversation with Imo. It was an honest mistake telling Graham and Jemima, and she couldn't bear to have them berate her for it. Jas asked about Sam's school, and in turn Sam asked about Layla's sleeping routine. Daisy chipped in here and there with comments and questions, but the energy in the room felt laboured.

'Something'll turn up,' Jas said absently about Daisy's fruitless job search as she rocked Layla in her arms. 'Are you back on the apps, D?'

'Why does everyone keep asking me that?' Daisy said with irritation.

Jas looked up at her with concern, as though breaking the polite rhythm was a grave sin. 'No, it's just that everyone says that's the only way you meet people now. I'm not saying you *should* be.'

Daisy tucked a strand of hair behind her ear and returned her voice to appropriately mild-mannered. 'I'd much rather meet someone in real life, like you guys got to. I don't believe that apps are "the only way".' In truth, she'd downloaded Bumble and Hinge since returning to Whitby and had been browsing profiles but couldn't bring herself to arrange an actual date. The thought of small talk with another adequate but uninspiring man filled her with gloom.

As soon as they finished lunch, Layla started crying again. Jas attempted to breastfeed but had difficulty getting her to latch. Sam and Daisy tried to reassure her that the noise didn't bother them, but Jas seemed stressed, mortified even, by her daughter's wails. She apologized and whisked Layla away into their bedroom, as though her friends' ears were too delicate for such noise.

'You guys should head off, go for a drink somewhere – don't let us hold you back,' she shouted from the bedroom.

Daisy looked down at her watch; they'd only been there an hour. 'Jas, it's fine. She'll stop crying soon—'

'She might not, Daisy,' Jas said, her tone exasperated.

Sam and Daisy looked at each other, then Sam called, 'Okay, Jas, don't worry. We'll get out of your hair. Let us load the dishwasher first though?'

'Honestly, it's fine, Ash'll do it when he gets home,' she called. 'You guys go.'

Stepping out onto the street, Daisy wondered what they were going to do for the rest of the day. She was expecting them to stay at Jas's all afternoon but now realized this was foolish when she had a newborn baby.

'Shall we go to a pub garden somewhere, get a drink?' Daisy asked tentatively, unsure if Sam would want to hang out, given her animosity earlier.

'I've got to head back really, need to plan an assembly for tomorrow.'

'Oh, okay.' A quiet panic settled over Daisy. She put her hands in her jacket pockets and kicked at the edge of a round manhole cover beneath them; she had no plans for tomorrow either.

'How about you come over to ours for a bit? You could pop over and see Derek and June while I work, then we could make tea together?'

Daisy looked up at Sam, wondering if the invitation was purely out of pity. 'You sure?'

Daisy spotted Derek sitting in the garden and headed out the back door to greet him. He was sporting a short-sleeved shirt the colour of peaches and a straw hat like someone on holiday in the Thirties. His face lit up as he saw Daisy.

'Well, well, well, the weary traveller returns! Welcome home, Daisy,' he said once he was close enough for her to hear his whispered voice.

'Weary's about right. You look well. Where's June?'

He pointed to their flat and said, 'I'll go get her. She'll be so excited to see you.' He reached for his walking stick, propped up against another chair.

'I can fetch her if you want?'

'No, no. The hip's always better over the summer. Give me my moment to show off.' He rose from his green plastic chair and slowly started the few metres towards the flat, adding an ironically laboured quick-step to make Daisy laugh.

Seconds later, June stepped out of the back door and marched towards Daisy with open arms. 'The traveller returns!'

Daisy smiled at the repeated greeting. 'Hi, aw, so great to see you both.'

'We got your postcard; still on the fridge, isn't it, Derek?' She stood back but continued holding Daisy gently by the elbows. 'And we're so sorry to hear of your grandmother passing. Samantha said it was a lovely send-off though?'

'It was. Thank you.'

'You sit down here next to Derek, and I'll get the tea and treats.'

★

The afternoon passed in a hazy mix of scones, biscuits, and milky tea. Daisy chatted away about Australia and her current set up in Whitby, and Derek and June ended up telling her all about Brixton and Herne Hill when they first moved there in the Seventies. The conversation flowed more easily than it had with Sam and Jas earlier in the afternoon, a particularly depressing realization. Sam had always talked about not having a community down in London – she had friends, of course, and Marvin's family, but she didn't have any of her own family here, and Daisy could completely understand why she'd taken to spending so much time with June and Derek.

She bid them goodbye in the late afternoon, moving inside to help Sam make dinner. They sat down to eat with a glass of wine, and the conversation relaxed, both of them laughing at memories of university – as though their shared past was more comfortable territory than the present. Daisy traced the rim of her wine glass with her finger, looking up fondly at her friend. As long as they saw each other regularly, they'd be back on track soon, more familiar with each other again.

Sam suggested Daisy stay for the evening to watch a film. 'I'll stack the dishwasher if you get the TV set up,' she said, clearing their plates.

Daisy was delighted by the extended invitation. 'Can we light these nice candles?' she asked, fingering the heavy glass holders on the coffee table.

'Sure, there should be some matches in the dresser.'

Daisy opened the drawers of the wide mid-century unit, revealing an assortment of keys, hair bobbles, and bills.

Reaching the bottom drawer, her eyes chanced on a book thrust to the back: *A Room of One's Own* by Virginia Woolf. She picked it up and smiled. It was a year ago now that she'd met Blake in the park, but the memory was still vivid. She flicked through the pages, surveying the length of the book, and a yellow Post-it note at the front caught her eye.

Daisy,

I thought you'd like this. Let me know if you want to discuss it over a gruesome fizzy drink some time.
 I'm sorry I left without saying goodbye.

Blake
X

His number was scrawled at the bottom in messy, black handwriting. The breath was drawn out of Daisy's lungs as she stood, rereading the note. Sam walked over to the living area, drying her hands on her skirt. She looked from the book to Daisy's face.

'You never gave me this?' Daisy said, looking right at her. 'You never even told me about it?' Her voice rose in volume.

Sam's eyes darted to the book, and there was a hesitation before she replied, 'Yeah, shit. Sorry.' She raised her hand and rubbed at the side of her forehead. 'Blake gave it to me after New Year's, and I totally forgot to pass it on to you.'

Daisy paused, studying her. 'His number's in here.'

Sam raised her eyebrows and opened her mouth to speak, but Daisy cut her off.

'Don't try and tell me you didn't know that. What the fuck?'

'Sorry!' Sam said, as though Daisy was overreacting. 'I had a lot of stuff on my mind.' She shrugged, staring down at the book. 'I must've forgotten.'

Her nonchalance was like whisky on open flames. 'You *forgot*? Like *fuck* you forgot that!'

'I did!' Sam laughed nervously. 'Are you trying to say I purposely kept it from you?'

'I'm saying exactly that.'

'Daisy, come on.' Infuriatingly, Sam laughed.

Daisy threw the book down on to the dresser with a clunk and spoke slowly as she said, 'I've been thinking about this guy for a year; I've been fucking *searching* for him online!'

'Then message him now!'

'It's too late!'

Sam swallowed and brought her hand to her mouth, biting down hard on a fingernail. 'Look, I'm sorry. I didn't realize you liked him so much. You'd only met him twice. And it's not like he was the only guy you were really into; you were mental about James back then.'

'*Mental*?' Daisy looked up at her. 'Is that really the term you're going for? I never even *liked* James that much – you were just convinced we'd be great together. And I was "mental" because he made out we were fucking *soulmates*, then five minutes later sacked me off like I'd imagined the whole thing!'

'That wasn't *my* fault!'

Daisy enunciated each word clearly as she said, 'I'm not saying it was your fault.' She ran a hand through her hair. 'Did you think I'd embarrass you at work if I dated him, that I'd mess him around or something?'

Sam frowned like she wasn't following.

'God, just be honest: you think I'm fucking up my life because I'm not ticking off all the boring conventions that you have—'

'What, get married and have a baby? Yeah, thanks for that reminder.'

'Oh, fuck off – that's not what we're talking about here!'

Sam scoffed, then stared back open-mouthed.

'I'm just saying' – Daisy took a deep breath before continuing – 'it's not all about you.'

'Right, so I'm self-obsessed as well as boring? Why are you even friends with me then?'

Daisy shook her head in disbelief. 'You're not listening to me.' She started gathering her things, snatching the book back up then turning in circles to look for her bag.

'Daisy . . .'

Daisy ignored her and marched through to the hallway, shoving her denim jacket on as she spat, 'I'd do *anything* to stop you getting hurt, and you couldn't even—'

'I know you would—'

'No, you don't!' Daisy almost shouted the words. Finally, the words.

Sam's expression changed then; her eyes searched Daisy's face in confusion as they stood in silence. 'What then – what is it? Is it Marvin, has he . . . what? Daisy, you're scaring me.'

Daisy dropped her bag to the floor with a defeated thump. 'Not Marvin, 'course not.'

Sam exhaled, seemingly grateful for this momentary truce.

Daisy folded her arms and cast her eyes to the floor as she said, 'I got pregnant, back in January.'

Sam laughed. 'What?'

Daisy met her eyes, her expression serious. 'It was James's; he doesn't know.'

Sam stared back, a strange smile frozen on her lips.

'I wanted to tell you at the time, but I knew it would hurt you too much,' Daisy said softly. 'I wanted you there . . . at the clinic.'

'You had an abortion?'

Daisy raised her eyebrows at Sam's apparent confusion but stopped herself from answering too bluntly. She lifted her shoulders for a few seconds before tentatively asking, 'Are you really that surprised?'

Sam stared at her and brought her fist to her mouth, pressing it against her lips as her eyes flickered over Daisy's face, her mind catching up. 'Jesus,' she said. 'Do Jas and Imo know?'

Daisy nodded slowly.

'So just me then.' She stared at Daisy, unmoving. 'I can't believe you didn't tell me.'

'I know. I hated not being able to; I've never had to keep anything from you before.'

Sam looked her up and down. 'How was it; are you . . . okay about it now?'

'Yeah. It was . . .' She bit her bottom lip, wondering how to explain it. 'It was painful but . . . actually not that big a deal.'

It was clearly the wrong thing to say. Sam laughed with harshness. '*Not that big a deal*? Fucking hell.' Her smile seemed fixed in disbelief, but her voice wobbled as she said, 'You were pregnant – how in the world is that fair?'

'It's not fair,' Daisy said quickly.

'Did you even consider keeping it?'

Daisy looked away. 'Of course, it crossed my mind . . .'

'It *crossed your mind*?'

'Would you rather I'd have kept it? Raised it right in front of you?'

'That's not what I'm saying; I just thought you'd show an *ounce* of emotion—'

'Emotion? I've felt completely shit about it all year because of your situation.'

'Oh, I'm sorry my *situation* has been such kill-joy.'

Daisy couldn't look at her. 'I shouldn't have told you.' She bent to pick up her bag, 'I knew you'd react like this.'

'Like what? Pissed off because my supposed best friend has lied to me for six months?'

'I didn't want to hurt you!'

'What, until now? I forget to give you a bloody book, so you decide to hit me with this? That's kind.'

'You know that's not what this is. And don't act like it was just a random book – this isn't all on me.' Daisy fingered the flap of her satchel as she waited for Sam to say something. 'Sam, come on . . .'

'No, fuck off now,' Sam said flatly.

They stood a few feet apart, Sam staring at the wall to the left of Daisy, arms crossed and jaw clenched. Daisy bit her top lip as she turned to open the front door with a trembling hand.

Sam

Marvin reached his hand out to Sam as they walked along the beach. She pulled the sleeve of her cagoule up to expose her pale, damp hand and grabbed his firmly.

'Oh, Lamp, you're freezing!'

'How are you not?' She peered at him from beneath her yellow hood as the rain pelted their backs.

'We've only got this stretch left – look, you can see the van.' The red camper van they'd rented for the week was just visible in a car park in the distance.

They carried on along the beach in silence, feeling the comforting sand beneath their trainers as the vexed sea slammed wave after wave on the shoreline.

It was Marvin who'd insisted they go away, insisted she have a break from it all over the summer holidays. Sam had spent a few childhood summers in Scotland, and Marvin had never been, so they booked a camper van for the very last week before returning to school. They'd spent the days driving to beautiful lakes, beaches, and mountains, pacing through the rain then warming themselves by the fires of cosy pubs. A true crime podcast had kept them entertained on the road, the words washing over them and erasing the temptation to dwell on their own thoughts. It wasn't their usual sort of holiday; previously they'd tended to go on European city breaks and stay in fashionable hotels, the sort with bookcases arranged in colour order and cocktail bars with brothel lighting and ironically drab, fringed lampshades. But those holidays hadn't appealed this year. They wanted a quieter time in the countryside, in nature. It was the kind of holiday Daisy would have loved. A month had passed since their argument, and they still hadn't spoken.

★

They reached the stone steps leading up to the car park. Sam turned to Marvin and saw that his glasses were dotted with raindrops, despite his cap and hood.

'Shall we run?' she called out, starting up the steps at speed before he had time to reply.

They raced to the top and were immediately engulfed by a fierce gust of wind and even heavier rain. Marvin's hood blew down, and he grabbed hold of his hat. They stood panting, looking out at the deserted beach. Sam squinted into the direction of the rain, spotting a new blanket of raging clouds.

'I think it's brightening up,' she shouted above the roar of the wind.

'Whose idea was Scotland, knobhead?' He bent over to pick her up in a fireman's lift. She squealed and smacked his back from upside down as he marched her towards the row of shops and cafés in the distance.

'Don't panic, lassie; you're all right,' he said in his best Scottish accent. 'We'll soon have you dry.'

'Marvin!' she shouted, struggling to get the word out as her weight compressed her stomach and laughter weakened her.

'You're all right! Just relax, pet.'

He put her down before they crossed the road, and she dusted herself off. 'You're ridiculous,' she said with a smile.

'D'you know what's ridiculous?' he asked, taking her hand as they crossed the road. 'This.' He gestured to the storm around them. 'This in *summer*.'

They entered the nearest café and ordered a pot of tea to warm up, shedding their raincoats and leaving them on hooks by the door.

'It's still fun though, right?' Sam said as they sat down.

Marvin took her hand. 'Hell, yes. I don't think I've ever been on a completely empty beach before. Yeah, babe, I love Scotland. This week's been amazing.' He circled her thumb with his.

With hesitation, she added, 'Sometimes I think we could still be happy if it was just the two of us, if it didn't work out and . . . and it was always just us two.' This wasn't entirely true: it wasn't a thought that she regularly entertained, certainly not without pain, but she needed to hear Marvin say it. Lately his endless hope was actually increasing her anxiety; it was as if he couldn't even confront the prospect that they might never have a family.

'Yeah.' His tone was questioning, and he cast his eyes upwards to find the answer. ''Course we'd still be happy, but it's not really what either of us want – just the two of us – is it?' He removed his hands from hers, and his eyes were drawn to something behind her.

'No, but I'm saying, *if*—'

'Pot of tea for two?' A waitress approached with a tray and a steaming white teapot.

'Yes, perfect, thank you,' Marvin said, smiling at the lady.

She placed the pot and cups on their table. 'Just give me a wave if you want to order any food.'

'We will do, thanks,' Marvin said as she turned to leave. 'So what time do we need to set off to get to your mum's for lunch tomorrow?'

Sam looked at him, deciding whether the moment had passed. She reached for the teapot. 'I guess about 9?'

Daisy

Daisy reached the cottage and unlocked the front door with the heavy iron key, a carved Russian doll swinging from the key ring. Maeve rushed in first, past Daisy's legs, and climbed up on to the fraying sofa in the front room. She rested her head on her paws, blinking at Daisy as she waited for her to get ready. Daisy closed the front door and leant against it, surveying the room. They'd sorted through most of Ida's things, and only a few books on the shelves remained. There were still basic kitchen implements for when any of them popped over, and the furniture remained untouched – though Daisy knew the house would be fully cleared soon, ready to sell.

She left the keys on a side table and climbed the creaking wooden stairs to the room on the top floor. A window spanned the back of the narrow attic, a desk set up against it, facing out towards the bay. Stooping in line with the pitched roof, she leant on the desk and looked out at the waves to assess the tide. She was a strong swimmer, but she wasn't foolish. Whitby beach was a far safer option, a harbour town with a small stretch of sand. But the last of the summer tourists deterred her, the ice cream vans and smell of suncream not what her heart longed for. Robin Hood's Bay was a rocky curve with dramatic cliffs and unforgiving tides, where seaweed gathered in mounds and tourists stuck to paddling on the shoreline before safely retreating to the pub. Daisy had been swimming there since she was fourteen.

Her wetsuit and swimming costume hung on the drying rack from yesterday, and she bent to check that they were fully dry, before pulling her clothes off and tugging the slick black armour on. Maeve barked as she heard her feet on the stairs, impatient to get down there. She grabbed the keys and a fleece from a hook on the back of the door and set out on the short stretch through the village, her feet constricted in her neoprene swim shoes and Maeve running ahead, wagging her tail. Daisy felt the familiar mix of dread and desire. She'd heard it was to do with the temperature of the water; your body's response to the cold becomes slowly addictive, though that couldn't be the case at this time of year. Nevertheless, she'd felt the pull of the ocean more strongly than ever these past weeks but could never quite beat the moment of trepidation before entering, the moment where her brain told her to stay in the warmth at home inside but her body knew better.

She'd returned to Whitby a few days after her and Sam's argument, reliving the conversation again and again, but it didn't feel real. She'd messaged her the following night:

> **Daisy:** Sam, I know it's unfair, but I didn't ask to get pregnant (as you know, I was on the pill). I've wished everyday since I found out that it had happened to you not me. I should have told you in January and for that I'm sorry, but my intentions truly were not to hurt you. X

Sam hadn't replied. As the days went by, Daisy switched between feeling anxious and sad about the silence to feeling furious. It hadn't been Daisy's fault; surely Sam could see that. The concealing of the book had been surpassed by the pregnancy revelation, but Daisy hadn't forgotten it. She couldn't understand why Sam hadn't given the book to her, and her mind was overcome with hurtful theories. What made it all worse was that she couldn't talk to Imo or Jas about it all. Imo had thawed a little since that phone call, seeming relieved at her parents' acceptance of Matilde. She returned Daisy's texts, but her responses were curt, and they hadn't yet spoken on the phone; there was no way she'd be willing to help Daisy out of the mess she'd created. Jas's messaging was sporadic and cooler than usual; she'd clearly taken Sam's side or perhaps just didn't have the time and energy to call Daisy now that Layla was here.

Daisy knew she'd been disproportionately upset about missing her chance with Blake, a man she'd met twice. Reading *A Room of One's Own*, she'd initially been distracted imagining him reading it, but as she'd read on, Blake was swiftly set aside in her mind. She was so blown away by the short book, she read it again the next day. She wanted to tell him of the irony of her eventually reading it when she didn't have an income or home of her own, though these circumstances were entirely her own doing. She felt the weight of those women before her who'd had to fight for so many of the things she took for granted: free education, employment, countless opportunities to create, not to mention reproductive choice. Yet despite all these privileges, what exactly had she created? She wasn't creating any of the adventurous stories her parents spoke of; she wasn't moving forward in any aspect of her life. The years were slipping through her fingers like water. And Blake was yet another missed opportunity.

Leaving her towel, fleece, and keys on the same rock as usual, Daisy tied her hair up and stood on the shoreline. It was her favourite time of day to swim – an hour from sunset where the sun hung low and the sky seemed to change colour with every stroke she made. She waded in, quickly but never at a run – the rocks could be slippery underfoot. Maeve bounded in with her, jumping the waves and running back and forth; she never went in too deeply and barked if Daisy went out further than usual – a personal canine lifeguard.

The water was warmer than usual, and Daisy barely registered it reaching her waist. Once she was past the breaking waves and up to her torso, she paused to pull down her goggles, then did a shallow dive and started her front crawl stroke. Apart from in the summer, it was too cold for long periods of immersing your head, so she made the most of the opportunity and kept the stroke up across the bay, her heart hammering in her chest after ten minutes. She came up panting and checked her distance, as well as checking for Maeve on the shore, then pushed her goggles up and relaxed into treading water as her heart rate slowed. It was a calm day, and the waves out this far were gentle movements, nudging her closer towards the beach.

Daisy had been attempting to sort through a lot of clutter in her brain over the last few weeks. Things had become overcrowded, obscuring the important parts. Her time in the water was when things seemed most clear, she wasn't overwhelmed by life – by the rise in right wing politics, the imminent climate crisis, or the abyss that had formed in her chest after the argument with Sam. She felt calm, alone but not lonely.

After a swim, she usually returned to the cottage, her mind clear. She'd found an old notebook in the attic and had taken to writing things down, exploring random trains of thought and circling around ideas as she smoked her one cigarette of the day. At the back of the book, she'd made countless lists of what was most important to her in life, what made her happy and how she would go about various career moves financially. But she couldn't yet see a clear path. Everything seemed unattainable or like she was too late – could she really imagine going back to university and being a mature student with eye-watering debts? All she really wanted to do was to talk things through with Sam, to dissect each option over endless cups of tea, like they used to.

She stretched out to float on her back, water flooding her ears and dulling the sound of the waves and gulls overhead, as the sun touched her face with its faithful golden fingers. Ida had taught her as a child not to pick out flaws and shortcomings with her body but to marvel at what it could do. She felt the pulsing rhythms of her body – the muscles in her limbs working to keep her afloat as her lungs expanded and fed them oxygen – and a calmness spread over her. Turning around, she swam back to her starting point with a slower breaststroke. Maeve swam out to meet her for the last stretch, excited to see Daisy coming back in, and they emerged together, two slick black creatures, exhausted and elated.

Sam

Sam climbed into the passenger seat, cutting the sound of the wind out as the door banged shut. She turned to Marvin in the driver's seat and rubbed his knee. He continued staring out at the empty campsite in front of them.

'Hey,' she said gently. 'That was a hard one, I know.' One of his oldest friends, Matty, had called when they were on their morning walk and told them his news. 'It'll be fine when the baby arrives – it has been with Jas – it's just the initial shock when they tell you that's worse.'

Marvin rubbed his hands up and down his face, making a rustling sound against the stubble that had grown in the last week, then brought his palms to rest together at the tip of his chin. 'I know, but he's like my little brother. I always thought it'd be me teaching him the good lullabies.'

Sam took hold of his forearm, unsure what she could say to comfort him.

'But maybe it'll happen for us this time,' he said, a spark of light returning to his dark eyes. 'They could even be in the same year group.'

No longer comforted by Marvin's endless hope, Sam faltered. 'Maybe.'

'Or if not this one, then soon, hey?'

He took hold of her hand, and they both gazed out at the unwelcoming grey sky as Sam's thoughts spiralled.

After digesting the news from the phone call, they seemed to move slower when packing up the van, eventually arriving an hour late to Sam's mum's house in the Wirral. They pulled up to the semi at the end of the cul-de-sac and climbed out, stretching their muscles after three straight hours' driving. Sam looked up at the house for signs of life as Marvin slid the door of the camper van closed.

'Hellooo!' Sam's mum opened the door and her arms to them. 'The happy campers arrive!'

'Hi,' Sam said as she was swallowed into her mum's bosom.

'Hi, Linda,' Marvin said, kissing her on the cheek as he stepped into the hallway. 'Have you decorated again?' he asked, looking around at the pale-blue hallway with an elaborate mirrored console table.

'Yes, d'you like it? I was bored of that wallpaper.'

'Yeah, nice – very understated.'

'I know Sammy won't like it. You love all that Sixties stuff that reminds me of your granny and grandpa—'

'I didn't say anything!' Sam said.

'Exactly,' Marvin and her mum said at the same time.

They headed inside to the grey glossy kitchen at the back of the house, and Marvin and Sam seated themselves at the small round table. Linda served them baked potatoes – crispy skins with soft, fudge-like insides – and filled the table with a variety of toppings and salad.

'Thanks, Mum, this is perfect.'

Her mum sat down and smiled at Sam for a little too long, examining something about her appearance. Sam ignored her and spooned baked beans onto her potato.

'Your roots are coming through, love. D'you want me to book an appointment with Melissa while you're up?'

Sam frowned at her plate as she picked up her cutlery. 'No, thanks,' she said through gritted teeth. 'I'm trying not to dye my hair for the next round because of all the chemicals. Anyway, it's fashionable to have your roots showing these days.'

Her mum looked at Marvin, eyebrows raised as though her daughter had lost her mind.

'I like it; pretty rock 'n' roll,' he said.

'Is that what the doctors have said then? No hair dye? Seems very strict.'

'How's work, Linda?' Marvin asked.

Her mum had worked as a legal secretary for the last ten years and loved to discuss the firm's ongoings. Sam thanked Marvin with her eyes and felt the familiar tug of gratitude for having such an emotionally aware husband. Admitting that the hair-dye avoidance was the acupuncturist's advice was not something she wanted to explain. She let the conversation wash over her as she forked food into her mouth like a conveyor belt, smiling when they laughed.

'And how's Daisy getting on?'

Sam met Marvin's eye. She'd told him, of course, calling as soon as Daisy had left after their row. He'd been angry too, though for a completely different reason: Daisy hadn't told James, putting Marvin in a hugely compromising position.

'Yeah, she's all right,' Marvin answered for Sam. 'I'm guessing she's not loving Whitby – not many friends left there and a bit stranded with her parents.' His tone was cheery but his eyes nervously flicked to Sam. She hadn't told her mum about their argument because she knew she'd take Daisy's side, and she couldn't bear it.

'Oh, but Whitby's lovely?'

'It is . . . but it must seem quiet after London.'

'Yes, but I can see her up there; Daisy's always been an old soul. She just needs to find herself a fella.' She stood and started clearing the plates, and Marvin copied.

Sam watched her with a flicker of irritation. 'She doesn't *need* to find a guy. Not everyone has to get married, Mum.'

'Who said anything about marriage?' she said, pausing with a plate in each hand. 'You just said she was lonely?'

'To be fair, Lamp, you are always wanting her to find a nice guy,' Marvin said as he stacked the dishwasher. They often did this joining teams charade, Marvin and her mum, conspiratorial side-glances that she used to find endearing.

'Isn't it more important for her to find a job, an income?' Sam said, repeating Imo's words from a couple of months ago, but they came off churlish and sour from her tongue.

Marvin walked over to her and put his hands on her shoulders, giving a faint squeeze. ''Course,' he said.

She wanted to shrug him off but managed a tight-lipped smile, aware of her mum's eyes on her as she returned to wipe the table.

'I'll do that,' Sam said, realizing she hadn't helped clear up and grateful for the distraction.

'Marv, I was thinking of taking Sammy out for a manicure this afternoon, a bit of girl time. You'll be all right to chill here for a bit, won't you?'

'Yeah, course. Nail varnish is okay, isn't it?' he asked, looking at Sam.

'Erm, yeah, there's certain brands that are non-toxic, so we could call them and check?'

Sam saw a narrowing of her mum's eyes, indicating that she clearly wanted to protest about the notion of nail varnish toxins preventing successful conception. Instead, she managed to smile and say, 'Great, let me get my phone.'

Sam put make-up on before heading out; her mum would assume she was depressed if she didn't. They left Marvin enjoying the luxury of the sofa and television after a week in the van, and walked the fifteen minutes to the salon. Her mum chatted away about people Sam vaguely knew – girls she grew up with who were still in the area and some of her dad's friends. There were some unfamiliar names but, comforted by her mum's gentle rhythm, she didn't stop her.

'Let's have a look then,' her mum said, taking hold of Sam's hand with new acid-green nails as they stepped back onto the street. 'You always went for the weird colours, even as a teenager. Always so trendy.'

'And you always went for fifty shades of pink.'

'This is violet!'

Sam grabbed her hand and held it up to the light. 'Mum, it's pink.'

Her mum tutted but stifled a laugh.

They wandered down to the local park and found a weathered wooden bench facing a small duck pond. Feeling the warmth of the afternoon sun on their faces, they leant back and watched an elderly lady feeding the ducks at the opposite side of the pond.

'So you've got a few weeks left until you have to start taking all the drugs again, then? Once you're back at school and settled into the new term?'

Sam replied, staring out at the water, 'Yeah, but I'm doing a natural round this time, so there's less drugs involved.'

'You mean none of those injections? That's brilliant news.'

People tended to assume that the injections were the worst part of the IVF process, but Sam had become so used to them. Instead, it was the endless rollercoaster of hope, grief, and uncertainty that was the bigger problem, but this was harder to explain. 'Yeah, definitely.'

Her mum shifted her hips on the bench a little and said, 'And, are you and Marvin okay, love?' There was a false casualness to her tone, unbefitting such a loaded question.

Sam looked at her and couldn't keep the frustration from her voice. 'What do you mean *are Marvin and I okay?*'

'What you're going through as a couple is very tough. Are you talking to each other; is he supporting you enough?'

'It's Marvin; of course he is.'

'That's good.' She leant back on the bench and flicked a piece of hair away from her forehead. 'I'm not nagging, Sammy; you just seem a bit . . .'

'What, sad? 'Course I'm—'

'Lost, actually.'

Sam held her mum's gaze for a second, then frowned and started biting at the newly painted nail on her forefinger. Her mum gently took Sam's hand and lowered it back down to her lap, as she used to do twenty years ago. Sam flexed her neck in irritation but didn't bring the hand back to her mouth.

'Is it work? Or are you missing Daisy? Imo's away a lot, I know, and it must be hard for you with Jas having the baby?'

'It's everything, Mum.' Sam paused, folding her arms and looking out ahead. 'Work's . . . rubbish.' She still couldn't bring herself to swear in front of her mum. 'I'm completely checked out, but I don't have the energy to leave – plus I wouldn't get mat cover at a new place if I did *magically* get pregnant. Daisy and I haven't spoken in weeks because' – she shook her head – 'because we had this argument and . . . it's complicated,' she added quickly, still not ready to discuss it. 'And it feels like everyone's *leaving* London, like I don't have that many proper friends down there anymore.' She looked up at her mum as she said, 'I think it was a stupid decision really, me moving down there, setting up so far from you. With Dad gone and everything . . . I think it was selfish, actually.'

'Honey.' Her mum's eyes narrowed with concern. 'Where's all this come from? You love London.' She put her arm around Sam's shoulders, an effort from her smaller height, and they both stared at the brown water in the pond, clouds reflected perfectly in the stillness.

'It just feels really far away, sometimes,' Sam said. 'With the burglary and everything . . .'

'That still would have happened whether you lived around the corner or in Timbuktu.'

Sam attempted to smile, but it didn't hold.

'I mean this in the nicest way, but I'm glad you moved to London—'

Sam scoffed, knowing this wasn't true, but her mum continued.

'No, I am. It's not exactly New Zealand, is it? Poor Denise only gets to see her daughter every couple of years! No, London's fine. Plus I get to show off to everyone at work about my daughter in the big smoke and all the exciting things you get up to.' She squeezed Sam's shoulder and added, 'And I think me and you work well in this set up, you know; real quality time when we get to see each other?'

'I guess.' Sam dipped her head to lightly touch her mum's for a second. 'But what about when you're old and decrepit?'

Her mum laughed at this. 'Then I've got your cousin Karen and Julie next door, haven't I?'

This did raise a smile for Sam; both women were the most overbearing and keen-to-help people alive. 'Of course, they'll be itching for your demise.'

'Exactly. And anyway, if you hadn't moved to London, you wouldn't have met the lovely Marv, would you?'

Sam drew her lips inwards and clamped them with her teeth as she considered what to say. 'D'you remember what you said to me when I came home from uni to see Dad, when Max and I had just broken up?'

Her mum's frown deepened with confusion.

Her dad was sick at the time: the cancer had returned that winter to ravage his body, a mudslide of disease. They'd moved his bedroom downstairs, setting up camp in the front room and transforming it overnight into a depressing bedsit of daytime television and a coffee table pharmacy. Despite her mum's around-the-clock care, open windows, and fresh flowers on the mantelpiece, the stench of the room was unavoidable. Gone was her father's familiar scent: an earthy pine mixed with varnish, permanently seeped into his being after thirty years as a painter/decorator. In its place hung an ugly odour of urine and the kind of sweat only produced by bodies pumped with medication designed to attack from within.

Sam had hugged him on arrival and tried not to let her shock at his appearance and the smell of the room show on her features. She'd spent the day helping her mum sort his food and medication out while he dozed in front of the television, waking only for mealtimes. The chemotherapy had damaged his hearing, and he struggled to get his new hearing aids in properly, so Sam had taken it upon herself to do this for him, thankful to have a task.

'He's like that most days now,' her mum had said as they stood side by side at the sink, Sam drying like a helpful robot. 'You're awfully quiet, pet.' Her mum had stopped washing to look at Sam. 'I know it's hard to see your dad like that.'

Sam had stared ahead, waiting for the next dish.

'He's so glad you're here, love. He really is. Anyway,' she'd continued, sensing Sam wasn't going to reply, 'how's Max?'

Sam had focused on the plate in front of her, running the tea towel over it in fierce circles. It was already dry. 'We broke up on Thursday,' she'd said flatly. 'He said he has "feelings" for this girl in his French module so . . . not much I can do with that.'

'Oh, honey! You should have said.'

Sam had continued drying the exceptionally dry plate. 'It's fine. He said nothing's happened between them; he just doesn't think we should carry on. It's nothing, you know, compared with . . .' She'd tilted her head towards the front room.

Her mum had turned her full body towards Sam, removing her rubber gloves while not taking her eyes away from her. 'Sammy, it's not nothing. You two were together for well over a year. Please don't feel you can't tell us things like that because Dad's not well.'

Sam's tears had fallen thick and fast then, a dam that had held beyond its limit. Her mum had reached for the plate in Sam's hand, then slowly grabbed the tea towel from her other. 'I think this one's dry, petal.'

Sam had slowly given the items up, then wiped her eyes and nose. 'I feel awful feeling sad about it, with Dad in there, like that.' She'd covered her face with her hands as her sadness escaped in heaving bursts. Her mum had taken her in her arms then, rubbing her back like she was a child. 'I just can't help but want him here with me, or to call him and tell him about Dad.'

'Of course you do.'

They'd extracted themselves from each other, and her mum

had passed Sam some kitchen roll to wipe her nose on. 'D'you know, if there's one thing I've learnt from being married for twenty-three years, it's this.' She'd leant back on the kitchen counter and folded her arms. 'Kindness is everything. Humour, intelligence, attraction, they're all important too, but kindness – that's the biggest one.'

It had dawned on Sam as she wiped her face that her dad was the kindest person she knew and, in that moment, the thought was so acutely painful that all she could do was dismiss it.

'Max knows this is a hard time for you – not just with your finals coming up – he knows your dad's dying, doesn't he?'

It was the first time either of them had admitted this fact. They'd stared at each other before her mum wrapped her in her arms again and said into her ear, 'Then a kindness would be to put you first right now; a kindness would be not having eyes for some French tart.'

Sam had let out a snort of laughter through her tears. 'She's not actually French, Mum.'

Her mum had released her, keeping hold of one arm. 'Sammy, he's not the sort of boy you want to be with, not for the long term.'

'I always think back to that conversation, you know.'

Her mum smiled widely, but her eyes shimmered with tears. She dabbed at them with one of her new pink fingertips and said, 'That was a rotten old time, wasn't it?'

'It was. But it was good advice.'

Her mum sniffed and said, 'So what are you saying: is Marvin not being kind enough to you?'

'No!' Sam folded her arms and leant back on the bench. 'The

opposite. Apart from Dad, I think he's the kindest man I've ever met. I think I took your advice very literally.'

'So, what's the problem then?'

Sam stared at two ducks swimming past, the mallard proudly leading the female. 'It just makes it even harder, breaking his heart.'

winter iii

Daisy

Daisy's freelance work had been sparse at best; it turned out many people wrote food articles for free these days, leaving little demand for her former specialism. She'd temped in a call centre in Scarborough for a few weeks, answering queries about boiler grants to desperate people struggling to pay heating bills, then worked on the reception at a local GP surgery with desperate people trying to make appointments. The roles made her previous job in London seem impossibly privileged, and she had moments of deep regret at having given it up so flippantly. But come November, she finally had a plan for a new career. It had taken months of discussion with her parents and brothers, and she needed to talk to Imo, to apologize in person. They'd spoken on the phone and messaged a lot over the last few months, but Daisy still felt things hadn't returned to normal between them. She was nervous about asking something of her cousin, aware that she'd become someone who was taking more than she was giving. But she knew that if she didn't act now, the opportunity would be one more thing that passed her by.

Imo answered the door in a chic cream blouse and dark indigo jeans, which probably cost more than Daisy's entire wardrobe.

A delicate silver charm bracelet dangled from her wrist, barely disguising the star tattoo that matched Daisy's own.

'Word up,' Imo said, standing back and making a swooping motion with her arm to usher Daisy in, simultaneously removing the moment where they might have hugged.

'Hey,' Daisy said, trying not to be offended by the lack of physical contact. 'Thanks for having me.'

Imo closed the door and said, 'Oh, you can fuck off with your *thanks for having me* bullshit – I cannot bear weird politeness from you.'

Daisy opened her mouth to protest.

'It was months ago, and I'm over it – I've told you already. Your big stupid mouth got you in trouble, but now it's fine—'

'But I wanted to just say, face to face, how sorry I am.'

Imo folded her arms, looking physically in pain from Daisy's earnestness.

'It was careless of me; you were right. It wasn't my secret to tell, and I am, truly, sorry. Okay?'

'It's *fine*,' Imo whispered the words, as though making them less audible was somehow less awkward. 'Now, *please*, let's just be normal. Tell me about life as a seaside pleb.'

Imo made coffee in suave smoked-glass cups, and they sat on the sofa, thankfully returning to their normal way with each other.

'So, something's happened . . .' Daisy began.

Imo's face remained expressionless as she said, 'Sam's hired an assassin?' She failed to remain serious and erupted into a smile. 'Just call her, for god's sake – it's been, what, nearly four months? She can't still be angry with you; she's been fine with me despite knowing I was "in" on the whole *deception*.' She whispered the word like she was enjoying the drama of the situation.

'I'm still angry with her too,' Daisy said, hearing the petulance in her voice.

'About the book thing?' Imo frowned. 'Not the same, mate. You trumped her.'

'I'm not saying it's the same. I'm just saying I have a right to be pissed off too. And why is everyone acting like I'm the worst person in the world? I didn't *intend* to get pregnant.'

'Oh, pity you!' Imo laughed teasingly. 'She's just hurt that you didn't tell her – you'd be the same.'

'She hasn't been in touch once.'

'Then be the bigger person and call her.'

Daisy considered her and exhaled in defeat. 'I will do, but can we not talk about it right now? I actually have some good news for once.'

Imo gestured with her outstretched palm to continue.

'You know how I've been jobless and homeless and wondering what the hell to do with my life?'

'You're joining the circus?'

'A while ago, Ida made this comment that I should be *making* food not writing about it, and it kind of stuck with me.' Daisy sighed, ready to defend herself. 'Sometimes I think we just go into office jobs because it's the normal thing to do if you're middle class and vaguely academic, but I'm not sure it makes us happy. Not all of us anyway. You said ages ago I wasn't made for an office, and you're right. I don't have it all figured out yet, but I've found this amazing cookery school, and I've been accepted onto their two-term diploma.'

'Okay . . . great! So you're gonna be like some school cook or something?'

'Well, I was thinking more like a chef or running my own food business. Not that there's anything wrong with school cooks.'

'I mean . . . there was *a lot* wrong with the ones at my school but, okay, I can see that.'

'But that's not the main news. The school's in London, and it's super expensive—'

'What are you going to do? Take out another student loan?'

'It turns out that Ida left me something.'

'Ooh.' Imo's volume increased as her interest picked up. 'God damn it, why isn't she on my side of the family?'

'I thought she just owned her battered old cottage that'd be divided between Graham and Uncle Wilfred and be sold off, but it turns out she also owned two flats in Scarborough.'

'The wily bitch. Well done, Ida. But wait, aren't flats in the north worth about thirty grand?'

Daisy swallowed the urge to call her cousin a tosser, then replied evenly, 'I've told you this before: "the north" isn't one place where everything's the same! And they're more like *a hundred* and thirty around there.'

'Oh, okay, and how are they being divided up?'

'That's the best part. Each of the Scarborough flats are going to Graham and my uncle. She left her house to me, Arkley, and Jez.'

'Babe! You love that place! Ah, let's celebrate!' Imo said, jumping up and swiping one of the three bottles of Champagne from the wine rack in the fridge. 'So, what's the plan? The three of you moving to Robin Hood's Bay?'

'Can you imagine? No, we've gone back and forth and eventually agreed. They both have places already and don't have as big an emotional connection to the cottage, so I'm going to remortgage it and buy them out. There's no inheritance tax as it's below the threshold. I'll have a pretty hefty mortgage, but it's still a life-changing amount and a way for me to finally own a place.'

'Definitely. So wait, you'll live up there after the course, on your own?' Imo couldn't keep the disbelief from her words.

'Maybe one day but, no, I'll rent it out.'

'Thank god! I was imagining you with a new career as a fisherwoman.'

Imo hooted as the cork popped, then poured the liquid into some stylish flutes.

Daisy explained how they'd been carrying out some basic repairs on the house and would soon put it on Airbnb, just until she could get a mortgage and buy her brothers out.

'Look at you, figured it all out. When does the course start?'

'Early January.'

'And where are you going to live?'

Daisy put her glass down and licked her lips. She gestured with her head to the door of the flat and stood up.

Imo frowned up at her. 'What? You've also inherited the flat across the hallway?'

'Just come see,' Daisy said with reluctance. She wasn't sure how this was going to go down.

Imo opened the flat door and peered out at the smart carpeted corridor. 'What am I meant to be looking at?'

Daisy again indicated with her head to the right of the doorway, and Imo leant around the doorframe to view the ginormous suitcase Daisy had travelled down with, tucked neatly out of sight. They both stared down at the beast, a canvas rainbow belt holding it together and an ancient CND badge fastened next to the handle from god knows when. It was a gamble to turn up like this, but Daisy felt she couldn't have asked over the phone with the atmosphere as it was between them.

'I'll barely be here,' she pleaded. 'I'm going to get a job and work evenings and weekends, so I'll be out all the time.' Imo's face still hadn't moved, so Daisy added, 'Or if it's too much, then no worries at all – I'll find somewhere on SpareRoom.' She tried to sound chipper but couldn't help but panic at this prospect; London rent would be impossible on a part-time salary.

Finally, Imo's eyebrows dropped, and she took hold of the battered navy suitcase, saying only, 'Jesus, Daisy, we need to get you some new luggage – is this Uncle Graham's from the Eighties? Fucking embarrassing,' as she dragged it into the flat.

Daisy laughed, relieved. Once the door had closed on them and the suitcase, now seeming completely out of place in the polished flat, she asked, 'Are you sure?'

Imo wiped her hands on her jeans as though the case had dirtied them, then said, 'Of course. Anyway, I've got some news of my own which might coincide quite nicely. No offence.'

Daisy met Jas the following day for coffee in Balham. Jas was running fifteen minutes late, despite it being around the corner from her house. Daisy chose a table outside on the street, hoping it would be less stressful for Jas if Layla was crying. She spotted them approaching from a distance and was struck by the strangeness of seeing one of her best friends pushing a pram.

Jas pulled up in a whirlwind of apologies, panting heavily.

'Do you mind if we go inside? It's a bit cold out for . . .' She indicated at Layla in the pram.

''Course, sorry, that was dumb of me,' Daisy said, standing and holding the door open for Jas to navigate the pram through, dragging it backwards up the step within.

There was some difficulty securing a table with enough room for them all, until two women eventually offered to swap their corner table for one in the middle. Jas thanked them graciously and tucked the pram against the wall, smiling at Daisy as they both removed their coats. Hot from the walk there, Jas pulled her sweatshirt off too as she sat down on the beech chair. Daisy spotted that the label of her pink T-shirt was on the outside, the seam clearly visible on each side, and decided she'd tell her when she'd settled down and caught her breath.

'Is she asleep?' Daisy asked, peering into the pram.

'Yes, thank god. You'd hear her otherwise. How're you?' Jas said, her eyes wildly flitting between Daisy and people around them at the café.

'I'm good. You?'

'Yeah, good. Knackered, you know.' She gestured in Layla's direction. 'Sorry, that's boring. What have you been up to in Whitby? Still working at the GP surgery?'

Daisy surveyed her friend and wondered with sadness when they became so polite. 'Er, I was . . . I'll fill you in on all that in a minute. Outside of work, not much really. Still swimming a few days a week though.'

'*Still*? It's November, Daisy. That's mad! I hope you're being safe?'

''Course. I joined a group up there, so I wasn't doing it

on my own anymore: seven of us, all women. "The Whitby Witches", we call ourselves.'

'Cute! Aw, I'm so impressed – I can't even cope with the English Channel in summer.' Jas picked up a laminated menu to look over.

Daisy continued, 'Imo told me her news yesterday – she said you already knew.'

'About Copenhagen? Yeah, amazing, isn't it? I just hope she comes back.'

'It's only a year's contract,' Daisy replied, defensive – the possibility of Imo staying hadn't even occurred to her.

They ordered coffees and cake, and Daisy relayed the inheritance and cookery school plans to Jas, who was predictably sweet and excited for her.

'Sam must be so happy to have you back down as well.'

Daisy scratched her neck. 'I haven't told her yet; we still haven't spoken since . . .' She jerked her head to their left, as though the abortion clinic was across the street.

'Shit, Daisy, all this time? Really?'

'It hasn't been that long.' Daisy drank from her coffee with an air of casualness, but Jas continued frowning at her. 'I messaged her; she's the one who hasn't replied.'

'How many messages have you sent?'

Daisy's shoulders slumped. 'Two. I messaged her again in September when their second round failed.'

'Two embryos that time as well.' Jas closed her eyes as though this was too much to bear. 'It's so shit for them.'

'I know.' Daisy grimaced.

'Chick, you need to call her. I'm serious; she's been going through hell—'

'I know she has.'

'Then *be there* for her!'

Daisy was so shocked by Jas's uncharacteristic sternness that she wanted to laugh. Instead, she gave an open-mouthed 'uh' sound.

'I geddit that you couldn't before because you felt guilty – about the pregnancy or the lie, I don't know – but she knows now, so it's time to get your arse in gear.'

Daisy slumped back in her seat and blew air with her bottom lip protruded, making strands of her hair lift upwards in the breeze. 'I'll call her today.'

'Good,' Jas said, satisfied.

'I've been putting it off, hoping she'd call me.'

Jas's usual nurturing manner returned when she said, 'It'll be okay; she'll understand why you didn't tell her. Are you still angry at her about the Blake thing?'

Daisy looked down at the pot of sugar on the table between them. 'Not really angry anymore, but . . . I still don't understand why she did what she did.'

'Are you sure it wasn't a genuine mistake, D? Like, why would she not tell you about his note?'

Daisy sighed. 'I could tell from her reaction that she was lying.'

'You don't think she's a bit in love with him or something?'

Daisy watched the couple behind Jas being served a pot of tea and smiled as the waitress made eye contact when she passed. She placed her elbows on the table to support her chin and said, 'I don't know. The thought has crossed my mind. It's easy to develop feelings for people you work with.'

Jas didn't disagree.

'Anyway, he doesn't even work at her school anymore or live in London.' Daisy gesticulated with her right hand, swiping the air to close the topic.

Jas stood up and peered into the pram as though she'd heard something from Layla. Seeing that she was still asleep, she mockingly wiped her brow. 'So, you're gonna be okay living on your own at Imo's? How long's the course?'

'Two terms; finishes early June. Yeah, I like being on my own.' Daisy smiled back, then resumed her serious expression and said, 'Actually I really don't; I don't know why I said that.'

The waitress returned with their coffees and a slice of lemon drizzle cake, which she placed in front of Daisy. They both stared down at the glistening moisture and snowflakes of sugar. Daisy swallowed and looked up at Jas. 'I haven't really had time to think about it. I'm just so lucky that she's letting me stay and only pay bills – particularly after I fucked up royally with the Mathilde secret.'

Jas scrunched her nose up, acknowledging the error.

Daisy picked up a fork and cut into the cake. 'I know we'd drive each other mad, but I was kind of excited about living with her. When I stayed there on my own in summer' – she held up a forkful of cake, addressing it as she spoke – 'it was actually quite hard.' She forked the cake into her mouth, the sweet citrus taste at odds with the memory.

Jas leant her head to one side. 'Hard in what way?'

'I dunno; it's stupid really.' Daisy finished chewing and swallowed, putting the fork back down before she continued. 'When I'm in Whitby and I'm on my own, it's lonely but not on the same level as here. London's hard to be on your own in; everyone's always doing stuff and having a great time.'

'That's just FOMO, chick. Totally normal – we all get it.'

'It's different,' Daisy said more forcefully. 'You have Ash and Layla now. I don't have that one person who checks in on me if I'm late or feeling down or whatever.'

'But you have us guys?'

'I know I do,' Daisy said, though recently this hadn't felt the case. 'I know there's so many people who are homeless or living with awful people or abusive partners, or just their sad-ass parents.' She pointed to herself, and Jas offered a small laugh. 'So I'll be incredibly fortunate to stay at Imo's, but last time I was there, I was lonely. I *am* lonely. All the time.' She put the fork back down and played with a granule of sugar on the table with her finger. 'I hate the idea that you need to be partnered up with someone in this day and age – the feminist in me is screaming that this isn't the case – but I keep finding myself . . .' Mortified at how desperate she sounded, Daisy shook her head, unable to finish the sentence.

There was a pause before Jas spoke. 'You're always fighting against your feelings, like you're disappointed in yourself for having them. Daisy, it's okay to feel lonely; it's okay to be someone who wants to be in a relationship, who wants to be in love.'

Daisy couldn't help but scoff at this, Jas could be so *Disney*. 'I feel like I'm one of your teens and you're Dr Jas'ing me.'

Jas laughed. 'Just listen! It doesn't make you a bad feminist if the desire is coming from the right place – as long as it's not some weird conditioning that you *have* to be with someone, which obviously you don't believe.' She looked Daisy over. 'I know you love the *idea* of being some unattached babe in your sixties who goes on Women's Aid marches at weekends and hasn't touched plastic in a decade—'

Daisy's laughter burst out.

'—but if actually in your heart all you really want to do is ditch the bamboo toothbrushes, shack up in Dorset with a man named Dave, and watch *Queer Eye* every night 'til you die, then, babe' – she reached across to squeeze Daisy's hand – 'that's OKAY too.'

'What about the 2.4 kids? Didn't Dave want them?'

Jas smiled. 'Ah, the average is 1.7 or something now, but yeah, you and Dave could have those too if you wanted, or *not*. Both are valid choices.'

Their eyes locked as Daisy took in her words. 'I get your point: I should choose a boring life if I want a boring life, and you'll still love me—'

'You should still love *yourself* is my point!' Jas laughed. 'And your life will never be boring.' She reached over to the pram and started rocking it back and forth.

Daisy continued, 'But *Queer Eye*?'

'The greatest show ever! Fine, you'd be watching some historical drama on the BBC.'

'Sounds about right.'

Their smiles faded, then Jas added, 'So, I know it's not the same, but I've been pretty lonely too, recently.'

For as long as Daisy had known Jas, her diary had always been overflowing with social events. 'Really?'

'I've been trying to do the NCT meet-ups and sensory classes and stuff but most of the hours of every week are just me and her.'

'As sweet as she is, I'm guessing she's not the best conversationalist just yet.' Daisy put her cup down and considered Jas. 'So tell me how it's really been: motherhood – I want the uncut version.'

Jas turned back to the pram and directed her words at it. 'Exhausting, monotonous, but also wonderful. When she smiles, I literally tear up at how cute she is; the level of love you have for them is *overwhelming*.'

Daisy propped her chin on the table and rested her head in her hand as she waited for Jas to continue. She couldn't help but wonder if she too would feel such love for a child, if she'd be missing out by not experiencing such an intense emotion.

'But she's had colic so she cries a lot. Like, *a lot*. Sometimes for three hours straight, and I feel like I'm losing my mind. I mean, they're literally helpless at this age but sometimes I get so frustrated it's bordering on rage. And then I feel awful, full on ashamed.'

'Jeez, Jas, three hours? Don't be feeling ashamed at hating on her for that; it's completely unreasonable of her.'

Jas offered only a faint smile that quickly vanished. 'I keep feeling like, why us? Look at Sam and Marvin. We've been given this amazing thing and, I don't know, I feel a bit lost with it all. Like, not confident about anything.' She bit down on her lip and paused, swallowing pointedly before she said, 'And I don't think I'm very good at it.'

Jas was one of the most assertive and confident women Daisy knew, and this admission was unexpected. It dawned on Daisy that perhaps Jas was another friend that she had neglected this year, that she'd been careless with. She leant forward on the table. 'Jas, you are. You really fucking are, okay? You're not going to be super confident about everything because it's completely new to you; you're still learning.'

Jas tried to smile, but her eyes were wet and disbelieving.

Daisy continued, 'And obviously I'm no expert, but everyone says it gets easier as the months go on.'

'I know.' Jas managed a weak smile. 'It's just such a mad experience – like, your whole identity changes overnight; I still feel like a weird imposter pushing the buggy.' She leant in as though telling a secret while her eyes scanned the people around. 'And dealing with her crying in public is *awful*.'

'Aren't people nice about it, though? What exactly can you do – babies cry!'

'I know, but I'm so used to being in control of situations.' She looked down at her stomach and added, 'And my body . . .' She puffed air from her cheeks.

'Your body what? Managed to build a tiny brain and spine? Don't tell me the queen of body positivity is having doubts about—'

'That's just it though,' Jas said, looking even more upset. 'I know it's *stupid* to be feeling like this, *shallow*. But I feel . . . not that nice all the time. None of my clothes fit: the maternity stuff is too big and all my old stuff is too small, so I wear the same shitty, vomit-stained stuff each day. My hair is falling out like you wouldn't believe and, well, everything just feels a bit stretched and . . . not *me*.'

Daisy sat back and surveyed her friend. 'Jas, do you think you could have some post-natal depression?'

Jas raised her shoulders limply, and her words came out in a whisper. 'I don't know, maybe. I've lost track of what's normal.'

'Look, why don't you speak to Kallie?' Jas's best friend from medical school was a GP. 'See what she thinks. You might feel better for it?'

Jas bit down on her lip and nodded a few times, attempting to look positive.

'And remember, you've *just* had a baby. It's been four months – of course all your old clothes don't fit. It goes without saying that you still look wonderful; no one else sees the vomit on your top or the change in your hair. They see a new mum with a precious little baby.' Daisy moved closer and softened her voice. 'You're still the same person – you're still Dr Jas: the girl who forgot where she lived in fresher's week, a psycho in a spin class, and the only person I know who still drinks Taboo and lemonade.'

Jas laughed through tears. 'It's tasty, I'm telling you!'

'You just have another string to your bow: motherhood. And you're smashing it.'

A tear spilt out Jas's right eye and ran rapidly down her cheek.

'Is now a good time to tell you your top's on inside out?'

Jas looked down and saw the seam. 'Oh my god. You see! I'm falling apart, Daisy!' She wiped her eyes and broke into a laughter.

Daisy grinned at her across the table, then continued, her tone serious, 'I'm sorry if I haven't been here for you enough. If I do get on this course and I'm going to be living on my own, I'd actually appreciate the opportunity to hang out with a newborn occasionally. It turns out I do not have enough friends.'

'Babe, you've got loads of friends; all you need is a few good ones anyway.'

Sam

Sam had been meaning to call Daisy for weeks. The problem was that every time she picked up her phone to dial her number, she couldn't think how to start the conversation. She'd tell herself she'd call her in a few days once she'd worked out what to say. When she saw Daisy's name flash up on her screen, she stared at it for several seconds, rooted to the spot as it vibrated before her, then eventually stopped. Before she could overthink things, she pressed redial.

'Hi,' Daisy answered, her voice tentative.

'Hi.' Sam paused before stuttering over the next sentence. 'I'm sorry I missed your call – I'm just out walking, in Brockwell Park,' she added, in case Daisy mistook the activity as some sort of impressive hike.

'Oh, you okay to talk?'

'Yeah, yes.' She stopped at a wooden bench at the top of the park and sat down, tucking her trainers beneath her. 'I was going to call you—'

'Thanks for calling me back,' Daisy said at the same time.

'Sorry,' they both said in unison.

Sam cringed at the formality. 'I really was going to call. I don't really know why I haven't.'

'Yeah?'

'Yeah. I'm sorry it wasn't sooner.' Sam pushed the phone against her ear to drown out the noise of a toddler wailing nearby.

'You never replied to my message.'

'I know.' Sam looked out across the park. 'I was still angry when you sent it that night, and then, as time went by, I guess, embarrassed – embarrassed about how I treated you that day.' She could feel Daisy listening intently. 'I should have called you months ago. I've just been dealing with a lot of shit and, well, I didn't know what to say.' Sam breathed deeply, then continued, 'Dais, I'm sorry. It was really difficult to hear and . . . I just lashed out at the closest thing to me. I wish that you'd been able to tell me at the time. I'm sorry that you couldn't.'

There was silence on the other end of the line, then Daisy said, 'I could've; I should have.'

Sam's heart hammered in her chest, relieved at the softness in Daisy's voice. 'I get why you didn't: I know I've been so wrapped up in all the IVF stuff.'

'Yeah, well, it's a stupidly intense process to go through.' There was a pause on the line before Daisy added, 'If anything, I should have been around more for you this year – you've been on your own with it all a lot.'

Sam held her breath, unable to reply without dissolving into tears; she'd never felt as lonely as she had in the last year. She continued after a moment, her voice tentative, 'Daisy, I'm really sorry for what I said about . . . about you not considering keeping the baby.' Sam brought her hand to her forehead. When she'd run over the conversation in her mind in the months that followed, she was most ashamed of this moment. 'I know we're in completely different situations and . . .' Her voice broke and turned desperate and whiny. 'I just felt really awful about what I said.'

'It's fine,' Daisy said quickly. 'I think I knew deep down that you were angry about the unfairness of it all rather than at me.'

'That was it completely.' Relief flooded Sam's veins. 'Marvin said you told James?'

'Yeah. Marv was right really: I should've told him.'

Sam felt she shouldn't ask anything more on the topic. 'We've never not spoken for this long.'

'I know.'

Sam picked at an area of dry skin on her cheek, her face cold against the late November chill.

'I know it's not as big a deal, but I still don't understand why you didn't give me Blake's note – and please don't say you forgot.'

Sam swallowed and gathered her words. 'I didn't forget. You caught me off guard, and I couldn't think what to say.'

'But why lie? All I can think is that you had feelings for him.'

'What? No! There were loads of reasons. For one, I still thought there was a chance for you and James—'

'Jesus,' Daisy said, exasperated. 'I kept telling you we weren't right for each other, and you wouldn't let it go.'

'I know; it was stupid. I just really wanted it to work.'

'For who? You or me?'

Sam sighed, defeated. 'It wasn't just that: you'd literally just broken up with Jono, and Blake had come out of an eight-year relationship—'

'You said that was over six months before!'

'But eight years doesn't just disappear! I thought it'd be a disaster for both of you and that I'd be stuck in the middle.'

'So you basically think I'm a mess who doesn't know what I want.'

'I don't think you're a mess! Daisy, when have I ever said that? And you say all the time that you're unsure what you want when it comes to kids and your career – and even with Jono.'

'But you said on New Year's that it was "my problem"?'

'I was wasted on New Year's. I don't even remember that!' It dawned on Sam that Daisy must have been holding onto these words all these months. 'Look, if I said that, then I was talking out of my arse. If anything, I admire your indecisiveness.'

Daisy scoffed at this.

'I do! You're so much more of a free spirit than I am. You just feel your way through things whereas I can't cope with any alteration to *the plan*.' She sensed Daisy softening at the other end of the line. 'I thought that it was bad timing with Blake, and I didn't want it to be awkward for me at work with him. I didn't realize how much you liked him. I'm sorry; I really am.' Sam traced the outline of her eyebrows with her thumb and middle finger as she waited for Daisy to reply. 'I really think that you should text him, D. It's not too late.'

'It's been nearly a year, and I only met him twice. He's probably shacked up in the Midlands with some English teacher by now.'

'But what if he's not?' There was a pause on the line, then Sam said, 'Anyway, are we okay?'

'Yeah,' Daisy said, somewhat cooly. 'But you know who actually isn't?'

'Who?'

'Jas. I think she's struggling more than she's let on, and we've potentially been quite shit friends to her when she's needed us the most. You have an excuse, but I don't.'

'D'you know what? I'm so sick of infertility being my excuse. Tell me everything and how I can help.'

'Are you in tonight? I could come over, if you want?'

'Tonight? Yeah, of course, but . . . you're not going to get into London until, like, ten o'clock surely?'

'Ah, yes. I'm not in Whitby. I've got a lot to tell you.'

Two weeks later, Sam accompanied June on a walk to Herne Hill market. It was a cloudy but still day, the sky overcast but the temperature mild, as though the clouds provided a welcome shield.

'So I'm having the transfer next week,' Sam said shyly, pulling her new teddy bucket hat down over her straightened hair.

'I thought you might be when you said you had an appointment – I didn't like to ask.'

'That's unlike you.'

June let out a tootle of laughter. 'True. I hope I don't ask too much about it?'

Sam turned to her and frowned. 'No, never. I was only kidding.'

'And they're putting two in again, are they?'

'Yeah, our last two embryos.'

June clutched Sam's wrist and said, 'Well, I'll be praying for twins everyday this week.'

'Thank you. Twins would be the greatest thing ever. Like, obviously *so* hard for the first few years but then, we'd be done. We'd have our family. I'd have to send one over to you and Derek every day. I hope you'll be okay with that.'

June winked. 'Maybe every other day.'

Sam caught herself and swiped the conversation away with her hand. 'Anyway, enough of all that. What have you two been up to this week?'

★

They reached the market, set within a small pedestrianized street at the centre of Herne Hill, framed by coffee shops, hairdressers and grocers. Sam had always loved the village feel of it, but June seemed dismayed at how busy it was each time they went. A few years ago, there were only a few food stalls, and now there were handmade cards and silver jewellery stands, as well as expensive artisan foods and even a lobster business. They passed a new stall selling colourful babygrows all adorned with pictures of exotic animals. Sam picked one up with koala bears on and felt the softness of the fabric between her fingers, imagining it on a baby in her lap.

'They're all handmade in the UK, organic cotton,' said the lady sitting down at the back of the stall in a thick padded coat.

Sam put it back down quickly. 'They're lovely.'

June appeared at her elbow, and Sam suddenly felt observed, caught out.

'They'll all be extinct soon though, won't they?' June said, eyeing the patterns.

Sam let out a burst of laughter. 'June!'

'It's true! So many children's toys and clothes these days have elephants and tigers on; who's going to explain to them in ten years that there's none left?'

Sam turned around, guiding June away. 'You sound like Daisy.'

'Sensible, you mean? She's got a good head on her shoulders, that girl.'

'Yeah, she cares about the important stuff.'

They wandered over to a bakery, and June bought two

doughnuts for Derek and herself after Sam declined the offer. She was being extremely strict with her diet for this round.

'So, what's Daisy up to at the moment?'

'She's just found a job in a restaurant, which is good, and, yeah, she's staying at Imo's and waiting for the course to start in January.'

'Ooh, how exciting! She'll make an excellent chef. I still think about that ginger loaf she made us last year.' She picked up a cauliflower from the vegetable stall. 'D'you know what my little sister used to call these? Broccoli ghosts.'

Sam laughed. 'I like that.'

'Quite a lot of male chefs these days, aren't there? I wonder if there'll be any handsome men on the course.'

'I don't think she's looking for anything like that at the moment.'

'Just because she's not looking doesn't mean she won't want it when it arrives. Not if it's the right person. No one wants to be on their own, do they?'

'Hmm. I think some people do actually, June.'

June stopped looking at the veg and turned to Sam. 'I suppose you're right, that's just me being old-fashioned. But does Daisy? I always thought she'd make a lovely partner for someone.'

'Yeah, I kinda thought the same,' Sam said noncommittally.

'Is there no one she likes?'

'Well, there was one guy but . . . they've lost touch.'

'Then she should make contact! When she's ready. I don't mean to be pushy; her career's more important obviously.' Sam smiled at June's attempt at modernity. 'But if you find someone you have a connection with, you shouldn't let them go. I knew from our first date that I wanted to marry Derek.'

'Did you?'

'Didn't you, with Marvin?'

Sam frowned. 'Not the first date . . .'

'But early on?'

'I suppose so.'

June raised her eyebrows to signal that her point was made then carried on choosing veg. Sam stared past June at the crowds around them meandering between the stalls: parents pushing buggies and couples holding hands, sipping coffee from small black cardboard cups.

'June, I'm going to grab a drink from here – do you want anything?'

'No, thanks, love. I'll come and find you in a bit.'

Sam ordered a green smoothie and sat on one of the metal chairs outside the coffee shop. She picked up her phone, determined, and found Ben's number.

Sam: Ben, hey! Hope your weekend's going well. Could I grab Blake's number off you?

She saw that he was typing back immediately.

Ben: Sure thing.

He shared the contact and then carried on typing.

Ben: I'm seeing him tonight if you want me to pass on a msg in person?

Sam: Ha! Thanks, it's fine, I'll just message him. You in Leicester then?

Ben: Nah bruv. He's moved back to London! Assumed das why you were texting

Sam gripped her phone tighter and started devising a message before she could change her mind.

Daisy

Daisy had spent the week pacing the streets of South London, handing out her CV to cafés and restaurants and scouring social media for job openings. Eventually she was offered a waitressing job in a new high-end burger restaurant in Wandsworth town and, after some persuasion, the manager agreed to hiring her to work in the kitchen. It was only the most basic of food preparation, but she relished the opportunity to see how a kitchen was run.

It was her fourth day there, and she was starting to understand how things went. She stacked tubs of coleslaw, vegan burger patties, and roasted butternut squash in the large silver fridge ready for the lunch rush. Leaning out of the kitchen doorway, she called to the young guy restocking the drinks fridge out front in the restaurant.

'Right, Olly, I'm pretty much done.'

He was nineteen with the thick floppy hair the upper class seemed to favour.

'Sick. You in tomorrow?' he asked, turning to her with a bottle of wine in each hand, amusingly suggestive.

'Yeah, but the afternoon shift.'

'Me too. I'll catch you then.' He smiled, and Daisy saw before him the hundreds of heartbroken girls he'd leave in his wake over the next decade. He was exactly Imo's type, fifteen years ago.

She threw her apron in the laundry basket in the staff room and grabbed her rucksack, shoving the door open with an enthusiastic kick. The sky surprised her in its greyness but didn't dampen her mood. The work in the kitchen was physically draining but, so far, she'd left each shift feeling satisfied. She liked the atmosphere: the chefs were only amusingly cranky and mostly good fun, and she still found it amazing that she was getting paid for making food – admittedly not paid a lot and not making recipes of her choosing, but she felt encouraged, like she was on the right track to something.

Imo was moving to Copenhagen in three days' time, and last weekend, in typical low-key fashion, she'd hired a private canal boat on Regent's Canal with a cocktail waiter as her leaving party. At last, they were all finally able to meet Mathilde. She was completely lovely and it was immeasurably enjoyable seeing Imo nervous. Mathilde seemed significantly older when Daisy first spoke to her, not necessarily in appearance but demeanour. She had a quiet confidence and assuredness as she talked about her work and her children. However, as Daisy observed her friends on their best behaviour, Sam chatting easily to her about fashionable neighbourhoods in Copenhagen and Jas listening in as she rocked Layla on her knee, it occurred to Daisy, with a sense of relief rather than woe, that they too weren't so young anymore.

She reached her bike and bent down to unlock it. Putting her keys and phone into the front pocket of her rucksack, she saw a message from an unknown number.

Daisy. Hey. I hope you don't mind me messaging you. I heard a rumour that you didn't get my note back in January – pigeon mail can be so unpredictable. I know it's been a while but I wondered if you wanted to go for a drink. With me. Blake x

Daisy read over the message several times, put her helmet on, then took it off again. Sam must have contacted him. She unlocked her phone and read the message again before zipping it into her bag and cycling home, her heart hammering in her chest.

Entering the flat, she collapsed on the sofa and read Blake's words again. The message was a regular text, rather than WhatsApp. Even this pleased her. She stood up and paced the room. She thought about calling Sam for advice, but there was a small part of her that wasn't ready to thank her for the gesture. She needed to reply. She was going to meet him; surely she was. She'd been thinking about him for over a year. Why hadn't she just texted him herself once she'd got the book? She honestly did think it was too late – where did he even live?

Daisy: Blake, hey. Thanks for getting in touch. Bloody pigeons ah. A drink would be good. I've just finished work actually, don't suppose your afternoon is looking as conveniently sparse as mine?

As soon as she pressed send, she was filled with regret – she'd painted herself as a loner with zero plans. She should have suggested midweek like busy and sociable people do; a Sunday afternoon was a strange time for a date. But what if he was only in London for the weekend? She needed to grasp these opportunities and not let things slip by again. She stared down at her phone, willing him to reply, then groaned loudly and threw it on the sofa, marching towards the bathroom for a shower.

Scrubbing her skin with a new ferocity, her mind raced with images of him reading her message and cringing. When she stepped out of the bathroom and wrapped herself in one of Imo's luxurious white towels, she couldn't resist plodding over to check her phone.

Blake: My afternoon's officially arid. Could you get to Monument for 3pm?

'Fuck,' she said aloud.

Two hours later, Daisy was standing outside Monument station, attempting to look normal. Usually she didn't think twice about what she wore, but she'd ended up changing outfits several times, eventually settling on some black jeans and one of Imo's expensive knitted jumpers worn under her denim jacket. She felt it was better to go underdressed rather than look like she'd made a huge effort; it was Sunday afternoon after all. Standing at the station now though, she looked down at her outfit and worried she looked scruffy. She straightened the strap of the tan leather cross-body bag she'd found at the back of Imo's wardrobe, grateful to not have her rucksack at least.

'Hi,' Blake said, suddenly appearing in front of her with a smile. He too was wearing black jeans and a checked flannel jacket of which the red, green, and mustard colours blended together like autumnal leaves.

'Hey!' she said, looking up with surprise. They both assessed how to physically greet each other and, just when she was about to move forward to kiss him on the cheek, he made the decision for them by purposefully stepping to stand by her side so that they were facing the same way.

'So, I thought we should climb it?' He looked out ahead of them, and Daisy followed his line of sight. 'Unless, of course, you've done it before?'

'Monument?'

He looked at her, a mischievous smile on his lips.

'I didn't even know you could climb it. Great idea,' she said, taking him in. He was just as she remembered: unruly brown hair cut longer than most men these days, swept back behind his ears, and a short, dark layering of stubble accentuating his jawline. He was a few inches taller than her and slim, as though he didn't need to work out but, even if he did, would struggle to bulk up like some men did.

They headed in the direction of the tall stone pillar, their pace slow as they adjusted to each other.

'I take it there's steps?' she asked.

'No, it's like an abseiling situation. Or you can do it freestyle; no ropes, just shimmy up like a spider.'

She turned to him. 'I thought you were serious for a second then, like it was the ultimate climbing wall or something.'

'Would you have been game?' He put his hands in his pockets and sounded impressed.

'Not for the spider shimmy.'

He laughed. 'No. No one wants to see me do that on the first date.'

The word hung between them as they walked on to join

a small crowd of people gathered at the bottom of Monument. Daisy looked up at the column properly for the first time; there was so much of the city that she blindly walked past. The overcast sky of the morning had cleared, revealing a sheer blue expanse with picture-book fluffy white clouds dotted around the impressive stone pillar. The queue only took five minutes, and they passed the time by Daisy quizzing Blake about the history of the tourist attraction from a Wikipedia page. She was grateful for the distraction, to be able to look down at her phone instead of directly at him when they were stood still and in such close proximity. She could feel his eyes on her as she read.

'Oh, this is our moment, our *monu-moment*,' Blake said, as they were ushered through. Then in a less excited tone, 'You know it's just loads of steps, right?'

'With great views, I'm sure.'

'Good point. After you,' he said, ushering her to the start of the spiral concrete staircase. The thought of him being able to look at her from behind for three hundred and eleven steps crossed her mind, but she couldn't think of a way to object.

They began the climb, falling into an easy rhythm, and Daisy filled Blake in on her last year. She was now able to put a positive spin on her stint in Australia – Victoria and Dean messaged her occasionally on Instagram, and she'd reached a comfortable acceptance of their friendship. She felt a sense of pride in telling him about quitting her job and enrolling on the cookery course. Torn between feeling ashamed about her privilege in receiving a significant inheritance and concern over coming across as someone who enrolled on expensive courses on a whim, she opted to give loose details of the inheritance.

Blake told her that he'd been back in London since June

and was living in Clapton; a friend who'd gone travelling for the year had offered him his place to stay in for a reasonable price. As Daisy steadily climbed the steps in front of him, she felt a warm glow in her stomach at the similarity of their present living circumstances – she was so used to feeling small and left behind when people described their £500,000 flats 'with great potential'. Blake was working solely on his furniture-making at present, at a studio in Hackney that Woolf accompanied him to each day.

Daisy's competitive spirit prevented her from slowing down but, after two hundred or so steps, her heart was thrashing in her chest and they were both struggling to keep up the conversation, their breaths ragged. A tall woman and her bored-looking teenage son met them coming down the steps, and they squeezed themselves against the wall to let them pass. Daisy was about to carry on, but Blake reached for her arm and said, 'Wait, two-second breather.'

She stepped back and leant against the cool wall next to him, their shoulders touching. On their separate steps, they were almost the same height. They both rested their heads on the wall, staring ahead at the dark chamber, and their breaths fell in time with each other, gradually slowing. It felt explicit being this close to him, panting heavily. She could feel the firmness of his upper arm against hers and didn't dare turn towards him.

They set off again, Daisy's legs shaky, and ascended the last few minutes in silence. As they reached the top, she was disappointed to find a chicken wire-like fence surrounding the viewing platform. She was unsure what she was expecting; it couldn't exactly be open. She turned to Blake as he stepped out and into the light, his mouth open wide in an overt display of awe, and couldn't help but laugh at his sarcasm.

'No, it is pretty amazing,' he said more genuinely, looking around.

Daisy peered through the fence at the city around them. The sun appeared from behind a cloud and flooded the buildings with light, transforming it instantly. 'It is actually,' she said, looking up at the impressive Shard. 'It's easy to take it for granted when you live here.'

Blake leant on the fence next to her and looked out at the view. 'Did you miss London when you were in Australia?'

Daisy shrugged. 'I wasn't really there that long. Although, I was in Whitby afterwards, so actually I was away for a while . . .' She let go of the fence and turned towards him. 'There were definitely things I missed: friends, obviously. And, yeah, I'd still say London's my favourite city in the world.'

'Big statement.'

'Yeah. I think I just realized that now.' She looked back out at the skyline, now shadowed as the sun retreated again. 'But I also don't think I want to live here forever.'

Blake seemed to study her, assessing her face for something unspoken. 'You say that like it's a bad thing?'

She felt shy under his examination. 'I have a kind of low-level panic going on about where I'll end up living. I've felt torn between here and Yorkshire for years, a bit lost between the two of them. And then I find myself looking at flats for forty grand in places like Armenia and convincing myself I could make a life there.'

Blake laughed. 'I reckon a lot of people in London are the same; everyone talks about leaving all the time, but then – like me – they're drawn back for one reason or another. I think it's best not to overthink geography; you'll find your place, in time.'

They squeezed past other people on the platform and started to make their way around the small perimeter.

'What about you?'

'What, London forever?' Blake said, finding humour in the question. 'Aah, I dunno. Not sure I'm a city boy, deep down. But where I'm living now in Clapton is pretty sweet, has a kind of village feel to it – living *and* working there, I can get away with hardly ever coming central. It took *a lot* of courage to come here today.'

She laughed. 'Did you have to pop a couple of Valiums before you got on the tube?'

'A couple? Try a bottle, love.'

'Ah, you sounded really Leicester then,' Daisy said, smiling widely.

'Did I? I can still hear your Yorkshire twang actually; you've not lost it.' He reached out and moved a strand of hair that had blown over her forehead, tucking it behind her ear and taking longer than needed to extract his fingers. She watched him, feeling strangely at ease, as though he'd performed the action a thousand times.

'Would you like me to take your picture?' said a smiling blond man with a strong, possibly German accent. He was wearing a full Dolce and Gabbana tracksuit, the logo splattered repeatedly over his entire body like a human advert.

Blake and Daisy looked at each other.

Blake turned to the tracksuit. 'Yeah, man. Thanks, that'd be great.'

Daisy raised her eyebrows at him, and he gave her a defiant

smile, as though it wasn't a strange situation at all. 'It'll have to be your phone though – mine's an ancient Nokia with no camera.'

'You're kidding?' Daisy said, digging around in her bag and then passing the phone to the man. She'd been thinking of coming off social media and getting an old phone for years.

Blake draped his arm around her, and she angled herself into his body as they both smiled at the camera.

'I take a few,' the man said, stepping further back and kneeling down for a different angle.

'Oh!' Daisy looked up at Blake and laughed at the photographer's enthusiasm.

'Beautiful!' he said, passing her the phone back.

'Thank you.' She glanced at the last photo taken, angling the camera to show Blake. It wasn't bad, but Daisy's smile was close-mouthed, wearing thin after posing for too many.

'Smashed it,' Blake said.

She put her phone back inside her bag. 'So' – she folded her arms and tilted her head as she looked up at him – 'what next?'

They agreed to a pub outside of the City, since it was a ghost town on Sundays. Blake had to be home to feed Woolf by seven, so they headed east so that he was closer and wouldn't have to rush off too early.

'You should have brought her,' Daisy said.

'Ah, I would have, but she gets jealous easily.'

'Is that right?'

They walked towards Liverpool Street, and Blake stopped suddenly in the middle of the pavement. 'Shall we get Boris bikes and go a bit further afield? There's some really nice pubs in Hackney. Unless that's really annoying for you to get home from?'

'Err.' Daisy hesitated as she calculated her way back to Putney. 'No, that's fine. Let's do it.'

They hired two bikes from Liverpool Street station and made their way out east of the City. The roads were quiet with it being Sunday, and Blake seemed to know a picturesque route, weaving along lines of beautiful Victorian houses and the bustling flower market on Columbia Road as it was closing up. Some of the houses boasted Christmas trees in their windows, despite it only being late November, and Daisy smiled, thinking of her parents' reaction – they insisted on putting their tree up on Christmas Eve.

On quieter roads, they attempted to cycle side by side so that they could continue talking, with Blake dropping behind when they reached traffic. His seat was too low for him, and Daisy kept wanting to laugh when she got close; he reminded her of a teenager on a BMX.

He told her about the places he'd lived in London, his year in Lisbon, and about an eccentric housemate in Devon. She felt he had considerably more life experience than her, more stories to tell. It occurred to her that her parents would like him, then she felt embarrassed for such a thought on a first date, imagining him reading her mind.

After twenty minutes, they reached Victoria Park. The bare trees stood prominently against the pale winter sky, a few with patchy brown leaves stubbornly clinging on, and the grass gleamed a brilliant green after weeks of recent rain. Blake cycled ahead, leading the way through the maze of paths to the north of the park. Occasionally, he looked back at Daisy with a wide grin, and she couldn't help but smile back. They passed young families heading to the playground and groups of young people crowding onto benches with coke-sized cans of beer and laugher that carried far.

They docked their bikes at the edge of the park, giddily clambering off like children returning from riding their new Christmas presents around the village, then walked up through Homerton to Chatsworth Road. The quaint street was lined with cafés and quirky independent shops. It was approaching five o'clock, and many of the shops had already closed or not opened at all, but there was still a nice feel to it. Daisy peered in the shop windows at the trendy homewares and observed the numerous fashionable people on vintage bikes, thinking how Sam would fit in well. They came across a plant shop that was still open, its windows lined with rows of exotic greens you'd usually see in hip hotels.

'I love these kinds of plants,' Daisy said, stopping to have a look. 'I know nothing about them, but I'd love to have one of those houses that's overflowing with greenery.'

'You should see my current place,' Blake said. Daisy couldn't think of anything suitable in response to this but, luckily, he continued, 'Legitimate jungle. I think that's why Chris wanted me to stay: water all the bastards.'

They stopped at a small café-come-bar that had tables on the street with red checked tablecloths; it felt like they were on a city break in some hip European neighbourhood. The conversation continued to flow easily, buoyed by their beers, and they walked on to another pub on the canal.

'This place is amazing,' Daisy said, taking in the large beer garden looking out onto the water as they sat down. 'I can't believe we're in Hackney. Hackney? Or Clapton?'

'Clapton is in Hackney,' he said, finding her amusing again. 'Can I ask you something?'

She pulled an awkward face. 'Sure.'

He folded his arms and sat up straighter as he said, 'How come you never messaged me? Once you finally got my number? Sam explained the whole thing.'

Daisy tilted her head to one side as she rotated the beer bottle on the table, twisting it around in circles and examining the pool of moisture left below it on the wood. 'I thought about it; of course I did.' She looked up at him. 'But I thought it was too late. I wasn't sure you'd remember me, and I thought I might have imagined a connection between us.' She returned to rotating the bottle and stared at the table.

He reached out and steadied her hand, keeping his hand around hers. 'I don't make a habit of buying books to ask women out.'

'You bought it?' she asked, laughing. 'It looked *read*.'

He took his hand away and drank from his pint, looking past her into the distance as he did. 'Had to rough it up a little, fold a few corners over.'

Daisy laughed loudly.

'I read it ages ago when I was working my way through this list: "100 books to read before you die" kind of thing; no idea where my copy is. A lot of effort went into that, and bloody Sam had to mess it all up,' he said without a hint of anger.

'But here we are,' Daisy said, drinking from her beer as she looked at him. 'It was a pretty cool way to be asked out.'

'I thought so.'

'Plus, I did read it. It's actually one of the reasons I applied for the cookery course; it made me really determined to sort my life out.'

'Really?' he said with wonder. 'I liked her whole premise of just needing some sort of living to get by: to have a space of your own to enable you to create. That's kind of how I try to live my life.'

Daisy opened her mouth to speak, but Blake interrupted.

'And I'm pretty sure I'm her target audience: white male, up against it all.'

Daisy laughed. She could not imagine having this conversation with Jono or James. 'Well, I feel like things have shifted since it was written. Women are now able to get jobs and have opportunities – not as many, but a hell of a lot more than a hundred years ago – but people are unhappier than ever. It's like we're doing the money-making part, we've got the room of our own, but we've got no time or energy to use it effectively. So maybe more burnt-out men should read it. Isn't the suicide rate highest in men in their forties?'

A shade passed over Blake's face, and Daisy wondered if she'd said too much. 'I'm actually not forty for eighteen months, so . . .'

She suppressed a laugh. 'Oh, well, not at all relevant.'

They finished their third round, and Blake dug out his battered old phone to look at the time. 'D'you want to eat?'

'Erm, yeah, always. But what about Woolf?'

'I'll have to pop in, but it's only around the corner – you could come with? Then we can get food after?'

'*After?*' Daisy clarified, the beers giving her the confidence to tease. 'Oh, after feeding Woolf, I see.'

He smiled as they stood up. 'Who's Woolf?'

★

It was pitch black outside by the time they left the pub, and Blake directed them to walk along the canal, quaintly lit up with streetlamps. Daisy took her blue beanie out her bag, pulling it down over her ears against the evening chill.

'It's this one here with all the plants,' Blake said, indicating a navy canal boat twenty feet away.

'A boat?' Daisy gasped. 'You never once said you lived on a barge.'

'Didn't I? Yeah, this is my mate Chris's longboat.'

Daisy stopped in front of it, running her eyes over its length. They heard barking from within, and Blake stepped down onto the front, reaching for his keys in his pocket.

'It's amazing,' said Daisy, in genuine awe. 'And massive. I see what you mean about all the plants.' The roof was full of plastic trays and ceramic pots of various flowers and stems.

'Yeah, it's pretty cool. D'you want to have a look in?' Blake asked as he unlocked the small door and flicked some lights on within. Woolf rushed out, and he bent down to greet her.

'Is that okay?'

''Course.' He reached out to help her down onto the boat.

She took his hand, stepping down and squeezing into the doorway beside him to peer in. The walls were lined with whitewashed wooden slats, making the space feel much bigger than she'd expected. Kitchen units made of mismatched reclaimed wood lined the near wall, and opposite was a small table with two wooden chairs painted in a bright orange. A small built-in sofa sat next to the kitchen, facing a grand wood-burner with Woolf's basket nearby, and a partition wall with a porthole cutout separated the bedroom area. Daisy could see some white sheets and a shelf of books above the bed. It was one of the most wonderful homes she'd ever seen.

'I can't believe there's a wood-burner,' were the first words she found. 'It's . . . incredible.' She turned to him, his face only inches away, and realized that he was watching her. His delicate smile faded when her eyes locked on his, and she felt her chest constrict under his scrutiny. Slowly, he raised his right hand and brought it to her mouth, gently tracing the length of her lower lip with his forefinger, as though it was a precious jewel he'd longed to touch. Her breathing quickened as his finger lingered, then his eyes moved back to hers and his hand dropped. Suddenly she was reaching for him. Their mouths met, and she felt the softness of his lips and his hands on her waist, clutching her to him. His lips moved down to her neck as her hands found his hair and their bodies pressed firmly against each other.

'Blake, we should . . .'

He straightened up to meet her lips again. 'We should what?'

'Get food,' Daisy said dreamily.

'Get food,' he repeated. 'We should get food.' He kissed her one last time, then stepped back, sweeping his hair back off his face and staring at her with a smile.

They both laughed and looked away.

'This wasn't actually my plan, by the way,' Blake said, stepping inside the cabin and reaching for Woolf's food from a kitchen cupboard.

'What, you really thought getting me back to this babe magnet wouldn't be any kind of aphrodisiac?'

He laughed as he poured the biscuits out for Woolf and changed her water. 'True. I knew exactly what I was doing.'

She leant her head on the doorframe, taking him in. 'So,

what do you want to do for dinner? Could we pick something up and eat it here?'

They ordered a Lebanese takeaway from a place nearby, then opened a bottle of red wine and moved the table and chairs to the small outside space at the back of the boat, draping blankets over their laps. Lights in the surrounding boats and tower blocks flickered on like fireflies as people made their way home. Daisy borrowed a thicker coat, recognizing the black puffer jacket from last New Year's Eve and gladly wrapping herself in his scent. As they headed out to pick up the food, Blake draped his arm around her shoulders – a new ease having developed between them – and they stopped to kiss several times on the ten-minute walk, Woolf watching them with confusion from the pavement.

Arriving back, Blake busied himself inside, lighting the wood-burner while Daisy poured more wine and found plates and cutlery from the small kitchen. A few stars were visible on the vast navy sky, blinking through the city glow, and the air was full of distant chatter from people on surrounding boats or walking the tow path. They unpacked the takeaway, and Daisy realized how hungry she was, grabbing a flatbread and loading it with baba ganoush.

They finished most of the food, chatting about their upbringings. Daisy usually dreaded explaining that her parents were academics; men tended to bristle and either comment on her extraordinary privilege or subtly belittle Graham's historical subject of expertise: the Yorkshire coast. But Blake only seemed interested, asking several questions about Graham's books and Jemima's work at York University. She sensed he was more comfortable asking questions than talking about himself.

He cleared the plates and passed her another fleecy blanket to wrap around her shoulders.

'I'm actually pretty warm, apart from my feet.'

'Pass them here,' he said, indicating her black boots.

She hesitated, then pulled the boots off and settled her feet on Blake's lap.

He took hold of them, wrapping them in a spare blanket.

'Thanks,' Daisy said, gathering herself as she adjusted to his touch.

He ran his right hand around her ankle, then traced it up her trousers, grasping the back of her calf before sliding back it down. Daisy felt her whole body respond, from her mouth opening slightly to her back arching.

'Sorry, carpenter hands,' he said, staring at her with a new seriousness.

'Can I ask you something?' she managed to say.

Hearing his own words from the pub a few hours earlier, he smiled. 'Sure.'

'Why did you leave on New Year's Eve?'

His hand stopped moving on her leg, and he brought it back to holding her feet. 'Ah.' He took a sip of wine and then looked back at her. 'Nothing major, but maybe not a conversation for right now.'

Daisy blinked and looked down, 'Oh.' She wondered if he wanted to challenge her about James but didn't want to destroy the moment.

'Sorry.' He brought one hand up and ran it through his hair. 'No, it was basically a family emergency. Just, not a good one, so I don't want to—'

'Oh, Blake, I'm sorry. Honestly, we don't have to discuss it.'

'It was nothing to do with you. I should have said goodbye, I know. I had to leave really quickly, and I couldn't find you.'

''Course, no. I just wondered. I kind of sensed that you were annoyed at me on the night – there was that guy, James . . .'

He shrugged. 'I could tell there was something weird happening there, but I figured you could handle it yourself. I didn't want to be that guy. You know the one: "Is there a problem here, sir?"'

Daisy smiled bitterly. 'I really thought I'd fucked it with you.'

He looked back at her. 'Anyway, here we are.'

'Here we are. Pretty average first date.'

He stroked her ankle as they stared at each other, their smiles fading.

'I think we should go inside,' Blake said.

'I think that's a good idea,' she said, and with that, the decision about her staying the night was made.

Woolf looked up from her basket as they entered the cabin, pleased for the company. The small space was now surprisingly warm from the wood-burner, and Daisy removed Blake's coat, hanging it on a hook by the door and settling herself on the narrow sofa with her glass of wine. They were onto their second bottle, and she was aware of a pleasant glow within her. Blake hung his checkered jacket on the next hook along and bent down to inspect the fire. Seeing it was now glowing a vibrant red, he sat down beside Daisy, one leg angled on the sofa to allow him to face her.

Neither of them spoke for a moment, and Daisy was aware of her heart rate quickening; she could feel her pulse even in her fingertips. Blake took hold of her wine glass then, gently releasing it from her hand and placing it on the floor behind, before looking back at her. Their bodies moved towards each other at the same time, grasping each other with renewed fervour as their lips connected. Blake tugged Daisy's jumper over her head and returned to kissing her as soon as she reappeared. She knelt forward and deftly removed both of his tops in one go, revealing his toned chest with a smattering of dark hair and faint tan lines still visible on his upper arms.

She noticed a thin silver chain around his neck with the letter A on and was temporarily distracted, but then she was helping him with her jeans, unfastening the button fly herself before Blake stood up to remove them. He did this slowly, ceremoniously even, dropping her clothes to the floor and staring at her. She looked up at him, feeling exposed, still sitting down below. Sensing this possibly, he held out his hand and pulled her up to him. They stood before each other a moment before Daisy reached out, placing her hands on his chest and kissing him gently. Blake ran his hands up her sides, wrapping one in her hair and grasping the back of her head as he slowly kissed her. He moved his lips down her neck and chest, finding her nipple through the mesh lining of her black bra.

Standing upright again, he said, 'This sofa is fucking ridiculous,' eyeing the three-foot-wide cushion below them. Grasping her waist, he lifted Daisy up, and she responded instantly, wrapping her legs around his waist and kissing him more urgently as he carried her through to the bedroom area. A loud crack tore through the air as Daisy's head clipped a lowered beam in the entrance to the bedroom.

'Oh, fuck!' Blake said.

Daisy brought her hand to the back of her head and clamped

her eyes shut as the pain radiated through her skull. 'Ow,' she said quietly.

'Oh god, Daisy. I'm sorry.' He laid her down on the bed beneath him, and she started laughing through the pain.

Blake started laughing too as he knelt above her, his hand clamped over his mouth. 'Shit, that was totally my fault.'

She opened her eyes and blinked back tears. 'It was going so well, as well.'

'It really was!' He laughed.

She traced the outline of his face above hers, mentally capturing the moment as they smiled at each other. She kissed him again, then firmly rolled him to her left, pressing her body on top of his as she said, 'Okay, I've recovered.'

Sam

Sam put the phone on loudspeaker to allow her to load the washing machine as she listened to Daisy. It was the first week of her Christmas holidays, her school having broken up exceptionally early this year.

'We've basically been living at each other's places since the first date,' Daisy gushed.

'What, every night?'

'No, we've spent one or two apart.'

'One or two!' Sam stood to turn the machine on and picked the phone back up, needing to be closer to the words. 'What does he do with the dog when he stays at Imo's?'

'We usually stay at his but, yeah, Woolf has come for

a sleepover a couple of times. Do not tell Imo! Woolf's the most well-behaved dog I've ever known.'

'I'm sure Imo won't even notice she's been.' Sam started wiping the kitchen surfaces, unable to sit still. 'God, I can't believe it. You're basically a couple.'

'It's only been two weeks. There's still plenty of time for me to fuck it up.'

'Daisy, you're not a fucker-upper. You've just been with the wrong people.'

'Maybe,' she said, sounding unconvinced. 'Did you ever notice he always wears a necklace with the letter "A" on?'

'Nope. Why don't you just ask him what it's for? He's a bit Clapton-cool, isn't he? It's probably just the first letter of the alphabet to be ironic.'

'That'd be funny. I don't want to seem nosy by asking.' She sighed. 'But, generally, yeah, I feel all glowy.'

'*Glowy*, says the girl with an English Lit degree.'

'But I do! And it's all down to you for getting in touch with him. I was being stubborn; I should have messaged him myself.'

'Mate, if it wasn't for me, you guys might have been together since January.'

'Hmm, I don't know now. I'm not saying you were right, but I feel like I've worked a lot of stuff out this year and I'm "in a better place to receive love".' She recited the phrase woodenly, as though reading it aloud.

'Well, I'm just really happy for you. Now tell me more about the course. I need to wee, by the way – don't be alarmed if you hear a tinkle.'

Sam sat down on the toilet, gripping the phone to her right ear as she listened to Daisy. Over the last couple of years, she'd developed a low-level fear of going to the toilet; a fear of finding blood in her underwear after two weeks of hoping against such an occurrence. But this time, she was so engaged with Daisy's news, the sight caught her off guard. She stared down at the streak of dark crimson, then touched herself, and her breath quickened at the obscene redness on her fingertips.

'Daisy.' Sam gasped. 'I'm bleeding.'

'What?'

'There's . . . there's blood. My period; it's come early again.'

'Oh, Sam . . .'

Sam's voice shook as she said, 'It's over.' She hung up and stared intently at the blood on her fingertips. She hated herself for hoping. Why would it be any different this time? Her body could not do what it was supposed to. A numbness spread over her, constricting her chest. No tears came. She sat for a moment, staring at the black-and-white tiles on the floor of the bathroom. The thought of calling Marvin or her mum or even the clinic threatened to loosen the restraints that were currently holding her together. After a moment, she stood up and wiped herself, then stared down at the bloodied tissue in the toilet bowl before flushing. She didn't reach for sanitaryware. She wanted to feel the blood, the wetness that kept her from motherhood; she wanted to mourn it.

Moments later, she found herself on the lawn in her slippers. It was still early, and there was a cool mist settling over the surrounding houses like a Victorian smog. She stepped forward to the white plastic chair in the middle of the small lawn and sat down. There was a familiar hum of traffic combined with some indecipherable music from a nearby house, and the combination set her teeth on edge. One of the flats above theirs had a window open, and the sound of plates and cutlery clashing added to the cacophony.

She looked down at her hands, the nails bitten down and the skin raw around her right thumbnail. The desire to hold a child in her arms had become greater over the summer; to have the weight and warmth of a baby against her, or the chubby fist of a toddler enclosed in her palm as it tottered below by her knees, looking up at her trustingly. She was tired of the emptiness: of her hands, her arms, her womb.

Sam didn't notice the sound of the back door or Derek's distinct slow footsteps, the tap of his stick on the hard ground. He hovered at the fence, and she turned to him eventually, as if in a dream. She noticed deep furrows in his forehead as his small brown eyes studied her. Then he glanced towards the floor, a visible tightening of his jaw as the news settled over him, her demeanour apparently transparent. To Sam's surprise, he turned around and walked back to their flat, leaving her to stare at the grass again. She hoped he hadn't gone to get June to come and talk to her. She needed silence.

Derek reappeared five minutes later. He let himself through the adjoining gate and set a cup of tea on a chair in front of Sam, then placed a blue tartan blanket around her shoulders. Sam looked down at the material draped over her chest and realized she was cold. She pulled it tighter around herself, the wool soft against her fingertips, then looked down at the pink floral mug – her favourite and one the Wilsons never failed to select for her – and tears finally came.

'Thank you, Derek,' she said quietly, not looking away from the mug.

'Do you mind if I sit with you while you have your tea, or would you rather be alone?' he asked.

Sam sniffed loudly. 'You can sit with me, if you like.'

He pulled up a chair and carefully sat himself down a couple of feet away from her, facing the same direction away from their flats. She turned to Derek, expecting him to ask something, but instead he gestured to her tea then leant back, looking out at the garden. They sat and listened to the hum of life around them for a few minutes, then Sam picked up the mug, the warm ceramic comforting in her hands, and took a sip of the hot sugary liquid with a loud slurping sound.

'You need some flowers out here, pet,' Derek said, interrupting her spiralling thoughts. He stood up, and Sam realized that tears had run down to her neck. She sniffed and wiped her right cheek, looking around the garden like she hadn't noticed it before. They never did get around to planting anything over the summer.

Derek took a folded handkerchief from his trouser pocket and held it out to her. 'It's clean, I promise.'

Sam took the pale-yellow cotton square, examining the embroidered blue trim before wiping her face and nose with it.

'Let me give you the grand tour of ours,' Derek said, holding out his elbow for her to take. 'We can get some ideas for yours for the spring.'

Sam looked up at him, unable to show any enthusiasm. He looked down at her, waiting, and she obeyed, standing and linking her arm in his, the blanket still draped around her shoulders. She felt some blood slide out of her as she stood, and wondered absently if it had seeped onto her leggings.

They squeezed through the small gate into Derek and June's garden.

'Now, it's not the best month to show it off, but I always

make sure there's colour through to autumn and winter.' He led her over to a vibrant purple flower, and they bent down to examine it. Derek's soft words, so filled with effort as his mouth had the soul duty of forming them, washed over Sam and instilled a particle of warmth. They headed over to a corner of the garden, and Derek let go of Sam's arm to take hold of another flower, cupping it gently in his pale hand like a fragile bird. He didn't speak at first, and Sam waited patiently, staring at the large pink freckled petals, its green stems threaded through latticing on the wall like veins between bones.

'We planted this one for Sarah, a year after we lost her,' Derek said. 'I replant the same every few years, when it gets a bit tired looking. Got used to her, I suppose.'

Sam reached out and took hold of one of the flowers, fingering the soft, speckled petals as though they were flesh. She felt her eyes filling with tears again and managed a smile as she said, 'It's lovely.' She dropped the flower and pulled the blanket tighter around her. 'I don't know how you did it, you and June . . . to come back from that.'

Derek reached out to a larger flower near the wall. 'We're not the same as before her, but you do, eventually, come back,' he said, nodding his head several times as he examined the flower. 'You have to find the beauty in the world, remind yourself of the good parts.' He took some small clippers from his pocket and cut the largest flower at the stem, then handed it to Sam, filling her palm entirely. 'It's tempting to turn your back on life, but you have to try not to.'

Sam bit her lip, her tears falling heavily. She looked down at the pink petals. 'Thank you, Derek. What's it called – the flower?'

He linked her arm as he said, 'Oh, it's just a clematis – *Clematis cirrhosa*. It was late November when we lost her, so we wanted something that flowered on the date, something beautiful.'

Realizing the date must have just passed, Sam wiped her eyes with the handkerchief and gripped Derek's arm as they moved on to the next plant, the soft petals a comfort in her left hand.

Daisy

Daisy arrived at Sam's half an hour after the phone call, her hair still damp under her beanie. She let herself in with the key she still had from staying there earlier in the year. The flat looked the same, with an eerie silence about it. She reached the kitchen at the back and spotted them. Derek seemed to be holding Sam up, or perhaps it was the other way around, his walking stick resting against the fence as he reached for the leaves of a fern in front of them. A tartan blanket around Sam drowned her narrow frame.

Daisy opened the back door and stepped out. They both looked up at the noise, and Derek waved.

Sam gave a faint smile and looked at the ground as she said, 'Hey.'

'Hi,' Daisy said. 'I thought you might like some company? I picked up Aunty Jocelyn's car on the way over, so we've got it for the day if we want it.'

Sam let go of Derek's arm and said, 'Ah, Daisy, I dunno. I just kind of want to curl up—'

'I know you do, but I really think in moments like this, really *shit* moments . . .' Their eyes met, and Daisy paused before saying, 'it's best to be by the sea.'

Sam folded her arms and didn't agree or object.

Daisy continued in a softer voice, 'I thought I could drive us out to Camber Sands for a walk; we don't even have to talk.'

'Camber's very beautiful,' Derek said, raising his eyebrows at Sam.

Sam looked down at a flower in her hand. 'Okay, maybe just for a bit.'

They parked up in the sparse grassy car park by the beach, its vast expanse a clue to the masses that would arrive in August. Daisy paid at the meter and placed the flimsy paper ticket on the wide dashboard of the BMW. Sam was slow to get out the car, seemingly weighed down by this continued emptiness in her life. They set off towards the beach, Daisy privately panicking that she'd made the wrong decision in bringing her here, that she was pushing her own love for the ocean onto Sam. It was a cold day, the wind blasting towards them from the sea, and the drive was longer than she'd remembered; Sam hadn't wanted to talk or listen to music, so they'd sat in an unyielding silence.

They reached the beach, and Daisy exhaled slowly, feeling instant pleasure at the altered proprioception as her trainers sunk luxuriously into the pliable sand. The tide was far out, and there were only a few dog walkers and couples on the seemingly endless stretch before them. The grey sky cast a cool hue on the sand, turning from golden to clay-like, reminiscent of childhood sandpits. They fell in step beside each other, and

Daisy tried not to keep looking across at Sam as the wind howled in the distance.

'Tell me more about Blake,' Sam said after a few minutes.

Daisy peered across at her from beneath her hat. 'Really?'

'Yeah, I need to hear nice things.'

So Daisy told her, reeling off the remaining details of their two-week 'relationship'.

When she'd finished speaking, Sam squeezed the back of Daisy's upper arm and said, 'I'm glad. Really, really glad.'

'Still very early days,' Daisy said, as was habit, though she didn't feel the usual resignation to it all ending imminently this time.

They continued walking with the wind against their faces.

Sam pulled her yellow hood over her hat, her face shrinking within the layers. 'I haven't told Marvin yet.' She looked down at the sand kicked up by their footsteps. 'I need to do it in person, when he gets home tonight.'

'I know you always hate that part.'

Sam grasped each elbow, holding herself together. 'I love him so much.' She locked eyes with Daisy. 'But all of this is . . . I read that you're three times more likely to break up after failed IVF.'

'Not you and Marv; that won't happen.'

'It better not.' Sam stopped and turned to the sea, then cast her eyes up towards the sky, littered with thick clouds.

Daisy followed her gaze and inwardly cursed the lack of sunshine.

'Can we walk to the sea?' Sam asked.

Daisy stooped to pick up some flat stones, and they headed out towards the water, the sand becoming hard then claggy. They stopped a few metres away, and Sam stood with her hands in her pockets as Daisy skimmed several stones out under the waves.

'Thanks for bringing me here,' Sam said quietly, still looking out at the sea.

Daisy spun around after a successful triple-bouncer. ''Course.' She gestured to the water. 'I always find it helps.'

'I think it reminds us how small we are,' Sam said.

'And it's beautiful, though not so much on a day like this.'

Sam wiped at the corners of her eyes with her forefingers and sniffed. 'That's the shittest thing in all this.'

Daisy walked back to her, eyebrows lowered into a question.

'I just feel like life is passing me by, like I'm missing the beauty of it and . . . I can't enjoy it anymore, even the good bits.'

Sam bent her legs and squatted down, placing her right hand in the sticky wet sand and watching as it engulfed her pale fingers. Daisy squatted down next to her, examining the hand like they'd stumbled upon a rare find as she waited for Sam to continue.

'I'm sorry if I've been a bit . . .' Sam stared at her hand as she said quietly '. . . horrible this year.' Daisy was about to laugh and disagree, but Sam looked at her directly. 'Snappy with you, then. Unkind.' She looked away, and Daisy wasn't sure what to say. Sam continued, 'I think infertility makes people a bit selfish, generally. It's not an excuse, but it does take over your whole brain and, well, there isn't always enough space left for other things that really matter.'

Daisy bit her lip as she considered her fragile friend before her. 'Too many beetroot recipes floating around in there?'

'Something like that.' Sam smiled for a second, then stood up and flicked the sand and water from her hand before wiping it on her coat. 'So, yeah, I'm sorry if I've been a shit friend this year.'

Daisy stood too. 'No need to get all dramatic about it,' she said with faux awkwardness, trailing her boot in the sand as though to detract from their emotions.

It made Sam smile.

They carried on up the beach, not talking, each lost in their own thoughts.

After a few minutes, Daisy asked, 'Have you got any more counselling sessions booked?' She knew Sam and Marvin had been to a few, preferring these to the support groups.

'You only get one per NHS round, so we've used our two. I looked into paying, but it's £90 a session.' She shook her head again to indicate this wasn't an option for them.

'What about online? You said you were following some good accounts now; could you chat to anyone on there about all this — you know, people who've been through the same?'

'Maybe,' Sam said, insinuating that she most likely wouldn't. 'There's all these people online, in the "trying to conceive" community, who call each other *warriors*. Fertility warriors, like it's a battle.'

Daisy asked with a soft voice, 'What's wrong with that?'

'Nothing but . . . I don't feel like a warrior. I don't feel brave; I feel *tired*.' Sam's voice broke, and a gust of wind whipped her hair around her face. She thrust the strands behind her ears. 'It just feels like everything's fallen apart this year: like it's affected *everything* in my life.' She turned her back on the sea and looked out at the beach, watching as two women caught up to their excitable Dalmatian, laughing as they tackled a ball from its teeth. 'I can't even remember who I was before all this. I think I used to be fun.'

Daisy took hold of her elbow gently. 'You still are.'

Sam smiled through tears as she said, 'I don't feel it anymore.' They walked on a few more steps in silence. 'Sometimes I can't even remember why I want kids. People often ask me – it's like they can't understand why I'm so upset – but I don't have an extraordinary reason. You don't have to want them more than the next person for it to still fucking hurt when you can't have them.' She looked at Daisy with pleading eyes. 'Maybe I just think I want them because that's what's expected of me or because I'm scared I won't *fit* in this world without them.'

Daisy looked at Sam properly then, this crumpled version of her person. There was a sadness in her eyes that ran so deep it frightened Daisy. She searched her gaze and said her name softly, 'Sam, surely you don't think that? The world has changed; look at Imo and me – we probably won't have children – what do you see when you look at us?'

Sam looked down at the sand, stepping backwards. 'It's different for you two—'

'How is it different?'

'Because you've never desperately wanted them. Your heart won't drop through the floor for the next forty years every time someone asks if you have kids.'

Daisy set her mouth in a line. 'There's your answer: your heart wouldn't hurt if you didn't truly want them.'

Tears spilt down Sam's cheeks, and her face crumbled.

Daisy added, 'But I don't want you to be thinking there's no place in the world for women without kids—'

'Of course, I don't think that. I don't know what I'm trying to say.' Sam sniffed and wrung her hands. 'I think, sometimes I'm hoping I'll have some kind of epiphany and realize kids aren't all that, and I'll stop wanting them so badly.'

Daisy linked Sam's arm, and they continued walking along the shoreline.

'What do you want to do next?' Daisy asked. 'Deep down, honestly, if it was just your decision and there was no societal or financial pressures.'

Sam looked down at the prints her shoes were making in the sand. 'It's not just my decision.'

'Yes, but, it's at least half yours.'

Sam sighed and thought for a moment. 'You know when we came up for Ida's funeral and we were in the pub with all your family?'

'Yeah. Well, only one brother but—'

'I know it was a sad day for you, but I looked around at everyone when we were outside and I thought *this*. *This* is what I want: *a family*. It always seems so quiet with just me and Mum – even before Dad died, always the three of us.'

'You've always said you wanted a big family.'

'Right, and even if a round of IVF ends up miraculously working, I don't want just one kid, so realistically how many rounds are we going to have to do?' Sam stopped walking then, turning to stare out at the sea. 'I just don't think I can carry on like this, on this endless rollercoaster, because I know there's a point where I won't come back from it, not fully.'

Daisy turned and opened her mouth to speak, but Sam interrupted.

'Daisy, I want to adopt.' She seemed to grow a little taller with the words, the confidence of the statement propelling her towards the sky an inch and her mouth set in firm determination.

Daisy nodded slowly, her eyes flicking between Sam's. 'Well, I think that'd be amazing.' She saw Sam's face switch to concern again. 'What?'

'But I know that Marvin's desperate for our own kids and—'

'Sam.' Daisy's voice was stern. 'You're the most important thing in the world to Marv. You've just told me that this is basically breaking you. When did you last feel truly happy?'

Sam raised her eyes to search through her brain.

'Marvin married you for you, not for your incredible genes. He worries about you all the time. Just talk to him – I really don't think he'll want you to carry on with this if he knows how you truly feel.'

Sam wiped at her eyes again. 'Maybe.' After a pause she said, 'Can you remember at our wedding when we were talking about the next decade? You said your mum described her thirties as *that time everything was on fire?*'

Daisy smiled at the memory. 'Yes, I do. And she wasn't even battling infertility or being completely fucking lost in life.'

They walked a few more steps before Sam said, 'I didn't really think much of it at the time – I thought our generation might be different – but . . . I think she was pretty much spot on.'

Daisy linked Sam's arm again. 'Well, we're only three years into our thirties; plenty of time to put those fires out.'

summer iv

Sam

Sam reached the Ritzy cinema first so took the opportunity to get beers at the bar and secure a table in the corner. After a brief glimpse of sunshine over the weekend, it had been raining all week, and the cinema was busy with people shaking off their macs and umbrellas and cursing the British weather. Marvin arrived on time and took a moment to scan the tables for her. She decided not to help him with a wave and instead sat still, smiling broadly at him until he placed her. He was wearing a green hooded jacket, rucksack, and new round metal glasses that were dotted with raindrops. He spotted her at last and smiled, pushing his glasses up his nose and heading over.

'Hey,' they said at the same time, kissing briefly.

He removed his jacket and bag, placing them messily under the table, then sat down and rubbed his hands together as he assessed the menu. They ordered burgers and filled each other in on their days at work before excitedly circling back to the adoption process, as was customary these days.

'So the open day's 2 to 6 p.m. on Saturday?' Sam asked.

'Yeah, four hours!'

'I'm nervous,' Sam said.

'Me too. I think they'll try and scare us off.'

'I don't think we'll be too shocked though; we've done our background reading.'

It had been a welcome switch that Marvin had taken the lead in all of the research and admin that came with adoption. Sam had felt herself slowly unfurling over the last few months. It wasn't a return to herself three years ago, nor was it an incredible metamorphosis – it was a glimmer of someone whom she recognized. She still felt the weight of grief, but it had transformed from a whole suit of lead to perhaps a few buttons that she carried around in her pocket, sometimes running her fingers over them to remember the pain and to accept that it might always be with her. And this transformation left more room for joy in her life.

When she'd returned from the beach that day, she'd seen a fiery glow from the back corner of the garden – a magnificent plant with stems the colour of molten lava. A note on their back doorstep read:

I hope you'll forgive the intrusion! She's called the Cornus Midwinter Fire and glows strong through winter. She reminded us of the spirit you have in you.

Derek and June x

PS If you hate her, don't worry; we can dig her straight up.

Sam had looked out at the plant each morning and was reminded of Derek's advice: *find the beauty in the world*. Telling Marvin the news that day had been as awful as she'd anticipated until she'd followed it up with her suggestion of adoption. They'd spoken about it in the past, but neither had broached the subject since starting the IVF process for fear of seeming uncommitted to what was at hand. Marvin had broken down when she'd finished speaking. They were tears of grief for the child they would never make, but they were also tears of relief; he had thought that adoption might no longer be an option, thought that she was so beaten down she couldn't continue the fight for a family. It transpired that his seemingly endless positivity hadn't been entirely authentic but more of an attempt to keep Sam's spirits up.

Marvin had already done a lot of research about adoption even before Sam had raised the topic. He knew that Black and mixed race children were more likely to be up for adoption in the UK – a sad fact that made them both more determined that this was the right path for them – and also that they would be matched more quickly if they were able to take on siblings. Although daunted, they'd both agreed that siblings were the right choice for them.

They knew that adopting children wouldn't immediately erase their desire to have a baby; they needed time to grieve for this part of their life. This was encouraged by the adoption agencies, who all stipulated a minimum of six months between completing IVF treatment and starting the assessment process. Sam and Marvin were accepting of this. They knew that in order for them to be the best parents possible, they needed time to come to terms with their altered plan to have a family. But they were fairly confident that, eventually, they would be accepted as prospective parents, confident that they would, in time, have children, and after the years of trying and treatment rounds, this certainty in their future was so unexpected, it felt like a gift.

'It'll definitely be intimidating when we get to the interviews and workshops phase,' Sam said. 'But that's not going to be for a while.'

'I don't think they'll make us do role-play or anything; it's not like an audition. We'll be fine: you're an early years teacher, for Christ's sake,' he said.

'And you're great at assemblies.'

'Put *that* on my gravestone.'

Sam laughed and drank her beer. 'I guess there'll be a lot of people who don't work with kids — at least we're used to being around them — but it's completely different, isn't it?' she continued, her tone more serious. 'Apparently, even babies taken from their parents at birth have usually experienced some kind of emotional trauma in the womb, from what the mother's been through.'

'I know. I read that too,' Marvin said sadly. 'But remember we'll have a lot of support, right up through school.'

'I just hope I'll be good at it, good enough for them after whatever they've been through.'

Marvin looked at her and said, 'Hey, you will be. You absolutely will be.'

Sam looked down at the table. 'You'll be amazing at it all too,' she said, meaning it. 'Mum's chomping at the bit, as well. Ooh, changing the subject, I wanted to show you something.' She unlocked her phone to find the webpage, then passed it over, nervously watching him read.

He looked up at her and smiled broadly, then returned to

the phone to read more. After a couple of minutes, he passed it back, folded his arms on the table and said, 'I think it's perfect.'

'Really?' she asked. She agreed, of course, but had been nervous he'd find fault with it.

'Similar salary, nice school, a step up in terms of responsibilities—'

'And right around the corner!'

'And right around the corner,' he repeated, his eyes lit up. 'A little too close, if anything. You'll see the kids everywhere.'

'I know, I'll have to wear a disguise at weekends. But it would feel like I'm kind of investing in the area, building my own little community.' Sam knew she'd have wobbles over the years where she'd feel the distance between her mum and herself more keenly, where she'd feel out of place in London, look at house prices in the Wirral, and spend a few hours imagining their life up there. But right now, she wanted to be here, in their little corner of South London, and she was making every effort to put down roots.

'What, beyond your little allotment club?' Marvin had taken to referring to her, June, and Derek as this, despite her still not having planted anything.

Sam laughed. 'Well, they'll remain president and treasurer, of course, but we've been thinking of expanding . . .'

He took her hand. 'Good plan. So let's crack on with the application this weekend then? Start date is September term, isn't it?'

They ordered margaritas and popcorn to take into the screen, sinking back in the wide armchairs in the cinema, the salt-rimmed glasses cool in their hands. As the lights dimmed, an advert about a father and his daughter filled the screen, the audience following the journey from her being a small baby right up to adulthood. Marvin took Sam's hand, and she braced herself for the familiar cloak of sadness as she watched yet another tender portrayal of parenthood play out. Tonight, however, buoyed by hope of the future, the warmth of Marvin's hand, and the delicious drink in her lap, her good mood was less penetrable. She felt merely a prickle of lacking, of loss, of the still childless existence they were sharing, and a gentle nostalgia for all the experiences she'd had with her own dad.

She squeezed Marvin's hand as the advert finished and the first trailer started, and leant over to whisper in his ear, 'Let's go dancing after this.'

He looked at her, amused. 'It's Tuesday!'

'Oh, come on, we don't have to stay out late? And soon we might not be able to do things like this.' She raised one eyebrow suggestively.

He touched her face with the back of his forefinger, and she could sense what he was going to say.

'I know it probably won't be that quick,' she said, getting there first.

Marvin rested his head on the back of the seat, and his face gave into a smile. 'Two drinks max and home by midnight.'

'Yessss.' Sam mimed a victory fist pump. 'Dogstar?'

'It'll be full of my sixth formers!'

'Perfect. Ooh, we should do shots! Though maybe a nice spirit like Amaretto?'

'Perfect,' he repeated, turning back to the screen. 'That'll really solidify our geriatric status.'

Sam could see the nudging of a smile that he was trying to suppress. She took hold of his upper arm and leant over, resting her head on his shoulder as they watched the trailers.

Marvin turned and kissed the top of her head lightly and said, 'I've missed you.'

Daisy

Daisy finished piping the icing on the strawberry and elderflower layered cake she'd made for Imo's arrival home that weekend. Mathilde was away for a fortnight with her children, visiting relatives in the US. Imo had feigned relief at having some alone time, but Daisy could hear the pretence in her voice down the phone and suspected she was hurt not to have been invited on the trip.

She stepped back and eyed her creation with pride. The course had brought her a newfound love of baking. Previously, she'd found sweet treats a waste of time, assuming people who were serious about food focused on savoury. But she'd discovered she had a bit of a talent for pastry and, under the gentle encouragement of her tutor, had branched out into desserts and intricate icing techniques. It had been six weeks since the course finished and, so far, all Daisy had done was increase her hours at the restaurant. She spent most of her spare time practising recipes at home and scouring restaurant websites for inspiration. But she didn't yet have a plan of what to do next, and she was growing tired of people asking her.

At five to seven, Blake buzzed the doorbell.

'Mamma mia!' he said as he eyed the cake, gripping her

waist and kissing her neck as Woolf jumped up at them. 'You did good. When's Imo back?'

'Tomorrow lunch time.'

'So we're just going to look at it tonight . . . no trying, no *checking* it for her?'

Daisy put her arms inside his open shirt, wrapping them around his waist and drawing him in to kiss.

It had been six months since the day they climbed Monument. They now viewed the column as a kind of symbol to the start of their relationship – she'd sent him a post card with it on when she was away in Whitby; they pointed it out to each other on the rare occasions it came into view on the skyline, and they amused themselves for hours sending photos of the stone pillar over text with the recipient responding in the nature of a dick pic: *so hard for me, baby!*

Blake made dinner as Daisy sat on the sofa with a beer and chatted to him throughout. They'd fallen into an easy routine of staying at each other's most nights, with an unspoken pact to have at least one or two apart each week.

She updated him on Sam and Marvin's progress with adoption as he chopped an onion for the lasagne. 'I'm so excited for them. It's amazing to think that their children are probably alive right now, somewhere out there.'

Blake dipped his head to one side. 'Probably not having the best time though, let's face it.'

'Well, they might be with lovely foster carers? Anyway, I was thinking . . .'

Blake stopped chopping and looked up with concern.

'It's a few weeks until the anniversary of Ida's death and

my parents want us to get together to scatter her ashes. I think Jez and Arkley will be there, plus Arkley's partner, Naomi, so I wondered if you wanted to come up for it?'

He smiled. 'Really? You sure you'd want me there?'

'Yeah, course. Plus, I'd like to show you Whitby.'

He looked at her, a warmth in his eyes, and said simply, 'I'd like that.' Then reached for a carrot from the side and continued chopping.

Daisy smiled up at him, then drank from her beer. She hadn't brought a partner home to meet her family in over five years and had imagined the invitation being much more complicated, practising the conversation in her head for the last few days. This was often the way with Blake; there was little he didn't take in his stride.

'So, you're at your brother's for the bank holiday weekend?' she asked.

'Yeah, sorry. I should have asked you to come.'

She shook her head quickly. 'No, sorry, that's not at all what I was angling for; I'm just organizing weekends in my head.'

'Well, you should definitely come up soon. They're all desperate to meet you. Particularly Amelia.'

Blake often talked lovingly about his two nieces. There was a fifteen-year age gap between the two girls, and he was particularly close to the eldest, Amelia.

'Aw, well, I'm definitely coming to her eighteenth in July with you, aren't I? So I'll meet them all then. How old is Etta now? Three?'

'Yeah, just turned three and a complete legend.'

An innate force within her found the image of him with

a small child particularly attractive. 'I bet you're really cute with her.'

He scraped the diced carrot from the chopping board into the frying pan. 'I'm not a bad uncle,' he said after a pause, as though putting forward a question.

Daisy watched him and noticed something shift in his face. 'What?'

He looked up. 'Nothing,' he said, too quickly. He put the knife down and turned to top up his red wine, the liquid glugging out heavily against the silence in the room.

'Shall we put some music on?'

'Sure,' he said, without looking up at her.

She walked over to the mint-green radio on Imo's kitchen countertop and selected a station. A dance song blared out, and she switched it quickly to a more mellow channel that her parents favoured.

'Want me to help with anything?' Daisy leant on the kitchen counter like a shy child hoping to help an intimidating father.

'No, I'm good. Thanks.'

The last word seemed uncomfortably polite, and Daisy ran back over her last few sentences, seeking the reason for his coolness. 'Have I . . . annoyed you about something, 'cause I'm getting the sense—'

He looked at her and frowned. 'No, 'course not.' Returning to chopping another carrot, he added, 'It's . . . yeah, no—' He put the knife down and picked up his wine glass. 'I think it's maybe time we talked about something.'

'Okay.'

Blake gestured to the sofa where they sat down a few feet apart before he shuffled closer, folding his right knee up, and turned to face Daisy. 'Can you remember that first New Year's Eve when I had to leave suddenly?'

They'd never talked about it beyond it being a family emergency; he hadn't elaborated further, and Daisy hadn't wanted to pry. It seemed so long ago now.

Blake ran his hand through his hair and put his glass down on the coffee table. 'My dad rang me. It was about my brother.'

'Nathan?'

'Yeah, he'd gone missing. You know he's bipolar? Well, he'd stopped taking his meds and not told anyone. I had to go back to Leicester to help find him; we thought something might have happened.'

'Shit, that must have been stressful.' Daisy was unsure whether to ask what potentially could have happened or if such a question would be too intrusive.

'He was okay, but he had a bad few months – that's why I moved back there last year. It's fine now.' He looked down at the coffee table and rubbed the palm of his left hand with his right thumb as though attempting to erase something invisible. 'My mum suffered as well; she was never diagnosed but . . . she had a bad turn when I was sixteen and . . .' He rubbed at his face with his hands. 'She killed herself.'

Daisy covered her mouth with her hand. 'Fuck, Blake.' He'd spoken about his mum dying young, but never the details. 'I'm so sorry.' She reached for his hand.

'Yeah, thanks.' His eyes flicked to hers then back down. 'A few years later, Nath had Amelia. He was only seventeen and, well, her mum wasn't the best back then. Dad tried to help, but he worked long hours, so me and Nath basically raised her together.'

Daisy twisted a piece of hair in her hand as she pieced the information together. 'So that's why you're so close to Amelia.'

'Yeah, Nath struggled a bit more in his twenties, so a lot of it fell on me. I'm not going to rose-tint it: we didn't have any money and, yeah . . . it was tough time.' He picked up his wine and stared at the wall as he drank. 'I decided back then that I didn't want kids of my own. I knew the reality of raising them, how hard it is, and I had Amelia; she felt like enough. So I had a vasectomy when I was twenty-eight.'

'Oh.' Daisy heard the word from her mouth.

'Two doctors refused to do it; the third agreed.'

Daisy leant back on the sofa, processing all of the information.

He turned to face Daisy and continued, 'I know it's only been six months with us but, with you talking about Sam and Marv, and my nieces. My ex said she didn't mind, but then – well, she did. She was actually riding on the hope that I'd try and reverse it.'

'Right . . . is that why you broke up, then?'

He shook his head. 'No, contributed I'm sure, but no.'

'And do you still feel the same? You don't regret having it?'

He stroked her right cheek, staring intently at her. 'No. I've had moments of doubt over the years, thinking it was a stupid thing to have done. But I kind of stand by my decision.' He closed one eye as he said this, as though holding something back. 'I really like my life as it is, Daisy. But I know it's a big deal, and you're younger than me, so . . . I didn't want to' – he gestured awkwardly with his right hand – 'lead you somewhere under a pretence.'

'Yeah, okay,' she said, somewhat dazed by his honesty. 'Well, thanks . . . for letting me know. Not sure why I've been on the pill all these months.' She said this with humour but it came off churlish – she'd been on the pill for years to control her painful cycles and had no real intention of coming off it. She leant away to reach for her beer and took a deep swig. 'So, I also don't think I want children. I've kind of been thinking that for years.' She opened her mouth to continue, but then stopped – did he really have the right to know, when it was her body, her decision? But as she met his eye, taking in the patient and concerned purse of his lips, she realized she wanted to share everything with him. 'I actually had a termination last year.'

'Shit. I'm sorry you had to go through that.' He leant forward.

'It's okay,' she said, embarrassed at having shared seemingly dramatic news. 'It was really early on and, well, I wasn't even with the guy anymore. It felt like the right thing to do, and I'm honestly fine about it.' She clamped her hands between her knees. 'I just didn't want it to be this thing between us that I'd failed to mention.'

'No, I get that. You didn't have to, of course, but thank you for telling me.'

Daisy found that she was surprised there was no mention of the unfortunate timing with Sam's situation, and she was glad of this. At last, it seemed the event was in her history and only hers.

'So, to be clear,' she carried on, 'if I decided I *did* want a child in future, you wouldn't ever consider adoption or . . .'

His brown eyes bored into hers, and he smiled sadly.

'No. D'you know what, I wouldn't even want to ask you to do that.' She stood up, suddenly hot, then sat straight back down and stared away from him at the wall in front. After a moment's silence, she said, 'I just didn't imagine that the option would be taken away from me.'

'I don't want to be the guy that took the option away from you.' He reached out and took hold of her wrist, making small circles around her star tattoo with his forefinger. 'This decision, it's bigger than me. It's bigger than us.'

She turned back to him. 'I think I need to make sure that, well . . . that I'm sure.'

He stroked a strand of her long hair down her back. 'Of course.'

'Blake? I'm really sorry that that happened to you, to your family. What was your mum's name?'

'Annie,' he said, subconsciously reaching for the chain around his neck, the letter A that Daisy had always thought was for Amelia, sitting closely against his chest.

She took his hand, and they both leant back on the sofa, staring at the wall in front.

A few weeks later, Blake joined Daisy in Whitby. He arrived the day before her brothers, which she was glad of – staggering the introductions seemed sensible. They were sitting on wicker chairs on the front lawn drinking elderflower gin cocktails with her parents. As far back as she could remember, Daisy and her brothers had been sent picking the white flowers from the surrounding hedges and woodlands in early June, so that Jemima could make a summer's worth of elderflower cordial. The sweet smell of the juice would always remind Daisy of home. She noticed Blake's glass was still full; perhaps he didn't like it. She swilled the ice in her own glass, defensive of her mother's recipe – what wasn't to like? – but then finally he took a sip, and another. It really was delicious.

She watched as Jemima listened intently to Blake talking about his furniture-making. He didn't seem nervous, though she suspected he was; her mother's hawk-eyed attention tended to have that effect on people, despite her generally thinking well of most. Graham smiled benevolently at Blake as he spoke, his demeanour warm and inviting. They both liked him, she could tell.

'Well, that's magnificent,' Jemima said with enthusiasm. 'What a wonderful thing to be able to do: to make something so worthwhile with your hands. We're both terrible at anything practical.' She indicated Graham, who looked startled, as though this was news to him.

'You're both good cooks,' Daisy said. 'That's practical?'

Jemima drained her glass and placed it delicately on the weathered table. 'Not like you and Ida; we just muddle along. But no, I meant more that furniture is so . . . long-lasting, passed down through families; I mean, without sounding morbid, I expect some of the pieces you make will outlive you, even? So I think that's rather special, the permanence of it.'

Blake looked from Jemima to Daisy. 'That's a really nice way of thinking about it.'

Daisy could tell he was piecing things together about her now that he'd met her parents and trodden the well-worn rugs of her childhood home. She'd spotted him tracing the floral wallpaper in the hall with his beautiful hand, glancing up at the antique brass light that had hung above the stairs for the entirety of Daisy's life. Introducing her parents and showing him her family home felt like opening one of the furthest compartments within her heart, then standing back and hoping he liked it.

They hadn't broached the subject of children since their conversation in the flat, but Daisy had thought about it a lot. She couldn't help but feel that Blake's seeming unwillingness to change his mind was a sign that he didn't care for her enough. It was an uncomfortable thought, immature perhaps, but she couldn't dismiss it. She'd spent a weekend at her brother's with her eight-month-old nephew and, in quiet moments, attempted to examine her absolute and honest feelings as she held him in her arms. He did look undeniably like her brother – strangely so, like a miniature version of him. It was impossible not to feel any stirrings of love and awe when he grasped her fingers and giggled at her expressions, but did she really want this for herself? Her biggest concern about not having a child was whether there was *enough* in her life without. Would Blake be *enough*? Was it *enough* to be an aunt, a godmother? The word had bandied around her mind so vigorously it had taken on a strange and ridiculous feel, and she was left with a hopeless sense of uncertainty.

She reached over and took Blake by the forearm. 'I might actually go for a swim before it gets dark – do you mind?'

'What, now?' Blake glanced at the retreating sun.

'You've probably got time if you head off soon.' Graham said, looking at this watch. 'Don't mind us; we're leaving shortly anyway.'

Her parents had tickets to the annual Soul Festival at the pavilion. Daisy had contemplated getting tickets and joining them, but it had sold out by the time she looked. It was probably better this way; she didn't want Blake to feel they were tied to her family for the whole weekend.

'Let's do it then,' Blake said, finishing his cocktail and rising from the table.

They headed down the coastal path together, Daisy's towel draped around her neck and their legs stretching out in unison as the gentle slope propelled them towards the town. Blake took her hand and pulled her closer to him, entwining his fingers with hers. They walked in comfortable silence to start with, evening birdsong from the surrounding hedges filling the air as bands of apricot ruptured the sky before them. Tomorrow, she'd show him the cove at Robin Hood's Bay, but Whitby beach would do for a quick swim this evening.

'I like your parents,' he said after a while.

'Me too.' She smiled and wrapped her hand around his waist, feeling his arm drape over her shoulder. 'I mean, they can irritate the hell out of me but . . .' She paused. 'Sorry, what a horribly ungrateful thing to say.'

He gripped her shoulder tighter and said, 'Dais, you're allowed to voice annoyance at your parents – it's a rite of passage.'

She nodded and tipped her head against his chest as the beach came into view.

She led him down to her regular spot, placing her towel and keys down on the usual rock. Apart from a few dog walkers and a young couple entwined on a bench in the distance, this end of the beach was empty.

'I won't be long,' she said, stripping down to her old navy swimsuit and piling her clothes on the rock.

'Take your time. It's incredible out here,' Blake said, sitting down on the rock and looking around.

Daisy walked quickly towards the waves and skipped through the first ones that crashed on the shoreline. The sky was now a vivid peach blanket, the sun starting to sink below the sea in the distance. Once the water had reached her stomach, she leant in and started a slow stroke out towards the horizon, her breathing steady in response to the familiar coolness that engulfed her.

It'd been months since she swam here. In London, she tried to get to lidos or the Ladies' Pond on Hampstead Heath, but getting to the coast was a stretch that she rarely found time for. She thought back to all her swims alone here last year, realizing now how grateful she was for that time – how restorative it had been. There was something pleasingly cyclical about returning a year later, with Blake behind her. She kicked her legs out, feeling their strength, and gazed up at the dazzling sky with its pastel ripples spreading far and wide; it felt like a spectacle especially for her. She thought of Ida and how she always made a fuss welcoming her home.

A gull squawked overhead, soaring sideways through the air before neatly settling on the gentle waves in the distance. Daisy heard calling from the shore, and her heart rate shot up for a moment as she worried something was wrong. But when she turned around, Blake was in his boxers, stepping through the first few waves.

'Dais, wait. I'm coming in!'

She laughed and started to swim back towards him. 'What!'

He was not a cold-water swimmer.

As soon as he was deep enough, he lunged his body into the

sea, letting out several growls as his arms divided the still water into an enthusiastic breaststroke. 'Fuck me, it's cold!'

She couldn't help but laugh at his expression, jaw tight in a grimace of actual pain. 'It's the bloody North Sea. Of course it's cold! Just breathe.'

She reached for his shoulders, and he stopped swimming, still able to touch the bottom, allowing her to wrap herself around him. He gripped her waist and brought his forehead to touch hers.

'What the hell are you doing?' she asked, her lips centimetres from his.

As his breathing slowed in line with Daisy's, Blake turned his head up to the fiery sky above them. 'Look at it; I didn't want to be the guy on the shoreline.'

She followed his eyes. 'No one wants to be that guy.'

He pulled his head away from hers so that he could properly look at her. 'Exactly. I wanted to be with you – to experience this with you.'

She kissed him then, salt on their lips.

'You didn't even bring a towel?' she said after a moment.

'I thought we could share. It'll be romantic?'

Daisy laughed. 'Okay. Shotgun using it first though.'

'Fair.'

He tucked a piece of her hair behind her ear, running his fingers down the wet ends. 'You're not even cold, are you? You're like a fucking mermaid-sea-warrior or something.'

Daisy smiled as this was how she'd always thought of Ida. And then she knew.

'Blake, I don't want children – I don't,' she repeated, noticing his startled eyes. 'I just want this: you – someone who plunges into the North Sea to be with me!' She laughed and let go of his shoulders, standing before him as the waves lapped at her chest. 'I've never really wanted them. I just assumed I'd end up having them because most people do.'

Blake ran a hand through his hair, leaving drops of water on his forehead. 'Dais, are you sure? Because I've been thinking about that conversation a lot, and I felt really shit about it. I don't want to lose you, so if it is something you really want then, I think, maybe—'

'It's not what I really want though; honestly, it isn't. And maybe I'll have moments of doubt in future, but I'm okay with that – it'd be the case either way. What I *do* know I want is to live by the sea' – she looked back at the quaint houses lining the shore – 'to have a job I love, to travel, and to have someone to do it all with.'

Dimples appeared on Blake's cheeks as he smiled and started treading water. 'Okay then, if you're sure.'

She drew him to her again, his mouth warm against the cold of hers, then they swam back to the shore, side by side, to their one awaiting towel.

winter iv

Sam

Sam whipped her head back to check that Marvin and June were keeping up as she reached the platform minutes before departure. Marvin was carrying their heavy rucksack as well as Derek and June's large floral suitcase, since the wheels were so worn down it no longer pulled. June was trotting alongside him, several carrier bags of snacks in her hands, and chatting constantly, turning towards Marvin rather than looking where she was going.

Reaching the train doors, Sam slowed her pace, coming to a stop and turning Derek's wheelchair around so that he could see Marvin and June behind.

The train staff were impressively accommodating, niftily adding and removing ramps, despite Derek's protests about the fuss. Once on board, Sam spotted him take hold of the young man's wrist as he was leaving them, bowing his head deeply and trying to give him a ten-pound note, which the man refused with a kind pat on Derek's shoulder.

Imo and Jas were already sitting at a table and stood to greet them with hugs. Derek and June's seats were at the end of the carriage where there was space for his wheelchair, and Sam felt guilty that they couldn't all sit together. She caught Marvin's eye and saw that he was thinking the same.

'I'm gonna sit up there with them for a while until the train fills out,' he said. 'Give you a chance to catch up with the girls.'

'Okay.' She squeezed his waist affectionately.

Imo seemed to have bought half of Pret a Manger and walked over to offer June, Derek, and Marvin coffee and pastries.

'I'm so excited to see them,' Jas squealed as she and Sam sat down opposite each other and the engine started.

'I know; I can't wait to see the coffee shop,' Sam said.

'I thought you'd seen it?'

'I saw it in October when they'd just got the keys, but not since the renovation.'

'Oh, but you've seen their house finished though?'

'Ida's? Yeah, it's so cute. God, I need to stop calling it Ida's. It feels different enough to when it was hers but still kind of has her charm. It's all stripped floorboards, white walls, and antique furniture. And they've kept her kitchen, just painted the cupboards sky blue.'

'Aw, it sounds so *Daisy*.'

'Yeah, I can't believe we didn't really see her returning to Whitby,' Sam said. 'Now that she's there, it seems ridiculous that she was ever in London.'

'I think we just didn't want to believe she'd leave us.'

'True. At least she moved to a place that's nice to visit. Bloody miles away but still. Marvin and I were saying we should make Whitby an annual holiday when we have kids. Like, we'll still go to other places, but we'll always do a week in Whitby with Aunty Daisy and Uncle Blake, without fail, and obviously we'll do lots of trips to the Wirral too. I don't want our kids to grow up with a kind of passiveness about the north – I want them to love it.'

'Of course, it's your roots,' Jas said, sipping from her coffee cup. 'I think those two'll always come down to London quite a bit as well. Blake seems to do a lot of his selling down here still.'

'Yeah, I think he's got a few good contacts now who sell his stuff, plus a few furniture fairs a year.' Sam looked out the window as the outskirts of London whizzed past, eager for the green fields to come into view.

'Have you heard anything from the adoption agency?' Jas asked.

'We're still waiting for a match, but it's only been three months since all the paperwork went through.'

Imo returned, and Jas stood to let her squeeze past to the window seat.

'Aw mate, you've got a little bump now,' Sam said, eyeing Jas's stomach from the side with wonder. Pregnant women still remained magical beings to her, but spotting this two years ago would have been too painful to comment on. Their eyes locked, and Jas seemed to realize this at the same time, which only made the moment sweeter.

'Yeah, think I've just popped,' she said, sitting back down. 'Fifteen weeks now.'

Imo shook her head. 'Can't believe you're doing it again, babe. Your poor, poor vagina.'

They changed at York and arrived in Scarborough for two o'clock. Daisy and her dad met them on the platform with much cheer and well wishes. Daisy grabbed Sam around the neck as you would a younger brother, then rushed past to greet June and Derek.

'Oh, Daisy, don't you look wonderful! The sea air obviously suits you,' said June, kissing her on the cheek.

'Thanks! How are you two?'

Derek took her hand in both of his and smiled up at her. 'Apart from this old thing' – he waved at his wheelchair – 'we're great. But I won't be in it for long!' He kicked the footrest with his heel in determination.

'Sam, great to see you!' Graham said, engulfing her in his green walking jacket before introducing himself to Derek and June.

They headed to the car park, where they'd arranged a wheelchair-friendly taxi. Daisy watched nervously as the driver helped Derek up the ramp, and Sam took her gently by the elbow.

'I'm worried about them getting around – all the cobbles in Whitby,' Daisy said. 'I offered them to stay at ours, but I think they didn't want to intrude.'

Sam glanced at the taxi as June climbed in next to Derek, who was now strapped in and beaming. 'They'll be fine. They've been excited about this trip for weeks.'

The rest of them climbed into Graham's battered old Defender and headed to the house in Whitby. Since there was more room at her parents' house, Daisy had suggested they all stay there, with the promise that she'd host them for a roast at theirs on New Year's Day, so that they could see the place. Jemima welcomed the six of them with open arms and a pot of loose-leaf tea. A fire was already lit, and they settled in the living room, helping themselves to the plate of shortbread. Sam could see Marvin taking the surroundings in and piecing it together with the Daisy he'd known for almost a decade. Sam was so well acquainted with the eclectic decor, cluttered with antiques, that she barely noticed the grandeur of it anymore.

Imo filled her aunt and uncle in on the latest with Mathilde.

'We're so sorry to hear that, Imogen,' Jemima said kindly. 'She seemed like such an interesting woman when we met her in the summer.'

Sam waited for a sarcastic retort but saw that Imo seemed to be gathering herself before speaking again.

'Well, we're just glad to have you back in London, babes,' said Jas over her steaming cup of tea.

Imo put on a brave face. 'Copenhagen was a bit of a drag. Everyone was so *nice*. And all those fucking bikes – give me an Uber, any day.'

They all laughed.

'It's fine,' she continued. 'We were at different points in our lives and, yeah . . .'

'D'you think you'll date women again?' asked Daisy from across the room, reclining with her feet up on a battered floral footstool. 'Like, are you officially "bi", or was it just her?'

'Oh, labels are so passé,' Imo said with her usual dose of sarcasm.

'Fine, don't label it then. I just wondered.'

Imo tilted her head to one side and said, 'I'm not really sure yet. I have zero interest in anyone else. But, I think I've learnt it's less about the gender for me, just the person. It's not a particularly radical notion.'

'Good for you,' Graham said with a slight raise of his mug.

At 4.30, Daisy drove them into town in the Defender. Jas sat up front, and Imo, Marvin, and Sam slid around on the benches in the back, singing along to Christmas songs which blared out of the old speakers. It was dark already, Christmas lights in people's windows flickering on, increasing the festive mood in the air.

They parked up on a steep hill a few streets away from the café. Sam couldn't help but feel a sense of pride that she, and only she, had visited it before. Marvin took her by the hand as they strolled down the hill, Imo carrying two bottles of red wine which Graham had handed to her on the way out. They rounded the corner onto a quaint road with old-fashioned streetlamps and only a few passers-by. Sam caught sight of it first; a streetlamp stood proudly to the side, illuminating the newly painted front. The faded cream paint of the summer had been replaced by a pea green covering the woodwork on the front and around the bay window, and cream lettering in simple typography spelt out *Daisy's Place* across the top. Sam stopped in her tracks and brought her hands to her face in awe.

Daisy reached her and stood by her side, looking up at it. 'I know, pretty egocentric. It was Blake's idea, and then we both couldn't think of anything better.'

'Daisy's Place!' Jas squealed from behind.

'D, it's amazing!' cried Marvin. 'Love the green.'

'It reminds me a bit of your ridiculous cast in Australia,' Imo said, studying the colour.

They all turned and stared at her.

'Obviously I'm joking. This is way more pea – that was emerald.'

Daisy folded her arms and stared back at it. 'I still feel a bit embarrassed about the name.'

'Daisy, no.' Sam stepped in front of her, aware that she'd

been struggling to decide on a name for months. 'It's perfect.' Feeling tearful suddenly, and foolish for it, Sam looked back at the café as she said, 'This is your place.'

Daisy smiled. 'Come on then, I'll show you inside.' She linked Sam's arm, and they headed towards the door, the others following. 'They should just be closing up.'

There was a series of gasps and compliments as they stepped inside. It was a mix of heavy rustic tables – all made by Blake – vintage chairs and eclectic lighting, from industrial brass pendants to cute vintage lamps. Only one couple remained, gathering their coats as they paid the bill to a young waitress who greeted their group as they entered. Daisy spoke to the waitress as the others milled around, taking in the place.

Hearing their voices, Blake came through from the kitchen, smiling broadly at the wonder in their eyes.

'Oh, here's the landlord,' Imo said, saluting him.

It had been Blake's idea to buy the place. Moving up to Whitby together had been a big step, and this was his way of grounding himself to the area, as well as having some financial independence – they'd converted the flat above the shop into a holiday flat that he managed. He and Daisy lived together in the house in Robin Hood's Bay, but strictly speaking, that was Daisy's and this was his.

Sam hugged Blake warmly. 'Hey! Have you been on food prep?' she said, gesturing to the kitchen where he'd come from.

'Hell no,' he said, hugging Jas before making his way to Marvin, while Daisy frowned and shook her head. 'She wouldn't trust me to do that. I'm just the handyman and the delivery dude.'

'We've had so many takeaway orders!' Daisy said, gesturing

for them to sit down at the largest table. 'It's actually quite a good money-maker as I'm not paying staff – Blake delivers most of them on his bike at the moment.'

'It'll be fun come spring, not so much in the depths of a North Yorkshire winter,' he said, picking up glasses from behind the counter and carrying them over to the table.

'Well, guys, I think it's absolutely incredible,' said Marvin, looking around.

Everyone agreed, and Sam caught Daisy and Blake looking at each other proudly across the table. Sometimes she couldn't imagine them not being together. Messaging him that day was one of the best decisions she'd made.

'Who wants red?' Blake asked, opening the first bottle. 'Not that we have a lot to offer without a licence – plenty of soft drinks and I got some beers in?'

Everyone agreed on red wine, and Daisy rose to get a ginger beer for Jas from behind the counter. There was a faint tap on the door, and they all turned to see June's face smiling through the glass. Remembering the steps at the entrance, both Marvin and Sam stood to help. Daisy beat them to the door, opening it and hugging June, who was gushing with praise. Derek was already shuffling forward in his chair, eager to get inside. Daisy and Marvin helped him up and guided him through the doorway, his weight leaning on his walking stick and Marvin, as Daisy apologized profusely for the lack of a ramp. Sam gathered the wheelchair from behind and guided it through, ready for Derek to sit down again once inside, but he was too transfixed by the place to notice her. He let go of Marvin and repeatedly patted Daisy's hand, which was gripping his left upper arm.

'Absolutely magnificent, my girl. What a wonderful place. Daisy's place.' His eyes twinkled, and Sam could see that Daisy's eyes were shining too.

They helped him back down into the wheelchair and made room around the large table, passing glasses of wine around and talking loudly over each other. Marvin pulled his phone out of his pocket and answered it, standing up quickly and heading through to the kitchen, presumably to escape the noise.

Five minutes later, Sam spotted him through the open doorway, hanging up and putting the phone away in his pocket, then clasping his palms over his nose and mouth. He turned and walked back to the group, and Sam stood up. Seeing her face, everyone stopped talking and looked back at Marvin.

'That was the agency,' he said as he reached them. 'We've been matched.'

'Already?' asked Daisy.

He nodded at Sam from across the table as though she'd asked the question, then walked around to take her hand in his and said, with the utmost tenderness, 'Lamp, it's twins. Sixteen-month-old girls.'

Sam took a shuddering breath in and brought her hand up to her mouth. 'Twins?' Her voice was barely audible.

Marvin bit his top lip and nodded; his eyes filled with tears.

The group remained quiet until June said, 'Oh my darlings,' shaking her head and clasping her hands together.

This jolted the rest of the group into action and half of them stood.

'Oh my god!'

'Twins!'

'They're so young!'

Marvin wrapped Sam in his arms and they stood hugging for several seconds as, next to them, June hugged Jas, Daisy grabbed hold of Derek's hand, and Blake and Imo crashed glasses together.

Marvin pulled away from Sam, whose face was now tear-streaked. She opened her mouth to ask more questions, and he said, 'I don't know any more details; they're sending the file over now.' He took her hand and squeezed it before saying, 'Babe, we can meet them next week if we want.'

Sam's mouth turned upside down as she clamped her lips tight, her tears falling thickly. 'Is this really happening?' she said, turning to Daisy now.

Daisy was standing with both hands clamped over her mouth, staring at the two of them, her eyes brimming. Slowly, she moved her hands to the bottom of her chin. 'I think it finally is.'

'It might not go through though,' Sam said, turning back to Marvin.

'We've been matched; it'd only be if we felt it wasn't right. Let's just have this moment, okay?'

'Okay,' she said, her voice a whisper.

They gathered into a huddle, hugging one another and wiping their eyes.

Blake skipped out to the kitchen and emerged with two bottles of Champagne. 'These were for tomorrow, but I think this tops New Year's for celebrations.'

Daisy grabbed water tumblers from behind the counter, apologizing for the lack of proper glasses. The cork popped, and they hooted and cheered as Blake poured the liquid into the hexagonal glasses that June passed around.

'What a day,' declared Derek quietly from below as he gazed at Sam and Marvin. Sam locked his eyes, and the memory of the two of them in the garden over a year ago passed between them. Sam thought of his daughter's flowers, took his hand, and squeezed it. Derek squeezed back, his face full – only, this time, of joy.

Sam hooked herself more tightly under Marvin's arm and felt him kiss the top of her head in response. She looked at her friends around her, laughing with their Champagne, and was transported back to their wedding day.

'I'd like to make a toast,' June began, and they all hushed. 'To Daisy and Blake for this wonderful place you've both created, and to Sam and Marvin and those two little girls. They won't know it yet . . .' She looked across at Sam before she continued, 'but they're lucky. Lucky to have found the two of you.'

They all raised their glasses, crashing into each other with vigour, as Sam's eyes met Daisy's across the table.

acknowledgements

Thank you to my brilliant agent, Viola Hayden, who believed in this book from the very beginning. I'm endlessly grateful for you (gently) pushing me to make it the best I could, and your guidance through an unfamiliar world has been the greatest comfort. Thank you also to Ciara Finn and Atlanta Hatch, and all the team at Curtis Brown for your exemplary direction.

I'm forever indebted to my amazing editor Clare Gordon who I have such respect for that scoring a laughing face or heart emoji in the comments section has been an endorphin hit like no other. Thank you for highlighting in an earlier draft that I'd made every item a shade of blue and had characters be eleven months pregnant; your keen eye saved this book in a myriad of ways. Thank you also to Grace Marshall and the rest of the team at HQ for shepherding this book into the world with such enthusiasm.

Thanks to Curtis Brown Creative for accepting me onto the course despite my complete disregard for punctuation back then (and a little now). My tutor, Chris Wakling, and course mates provided invaluable feedback, particularly Grace Wingate, Steph Sowden, Heather Darwent, and Michelle Heng, who continued reading my work after the course had finished.

Thank you to Susanna Jones and the Pebble Beach Writers

Group for welcoming me so warmly and for helping pin down the final scenes of the book, and to the debuts 2025 group which has been unequivocally supportive and a hive of knowledge during a time of such change.

The end of Sam and Marvin's story was inspired by an interview on The Big Fat Negative podcast; it brought me hope in a time of great doubt and I'd like to thank its hosts Emma Haslett and Gabriella Griffith for the amazing work they do.

To my friends who I'll lazily categorize by WhatApp groups: Sexy & Cool Crew, Schoolies, 6ix is better than 5ive, Wings Bitches, Hen, Book Club, plus a couple of special outliers who know who they are, I'm glad we've managed to navigate the differing branches our lives have taken in our thirties better than Sam and Daisy did. Female friendship, in all its complexities, has been one of the greatest joys of my life – of course I'd write a book about it. A special thanks to Vicky Ginyatov, the Jas to my Sam, for all her support over the years and for answering an abundance of questions about ovaries.

Thanks to Cheri Ellis for not laughing when, seemingly out of nowhere, I decided to write a book when we were living together, and for keeping my early attempts a secret. Dissecting James's dastardly ways, and our numerous discussions about the trials and tribulations of being child free, improved the story more than you can know. And thank you for being there for me when it felt like everything was on fire.

A special shout out to an early reader, Gemma Dunn, who consumed most of the manuscript while in labour with her daughter. You said it was great, but perhaps that was the drugs talking.

Thank you to my mum for teaching me to imagine things,

and for instilling a love of reading in me from a young age; I still remember coming home from Scotland to find *The Philosopher's Stone* on my pillow. Thanks to my dad for always encouraging me creatively, from paper mâché cats to stupidly ambitious renovations, your belief in, and excitement for each project has made them all that bit sweeter. Idolising my older sister as a child led me to copying her handwriting – to this day I still have an uncannily similar yet messier version – so thanks for our stylish scrawl; and exposure to my teenage brother's music reverberating from his room obviously made its mark as, like Sam, The Smiths stir up a nostalgia so powerful it stings – thanks for having great taste. Thank you to my in-laws, all eight hundred of you, for your support and excitement about my writing, and for looking after Ezra so that I could edit this book.

Thank you to Matt for encouraging me to write; for believing, with little to no evidence, that I could do this; and for being the best and kindest companion on our own journey to parenthood. And to Marnie and Ezra, who stole my sleep and my heart.